DAYBREAK

DAYBREAK

Ellen Connor

B

BERKLEY SENSATION, NEW YORK

THE BERKLEY PUBLISHING GROUP
Published by the Penguin Group
Penguin Group (USA) Inc.
375 Hudson Street, New York, New York 10014, USA
Penguin Group (Canada), 90 Eglinton Avenue East, Suite 700, Toronto, Ontario M4P 2Y3, Canada
(a division of Pearson Penguin Canada Inc.)
Penguin Books Ltd., 80 Strand, London WC2R 0RL, England
Penguin Group Ireland, 25 St. Stephen's Green, Dublin 2, Ireland (a division of Penguin Books Ltd.)
Penguin Group (Australia), 250 Camberwell Road, Camberwell, Victoria 3124, Australia
(a division of Pearson Australia Group Pty. Ltd.)
Penguin Books India Pvt. Ltd., 11 Community Centre, Panchsheel Park, New Delhi—110 017, India
Penguin Group (NZ), 67 Apollo Drive, Rosedale, Auckland 0632, New Zealand
(a division of Pearson New Zealand Ltd.)
Penguin Books (South Africa) (Pty.) Ltd., 24 Sturdee Avenue, Rosebank, Johannesburg 2196,
South Africa

Penguin Books Ltd., Registered Offices: 80 Strand, London WC2R 0RL, England

DAYBREAK

Copyright © 2011 by Ann Aguirre and Carrie Lofty.
Cover art by Gene Mollica.
Cover design by Lesley Worrell.
Interior text design by Tiffany Estreicher.

PRINTING HISTORY
Berkley Sensation trade paperback edition / December 2011

ISBN: 978-0-425-24340-4

An application to register this book for cataloging has been filed with the Library of Congress.

PRINTED IN THE UNITED STATES OF AMERICA

10 9 8 7 6 5 4 3 2 1

To our readers,
whose support made this journey epic

ACKNOWLEDGMENTS

It's time to mention the people whose expertise and support made this novel possible. Thanks to Laura Bradford and to Cindy Hwang for believing. The Penguin team is likewise fantastic . . . with renewed appreciation for artist Gene Mollica for such gorgeous covers. You brought our vision to life.

With love and gratitude, we thank our families for their fortitude in the face of leftovers and distraction: Andres, Andrea, and Alek, as well as Keven, Juliette, Ilsa, and Dennis and Kathleen Stone.

Additional thanks to the Peeners, the Broken Writers, plus Larissa Ione, Sasha Knight, Jenn Bennett, Zoë Archer, Lorelie Brown, Patti Ann Colt, and Kelly Schaub. Your unstinting and unshakable friendship means the world to us. Thanks, as well, to Fedora Chen for the best proofreading in the business.

To our readers, we offer sincere appreciation. *Daybreak* ends this journey, but as always, we deliver the happy ending the hero and heroine deserve. You can email us at author.ellen.connor@gmail.com.

ONE

From the great water, a leader will rise up. He bears no magic and yet those who fly and cast and shift their skins will follow him.

From great sorrow a flower blooms in a woman's shape. A lion prowls in her shadow. She may be born again in the beast's mouth.

The flower balances between lion and leader, and she must choose. In such days, an island kingdom may found an empire that spans a hundred plus a hundred years. The world holds its breath.

—Translated from the ancient Chinese prophet Xi'an Xi's personal writings

Pen Sheehan twisted her right forearm. Wire dug in where guards had pinned her arms behind her back. The slack meant she could slip free. With time. But no telling how much she had. The camp could be anywhere, from a few kilometers away to a few hundred.

Only, she couldn't work any faster. Just slow, patient movements. Should her unconscious mind tumble ahead of her goal, she'd panic. She'd realize just how terrifying it was to be bound as a sex slave.

Visceral fear jabbed at her, as real as the gouging strand of wire along the thin skin of her inner wrist. She closed her eyes and breathed steadily. But she only ever found her mother in the dark—her mother, Angela, who had been dead nearly twelve years.

Her pulse jumped. The tingling ache that radiated out from her marrow said she was too close to losing control. Panic meant transporting. Involuntarily. She'd blink the wrong way and find herself by the side of the road somewhere.

And with her magic, panic could mean much worse. So much worse.

As much as she'd love a breath of air untainted by filthy, sweaty bodies, she needed to stay put. Stay in the truck. Make it to camp.

She opened her eyes and met another woman's wide, terrified gaze. Thin and grimy, she should've resembled muck hauled from a pit. But she had amazing cheekbones, smooth skin, and a remarkable figure revealed by tatters of dark wool. O'Malley would earn a fortune on her, especially if she was free of disease.

Wire wrapped the woman from palm to elbow, securing her arms overhead on a rusted hook. At least Pen didn't have to wiggle out of *that* serpentine fastening. She might not have been able to hold back her terror.

Using magic wasn't the problem. It was the dizziness and half-starved weakness that came from it, especially emergency bursts designed for self-defense.

And then there was the unpredictability.

She needed to arrive at camp strong and in full control of her senses. Anything less meant failure. No more innocents would die because of her.

She cleared her throat and locked eyes with the woman across the way. "What's your name?"

No response. Only the shy skitter of a gaze that touched the two armed guards at the back of the truck, then ducked away to a neutral place on the truck's filthy floor.

Pen sighed. While she struggled with the occasional flash of alarm, at least she had recourse that the other two dozen captives lacked. Not only could she heal and produce at will, a host of spells, but she was in the truck by choice. The Change had done its best to wipe out humanity. She refused to let the nastiest surviving strain obliterate the remaining good.

Purpose infused her with new strength. She braced herself for the pain. With a quick jerk, she wrenched her elbow; the wire gave up a half inch of its grip. Blood dripped along the pad at the base of her thumb.

The boy trussed to her right ducked away. He cringed. No one wanted to be associated with a rule breaker. Rage simmered under her breastbone—a quiet burn that matched the ache at her wrist—at seeing people so victimized. She kept working, occasionally checking the guards. The bastards were, as always, distracted by the merchandise. One of them might find *her* worth staring at, which could be disastrous for her plan.

At least she didn't fear rape. None of the slaves did. Not in the truck, anyway. Later, after a sale, daily abuse became a fact of life. But for a guard to sully the goods meant the loss of his dick. She'd seen O'Malley thugs stripped of all four limbs and left alive to serve as an example. A man who stole from General O'Malley might as well find a rope and hang himself.

Her hand went numb. Her knees, too, ached from the way she'd been forced to sit. Hunger gnawed at her belly. The hot wind snaking between gaps in the tarpaulin left her missing her cloak, because that would've kept the dust out of her mouth. She adored that damn cloak. Blanket and disguise and protection, all in one. But giving it up had been essential. Be meek. Be subservient. Anything else risked betraying her real purpose.

Taking a break, gathering her patience once again, she craned her neck toward the truck's covered top. A gray-green grime covered the canvas like mold. Elaborate twine stitching revealed where scraps had been pieced together to form a whole sheet of fabric, or repaired through the years. The tarp stretched over a lightweight frame of sturdy chicken wire that arced like an igloo over their heads. Hooks stuck out from metal studs spaced two meters apart. Loops screwed into the floorboards held fast to chains and shackles.

Custom-made for hauling human beings.

Red soaked over Pen's vision. Hatred and purpose fused. She yanked hard. Her wrist popped free, smeared with her own blood.

She quickly turned her back to the guards and set to work on her other arm. The tingling in her fingertips as sensation returned was almost as painful as the gash on her wrist. She ignored it, concentrated, freed herself.

"Hey!"

Pen froze.

Damn.

Slaves pulled their bare feet back from the guard's boots as he used the handholds along the studs to maneuver toward Pen. "Face front, you!"

She tucked her hands out of sight, slipping her wrists back into the loosened restraints. Worst case, she'd disorient him with a touch of magic. Again, she'd be left vulnerable and depleted, but it was a better option than losing control.

Stay in the truck. Keep the prisoners safe.

With her shoulders hunched forward, she angled her body to face forward once again.

"Look at me." The guard used the toe of his boot to raise her chin. The stench of mildewed leather dominated her next breath, as if the rot of the Everglades had hitched a ride.

Long ago, when the Change upended the whole world, Pen had been a frightened little girl. She didn't like how easy it was to return to that feeling. But it always came back, as did seeing her mother when she closed her eyes. She channeled that helplessness and utter despair.

Whatever she dredged up from those dark places must've been enough to satisfy the man. He didn't check her fastenings. Only grinned. A puckered scar that looked like a silver ladder ran down his throat. It shook when he chuckled.

Strange that of all the disgusting sights and smells in the truck, and of all the horrors that likely awaited her at camp, Pen shuddered because of his scar. She couldn't say why. But the revulsion and fear he'd needed to see in her eyes felt real enough. She couldn't look away from his ruined skin.

"Another pretty one," he said. "O'Malley will be pleased. We don't get many as pretty as you up in the mountains. Man'd have to turn queer or fuck a pine tree just to give his hand a break."

Pen grabbed the man's flash of memory. She could discern geographic features and weather patterns, although not as precisely as an actual map. She squirreled away the clues he inadvertently provided. Rumor had long since suggested that General O'Malley lived in a fortress hideaway, somewhere in the Appalachians. What this guard revealed didn't change her best guess. But she still needed to confirm its location, which meant arriving at an O'Malley camp staffed by more than just hired thugs.

Only then might she be able to convince the Mäkinen camp to mount an army. She'd die for the right cause, but trust her own leadership? No way. Too many ghosts and auras and blood-streaked memories made her doubt her sanity, let alone her ability to see to the safety of others.

But that meant finding the camp. Arturi Mäkinen was as much the stuff of legend as she was. Only, what if the pull she felt toward his haven was just another of the crazy voices she'd battled for years?

Pen fought her despair, only to find the guard leering at her breasts. *You'll never get a taste.*

A guard like him wouldn't ever earn enough to sample the flesh he peddled. Not unless he turned on his boss and went rogue. And that never ended well.

The brakes squealed. The truck lurched as it slowed.

With his hand only loosely gripping a handhold, the guard tumbled toward the front. Pen fell from her relaxed restraints and somersaulted into another woman's thigh, killing her momentum.

Another shriek of the brakes brought the truck to a full stop.

She threw a glance over her shoulder. The other guard was too busy checking his weapon to notice her. Keeping low, she crawled back to her spot. But before she could return her wrists to the wire fetters, she froze. A tingling prickle of awareness clawed like a cat walking up her spine. Someone was coming. Someone with magic.

She knew the difference between ordinary humans and those blessed—or cursed, depending—with gifts bestowed by the Change. No one in the truck. Whoever she felt was coming from the outside.

Two shots fired. Shotguns, by the sound.

The guard with the scar scrambled to his feet. He made it to the middle of the truck, halfway to his partner, when he froze, too. Likely not because he felt magic.

Likely, it was because of the lion's roar.

The hairs on Pen's arms lifted. From deep in her chest came a primal response. In ancient times, men had learned to craft weapons to defend their families from that sound. Hunter and hunted. Kill or be killed. Predators fighting for control of their territory.

The roar came again, this time as the rear canvas split down the center. A huge male lion leaped into the truck. Captives screamed, but none so loudly as the guard at the back. His frantic burst of terror didn't last long. The golden beast's powerful jaw cut it short. A quick shake of his massive neck ensured his opponent was dead.

Pen gave up on pretense. She freed her arms and scrambled to the end of the truck nearest the cab. The guard with the scar stood between her and the massive cat. No telling what the beast intended. Feral skinwalkers were as much a danger as human scum like O'Malley's people.

The guard raised his weapon—something automatic with a sight for night vision. Leaping, the lion closed the half-dozen meters and landed on the man's chest. The gun fired. More than one bullet. Screams erupted from the back of the truck. The guard hit the bed of the truck with the sickening crack of fracturing bone. Maybe his sternum? His spinal column? Not that it mattered. He lay motionless, eyes blank, beneath the lion's broad paws. The impressive weapon lay idle in his lifeless hand.

Pen scoped out the situation. She'd have only a second of warning if the animal went for the prisoners.

Instead, the lion sniffed the air. He swiveled his strong neck, thick with a wild mane, as if appraising the truck's contents. An eerie, sky-blue gaze locked with Pen's.

A hot spark of déjà vu replaced cold fear. She frowned. The lion sniffed again but moved no closer. She stood, her fingers at her back to use the chicken wire as support. Her thighs trembled, but the tingling return of sensation to her lower legs bordered on misery.

"May I have the gun?"

Her voice sounded peculiar in the near silence. No engine noise. No shouts. Only a few sniffles as the slaves took stock of the mangled bodies.

The lion glanced at the weapon in the fallen guard's useless grip. He almost seemed to . . . shrug. And turned away.

Pen wasted no time in claiming the weapon. Staying in the truck was useless now, her mission scrapped. Even if the lion had left any of O'Malley's people alive, they'd be unlikely to give up additional details of the camp's location. The best she could do now was free the captives and see that they escaped.

Her best opportunity. Ruined.

Finger on the trigger, she was tempted—just for a moment—to take out her frustration on the lion as he stalked away.

But he had obviously acted with purpose. Killing the guards. Walking away from the defenseless. Some skinwalkers became entirely animal—not as vicious as the demon dogs that still roamed unchecked, but without enough humanity to make distinctions. Flesh was food. Simple as that.

This big cat obviously thought otherwise.

Pen followed him, signaling the others to remain still. She kept the gun at the ready, although she doubted her reflexes. The guard hadn't stood a chance when the lion decided to strike.

The air at the back of the truck glowed. Warmth coated her exposed skin like the sun emerging from clouds. Pen stared in momentary amazement as the lion shifted. She rarely got to witness the transformations. Jenna Barclay, one of her guardians for many years, had been a skinwalker unashamed of her abilities. But most lived like creatures in the woods, unwilling to be seen. Others retained their human forms within little clusters of society, because O'Malley had hunted them since he came to power.

This . . . this was incredible.

The lion's skeleton realigned, shrinking and warping into the form of a naked man. His lean street fighter's body was a map of sinew and defined muscle. Fur retracted to reveal skin. Pale skin. Dark hair. She stared for long moments in captivated silence. Something about him plucked at her memories.

Pen hadn't expected goose bumps. But then, she hadn't expected to recognize him either.

"I know you," she whispered. "I *know* you."

He raised a brow. "Then what's my name?"

"Tru Daugherty."

TWO

Tru stared. The woman's words snared him because he'd told so damn few people his real name. This world didn't call for intimacy. Didn't call for anything.

Nietzsche would've loved the hell out of the Change.

Though he was naked, he took his time studying her. His gaze skated over her dirty face. Decent bones, good body—if a little thin, but that was common. Few people had the luxury of overeating. She had killer eyes, indigo like a night sky over the ocean, fringed in dark gold lashes, and snapping at his scrutiny. Great mouth. If he hosed her off, he could have some fun with her.

Just fun. Nothing deep. He'd given up on that idea long ago. When stopping the truck, he had been looking for one of two things: sex or death. And he wasn't picky about which won the coin toss. The lion rumbled in his head, disturbed by his kamikaze attitude. In sharing the same skin, they were codependent.

She made an exasperated noise at his continued silence. Despite himself, Tru studied her slender neck, revealed by her short hair. Lovely. He'd always had a thing for that hint of feminine vulnerability. The lion rumbled in agreement.

He lifted his shoulders in a shrug. "You were saying?"

"Do you remember me?"

"You seem to think I should." In truth, she held a hauntingly familiar air, but if he admitted he recognized her, then she'd probably expect him to help—save the orphans or the slaves, whatever her crusade.

Tru wasn't the hero type. Not anymore. Some people could get up after profound failure, dust themselves off, and become better. Stronger. Fight harder. He wasn't that guy.

"It doesn't matter. We need to stop the bleeding, here—"

"Good luck with that." He turned away.

He'd just wanted to screw with O'Malley, and then grab the prettiest girl for a little private party. He wasn't in the business of hopeless causes.

Not since one very dark day when he'd lost everything. Only pain came of being selfless and optimistic.

The truck contained plenty of wounded, some bleeding more than others. They wouldn't be any use to him, nor he to them. No solace left to offer.

Some stared at him in dazed terror. That was unsurprising. Few people got used to seeing a man crawl out of an animal's skin. Most days, life as a lion was a hell of a lot simpler. But since he didn't know any compatible shifters—he'd left those contacts behind long ago—he only prowled for sex in the shape of a man. These shell-shocked folks looked like a buffet of possibilities. Likely any one of the women would go with him in gratitude for his rescue. But first he had to show he meant them no harm.

He was an expert at getting what he wanted. These days, that skill was all he had left. It permitted him to forget, albeit briefly, that he'd ever been anything more.

Sliding past the bound captives, careful not to touch, Tru selected the guard who had died cleanest. He stripped the man's clothes, shook them out, and dressed while the scruffy, familiar woman watched in astonishment. Her lovely mouth parted, as if she didn't know what to say to him or how to say it.

Then she, too, went to work, but with a different end. A soft glow kindled about her as she bent to minister to those weeping in pain. *Like a fucking angel.* Her silence triggered the memory, more than her words could. Because the girl he'd known rarely talked to anyone.

But she'd spoken to him.

"Penelope," he said with a slow smile. "It's been a long time. You look . . . good." He rendered another visual inspection, judging her tender curves. Short blonde-streaked hair revealed a graceful sweep of neck.

"Pen," she corrected in a tight voice, not even looking at him. Busy, elbow-deep in blood.

Fuckable.

But it would be weird and complicated. And she'd expect him to stick around because of their shared past. At seventeen, he'd left the home Jenna and Mason had built. They'd taken in Penny as well, after her mother died, and Chris Welsh moved on. They were the reason he'd survived the first, awful winter after the Change. Mason taught him everything he knew—the closest thing Tru had known to a father. Never once had he considered heading back to see how they fared, if they had kids, or if their homestead prospered. Sometimes it was better to imagine the best.

Given his grim history, he wouldn't be able to bear it if the people who'd saved him were gone, too.

Tru shook his head. Penelope would not be the woman he carried away from the truck. She seemed to be healing some of these folks, meaning she was a witchy do-gooder. He'd fare better with someone else.

His gaze lit on a pretty thing chained up by her arms. She seemed less terrified, watching him with eyes afraid to hope. He found a knife in the guard's pocket and moved in, slow and cautious.

"I'm going to cut you loose," he told the girl. "Do you speak English? *Hablas inglés?*" That was pretty much all the Spanish he knew. If they didn't share a language, they were boned.

"Yes," she whispered.

"Hold still, then. It'll take me a while to saw through the wire. I don't think I can untangle you without freeing this end first." He flashed a roguish smile. "I'll try to be gentle."

She smiled back that time, responding to his practiced charm. "Thank you."

Nearby, Pen made another sound. He couldn't tell what emotion it represented, and he didn't much care. This was the woman he would take out of the truck and call his own for a while. Oh, he'd find somewhere safe to leave her once he was sated. But until then, they'd have a great time in bed. So for today, sex won.

Death could wait a little longer.

She needed a bath and time to recover, but if he played his cards right, this little bird would creep into his bedroll, trembling with excitement and appreciation. That was his favorite part of the chase— when the prey didn't even know she was being hunted. A thrill of arousal shivered through him, but he didn't let on, merely kept working the blade against the wire.

Pen was still working behind him. The air gained a visible charge, like sunlight reflected on a new sidewalk. It had been a long time since he'd seen that, but he'd never forgotten the shine. Hairs on his nape lifted as she murmured something, almost a chant. Hella distracting. Fine, she could save them. Teach them to read and make pottery, whatever industrious females did these days.

"What's your name?" he asked the girl.

"Calla."

"That's pretty."

"It's Greek," she volunteered in a tiny voice. "My mother told me it means 'beautiful.'"

He smiled. "You are. Eyes like pansies. It's terrible what these bastards did to you because you're young and gorgeous."

"You think so?" Those eyes beamed more hope up at him.

She should really know better by now. None of us can be trusted, especially me.

But he offered his best smile. "I promise. How old are you?"

He retained some pre-Change scruples. Some men didn't. Just as some skinwalkers had gone cannibal, some men had lost all sense of who might be a suitable sex partner. Tru wouldn't touch a girl if she said she was fifteen. That was how old he'd been when everything fell apart.

"Eighteen," she answered.

Old enough. He'd be twenty-seven soon. People grew up fast in this life. Her age might prove a bonus because she'd be infatuated with him for a short time. She'd get over him when he left, and find someone to build a life with down the road. Older women were more dangerous, mature in their emotions and their attachments. When a thirty-something woman told him she loved him, she meant it. Tru still moved on, though he regretted any lasting harm. He couldn't stick around after dealing with the fallout when he did.

With a ping, the wire gave and he freed it from the coils around Calla's forearm. That left only one to go. Before moving on, he set his hands lightly on her arm and rubbed the circulation back. Her throat worked and her eyes fell half closed. It was almost too easy with this one. Given half a chance, she would curl into him like a kitten. Women desired men they saw as saviors.

"How come you're helping me?" she asked. "Other people need you more. I'm not going to die or anything."

"You're special. I knew that as soon as I saw you." He spoke the lie without a tell.

Another of those sounds from Pen. He ignored her, but Calla cast the other woman a questioning glance. "Do you need his help? I can wait."

"I'm fine," Pen muttered, but her voice had a thick, dazed sound.

Annoyed, Tru turned. The clammy pallor of her face was visible even beneath the dirt. She knelt over a girl who definitely wasn't going to make it. He could have told her that and saved her some time. A silver glow kindled from her hands, radiating steadily.

"She doesn't look good," Calla observed.

Dammit. He should have his pick hauled out of the truck by now. But her pansy eyes said she would be disappointed if he didn't pretend an interest in helping the others. If he hadn't already set his course and claimed Calla was special, he'd pick a less idealistic, more grateful girl. But full on, as they say.

So he put down the knife and crouched beside Pen. She was still trying to save the patient, but he didn't think it was possible. "She's not going to make it."

He pulled her hands away, interrupting whatever the hell she was doing. That touch gave him a crazy shock, like grabbing a live wire—if anything still ran on electricity, which it didn't.

The jolt from her skin left him tingling and dizzy. "Fuck."

"Asshole!" she shouted. "You killed her."

"No, the guard did that." He tried to keep calm, to make her see reason. Why, he couldn't be sure. "You were just prolonging it. You've got some mighty mojo, but she's not gonna live. Look at the hole in her gut. Move on to those you can save."

Because he knew Calla wanted him to, he ripped some bandages from a dead guard's clothing and helped Pen with the wounded. Not something he'd normally do, but he was getting hungrier by the minute. Shifting took a lot out of him. Soon he'd look as fragile and pasty as Pen. Women didn't respond to weakness. If he wanted Calla to go with him, he had to show her he was strong and capable.

"There, that's the best I can do here."

At last he and Pen had bound the wounds, their supplies crude and their patients edgy for freedom. Tru returned to Calla. By sheer effort of will, he concealed the light tremor in his hands as he sawed the wire. She was gazing at him like he was a proper hero.

Game, set, and match.

He freed the girl and extended a hand. "Come on, precious. We need to make tracks before O'Malley misses this shipment."

It gave him a little burst of pleasure when her small fingers touched his. She stepped from the truck, his hands on her waist. She took a step toward him as if unable to help herself, seeking his proximity. *Mine. Soon.* The lion in him gave a lazy growl of approval. He needed a fuck so bad.

The girl drew up short then, glancing up at the truck. "But what about the others?"

"I'll help them get to safety," Pen said firmly.

But she looked winded and wan, hardly able to shepherd a motley group of refugees. Tru gave them half an hour in the wasteland. Tops. *Not my problem.*

Until Calla said, "We'll help you."

Shit. Tru glared. He could get to hate Penelope fucking Sheehan.

THREE

Pen stared back. But mentally, she changed him into the boy she'd once known. This version of Tru, grown-up and beautiful, was a selfish bastard.

The young woman, Calla, stared at him with the eyes of a little girl at Christmas. Pen remembered feeling that way. She'd sat on her mother's lap, determined to stay awake long enough to see Santa come down the chimney. She'd never managed to do so, but neither had she lost faith.

The Change had taken it from her instead.

Trying to heal that wounded prisoner had taken a lot from her, too. She hated that Tru had been right about the poor kid. The girl just bled and bled. Pen had been willing to try her most dedicated spell, knowing the risk. She hadn't been allowed that chance.

Now she had a whole truckful of captives to protect, and the only viable partner in her task was one surly, selfish skinwalker.

Pen grabbed a cloth from the pile of rags the guards had confiscated from their quarry. After wiping her hands, she dug a little deeper and found her cloak. And her belt of knives. She didn't know what god to thank anymore when things went right, so she always just thanked her mother—the closest connection she maintained with the divine.

Wrapping that fine, familiar wool around her shoulders, she held her dizziness at bay. She needed food and sleep. That was the counter to the energy expended for her spells. With another glance at Tru, she knew he suffered the same ailment. Magic could be a fine thing, but it made unearthly demands on the body.

"Calla," she said evenly, taking a knee. "Would you do something for me?"

The woman nodded. She really was an incredible beauty. But there was a time and place for everything. In the Changed world, Pen couldn't imagine any benefit to being so attractive. It only meant attention that few females desired.

But then, Tru had chosen Calla from two dozen possibilities. She would live because of his attention, and because of her pretty face.

Some things hadn't changed at all.

"The driver. The guards. They must've had food somewhere. Will you look for it?"

As if asking for permission, Calla flicked a glance toward Tru, where he lounged against a tree trunk, arms folded over his chest.

He simply shrugged. "Can't hurt."

Maybe the girl wasn't so oblivious as Pen had first assumed. "And you *will* help, yes?"

Tru sighed, shook his head in resignation, and pushed away from the tree. Calla rustled through the pile of clothing and found a jacket with shredded sleeves. Who knew if it was actually hers, but she seemed compelled to cover up. Yes, she had a little sense after all. Then she was gone, hurrying off toward the front of the truck.

"You could be sending her to face an armed driver," he said, strolling to meet her. He yanked aside the canvas flap.

"You don't leave wounded if you attack." She met his gaze. "I'd stake my soul on it."

He snorted. "Soul. Good luck with that."

"Tell me I'm wrong, then. Tell me I just sent that girl to her death."

"They're dead. She'll be fine."

Together they helped the prisoners from the truck. The process was arduous, as most were hobbled by injuries or pure, cold fear. But at least Tru stuck around long enough to offer his aid—no matter the don't-give-a-shit smile on his lush lips. Despite the grace and power in his sleek body, Pen noticed that his arms shook. Shifting depleted him as badly as magic did her.

After boosting herself into the truck, she worked on freeing the rest of the bound prisoners. Had she been truly tied or wired in that chicken coop of a vehicle, she would've behaved like a wolverine. Chew loose. Escape by any means, even without her magic. But most of the prisoners simply languished. Hoping for rescue in this age was the same as waiting to die.

She couldn't relate, but she sympathized.

One captive, however, was not so passive. Tru had climbed inside to join her and worked to loosen fastenings on the truck's left side while Pen faced the boy who'd sat beside her for the whole journey. He'd cringed when she worked to wrench free. But with the guards dead, he didn't cower anymore. She wiped blood on her leggings and got a better grip on her knife, ready to help.

"What's your name?"

Keen brown eyes above a wide mouth watched her face as she worked on his ties. He had lovely dark skin, all smooth and free of the worry he must feel. "Adrian."

"You ready to get out of here, Adrian?"

"Yes, I am." He hesitated, not even speaking when he brought around his free hands. Fingers petted wrists, almost nervously. "You're . . . You're her, aren't you?"

She stilled. "Who?"

"The Orchid."

Those remaining in the truck fell silent. If she looked behind her, she'd find what she always did: a mixture of awe, fear, and reserve. The Orchid inspired that in people—just as she'd intended years ago. Pen had found the strategy useful when rallying troops against impossible odds and providing comfort for the fallen. But the legend had outpaced her abilities.

"My name is Pen," she said quietly. "You may call me that."

Adrian seemed only a little chastened. He continued to watch her with a gaze bordering on worshipful.

Fantastic. Both she and Tru had acolytes. But they could be of use.

She freed the boy, then faced the remaining captives. "I'm looking for Arturi Mäkinen's refuge. Can anyone tell me where it is?"

Silence. But Pen had opened her mind, catching glimpses and fragments and pieces of scattered puzzles. She saw a beach—dunes along the ocean. A word: Hatteras.

That, too, confirmed her collection of rumors. Cape Hatteras it was. She only hoped the other scattered intelligence she'd gathered about O'Malley's fortress would be useful, and that the man named Arturi would be willing to take his people to war. By all accounts, he was a man of peace and seclusion. But if the talk was to be believed, he'd also amassed the largest human settlement in the Changed world.

It was worth the risk.

After Tru had freed the final prisoner, she asked, "Can you hunt?"

He shot her a sidelong glare. "No. But I think you knew that. Why rub my face in it?"

"So you'll remember you're a human being and leave that girl alone."

A patronizing smile turned his pretty mouth into something fiercer, the smile of a predator. But with fair skin and the clearest blue eyes in creation, he remained almost unimaginably beautiful. "She doesn't want me to leave her alone," he said smoothly. "Haven't the last twelve years taught you anything?"

He should've patted her on the head after that high-handed dismissal. Instead he stood and stretched. Some might have called him lanky, but they'd be wrong. He was too powerfully muscled. The grace he carried just under the skin was a constant reminder of the lion inside, as was the faint glow of a gold aura that enveloped him like a halo. She knew that was one of her particular gifts—sensing the auras of other magical beings—but it only added to his majesty. Dark hair tumbled across his forehead as if blatantly disregarding his hard facade.

Tru Daugherty had matured into a stunning man, and he eyed Calla's return with unabashed lust.

Pen had got him wrong. He wasn't a predator. Not really. Predators protected their territory and battled enemies that would do harm to their kind.

This man was a vulture. A beautiful one, to be certain, but picking at carrion on the edges of civilization. Pen found herself oddly . . . disappointed.

"I found these," Calla said excitedly, meeting them at the back of the truck.

She knelt beside Pen and laid out a selection of foods, mostly fruit. Malformed things that looked like bananas, or maybe plantains. A few small, hard oranges. Like the roadside foliage left to grow wild, no one remained to tend fruit trees. She'd also found a hunk of what looked like unleavened bread.

But no protein. It would have to do. Pen ripped the skin off the banana and forced the dry, sticky fruit into her mouth. Bite after bite restored balance to her brain, even if the mush tasted like bitter sawdust. Pen finished the hunk of bread and swallowed thickly, sharing with the worst of the malnourished prisoners.

She tried to get a sense of where they were. Still in Florida. Or close to it. The trees along the roadside were fat with clinging moss. With few people left to indulge in things like trimming branches, nothing restricted the swamp's rabid growth. Just heat and greenery and a cloying humidity that made her dizziness no easier to handle.

Adrian stayed by her side as she worked, helping the others collect their belongings from the heap of clothes. She reclaimed the guard's weapon in order to break up a fight between two emaciated, foulmouthed women who looked alike enough to be sisters. Maybe they were. Desperation weakened even bonds of blood.

Prisoners fled into the swampy overgrowth. Unable or unwilling to free themselves, they certainly had no problem fading into the wild when given a split-second opportunity. Adrian stayed. Calla stayed. Most of the others were gone before the sun pulled fully over the horizon.

Pen watched the bickering sisters disappear over a distant crest of road. Just like that.

"Were you expecting thanks?"

Tru's voice was low, but not like her memory of Mason's. The grizzled warrior who'd raised her since her mother's death had sounded oddly broken, as if his vocal cords were damaged. The deep rumble had more power because he never quite seemed in control of it.

With Tru, however . . . his voice was just as deep, but with the mesmerizing daze of a snake's hiss. Fascinating and dangerous. No syllable out of place.

"No, of course not," she said, still watching the now-deserted road. "That wasn't why I was there."

"No, the divine Orchid rides with O'Malley scum all the time."

Her attention caught on the cynical twist of his lips. Did he ever speak to anyone without condescension? Had he ever? But thinking back to when they'd both been under Mason and Jenna's care was painful. She had been . . . broken. Shattered by her mother's death. The little comfort she found in the following months had been with Tru, but those instances were so rare as to be priceless. His reluctant laughter and stupid jokes, always quoting words that made little sense to a lonely nine-year-old. Hadn't needed to.

But then he'd left. Just when her thoughts had started making sense again. Gone.

She took a breath. Memories locked away. Where they belonged.

"I was trying to infiltrate the nearest O'Malley camp."

Those pale, pale eyes bored into hers. "And why would you want to do that?"

"To learn the exact location of O'Malley's fortress, helping as many as I can along the way. Ultimately, I'd like to see the whole damn organization dismantled."

"By yourself?"

No, never by herself. She couldn't be trusted to lead, not when her powers made her so unpredictable. That potential to lose control . . .

She'd done well with the resistance in the west. Healing, mostly. Identifying other practitioners of magic, then instructing them in how to channel their new, often confusing abilities.

Penance for the damage she'd already done.

Her reputation had grown then, as a patron saint among the rebels. Most people considered her one step short of sacred. But that also meant they'd looked to her for direction. For guarantees. With no such faith in her divinity or self-restraint, she'd slipped away and headed east—where no one would know her name.

And yet the legend of the Orchid had followed.

"No," she said. "Not by myself. I'm not a leader. Now it's time for new allies."

"You're an idiot, you know that? And here I thought by your reputation, that you must be pretty amazing."

"And what reputation is that?"

The skin around his eyes tightened as he stared her down, as if probing deeper. "From what I'd heard, the Orchid is a goddess on earth, a benevolent healer, and a good-luck charm for those who choose rebellion over obedience." His grin turned dirty. "To a chosen few men, she offers the sanctuary of her chaste flesh. Only, I never got that part. Seems the virginal bit would wear off after the first lucky bastard. You running some scam?"

She forced herself to relax. "You can stop now."

"Fine by me. You're welcome, by the way."

"Now who expects thanks?"

"Oh, that'd be me," he said with a clipped grin. "I kept you from being thrown into a goddamn sex dungeon. Lavish praise would be appropriate."

"You interfered for what? You were poaching girls as much as O'Malley's men do."

"Hardly."

Pen laughed, revealing her disgust. "And what you're offering Calla is so different?"

He surprised her by cupping her cheeks—broad palms with long, elegant fingers. A little too roughly, he pulled her face up so that their eyes could throw daggers at very close range. His thumbs stroked the tops of her cheeks, brushing at the dirt. Only his sneer kept it from feeling like a caress.

"Calla will eat. She'll relax, knowing she's with the baddest mother-fucker around. And I'll damn well make sure she comes. She gets *everything* with me. While the Orchid gets the satisfaction of a job well done . . . and maybe a little slap and tickle with the kid." He released her and stepped away, sketching a bow. "I hope he's fun, but I hear training boys can be frustrating."

FOUR

Green. It should have been a lovely color, affirmation of life and all that. Instead it drooped and slithered, sank damp fingers into his bones. The heat created a sheen on Tru's skin, exacerbated by the humidity. This was where fungal infections set in. Wanting to get out of the cold, years ago, he'd come south. But this was too much. Lions thrived in dry heat. Maybe he'd be better off in what used to be Arizona.

They had been walking for hours. Penelope the Good Witch claimed, after peering at some dirt in cloudy water, to see shelter not too far away. While she might, indeed, possess such crazy powers, he didn't like having them too close. Magic after the Change wasn't a benign force, so far as he'd seen. People used it to usurp authority to which they had no rightful claim. He was better off removed from the world.

Tru had stowed his belongings not too far up the road—a change of clothes, some odds and ends he'd picked up along the way. More importantly, he'd also stashed some food. It wasn't greed that made him devour everything he'd put back. If he were to be of any use in protecting the girl he'd chosen, he needed to refuel. And he wouldn't be able to go lion again until he snagged a hefty dose of sleep. The laws of nature could only be bent, not broken.

"You don't intend to share?" Pen asked.

"Share what? It's gone."

"Asshole," she muttered.

Whatever. He just needed to find a quiet place to rest and then he'd take Calla someplace safe. And private. She seemed like a sweet girl. The lion in his head didn't register much opinion on her otherwise, but the beast agreed she would do. *For now.*

"How did they grab you?" he asked over his shoulder.

Calla hunched her shoulders as if she didn't want to talk about it. And the way she held the gun? Sloppy. Inattentive. *Mason would have kicked my ass.*

Pen led the way, Adrian behind her, while Tru fell back to try explaining some of the finer points of handling a weapon. Calla stared at him, puzzled, as he talked. Yeah, men probably didn't try to teach her not to need them.

Calling it a loss, he stepped up his pace and pushed past Adrian to ask Pen, "How much farther is it, O mystic one?"

"Half a kilometer. I think."

"You're not sure?" It was fun to bait her.

"Scrying is not a precise science. Be patient or go find your own love nest."

Before Tru could reply, everything went to hell. He wheeled as six feral shifters burst from the swampy undergrowth. He should've sensed their presence, but fatigue was no excuse. They pounced on Calla. She panicked, flailing instead of shooting. Her scream died to a gurgle as they went for her throat. She dropped her gun as Tru brought his own weapon up, cocked, and fired. The pack snarled, dragging off their prize for a private feast. He nailed them repeatedly, but it was too late to do Calla any good.

Pen fought coolly at his side, aiming and shooting with more finesse than he would've thought possible for a do-gooder witch. Her composure earned his grudging respect, even as adrenaline and remorse mixed a sick cocktail in his veins. Adrian shook but still tried to defend.

He needs teaching. Mason would have taken him in hand.

The skinwalkers died like animals. Just as they'd chosen to live. Their corpses twitched, matted fur yielding to human form. Three men, three women.

This was his nightmare. *If I'm not careful, this is how I'll end up.*

Without looking at the others, he strode over to Calla's body. He could tell she was dead even before he knelt, but he brushed hair away from her blood-smeared forehead and gazed into those pansy eyes one last time.

He'd chosen her. That made him responsible for her, at least for a little while. And he'd let her down. It was part of the sexual compact that the lion guarded his mates, however long he chose to stay. Lions were notoriously lazy, of course, and let their females do most of the work, but they did scare off other predators, sometimes with nothing more than a roar.

I got complacent. An echo of old failure—the one that had cost him so dearly—cut to the bone.

"Sorry," he whispered. He closed his eyes so he didn't hurl. After two deep breaths, regaining his composure, he pushed to his feet. "Shall we?"

Pen didn't argue his decision to leave Calla. He guessed she was more practical than she appeared. They couldn't afford to remain vulnerable. There might be others nearby, who would be drawn to the stink of carnage. Without ammunition or physical reserves, he wouldn't be able to fight off half the swamp.

"It's not too much farther," she said, low. "We'll make it before dark."

A grim and silent trio, they trudged the last leg of the journey. Just before sunset, Tru shaded his eyes and registered what she called shelter. No more than a tar-paper shack, long since abandoned and claimed by the elements. Some eccentric had used all sorts of rubbish to build his home; Tru would be astonished if the place wasn't crawling with vermin. But at least it would keep them hidden. And if the clouds overhead were any indication, they were about to get a shower.

The shelter was mildewed inside, stuffed with piles of broken junk that testified to its abandonment. A skeleton sat in a half-rotted wooden rocking chair. As Adrian watched with dawning interest, Tru picked up the whole mess and carted it outside. He remembered feeling just that way, confronted with an adult who didn't look piss-scared over every little thing. Mason had been his first experience with a man who didn't scream, lash out, or drink himself stupid every night.

The boy nodded to the skeleton. "What do you think happened to him?"

He shot himself, kid.

Tru recognized the damage to the front of the skull as a bullet wound, not a blunt instrument. If he had to guess, he'd say the man saw the beginning of the Change and decided he didn't want to stick around for the closing credits. Some days that felt like the smart move.

Instead of saying that, he merely shrugged and erred on the side of kindness. The good witch must be rubbing off on him.

"I need you to take first watch," he told Adrian, who straightened his shoulders at the brusque command. Tru knew how that felt. The kid was probably thinking, *You trust me? Seriously?* "Penelope and I need sleep in the worst way. We'll be able to protect you better once we rest. Until then, it's all you. Keep your gun trained on the door and shoot anything that moves. If it's not trying to kill us, we can cook and eat it for breakfast."

The boy laughed but soon quieted, as if he wasn't sure the remark was meant to be funny. Tru let himself smile, but inwardly he groaned. This was why he never stuck around. People got attached. Roots turned into chains, expectations into demands. And it hurt too much when those chains were severed. He didn't like remembering that he'd once worn them with sheer joy.

He revealed none of those thoughts as he cleared a space and stretched out. "Wake me in three hours."

Adrian nodded and settled into the doorway.

Tru's skin prickled from the weight of Penelope's regard. He cocked a brow at her. "Can I help you?"

"You were nice to him."

He gave her a lazy smile. "The sun rises in the east, too."

"I wouldn't have thought he'd be worth the bother since you can't sleep with him." And then her pretty face froze, eyeing him with speculation he didn't like. "Unless . . . no, I won't *let* you."

He knew what she suspected, despite her garbled outrage. It shouldn't bother him. And it didn't. Much.

"He's too young for me," he said.

Let her make of that what she would. He didn't begrudge people finding pleasure where they could, regardless of the labels it earned them. Just . . . not with kids, despite his prior teasing.

He'd killed for much less.

Ignoring the other two, because he was fucking done, he rolled onto his side, wrapped up in a blanket from his pack, and went to sleep. He woke just before dawn. Sunset to sunrise, he'd slept like an animal.

The kid hadn't just taken the first watch; he'd stood *all* of them. It was the kind of crazy-gallant thing Tru would've done early on, trying to earn Mason's respect. But it also lacked foresight because now they couldn't move until noon. Adrian needed rest or he'd keel over on the trail.

The boy sat with glazed eyes still trained on the door, gun in hand. Tru crept over to him. "Get some sleep. You did good." The words sounded rough to his own ears. He hadn't provided positive reinforcement to a child in years.

But Adrian relaxed and put down his weapon. Fighting the urge to curse, Tru handed over his own blanket. He could feel the knots tightening around his ankles; he might have to chew his own foot off to get away.

Like the predator he was, he stole out into the pearly light, weapon in hand. They had no food, which meant it was high time he found some. In a place like this, he could count on alligators. They were tough to take down but provided a ton of meat beneath thick hides. Gator meat was lean and mild, though prone to going dry and crumbly when cooked. They needed fat to keep from starving, but the protein would keep them going.

"Deserting us?"

Penelope stood in the shack doorway, her short, gold-shot hair tousled from sleep.

In the faint morning light, her eyes were luminous, dark, and haunting blue. She'd grown up to be beautiful and . . . good. And he disappointed her. He'd seen the flicker of it in her eyes—that he hadn't turned into a hero who could heal the world of its sorrows. He remembered with uncomfortable clarity the way she used to cling to him, the way she followed him and watched him, and put her small hand in his.

This version of Penelope Sheehan looked harder, less vulnerable, and yet she hadn't stopped trying to help. In Tru's book, that made her crazy.

He lofted the rifle in his hand. "I thought I'd get breakfast, actually."

"So you're going hunting." Was that relief in the softening of her mouth?

"That was my plan. I'd invite you along but somebody needs to keep an eye on the kid."

"You're good with him," she said. "Just like Mason was with you."

Oh, low blow, lady. Low. Blow.

He wondered how much she remembered of their time together. If she recalled whispering in his ear when she wouldn't talk to anyone else. If she remembered climbing into his lap after she had a nightmare. It felt weird being confronted with her as a grown woman. He hadn't seen any of her awkward, intermediate stages, as if she'd transformed from caterpillar to butterfly without need for a chrysalis. If that wasn't magic, he didn't know what was.

"And?"

"How long do you plan to stick around thereafter?" she asked.

I don't. Calla had been his incentive to play along.

Penelope must've read the truth in his eyes. She smiled at him, really smiled—and the sight stole his breath. But her eyes held an assessing look, as if she had some scheme in mind. Tru admired a clever female, even if they were often more hassle than he desired. This one promised to be more work than ten women.

But when had he last set his sights on anything other than quick and easy? A challenge might be . . . interesting.

"When you get back," she said, still smiling, "I have a proposition for you."

FIVE

Pen didn't expect him to come back. Worse than that, she didn't *want* to expect him back. But the idea she had for continuing her work against O'Malley never left her mind.

She collected water from the swamp, which was revolting. For a fire she had gathered branches from one corner of the shelter, which looked to be an abandoned animal's nest. Even if Tru returned, and even if he found game, they would still need drinking water. And she desperately wanted to get clean.

The morning was sticky and warm. She'd sweated like hell in the truck, and the brief subsequent rain hadn't brought a hint of cool. Now the challenge was drawing an easy breath. Heavy humidity sat on her chest like a stack of stones.

She found Adrian still awake on the pallet he'd made of Tru's blanket. Exhaustion added a waxy pallor to his dark skin. The whites of his eyes were far too big, as if he always looked at the world in a state of surprise.

Maybe he did.

"You should sleep." She touched his forehead. No magic with this touch, although rest and food had restored her to full potency. Just the comfort skin could give to skin. He sighed quietly as his eyelids dropped.

"He won't be back," Adrian said, his voice a whispering rustle. "Will he?"

"Best to prepare yourself for the worst, I think. People don't come back. Or they die."

"Like Calla."

Pen stopped, swallowing a surprising clench of sadness. She spoke frankly about death because that was what needed to be done. She wasn't used to . . . revisiting. Certainly not dwelling. But Calla's panicked eyes wouldn't leave her be. The girl had been so scared. And then she was gone. Just like that.

"Yes, like Calla."

When was the last time she'd stopped to mourn? She couldn't even recall. Grief was a wound that wouldn't heal. As long as she had people to help and knowledge to pass along, she didn't feel so helpless. A pack of feral shifters couldn't wipe out humanity with one surprise strike. But they'd snuffed out one young woman.

I don't do helpless.

She thought it even as her hands shook. "We'll move at midday."

"Where to?"

"We'll figure that out when you wake. No sense borrowing trouble."

With a deep breath, she forced away the obvious. Nothing to be done. Move on. Help someone else. She stepped out into the morning. The swamp was just *noisy*. If she hadn't known better, she'd imagine the absolute worst. Shadows and shades creeping between the branches, death on two feet. But she wasn't a little girl anymore, huddling against her mother's side when tales from the Brothers Grimm had become too intense. She no longer needed to imagine the worst. She'd fought it. Survived it.

She'd even perpetrated it.

With the dead branches stacked in front of the shelter, she rummaged through the detritus they'd scavenged off the guards and from the cab of the truck. Although no one owned lighters anymore, most carried flint. Or magic—a kind she didn't possess. She found a shard of flint wrapped in a shredded piece of cotton, protected as the special resource it had become. Soon she had the makings of a fire.

Then it was just about waiting. For the water to boil. For the swamp to close in on her in a flurry of fangs and teeth. For Tru to come back. Pen sat on the shack's ramshackle porch and shook her head. Best not wait on that.

She'd give him till high noon. Then she and Adrian would continue on their own. With one of the semiautomatic weapons across her lap, she leaned against the wall.

A distant gunshot yanked her to her feet. Only one shot, no matter how hard she listened for another.

With the water boiled and her nerves stretching thin, she set about washing her body, hair, and clothes. Something to do. Something to keep her mind from crawling out of her skull. Wrapped in her cloak, she scrubbed her leggings and shirt, not holding out much hope they'd be dry by midday. The air was humid, but the fire might help. She needed to try. The opportunity was too good to pass up.

With a makeshift washcloth, she indulged in the simplicity of getting clean. The hot water provided some relief from the sticky dawn as it dried on her skin.

"Goddesses need to wash?"

Pen prided herself on not making a sound. A little flinch. But no gasp of surprise. She didn't want to increase her chances of turning around and finding him smirking.

She turned. And he *was* smirking. Of course he was.

He was also holding the tail of an alligator. The beast dangled headfirst over his shoulder. He propped the weapon against the other, looking like some exotic game hunter. Her mother had loved elephants, and the wildlife videos Pen had watched before the Change made men like Tru out to be the villains. That didn't quite sit right on him. Not entirely. Because at that moment he'd brought them food.

And he'd come back.

What's more, she bet the single shot had come from his gun. That alligator would have only one bullet in its brain.

"I wash," she said tersely. "And I'm not a goddess."

"Nope. You're not." Tru nodded toward the shack. "But do you think Adrian in there knows that?"

"Doesn't matter what he thinks of me. He's got you."

Tru sloughed the alligator onto the ground. "Either take your cloak off or shut up."

"What, you can only handle conversation if you get a reward?"

"Pretty much."

"Human beings communicate. Through words. That's what sets us apart from the animals."

"That so?"

The way he watched her, tracked her with his eyes, was an ever-present reminder of the animal inside his Changed cells. She wasn't surprised at all that he'd become a skinwalker. A preternatural feline grace had been with him as a teenager, even when he clunked around the nature station in too-large combat boots. Back then, he'd done everything he could to be blunt. Now he was all smoothed edges and silken charm.

Which meant she watched him right back, unable to look away.

He pulled within arm's reach of where she stood by the metal pot of water. Pen tightened the cloak around her body, even though his intense gaze made her feel as if the black wool were invisible. She wasn't a virgin. Far from it. But still, most men received her attention as a gift. Something she bestowed when they sought a sort of healing that her magic didn't provide.

Tru looked at her as if he didn't want a gift, given freely. The predator wanted to take.

He slid a finger down the side of her neck, where the fringe of short, wet hair clung to her skin. "If I stuck my hand in that fire, would you heal me?"

"Why would you ask that?"

"Curiosity. And to point out your nonverbal communication." That single finger traced the seam of her cloak and pushed between, still following skin. "You flinched. That was obvious enough. A startled response to an unexpected question. Your heart rate picked up, too. I can see there at your jugular. Pupils dilated. Even your scent changed."

He grinned. Nothing about the expression was pleasant, even as his touch flirted with the inner curve of her left breast. He remained as closed off while smiling as he did when scowling.

Pen gave him blankness right back.

"My scent?" She shoved his hand away. "You think you're amazing, don't you?"

He shrugged, then washed his hands and face with efficient motions. "Still doesn't answer the question. Would you save me, Penelope?"

"Depends on whether the expended energy was likely to garner anything useful."

"How about some meat? Maybe that's a fair trade for healing." Without even looking toward Pen for permission, he grabbed one of the knives off her holster where it draped across a low branch, and used it to gut the fresh kill. "Seems you already think you can buy my services. That makes you no better than me."

"Why are you doing this?"

"Like I said. Curiosity. I never met a living deity before."

"A living—?"

"So I figure I better make sure I have what it takes to hang with such august company."

Pen ran her tongue over her teeth, grounding herself in that sharp pain.

But even as he nettled, he never stopped working. Each slice had purpose and symmetry. Sunlight climbing to a steeper angle cast heavy shadows below his prominent cheekbones. Sweat gathered on his upper lip. The cotton of his shirt was thin, patched, and often worn.

She needed him—for more than just his hunting skills as a lion and as a human. She traveled alone for a reason, always keeping her powers in check. Otherwise she risked lives. Had she been alone, she would have no trouble tracking down the Mäkinen camp. No life to risk other than her own. And no humiliation if it turned out to be a wild-goose chase, one born of her own lunatic brain.

Adrian complicated matters. He was young and needed protection. His worshipful attitude meant he wouldn't question her leadership at all. She didn't trust herself with that responsibility.

Watching Tru in silence, she lost track of the conversation until he stopped. Faced her. "What do you want?" He stressed the last word with low, husky insinuation.

She shivered. Naked beneath the cloak, her body responded with a jolt. Part sexual awareness. Part nerves that he could rile her so easily.

"The truck was heading north toward the mountains. Rumor has it that O'Malley himself makes his home there, in a fortress bounded by woods. The guard on the truck confirmed at least that much. I would've liked to learn more from men like him, but a lion appeared out of nowhere."

He grinned. "Gonna introduce yourself to the general?"

"He needs to be killed and his organization dismantled."

"Says who? We have bullets because of O'Malley. People like him make the wheels turn." Another one of those infuriating shrugs.

"You'd trade Adrian to reload?"

"What does this have to do with me?" he asked, folding his arms with deliberate patience.

She forced a breath of calm, although the ache he caused wouldn't dissipate so easily. "The prisoners on the truck confirmed what I suspected. There's a camp organized by someone named Arturi Mäkinen.

He has powerful magic, but is reputed to be a man of peace. Rumor has it that's changing, that his people plan to take on O'Malley—a real resistance here in the east. Free those who've been taken hostage. Take down the general."

"And you want me to what—*help* them?"

The idea of this grown-up, callous Tru actually helping her struck her as funny. Sickly funny. Pen choked out a laugh. Because she didn't want her hopes to be ridiculed. It was either laugh or face how his cynicism wore down years of trying to make something good out of this world.

"No, I just want your help getting us there. Alone, I'd be fine. But Adrian needs more protection than I can provide."

"You carry knives." He angled his head toward where her belt hung next to her drying clothes.

"For self-defense, mostly. But I'm not good enough to take on a whole group of O'Malley thugs." She sighed. "He's just a kid. If this camp is what I hope it is, he'll be safe there. Unless you'd rather I leave him behind."

The skin around his eyes tightened. Such a small tell, but she read it loud and clear. Adrian was a liability and he didn't like it one bit. "Two's no more trouble than one."

"Good. We'll eat, wake Adrian, and get going."

"Not so fast, Penelope. I said I could do the job. Not that I *would*. Give me some incentive here."

"It's not enough to help—" His laugh interrupted her before she could finish the thought. An angry flush heated her cheeks. She'd known the answer, of course. She was just stalling. "Fine. I know a group of people in what was once Georgia. They have some good weapons stockpiled. You can have your pick."

"I can get my own guns," he said silkily.

"Then healing. You never know—"

"Generally, I'm smart enough not to get hurt. If I do, then I deserve the pain as an object lesson." His eyes were such a pale blue, almost gray in some lights, eerie against his dark hair, like a morning sky over bleak mountaintops.

She'd be backed into a corner if he turned down her last gambit. "Arturi's people will reward you, I promise. Whatever you need."

He shook his head, still smiling. "I don't work without payment up front. If there's nothing else, I better roast this meat before it turns, and head out."

"You're going to make me say it, aren't you?"

"You know I am." His gaze heated, making promises she couldn't ignore.

"Fine." Back straight, knowing she'd faced much worse, she took his challenge head-on. "Get us safely to the rebel camp, and I'll have sex with you."

SIX

Tru feigned amusement, as if he didn't take her offer serious as a heart attack. He'd gone breathless the minute the words left her lips. He hadn't figured he could get her to say them, no matter how much he teased. Up until that moment, the game hadn't been one he expected to win.

Penelope Sheehan was a fucking legend in the wasteland, though he hadn't known her real name until now. But of course he'd heard of the Orchid. Who hadn't? He'd imagined she was a saint despondent folk had invented to create hope in desperate times. Not a real person.

Not a woman with great fucking tits.

He propped himself against the wall of the shack, ignoring the field-dressed reptile behind him. Not exactly the setting for seduction.

"Under what conditions? How often?"

Her chin firmed. "We'll negotiate along the way."

"I find it's better to have things out in the open," he drawled. "No potential for misunderstanding that way."

How far would she go with this? He couldn't believe she wanted anything bad enough to bargain with him. The entire conversation should have seemed tawdry, her offer half a step above prostitution, but now he was caught, intrigued by the flicker of fire beneath her layers of ice. Nobody had truly awakened her sexuality; he'd stake *her* life on it. He imagined neat and tidy encounters, born of impulses higher than the primitive desire to mate. The idea of making her crazy—when she neither liked nor respected him—rang all his bells.

She exhaled a slow breath, shooting an appraising glance toward the shack. But Adrian was still sound asleep. Just as well. The kid would stab him in the neck for considering this proposal, even if Pen had made it only for Adrian's sake. Despite Tru's prior taunts, the boy's adoration didn't seem to hold a carnal tinge. Some people were content with worshipping from afar.

Pen's eyes looked huge. Maybe she was rethinking the offer. Too late. He liked the faint hint of nerves in the cant of her head.

"I need a few days so we can get reacquainted. I can't just . . . lie down for you."

"It wouldn't be like that," he whispered, prowling closer—and she responded with a parting of her lips. Instinctive. "Even right now. You want me a little."

Pen backed up a step. "I don't. I never said that."

"Not with words." Her gaze followed every movement. Hungry eyes, though she didn't seem to know it. Starved for pleasure. "But that scent I mentioned? Sex, Penelope. You smell like a woman who wants sex. With *me,* unless you're saving yourself for Adrian."

"You're foul." Something flashed in her blue eyes, but the emotion raced too quick for him to identify. Not that he was an expert on feelings these days. He'd spent too long intentionally severing all ties to his emotional side, the side that had burned in a fiery ruin.

He didn't want it back.

"I'm a man. A real one—not a grateful disciple. Get used to it."

She swallowed . . . and he watched her throat work. Vulnerable. Graceful. "Back to our bargain, Tru. You need sex. I can supply it."

"I'm not interested in fucking a martyr. When I collect my reward, you'll enjoy it as much as I do."

"Don't be ridiculous. I can't promise that."

"I can." Tru leaned in, close enough to touch her. He didn't. Just stood with his cheek by her delicate jaw and breathed her in. "You just have to let me."

"Right," she scoffed. "It's always sighs and ecstasy, I'm sure."

Maybe sex had *never* left her breathless. That meant she was frigid or her partners had been clumsy. Or so awed by her mojo that they felt she'd bestowed some grand favor by letting them touch her at all.

It couldn't be easy being the divine Orchid. Tru quelled the sympathy with a mental head shake. He didn't want to feel *for* her; he just wanted to feel her up.

Softening his voice, he angled his head to whisper in her ear. "So you've never had your pulse speed, your breath catch? Haven't ever gone flushed and soft, aching to be stroked?"

She didn't answer, but he saw response in the lift of her head, the way her nipples peaked against the fabric of her cloak. The scent of her intensified—sweet, clean, aroused woman. He should back off and give her space. He would, if she were any other female. But he didn't want to. The impulse amped in his head. He wanted to push her to the edge. The lion growled in anticipation. *On her, from behind, teeth on her neck.*

With some effort, he drove the beast back. *Too soon. Dial it down.*

He made himself withdraw. "If we're going to have some fun, that means you stop thinking, calculating, judging. It means turning yourself over to me. Can you?"

"I don't know." She was honest, at least, her voice unsteady.

He wanted her, fiercely. No explanation for the brutal bite of desire, but there it was. She was so different from those he ordinarily chose. Maybe that was it: variety. The spice of life and all that. When he made her come, it would be incredibly satisfying.

"Relax," he said softly. "Nobody goes from zero to sixty in a day. We'll take our time."

He conceded the getting-to-know-you period she'd asked for

because that fell in line with his usual process. Tru never fucked a woman on the first day, and though they'd known each other as children, that shared past offered no basis for a sexual liaison. Those were just memories, bittersweet and best forgotten. He'd been alone for years, with so much loved and lost since then. If he let himself, he could count the exact number of months and days. But to do so would mean going back in his head, and that he couldn't do.

"You'll take too much," she said sharply.

"Not more than you want to give, precious."

"Don't call me that. You called *her* that."

Her? Calla. Shit, yeah.

"Sorry," he said with real remorse—and not just because her body language closed off completely.

Goddamn, when had he become so cold? But with Pen watching him, he tucked his doubts alongside the bad memories.

He cleared the tightness in his throat. "I have a counteroffer for you. Today, we seal the deal with a kiss. Tomorrow I get two kisses, unless you choose to give me more. The next day, we'll play it by ear. And when I get you safely to our destination, we sleep together. Does that sound fair?"

Her mouth tightened. "Fair."

"In exchange, I'll protect you and Adrian. Yes, better than I did Calla." He forestalled the objection before she could make it.

God knew, she couldn't make him feel worse than he already did. He'd learned early on that he took failure hard. When he'd let himself get close to people, he let them down. Spectacularly. Which was why the self-preservationist part of his brain was screaming like a lunatic. *Run, run, you moron!*

Tru ignored it.

She exhaled sharply. "You want to do it now?"

Do it? What? Oh, the kiss. Right.

"Seems like the opportune time."

Seeing as you're naked.

Her blue eyes snapped, telling him she knew what he was thinking. An amused smile curved his mouth. Tru set a hand lightly on her shoulder, careful not to pull her cloak out of place. She closed her eyes and tilted her chin. Lips closed, he noted. That was the face a woman presented with the expectation of a chaste kiss, so he didn't disappoint. Best to leave 'em wanting and wondering anyway.

He tasted her lower lip, nuzzling with gentle pressure. No teeth, no tongue. Just his flesh meeting hers. Then he drifted to the pert curve of her upper lip, offering the same tender treatment. From experience, he knew these soft little kisses built a hunger for more. He took his time—never pushing, never rushing—and when she parted for him on a small sound, he raised his head.

"Huh," she said.

He saw no helpless desire in her. Instead, she stared up at him with puzzlement and . . . curiosity? As if his kiss had surprised her but hadn't left her dazed. No revulsion, at least. Whatever her life had been, she might still find pleasure in a man's touch. But he had his work cut out for him. Instead of dismay, Tru felt a frisson of anticipation.

He offered an easy smile, the one he wore most often when he was thinking. While he went to work on the fire she'd started, arranging it so he could cook the meat, he considered his strategy. Keep her off balance. Thaw some of that ice. The way to do that would be to alternate gentleness and ferocity, but she was smart enough to see a pattern in his approach, which might ruin everything. Maybe it would be best to watch her mood and respond accordingly.

Penelope was quiet, too. Pensive. And he hadn't given her a second thought in years.

By noon he had prepared the gator for travel in dry, flaky packets. Adrian emerged from the shack, rubbing his eyes. "Smells good."

"Afternoon, kid. Hungry?"

"Like you wouldn't believe."

"Action and mayhem have that effect on growing boys."

"I don't know if I'm growing," Adrian muttered. "But I hope so."

"You will."

But the kid was right. He was small for his age. Pretty too, which was why he'd ended up in the O'Malley shipment. If he'd reached that camp Penelope had been going on about, they would have castrated him to keep him soft. That should outrage Tru—and it *did*—but he was a realist. There was no saving this world. One could only find a quiet corner of hell and make the best of it.

You're alive because a mean son of a bitch made an exception for you, a little voice reminded him. *You owe it to Mason to pay it forward.* Tru heaved a sigh and agreed with his inner critic.

Fine. Even after the thing with Penelope went pear-shaped, which it would, he'd look after Adrian. Shouldn't take more than a year to sort him out.

Assuming Tru could teach as well as Mason. *Why do I have the feeling my life just got impossible?*

Shoving down his foreboding, he finished packing up after they'd all eaten. "Well, the camp is north. Duh. So I guess we start walking."

She cocked her head. "We should be wary of O'Malley convoys. They're not my biggest fans." Something in her impish expression told him she'd done some impressively awful shit to earn that reputation.

Tru wanted to hear the story. Therefore, he resisted the impulse to ask and get to know her better. Which was, ironically, what they were supposed to be doing. Damn, complicated—

"I don't want to put you at risk." Adrian shot Pen a soulful look.

I can't take this bullshit.

But a deal was a deal. Tru wasn't such a reprehensible human that his word meant nothing. That was why he seldom gave it. And she was right. Under no circumstances could he leave Adrian to her care. They'd die.

He scrubbed a palm across his face, shouldered his pack, grabbed a rifle, and headed out. "Stay close," he muttered. "I want you both tight on me, so if we run into ferals, I can drop them before they're on us."

"We," she corrected quietly. "*We* can drop them. We're in this together." Her wicked smile sparkled, kindling in him a reluctant, responsive joy. "Truman."

Fuck. Why did she remember his full name? *Why?* He felt like he was fourteen and in the principal's office again. By her smug look, she knew. Her gaze spoke volumes. If he pushed her buttons, she'd push his back.

Yeah, he got it.

As he turned north, Tru suppressed a smile.

SEVEN

The heat was a monster in her lungs. But Pen pushed on. She couldn't remember a time when she'd done otherwise. They stuck to the roads as much as possible, although they weren't the roads she remembered from childhood. Those smooth expanses of blacktop had long ago deteriorated into pitted ruts and ankle-high foliage. The worst had been a few years back, before the weeds grew in so thick that they softened the way.

Tru tripped on a knotted vine and cursed. She hadn't expected such clumsiness from him, but it wasn't the first time his body seemed to rebel against his mind.

Maybe because it wasn't the right body.

"How long has it been since you've been human?"

"Don't remember," he said. "A couple months, maybe."

Pen frowned. "And you just . . . live as a lion?"

"Mostly." He angled her a smirking smile, then dipped it toward her breasts. "I shift for various reasons."

"Other lions not doing it for you?"

"Wouldn't know. I haven't found any." With another curse, he kicked at the heavy piece of asphalt that had grabbed his toe. He shifted his pack higher on his shoulder. "Just walk."

"Quite the seduction you've got going on. I don't know how I'll stand the anticipation."

He glared as Pen moved on to Adrian, hoping he might be better company. But Tru cocked his head and grabbed her arm. At first, she couldn't hear it. And then the sound rumbled in distant vibration. An engine.

Trucks were few and far between, even on a main trading route. His mouth twisted. Not overt. Nothing about him was. But she liked that she was getting to know his subtle tells. She knew to get off the road long before he gave the signal.

"Stay low," he said to Adrian.

The younger man nodded. Pen flicked Tru a look, ready with some quip about his new protégé. But he didn't seem to be in the mood for gibes, so she let it die unsaid. The responsibility he felt for Adrian's safety was as clear as his eyes.

Crouched in the dense overgrowth, Tru stayed watchful as the vehicle rumbled closer. That extra edge of determination turned him into someone Pen could trust. She forced herself to look away from his profile, although she wanted to linger on the hint of red that tinged his two-day growth of stubble.

He'd kissed her. And she was already thinking about when he would kiss her again.

The truck was larger than the one she'd been stuffed into. "That one's valuable," she whispered. "Petroleum, maybe."

O'Malley controlled all the fuel stores that remained. Therefore, only vehicles that belonged to him—or had been stolen from him— ran on the east coast. And once the supplies vanished for good, there would be no more. The ability to drill and refine oil had been lost in the Change, like so many technologies, some of which she barely remembered.

Tru squinted, as if giving the scene another pass through his quick mind. "Because of the armor?"

Nodding, Pen ignored the weird stench of the muck they were

lying in, bellies to the ground. "More guards, too. Two on the roof, at least. And one of them's a skinwalker."

"You can tell?"

"Anyone with magic. Sometimes it's an aura I can see. Colors. Other times it's a prickle behind my ears."

Moving just enough to bring his hand around, he touched the spot she'd mentioned. "Here? You feel me here all the time?"

She shot him a killer stare. He only grinned and turned his attention back to the road. Minutes passed as they waited in stillness. The noises of the swamp took the engine's place as the truck rolled out of sight. Tru began to move, but she grabbed his arm.

"Listen again. Wait for it."

Rather than arguing, which she was fully prepared to counter, he did as she said. His eyelids seemed perpetually at half-mast. Lazy and insolent. That hardly changed when he was concentrating, but the shape of his mouth did. Full lips drew in—the exact opposite of his don't-give-a-damn smile.

Recognition changed him again, just bordering on surprise. "Shit, you're right."

"Big shipments always travel with a tail, way back. O'Malley learned the hard way that some of his drivers couldn't be trusted. He sends guards to watch the guards."

"You and the others weren't valuable enough for that yesterday?"

"Two dozen scrawny slaves. We're a dime a dozen compared to enough refined crude to power O'Malley's entire fleet for a week."

"Fuckers."

Pen smiled at his indignation.

On his other side, he hustled Adrian back into the covering foliage. Funny, but the boy stuck close to Tru, not her. The Orchid, for all the reverence people laid on her, couldn't match the pull of a father figure. Shades of Mason all over again, which gave her hope that Tru would get them safely to North Carolina.

She had no such confidence in her physical appeal. Conquest

was conquest. He'd get what he wanted out of her and move on. Fair enough. She just didn't want it to happen before reaching her destination.

The truck's tail was smaller, just an old vehicle—so old it lacked a computer chip. Those all fried during the Change. No one sped, not even in a vehicle so small. The roads and the overall lack of fuel meant driving to minimize repairs and waste.

"We have about a minute to decide," she said. "Take it or stay on foot."

"What mojo can you offer?"

"I could distract the driver."

"We don't want him to crash."

She grinned. "Not my first time. He'll just . . . forget to keep his foot on the accelerator."

"Nice trick, witch." Tru frowned. "Shots carry . . . the lead truck will hear them."

"I have knives."

"You skilled?"

"Wouldn't bring them up if I weren't."

"Even after a spell?"

"Four or five seconds."

Something flickered in his eyes as he assessed her, quickly but more deeply than before. She felt as if he'd finally looked past her body and her promise. "But you're a healer."

And a killer.

They didn't have time for issues of conscience or specters from her past. Instead she blew him off. "So many questions, Truman. Don't tell me you give a shit."

"Whatever," he said tersely. "You distract the driver. I go lion. We take them as quietly as we can."

Adrian tugged on Tru's sleeve. "And me?"

"Stay put. Do me that favor, kid. I don't want to split my concentration."

"But I want to help."

"Later. I'll teach you how. Promise. Got it?"

He waited until Adrian nodded before he stood. The artificial thunder of the ancient engine was almost upon them. "Afterward, I'll stay lion and go hunting. You two keep the meat from this morning. I'll feed myself and catch up."

"We'll head east," she said. "Then take the first road north along the coast. At nightfall, we'll make camp. I'm sure you'll be able to find us."

Tru appeared to run the numbers, mentally charting where she and Adrian should end up. Then the human part of him vanished. His transformation charged the air with a sticky sort of energy, as if individual flickers of bygone electricity had been slowed to half speed. The golden-wheat glow of his aura surrounded him, blazing with intensity. Although Adrian wouldn't be able to see that indicator of magic, he still stared, openmouthed.

Pen turned her back as Tru gave himself over to his animal incarnation. She had work to do, too.

On her knees, she edged toward the side of the road. Just enough to see the oncoming driver. Not enough to be seen herself. Pressing her palms together at chest height, she bowed once before angling her face toward the sky. Her ritual was necessary. Not only did it channel her powers, it kept her from yielding to the impetuousness that could get her friends killed. For their sake, she would never alter her routine.

Eyes closed, she recited a thanks to her mothers—Angela Sheehan, the woman who had given her life; Jenna Mason, who had worked hard to keep her safe and raise her well; and to the earth and heavens and all the mystery in the layers between. "Thank you, Mothers, for all the days I've breathed and for all the breaths I've yet to take. I entrust my body and my soul to your care."

Thanking them meant acknowledging them. And by acknowledging them so overtly, she found the key to tap into their strength.

Like unlocking a door she couldn't see or touch. In her own mind. In her cells or her blood. That strength compounded until she no longer lived in her own skin. She was part of the trees and the sky, although her body never left that damp patch of weeds.

Eyes open, seeing with so much more than her physical abilities, she located the driver behind a filthy windshield. A spiderweb of cracks laced the glass. Heavy beard. Mole on his left cheek. And finally, a glimpse of his eyes.

Pen bore down, as if gritting against a punch to the gut. Muscles tight. Tendons cramped into knots. All the power she'd been hoarding burst out in a rush. She felt it but saw nothing. The only visible effect of that effort was the gradual, inevitable slowing of the small truck.

The driver shook his head, but it was too late.

Tru bounded past in a blur of golden fur. She stared as the rush of her spell wore off. He took out the nearest guard with a single leap, as he had done in the back of the slave truck. Just a pounce and the sickening crack of bone. He turned with his massive forepaw raised, knocking another man into the bushes.

Pen jumped to her feet. With knives in hand, she first took out the man in the bushes. Glad she checked. He'd been stunned but not dead.

She crept into the fray, behind a man who took aim at the lion annihilating his cohorts. Bullets would warn the truck ahead. And bullets meant the possibility of harm coming to Tru.

Still glowing with the afterbuzz of her spell, she felt no fear. Simply jammed her knife between the vertebrae at the base of his neck. He collapsed into a paralyzed heap. From that vantage, creeping in behind while Tru took them head-on, she felled another man.

But not before he opened fire.

She couldn't worry about that now, only be thankful that none of the bullets hit Tru. The guard spotted her approach before she could attack. He spun, using the butt of his rifle to knock the air from her stomach. Pen doubled over. Spots shimmered in her eyes, but she adjusted her grip on both knives. The bastard made the mistake she'd known he would. Rather than keep beating with the blunt end, he insisted on making it messy.

He flipped the gun. Or attempted to.

Pen didn't let him get that far. She surged up from below, using her shorter stature against him. Forget the armor on his chest—she went for the femoral artery in his thigh. And for his groin, because he'd put her in a bad mood.

The man sagged on a scream, hands clasping his crotch. Pen kicked the rifle away. She ran to the driver, whose eyes she'd only seen with her amplified sight. Now she stared at him, face-to-face. Green eyes. Like moss. But his mind was still fogged from the spell. He simply sat there, both hands on the wheel, the engine idling in neutral.

Good. Just as she'd intended. Precise and intended only for her chosen target.

No torture for this one. She hauled him out to the rough, weed-eaten blacktop and cut his throat.

By the time she looked over the mess, she realized the quiet. All clear.

Tru, in lion form and crackling with that beautiful golden aura, circled the truck. He nosed every corpse, apparently double-checking. The tufted tip of his tail twitched as he walked. Long bunches of muscle flexed beneath his pale yellow pelt. A spectacular mane framed that lion face.

But he was in there. Their gazes locked and Pen felt it.

"Adrian, you can come out now," she called, not looking away from Tru. Later she'd be able to justify having Adrian there. She was talking to the boy, not an animal. But even then she knew that wasn't the case. "Shots were fired. They'll send a team to investigate. We're turning the truck around and heading back to that last road, then turning east. We'll head to the coast, away from O'Malley's shipments."

"How much gas does it have?" Adrian asked.

A quick check revealed a busted instrument panel. "No telling.

But we need to get away from here. Gather our stuff. I'll get these corpses off the road."

She could kill. But the memory of running over dead bodies, years ago, made her want to vomit. Her stomach hurt enough already from that rifle butt.

The lion made a low noise. She turned to watch in fascination as his massive serrated tongue flicked out, licking his jowls clean of blood.

"You'll come find us, yes?"

He didn't answer. Might not have, even if he'd been able. The lion strolled out into the swamp, his tail still flicking. Pen only hoped he'd bring Tru back.

EIGHT

Tall grass. Trees. They had names, but he couldn't remember them. It always took a while to lock into his new range of vision, greater in the periphery. Fewer colors. Better detection of noise, smell, movement. His ears pricked up, as he scented something delicious in the distance.

Salt tinged the air. Beneath it, animal musk. It was clean here. Mostly. Few humans. That made stalking easier.

Crushed grass led him onward. He knew the hoofprints and the trace of prey intimately. There were few hunters to cull their numbers these days, so the deer ran free in lands that had once been settled. Sometimes he passed the ruins of human places, littered and fallen into disuse. He skirted those areas in case danger lingered. Even in this form, he knew not to trust his fellow man.

The lion only needed one deer. Hunger snarled in his belly, making him impatient. He needed to strike. *Eat. Move.* Urgency, but why? There was another task, something he'd forgotten, but he put it aside and focused on the hunt. The delicious scent lingered in the grass, on leaves the herd had passed in its quest for fresh water. He crouched, slinking closer.

They grazed, unaware of the danger, white tails flicking in the hot breeze. With keen eyes, he chose his target. Muscles bunched, the lion sprang and brought down a young buck, just barely coming into his antlers. A clean kill. Blood spilled down the lion's throat as he devoured his prey in great gulps.

With lazy arrogance, he settled to indulge himself as panicking animals fled in all directions. In this land, the only creature that could challenge him was the alligator. And so on land, he ruled over all he surveyed. A good life, full of contentment and simplicity.

For a while he'd searched for lionesses—coming close to the perfect mate, once. Long ago. Long gone. He ought to have a number of females pacing around him in teasing circles while he lay at the center of their number. But there weren't any like him here. A few smaller cats who spooked at his scent. Wolves who growled and drove him away when they didn't attack outright. It was hard, sometimes, being different.

He'd gotten used to it.

Once, he'd had a place. Now he wandered.

The lion stretched, full and content. The sun shone down on his heavy pelt, and with a growl of a yawn, he rolled over for a nap. It was much later when he roused, though in this form he lost some of his awareness of time. He had something to do. Somewhere to be.

The man part that had a name—Tru—roused with a start. Remembered the woman's words. *We'll head east, then take the first road north along the coast. At nightfall, we'll make camp. I'm sure you'll be able to find us.* That was right. He had a pride now, a small one, and he would look after them. He needed speed.

East, toward the water, north. Those words meant less to him in lion skin than they would later. But loping toward the sea, he caught the faint scent of people-things. Smoky, oily stink lingered in the wind, carried over distance. More certain, he loped off in that direction.

Because he'd spent the afternoon napping, he did not find them until full evening. They had done as promised, using the guards' belongings to make a comfortable camp. Tru shifted in the shadows, not wanting to startle either Pen or Adrian by padding in as king of the jungle, though in all honesty he preferred the power of his animal form. His needs were so much simpler.

One day he'd lose the knack for human socialization altogether. Aside from the fear of turning into a feral skinwalker that fed indiscriminately, he longed to leave his humanity behind. Nothing left worth sticking around for anyway.

Silently, he found his backpack. Pen—or possibly Adrian—had been kind enough to toss it into the back of the truck. He dressed in silence, needing those moments to get used to his arms and legs again, and the idea he had a voice instead of a roar. At such times, he lost his customary grace, fumbling with fingers that felt unfamiliar. Occasionally he stopped himself from reaching for things with his mouth, a sure sign he'd spent too much time in lion form.

With a faint sigh, he joined the other two at the campfire.

"You're back." Penelope's tone held a chiding note, as if she'd waited up for him.

It *was* late. Adrian slept, whereas Tru felt wide-awake after his nap. Not the most considerate decision, but satisfactory after a venison feast. The flickering light didn't give any hint beyond the faint rebuke in her words, so he had no idea if she was surprised to see him, or relieved.

"I told you I would be."

"Can I trust you to keep your promises?"

"Yes," Tru said seriously.

If he was a bastard, he was an honest one. He'd never promised a woman anything he couldn't deliver, not even to get what he wanted.

And he wanted Penelope Sheehan. A lot.

"I wondered. Not for me," she said, hunching her shoulders. "It would hit Adrian hard if you vanished on us. He's starting to think he can trust you."

Now he wasn't sure if she meant Adrian . . . or herself. He needed to tread carefully, reassure without making more promises. Not an easy task when she looked so tired and worried, the weight of the world on her shoulders. The unfamiliar urge to swear he'd make it all better, somehow, bubbled up. Through sheer will, he quashed that impulse.

"I'll stick to the terms of our agreement. I won't disappear."

That should satisfy her. And tomorrow he'd kiss her again. Tru was surprised how much he looked forward to that. Just a kiss. And to seeing if he could rouse her to a little more enthusiasm.

A shimmer of awareness prickled over his skin. He shifted and saw that she was watching him.

"Thank you," she said, voice low.

Those words couldn't come easy; she was used to people giving way to her. She wasn't accustomed to bargaining for what she needed. The Orchid gestured, and people made room. Maybe she did need somebody like Tru in her life, at least for a while. To remind her what it was to be human. Ironic, that, when he'd almost forgotten. They fell on opposite sides of the spectrum. He was too much animal, and she was too much magic.

"Long day?"

When Pen nodded, he eased in behind her. Her quiescence moved him to unexpected optimism. *She must trust you a little to allow you her back.* Without asking permission, he rested his hands on her shoulders, finding the knots that came from hours behind the wheel. Someone unused to driving would hurt after hours of it, both from bad roads and from wrestling the truck.

"Go ahead." Her words were soft, even if her body was tense.

People don't touch her like this.

In a way, that permission was more intimate than sex. Which should have put him off. But he'd gentled women this way before, conditioning them to crave his touch. It wouldn't be any different this time. *Would it?*

With light pressure, he rubbed the tension away, thumbs circling counter to his kneading fingers. First she sat still, but the longer he worked, the more she leaned, tipping forward so he could reach more of her. He didn't comment on the silent invitation, merely worked his way down her spine in confident strokes. She made small sounds now and then, but it wasn't sexual, only the pleasure of relaxing muscles. Soon he was simply caressing her back in delicate passes while little shivers stole up her spine.

"Is this where you seduce me?" she asked, amusement threading her tone.

But she didn't sound wholly unwilling to go further. He'd love to draw her back against him, her tempting ass against his hard cock, and kiss the curve of her throat. Too soon for that.

He chuckled. "Hardly. I just thought I'd make you feel better. I promised to take care of you, after all."

"So you did." Thoughtful tone. "My ass is sore too, you know. You want to rub it for me?"

It was a joke.

Maybe?

She wasn't flirting, he thought, or daring him. More curious, as if she wanted to see how far he'd go, if he believed it was beneath him to provide a kindness without the hope of immediate sexual gratification. He decided to surprise her.

"Roll over on your blanket, and I will."

She eyed him. "Seriously?"

"Sure."

"You won't try to take my pants off?"

That conjured all kinds of delicious images. It had been a long time since he'd kept a woman long enough to lick her all over, get lost in her body, and drive her out of her mind. He wanted to start at her toes and work his way up.

To cover the sharp intensity of that need, Tru winked. "It's not on the schedule, Penelope."

He waited to see if she'd trust him. The moment slowed, incredibly long, as she gazed at him. With a languorous grace that left Tru slack-jawed, she pushed to her knees and walked on them to her blanket. Skirting the fire, she settled in as he had instructed.

Wow. Unexpected. But okay.

He moved alongside her, because kneeling over her would seem overtly sexual. Schooling himself, he settled his palms and went to work, moving his thumbs in slow, gentle circles, palms splayed on either side. He manipulated the base of her spine first, easing down so gradually that she didn't even tense when he touched her butt. It required all his self-control not to cup and fondle, but rather to massage and soothe.

Watching her responses, listening to her breathing, Tru alternated the pressure, gentle and firm, until she relaxed beneath his touch. Her thighs fell open; he took that as her cue to rub them, too. Beneath the fabric of her pants, her legs clenched. But even those tight muscles eased as he continued his steady caress. He tried to keep it impersonal, but Penelope didn't help when her hips shifted, just a little rhythmic push against the blanket. Her scent changed slowly, deepening with the greater heat. Though she might not realize it, she'd hit the first stage of sexual arousal.

He could tease her inner thighs, make her crave release. Quite desperately, he wanted to roll her over, unbutton her pants, sink his fingers into her, and stroke until she came.

But he'd promised he wouldn't go that far tonight. Fucking *promises.*

Instead he left her, sleepy and soft, moving restlessly, and found his own blanket—padding for sleep, not for cover. Even in the dark, it was hot as hell. She murmured something indistinct, her head pillowed on folded arms. Before long, her breathing evened. So relaxed. Not thinking or worrying.

All told, Tru felt like he'd done a good, good thing.

He still wasn't tired, so he settled in to keep watch. To make matters worse, his cock throbbed like a wild thing in his pants. If it didn't seem indecent with a woman and kid sleeping nearby, he'd give himself some relief. Instead, Tru forced the erection down with bad memories. Didn't take long.

He gazed into the fire and hoped for a future brighter than the nightmare of his past.

Faint hope, indeed.

NINE

Pen awoke with a start. She sat up in the near darkness and searched for a clue as to what had woken her. A glimmer of light on the eastern horizon seemed even brighter for the nearness of the ocean, reflecting off the distant water. Too far away to hear the waves, but near enough to taste the salt on the back of her tongue.

An hour left till the sun rose. Then they'd move again. The condition of the roads meant she hadn't risked night driving. Too many truck-size craters that would consume their rickety vehicle. And though she'd never admit it, she hadn't wanted to make it any harder for Tru to find them.

He acted as if nothing mattered. No big deal. She'd intended not to let his seeming nonchalance burrow under her skin, but that was a futile hope.

Touching her. Hands on her. Again . . . no big deal.

"You should be asleep," came his voice, quiet as the rustle of leaves. Even as a human, he remained a seamless part of nature. Closer to it, somehow, than anyone she'd ever known. Only occasionally did she feel that way when she cast her healing spells and saved lives. The world came into alignment under her sternum. Heart beating. Everything making sense. Transcendent moments to be treasured.

Other times were pure chaos, when her powers made her wonder if she deserved to be around people at all. Forget the Orchid. She always considered herself one step short of a full-fledged lunatic.

Who else would follow gut instinct and voices on the wind?

Who else would dream of a rope ladder leading into the trees and awaken shivering, cold, crying?

I gave you my all, love. I did, I did.

She shook away the remains of her old, ghostly nightmare—the same she'd repeated since her teen years, when her powers had pulsed like a wild wind storm under her skin.

Old insecurities aside, she should've been startled at the sound of Tru's quiet words. Instead, she'd already known he was awake, too. That magic tickle behind her ears might as well have been his fingertips. Or his tongue. Tasting her as he tasted the air, searching for whatever he desired.

"Something woke me." She didn't speak much above a whisper, unwilling to disturb Adrian's sleep.

"Bad dream?"

"Would you care?"

"Depends on if I was in it. And if you're prescient."

Nope. Just crazy.

The faint predawn light did little to illuminate his face. He lay on the ground with only his blanket beneath him, arms behind his head. The pose stretched his body, lean and long. The hem of his shirt had ridden up, revealing his pale stomach. Thoughts of tasting him trickled into her mind. She would lick him there. One day. And he would shiver.

Pen wanted to close her eyes against that sudden flash of desire. She *wasn't* prescient. At least she hoped not. Just one hideous dream that left her quaking and praying it never came true. Because frankly, insanity held more appeal than the abject grief that always accompanied her nightmare. Why a rope ladder? And why those forlorn words? To love so intensely . . . and to lose it. She shivered.

"It's not a talent of mine, no. And as for last night, I can't remember specifics." She certainly didn't want to try to explain something that seemed so completely irrational.

"Then I must not have been in it."

"Why, because I'd have been sure to remember?"

His chuckle was impossibly quiet, like thunder a thousand kilometers away. She would've felt it, though, had her head lain against his chest. "Something like that. Good or bad, Penelope, I'm memorable."

Damn, but he was. How many times had she thought of him through the years, wondering what had become of him? She liked to think it was because of the Change. Everyone she'd known from Before was dead. Simple fact. Hard fact. The people she'd come to know since—really come to know, rather than meet in passing—were so few. Jenna and Mason. Dr. Chris. Tru. They came to her as hopes and bittersweet memories, often all at once, when her loneliness and isolation hit hardest.

The Orchid walked a different path.

Jenna and Mason would live happily until, one day, they went down fighting. That, too, seemed such a clear, clean fact. Chris . . . Sometimes she dreamed of a dark-haired woman and a tiny town in the desert. Pen would never know for sure, but she felt certain that Chris was there—safe and happy and loved.

And Tru. There he was, smirking at her in the gathering daylight. Over the years, she'd thought of him most of all. Which probably explained the depth of her disappointment.

Only, that wasn't fair either. The shock of his initial behavior had softened. He was simply Tru again, a more potent version of the boy she'd known. Faults and all. And his faults had always been most entertaining. Irreverent. Cynical. Still charming as only a bad boy could be, the kind no mama ever wanted her daughter to notice.

Her stomach made a loud cry for food. Tru's chuckle sounded again. "There's just more gator, I'm afraid. But even if we had venison, I don't suppose you'd want to eat it raw anyway."

She didn't smile. Only pulled the cloak tighter around her shoulders. "Wouldn't be the first time."

"Oh?"

How did he manage to make *no* noise, even as a human? He sat up, stretched, and joined her. Just sitting. Shoulder to shoulder.

"Is this my invitation to open up and tell you my life story?"

"No," he said. "You can leave out the parts before the age of eleven."

"A trade."

"Hmm?"

"A story for a story. I want to know how you first shifted. When you learned."

He turned to look down at her. Already the sunshine was strong enough to brighten his eyes, lighting them with pale fire. "And you'll tell me when you ate raw meat."

Some deep instinct told her that pointing out every time he hid the truth from her wouldn't help. He'd only tuck deeper in his defenses. She was just getting used to hearing what remained unsaid. But she wasn't used to his breath so near. That heat. That . . . intimacy. He leaned closer, until his nose brushed her temple. Pressing deeper, he nuzzled the short hair just above the curve of her ear.

"Tell me," he whispered, lips touching her as he spoke. "Don't think."

Pen nearly called it off. Five throwaway words had landed her in this moment. *Wouldn't be the first time.* Because she had eaten raw meat, just to fight for the privilege of seeing another sunrise. That didn't mean she needed to rip open that scar for a callous bastard.

But Tru. He would know what it was to endure ugly things. Maybe more than anyone. He might even understand why she'd left home . . . because she had to be worthy of the life her mother had died protecting.

"A year or two after I left Jenna and Mason, I was in the middle of the country. Old Kansas? That area. Sprawling wheat fields consumed by bugs and weeds. The voices I used to hear—they called me, leading me."

A shudder shook her upper back. She wouldn't mention how many of those voices still called to her. One in particular. Finn. The imaginary friend who'd helped her through so many dark times. But what full-grown woman still heard the call of imaginary friends, let alone thought about replying?

She huddled more tightly into herself and didn't protest when Tru pulled her against his body. *Don't think.*

"O'Malley's men picked me up. I magicked their leader into thinking I'd be more valuable if I remained pure. That he'd be rewarded if he brought such a prize to his bosses. We never made it that far. Demon dogs attacked—this massive pack. I hadn't seen anything like it since our first winter, when they all worked together, trying to break in. Do you remember?"

The feral skinwalkers who ate human and animal both had culled the dogs almost entirely. Pen couldn't recall the last time she'd seen one of those nightmare beasts.

Tru was quiet for a long time, long enough that she didn't think he'd answer. But he tightened his hold and whispered, "I remember."

Something bunched and painful unfurled in her chest. Releasing her. The frantic rate of her heart slowed just enough to regain her calm. She'd lie to him, just a little, but most of the story could be told.

"The guards fought. Fangs versus bullets. I huddled with four girls in the back of a nasty old van, holding them as they held me. The monsters won. We were trapped in there, half mad from entire nights filled with their howls. Claws on the metal. Their bodies slamming into the sides. For *days* this went on."

He smoothed the hair from her face, cupping her cheeks. "Hey. You don't have to tell me this."

"The other girls died," she said, talking over his kindness—hoping he wouldn't ask about those deaths. "I tried to help them, healing as their bodies shut down. But I couldn't keep it up. My own survival instincts only let me give so much. I shoved the bodies out of the van as a distraction. Just . . . *weak*. Exhausted. But I got hold of a gun and held them off, one bullet at a time, until I found the keys to the van."

"Jesus."

"I drove until I just couldn't anymore. Maybe an hour. I would've died. I knew it even at the time, that I was dying. But I hit a deer. Out of nowhere. It ruined the van. I cracked my head on the steering wheel." She closed her eyes. "But I ate that night."

Her body shook as if she faced that choice all over again. It hadn't been a choice at all, perched on the edge of starvation.

"You hate them, don't you? O'Malley and his people?"

"Individually? No. Like those men we killed yesterday. I mourn them." Letting go of the hard memories, she licked her lower lip. "But the organization? And the general? Yes. They're the worst of humanity. They'd have us eating roadkill for the rest of eternity if it meant amassing power enough to buy and sell little boys. We're meant for better than that. I can't believe the Change came along so that so much revulsion and agony would be our fate."

"You think it had a reason? No way."

She ignored his mocking tone, and tried to ignore how he let her go. "They don't get to win, Tru. That's all I know."

"Think what you want."

They can't win. Otherwise all of her sacrifices would be for nothing. That thought left a sick, dark hole in her gut.

Though he didn't move, she sensed his emotional withdrawal; the moment of closeness evaporated. But then, so did the suspense of her story. He acted caring and sympathetic—probably had done so for a dozen girls, all with sob stories of how the Change had left them hurting. And dear, smooth-talking Tru would kiss it better.

"You owe me," she said.

He considered in silence, face half in shadow. The hair over his brow made him appear impossibly boyish yet heavy-lidded eyes maintained a cold distance, even after what she'd just described. Hard to believe he must feel more than he revealed. Pen looked away. *Never mind*, she thought. She didn't need a confessor or a confidant. She needed a hard man who could get her to a civilization worth fighting for.

For the first time she wondered if she'd actually find such a place. The words "wild-goose chase" hit along the inside of her skull like a ball bouncing loose. She'd been searching for years. Listening to the voices that said she was a prophet or a lunatic. What would it be like to give that up? Just find a quiet corner of the Changed world and piece together a little happiness?

She couldn't even imagine it.

The soft whisper of his movement was all the warning she had. He shifted, kneeling before her and took both hands in his. The sunlight was stronger now. No one should have eyes that beautiful, that soulful—and yet so empty inside. Only, when Pen looked this time, he was right there with her. *Present*. Some inner rooms remained shut up and locked tight. A man like Tru might never throw open all the dark closets. But he wasn't leaving her behind. Not yet.

"I was eighteen." His voice took on that hypnotic quality, as if the sound could lull a restless child. She'd been that child once, but no longer. Now his voice melted her by slow degrees, warming and opening a tight place deep inside. "On my own for, oh, a year? Kinda high on it. All those skills Mason taught me kept my ass out of trouble, mostly. Until I got backed into this canyon. Demon dogs were thick on the ground back then."

He dropped his gaze to the damp dirt. "It didn't take much. Just that moment I realized I wasn't going to make it. Something snapped in my head. I woke up two days later, sprawled at the base of a tree. Clothes gone. After that, it just became . . . simpler."

Two blinks later, he retreated, and then gave Adrian a nudge with the toe of his boot. "Up and at 'em, kid. Time to move."

They packed the truck quickly. Tru stood guard with a rifle as

Adrian ate some gator for breakfast. Ten minutes later, still in silence, they yanked the rusted truck doors shut and headed north. Tru drove. Adrian slept in the back. Sitting in the passenger seat, stomach still rumbling, Pen couldn't eat. Her mind was lost to the pain of the past, the muddled emotions of the present, and the unknowns of the future.

TEN

Relief spilled through Tru's veins. It hadn't been as bad as he imagined after seeing her bleak expression. He had been afraid, as he seldom was—at least not since he learned to shift. And that bothered him. He hated this fucking vulnerability. Didn't want to care.

Honestly, Tru had expected a rape story. Sad as hell that they lived in such a world, but it could have been worse. Maybe Pen didn't think so, but she'd probably never found a girl dying on a dusty road, her face mutilated to match her genitals. Or maybe she had. It was hard telling what horrors she'd experienced, hidden behind her dusky blue eyes, behind her silence and reserve.

Driving occupied his attention, between the bad road and wildlife that darted in front of the truck. They kept moving even through mealtimes, stopping only for quick bio-breaks. The scenery changed gradually to tell him they were out of Florida. Wind rushing through the open window stole a little humidity, though it was still hot as hell. He'd give a lot for a dip in a cold lake.

With the busted fuel gauge, he had no idea how much gas remained in the tank. "Keep an eye out for any machinery," he said.

Adrian nodded, craning his neck to look out the window. "On it."

But the few shacks they passed were so humble that they boasted no equipment at all. Tru couldn't bring himself to terrorize anybody for no good reason. Their possession of an O'Malley truck wouldn't win friends either. One faction would fear them, and the other would try to kill them.

Near noon, the vehicle sputtered. Eventually it coasted to a stop in the middle of nowhere. Which was the whole damn world, compared to what it had been.

"I guess we're on foot from now on," he said, opening the door.

Penelope waited until Adrian got out. She followed and stretched with deliberate grace. "It shouldn't take us more than a couple of days from here, even walking."

That was true, as they'd already covered a good distance. Jacking the vehicle made for faster travel, but it also accelerated their time-table in a way Tru hadn't expected. He needed to step up his game, but the better he got to know her, the more reluctant he felt about sleeping with her. His usual methods seemed . . . wrong. Without a quick course correction, they'd wind up talking about feelings. Already they'd come perilously close—opening doors to intimacy that should be shut and bolted.

To get away from his unsettling thoughts, Tru beckoned to the kid. "I don't know about you, but I'm tired of gator meat."

"I could eat something else." But Adrian diluted his wishes with a shrug, as if he didn't expect them to be heard, much less granted.

"Let's do some foraging." At the boy's questioning look, Tru added, "It means looking for edible plants."

"Oh."

"You never did that before?"

"I grew up on a farm," the kid said, eyes distant. "I don't remember much from before the Change. Except I know Pop had to kill scary stuff from time to time. Afterward."

An unsought confession. He guessed the boy wanted to connect with him, and he imagined sharing was the way to go about it. Tru hadn't let himself get into this position in years, which meant he needed to decide whether to encourage this or shut it down. He settled on a quiet nod. Let the kid choose to continue.

"Two years ago, my dad died. Ma didn't do so well after that."

Tru could imagine. Women and children were fodder in the Changed world. "I'm sorry. Did you have brothers or sisters?"

Why the hell did you ask? Idiot.

"I had a sister, but she died in the Change."

Tru remembered all too clearly the result of those first, failed shifters. How good people had turned inside out, their bodies unable to meet the magic's demands. Bad people became demon dogs on the prowl.

Before Adrian could share something else, Tru started a monologue on the plants he was gathering: mushrooms that may have been chanterelles, watercress, plantains, possibly dandelion greens. A strange salad, but his human side needed something besides meat— yet another reason why he spent most of his days as a lion. Dinnertime offered no difficulty.

They walked east toward the water, over a rise, to where enough dirt produced fertile ground. Down the slope lay the beach and the ocean itself. Adrian stared, wide-eyed.

"First time?" Tru asked.

The kid nodded, speechless.

"Why don't you do a little wading? I'd suggest a swim, but we don't have a way for you to rinse off. Salt water's itchy as hell if you get it all over you."

Adrian wouldn't appreciate Tru worrying about tides, undertow, and currents. This was better. More tactful, less an insult to the kid's delicate pride.

"I don't know how to swim anyway."

Tru nodded. "Then let's go get our feet wet."

Their original mission postponed, he trailed the boy down the beach. It had been a long time since he'd seen the sea. Tru knew how to swim, thanks to summers at the Y, where they never let him forget he was a charity case.

That world was dead and gone. Kids had it tougher these days, crazy as that sounded.

He mustered endless patience while Adrian danced in and out of the waves, never mentioning that they would lose the light, with nothing collected to eat. Instead Tru played some. Mostly he watched with a sharp pain in his heart, remembering, *aching* because of a loss he'd spent years trying to escape.

But this . . . there was no denying this. His world had stopped making sense days ago.

Adrian pulled himself from the waves one last time, then glanced at the setting sun. "I guess we'd better get to work. This was fun, though."

Something you've had too little of, I suspect.

On the way back, they cruised the green hills and came back with shirts full of goodies. At the derelict truck, Pen had set up camp; she watched their approach with a lift of her chin. Deliberately, Tru settled on the opposite side and laid out the bounty on a blanket. They had no plates or silverware. He never traveled with such niceties. In fact, he only owned one change of clothes and a few odds and ends. Nothing to remind him of his former life.

What was gone was gone. Burned. Lost forever.

After a few bites of his strange, slightly bitter salad, he looked at Pen across the small clearing that sheltered their camp. "How were they, before you left? Mason and Jenna."

"That was a long time ago," she said.

"I'm aware."

"They were good. By then, they'd gotten the knack of farming and making their own medicines. And they had a baby."

He didn't know why that news gave him a twinge. Tru was sure they barely remembered him. He'd stayed a couple of years, just long enough to learn what he needed to keep from becoming a helpless victim. Then he'd gone off to find his own place in the world.

Adventure, first . . . and then belonging. A couple of lines from a poem flickered in his head. *So dawn goes down to day. Nothing gold can stay.* Years had passed since he'd thought of the pleasure words used to provide. As a kid he'd spent most of his time lost in books, bathing in other people's pain—dulling his own with that stark beauty.

"Boy or girl?"

"Boy. They named him Mitchell. But they might have had more after I left."

"Brave of them. I wouldn't want the responsibility."

Not ever again.

He returned to his salad, determined to eat rather than dwell. His lion side encouraged him to live in the present, and that simplicity kept him sane.

But Adrian must have heard something different in Tru's evasive words. "You don't have to be responsible for me," the kid muttered.

Tru didn't make the mistake of trying to salve his wounded pride. "What the hell?" He spoke sharply. "Don't be stupid. You're almost a man. I was talking about some toddler who can't figure out where to piss without help."

"Oh." A bright smile lit up the boy's face, and Tru felt like a bastard.

Not that he'd lied. But he didn't want that kind of influence. Considering he'd gotten into this mess by following his prick, he hoped he wouldn't have to cut it off in order to escape the closing trap.

Pen glanced between them with an unnerving expression of comprehension. Her look gentled, making him think she liked this side of him. Whatever. He scowled, his mood darkening. Probably sexual frustration, and since they only had a few more days before reaching their destination, he ought to do something about pushing for deeper contact. His unwillingness to proceed still mystified him.

After the salad, they ate more gator meat. Protein and greenery would keep them from malnutrition on the journey, but once they arrived, everyone needed to eat bread and butter. Lots of butter. Adrian especially needed the fat to fuel a growth spurt.

I wonder if babies born after the Change will be shorter, due to a lack of variety in their diets. An interesting question, but one the demands of survival meant would likely remain unanswered.

And why the hell was he thinking about babies?

Watching Adrian play in the ocean, he decided, and the news about Jenna and Mason's son. Maybe one day he'd head west, surprise them with a visit, and play the cool uncle for a day or two before hitting the road.

Satisfied with that plan, he settled on his blanket with the intention of turning in. Not because he was exhausted, but because he was tired of people. Tired of conversation. If it wouldn't be an impractical allocation of resources, he'd shift and sleep as a lion to further discourage interaction. And unwelcome memories.

As before, Adrian went to sleep first. And then Pen did something unusual. She came to him.

"What do you need?" He didn't want to argue with her, nor did he want to negotiate.

"Have you forgotten the terms of our agreement?"

Doubtless she was about to produce some clause that required him to do her bidding. He arched a brow in what he hoped was a discouraging fashion.

"*Two* kisses today, you said."

"Don't worry about it," he muttered. "We can defer them."

"I pay my debts."

"I don't want 'debt kisses' tonight. And I'm in no mood to persuade you to make them something else. So it's better if you leave me alone."

"What's the matter?"

As if she hadn't created the problem with her constant talking.

There's only one way to shut this woman up. When he claimed her mouth, Tru kissed her with driving demand and a thrusting tongue. He permitted no distance, no reserve, and pushed past her lips to delve into her mouth. She made a small, surprised sound, but he ignored it and dragged her into his arms. She had been treated with too much delicacy, not like a woman a man intended to fuck.

After settling Pen astride his lap, he made love to her mouth for endless moments. It gave him a jolt of intense satisfaction when she wound her arms around his neck and pressed closer. Her lips warmed as he nuzzled them, went swollen from the little nips, from the way he sucked gently at the lower, before teasing her tongue with his own. He wrapped his hands around her hips and rocked her against his hard cock as she learned how to kiss. God, he could almost swear nobody had done this with her before. But she was a quick study, working out how to breathe through her nose. Her response became hotter, more ferocious, as he cupped her ass and worked her body against his.

He nibbled his way down her jaw to her throat, sucking, kissing, licking. Her nipples peaked and grazed his chest. An actual moan escaped her. Fucking beautiful. Music to his ears.

And that was when he stopped.

Her eyes were glazed, mouth parted. She panted, hands on his chest. "That was more than two kisses."

"Technically, no. I never broke contact."

Dazed, she seemed to think about that, obviously trying to find a flaw in his logic. Then she leaned in. "Time for round two."

That made him smile. But Tru stopped with her a touch on her shoulder. Now she looked worried, as well she should.

"I don't want this kiss on your mouth," he whispered.

"Where, then?" She didn't try to argue. In fact, he'd almost say she looked . . . intrigued.

Or maybe he just wanted her to.

"Here." He unbuttoned the top two buttons on her shirt—once a man's garment, he thought, cut down to fit her. Delicately, he pulled the fabric aside, exposing a small, pert breast to the night air. It wasn't cold enough to explain her taut nipple, so she must feel . . . *something*.

He'd call it desire.

Tru urged her to kneel over his lap, bringing soft flesh right to him. He kept his hands on her hips, touching her upper body with nothing but his mouth. A soft kiss, first, and then a sweep of his tongue. She tasted faintly of salt. As long as he didn't break contact, he could do this as long as he wanted, as long as she'd let him. Her gasp told him she liked it, especially when he sucked the tip into his mouth. She wrapped her arms around his head, urging him closer.

For a delicious eternity, he played with her, sweeping his mouth back and forth between breasts. He nuzzled and sucked them both, until she seemed unable to control her breathing. Tru felt just as crazed.

At last, he eased back and fastened up her shirt. She trembled in his arms, and he didn't have the heart to push her away immediately. He was masochist enough to want the pressure on his aching cock.

To his surprise, she curled into his lap, tucking her head beneath his chin. That roused an unnerving sensation, as if this was precisely where she belonged. He'd only experienced that peace with one other person, a thought that nearly had him scrambling away from the woman he'd just kissed senseless.

"Now I see why you have no trouble getting laid," she said softly.

Tru swallowed. "You didn't before?"

"No. You're kind of an asshole."

"No more than anyone else," he said with a shrug. "Less than some."

She frowned up at him. "But *you* should be better."

"Why the hell would you think that?"

"Because you're Tru."

His heart twisted. That would have started an argument of epic proportions, except that she fell asleep in his arms. He didn't know what disconcerted him more. That she could set sex aside so fast, or that she trusted him enough to do so.

Whatever. Despite his better judgment, Tru held her long into the night.

ELEVEN

Pen rubbed her aching neck and came away with the smear of a mosquito on her palm. She hefted the rifle on her shoulder, wondering when the busted blisters would form calluses. Maybe never. Even after Pen healed them—for herself, Adrian, and a begrudging Tru—they came back. Just endless wear and tear on human bodies.

The soggy ground and constant sweating meant no time for the skin to dry and toughen. Trudging behind Tru, she kept her eyes on the soles of his boots. Wet sand caked the waffle pattern as they continued the trudge through an unkempt waste of overgrown dunes.

The ocean had stopped being interesting three days ago. Now the waves were a constant drone, numbing her mind. *Just walk and keep walking.* The bright summer sunshine reflecting off the mica burned her eyes, so that even closing them—if she'd been able to—only hurt worse. Quick blinks to get rid of the salt and sand. Unable to wear the cloak because of the heat, her skin blistered daily. She used minimal magic on the worst of it, to keep from getting sunstroke or burns that would leave her with a fever. But mostly she sucked it up and saved her resources for bigger trouble.

And for more walking.

Her unlikely companions filled more dead air with talk than she did. Adrian had opened up, not so much about his past. Maybe he sensed that Tru wouldn't respond so well to that type of confidence. But he opened his mind. Question after question. He soaked up every answer, which triggered more curiosity. Pen could only wonder how he'd lasted this long. Cared for by a sexual master? It was the only answer that made immediate sense, and offered another reason why he wouldn't be eager to offer up his experiences for others to hear.

Three days.

And at the end of each day, after Adrian fell asleep, Pen went to Tru. An added kiss for each day. The night before, he'd used up one of them on the end of her nose. His mouth had been swollen and wet from the delicious madness he inflicted on her breasts.

"Now somewhere new," he'd said.

But not her navel or the aching hollow between her legs. Her nose. As if he had all the time in the world and could blithely waste opportunities. She hadn't ever known anyone to behave that way.

Their sessions had started to feel less like payment and more like reward. Her reward. At the end of a long, tedious day of walking, they worked out the kinks and aches in each other's body, first with nearly medicinal massage. Then with kisses that set her insides alight. She was achy and tired, eager to reach their destination—if only for something new to occupy her mind. But she could've continued indefinitely with the promise of spending the night in Tru's arms once again.

Soon they'd reach Arturi's camp. And Tru would leave.

She would enjoy him while he was there. That was the only option, knowing his desire to run outweighed his greed for her body. In introducing Pen to sexual passion, he would never disappoint her. Best to keep to fields of play where his cynicism wouldn't ruin what fragile regard she had for him. And guard herself for that moment. She wouldn't be able to watch him go, whether he did so as a lion or a man.

But it was for the best. Pen couldn't trust herself, her judgment, her magic. Why would she ask anyone else to do the same?

A distant rifle shot snapped her out of that trudging stupor. She dropped. Tru and Adrian were already belly down in the sand. With a quick flick of his wrist, Tru motioned for them to stay put. He crawled up the dune, using tall sand grass as his cover.

Pen slid up to lie side by side with Adrian. "Don't follow me. Stay absolutely still. Understand?"

The boy nodded, eyes no longer so wide in the face of situations that required quick thinking.

She returned his nod and shimmied to meet Tru at the dune's crest. Mouth pressed nearly to his ear, she whispered, "Standard plan."

"Yup."

They'd come up with the protocol on their first day walking, same as when they'd taken the truck. If Tru needed to shift, he'd go hunting and meet them at dusk at a camp due north. They hadn't needed to use the plan again, but it made emergencies less frantic. He would be there.

For now.

"I can't see anything," he said, voice clipped. "And the wind's blowing the wrong way."

"Shift now?"

"Could be nothing. Just a local hunter after game."

"Then let me work."

He quirked an eyebrow but asked no questions. "I'll cover you."

Three simple words. A hot fissure of something close to hope fired down her spine. What would it be like to know this man had her back? Always?

Another rifle shot. The sound ricocheted closer this time, glancing down across the beach.

Pen shook out of that daydream and lay on her back. Kneeling was out of the question, not if she wanted to keep her head attached to her neck. But she needed her ritual. Needed to keep control, even though the moment demanded speed.

Palms together. Eyes down. Then to the sky. She said her thanks and found the moment that unlocked her to the rest of the universe.

Still dazed, as if her arms and legs were made of fog, she turned back to her stomach. Sight beyond sight. Vision so far off that it couldn't be human.

"A man. Midforties. Aiming at waterfowl. Two women with him. One dark-skinned and slim, one short and fair. They're watching him. Seems to be the only rifle between them."

"Magic?"

Pen extended her sight even farther. A feathery tickle brushed behind her ears, and a bright leaf-green aura emanated from one in particular. "The woman with the dark skin. Something like me, but not a healer."

"Violent?"

The touch of another mind pushed her back. Gently. A warning, it seemed, to be polite. She jerked and panted. Her head felt heavy, so she let it drop to the sand. Tru put a hand at the back of her neck and kneaded.

"You have to tell me. Any trace of violence from her?"

"No," she whispered, head still bowed. "She seemed . . . curious? As if she recognized me? That can't be right."

"I'm not taking any chances. Either we walk past them or we go meet them, but I'm shifting before we do."

"You sound like you're leaving that decision to me. Why?"

"You're the Orchid," he said curtly. "Something special, right? So prove it."

Pen twisted her bottom lip between her teeth. *Something special, all right.*

But Tru didn't appear ready to change his mind. He waited, arms crossed, looking impossibly self-assured. He wouldn't walk blindly into danger. Although he called her the Orchid, he was no blind, obedient follower.

She glanced behind her, down toward the ocean. Cloaking mounds of sand to the west. Great waves crashing in from the east. "We could walk between the water and the dunes, risking that they won't spot us. But that would also risk meeting them from a vulnerable position. They don't outnumber us and they don't appear to have more weapons." She shrugged. "They might know something about the camp. We have to be nearby now."

"Lots of talk, Penelope. Gimme a straight answer."

After a deep breath of salt-laden air, she met his gaze. The sky matched his eyes today, clear and eerily pale in the bright sunshine. "Let's go meet the neighbors."

He nodded. "Would be my call, too. You and Adrian can cover me with the rifles."

Despite her nerves and the exertion of her magic, she grinned. "You think you're special?"

"You know it. And even a good judge of character has trouble reading an animal."

He slithered backward down the dune. Pen followed, trying to shake the feeling of foreboding out from under her skin. The vibe she'd gathered off the trio wasn't violent, but neither was it honest. One of them crackled with deception.

Tru outlined the plan to Adrian when they met at the bottom of the dune. From her pack, Pen grabbed a slab of fish they'd caught and cooked that morning. She stuffed a quick handful in her mouth and swallowed it down, despite how the salty flesh turned her stomach. The light-headed feel that always came in the wake of using her magic was nearly gone by the time Tru had shifted.

She sat on the beach. And stared at him.

Even if she could get used to the sight of a fully grown wild cat striding five meters away, she couldn't reconcile him against the backdrop of the sea. Lions were supposed to be on a savanna somewhere. A huge, beautiful male lion with blue eyes was never supposed to prowl along the eastern coastline, his paws leaving gouged prints in wet sand.

But there he was. Tru. The wind fluffed his mane and skated ripples along the short fur of his back. He tipped his face toward the sky. Quick inhales wrinkled the bridge of his nose and flattened his nostrils. His tongue lolled out in a giant yawn, as if he'd just awoken from a nap—the opposite of preparing to meet a potential enemy. Yet, that was Tru, too. Casual insouciance in the face of the worst situations. Maybe that lion side had always been a part of him, just needing the Change to fulfill its most impressive potential.

"Ready?" Pen asked Adrian.

The boy nodded, carefully wiping the sand from his palms as Tru had shown him. *Keep the rifle clean. Never risk a misfire.* It was as if Mason had come with them to the Carolina coast.

She stifled her slight smile and checked her own weapon. One day she wouldn't need to carry one anymore. One day. On a day of peace.

But that seemed far off.

With a nod toward her animal guardian, she crested the dune. It took no more than a minute to pull within human eyesight of the unknown trio. Tru prowled between her and Adrian, then set off at a casual lope to circle around from the other direction. Not so far that he'd be out of leaping distance. But far enough that the man with the rifle would need to split his attention between human and beast.

The darker woman spotted them first. She locked eyes with Pen, and again that fissure of recognition threatened to unnerve Pen's concentration. Tall and slender, but with a nicely athletic build, this woman did not look like the malnourished sex slaves Pen had often aided. She held herself with a warrior's confidence, larger than life in the way Jenna had been to Pen's nine-year-old eyes. High, wide cheekbones offset her dark and inquisitive stare.

The act of lowering his rifle brought the man back into focus. Pen blinked and hefted her own weapon. "Don't move," she said.

A quick glance to her right showed that Adrian, too, had the man in his sights. His hands didn't tremble as he kept the rifle level. *Look what Tru has accomplished.*

In just three days. What could a boy like Adrian learn with a lifetime of such guidance?

But Pen shunted that impossible thought away as quickly as it appeared.

"No one wants a bloodbath." She tipped her head to the man's right. "And he's one of us."

The man didn't look at Tru, but the two women did. The shorter blonde one, who on closer inspection appeared too small to be fully grown, watched the lion lazily circling their position.

Gaze still steady on Pen, the other woman raised her hand and laid it slowly, carefully, on the barrel of her companion's weapon. "Put it down, my friend. Nothing to fear here."

Pen didn't exactly agree. Adrian could panic, or Tru could twitch his tail the wrong way. Fear was everywhere in their little circle—everywhere but in that woman's impossibly dark eyes.

"We're heading north," Pen said. "Not looking for trouble, don't want any following us either."

"Neither do we. Perhaps we can make introductions?"

Something about the woman's voice was hypnotic, as if she'd worked for years to find the perfect soothing pitch. That might have been her magic, but Pen didn't believe it. She was capable of more. The only question was whether that something else constituted a danger.

Pen inhaled past a bubble of panic. She wasn't a leader. She didn't have the control for it—her magic was too unreliable. Adrian . . . Tru . . . They depended on her to make the right decision.

But this moment had nothing to do with magic. Just people. Just a judgment call that could mean their lives.

"My name's Pen. This is Adrian and the lion is Tru. We're heading north to a camp. Maybe you know something about it."

"Arturi Mäkinen's camp."

Pen blinked. "That's right."

The woman offered a brilliant white smile that contrasted with her complexion. "Good. You're just the people we were coming to see. This is Jack, Shine, and I'm Zhara. Arturi Mäkinen is my husband. And you, Penelope—I've been expecting you."

TWELVE

Tru shifted to back to human.

In lion form, while he retained memories, he wasn't exactly himself. He lacked the ability to make logical decisions. Needs became simpler and more primal. This situation called for human sophistication. So at Pen's cue, he responded. She and Adrian stood at an impasse with the three newcomers, while he quickly dressed. He didn't think the confrontation would come to bloodshed. These people wanted something from the Orchid.

Big surprise. Everyone seemed to.

"Better?" the tall woman asked.

Tru smiled lazily. "It is for you."

Zhara turned to Pen. "Arturi bade me go and guide you to our camp. We're well hidden from our enemies."

So far, Jack and Shine hadn't spoken a word.

"You promise safe passage?" Pen asked.

The tall woman shook her head. "I can't, can I? But you will come to no harm from us."

"Our boat's anchored a mile up the coast," Shine put in.

A boat? Tru banked a flicker of interest. He'd never traveled by water, despite a history of exploration. Few people had seen as much of the Changed world as he, though he usually saw it in lion form. Not this time.

Tru waited. This was Penelope's operation.

Finally, she nodded. "Lead the way."

Adrian dug into their provisions and handed Tru a couple of fish to eat on the move. An efficient use of time and resources. Little conversation passed between the two parties. The younger female eyed Tru with a carefully blank face. He obliged her with a toothy smile, but she surprised him by responding with a wink before striding ahead.

That left the man walking between them. It was a good move. Protective.

"You tried to scare her," Adrian said to Tru.

"So I did."

"How come?"

"Because she stared at me. She should be used to skinwalkers, but maybe my ability isn't why she was looking."

"I think it's amazing." The kid's tone held a wistful edge.

"You wish you could shift?"

"Hell, yes."

That was how he'd felt upon first learning of Jenna's ability. "Well, I was older than you when my lion kicked in. So maybe you'll change too. At the right time."

Adrian seemed cheered by this possibility. They lapsed into silence, putting one foot in front of the other. Tru didn't trust this group or their timely intervention, but then, he was a suspicious bastard. Penelope's magic would detect hostile intentions. Wouldn't it? He couldn't bring himself to ask her, and certainly not in earshot of the newcomers.

"You've just about kept your promise," Penelope said softly. "We're almost there."

"Just a boat ride now. It'll be a welcome break from walking."

Her voice dropped to a husky timbre. "But we still haven't slept together."

That no longer sounded so pleasing as it once did. Oh, he still wanted her, but . . . not on prescribed terms. What he wanted would never come to pass. The Orchid wasn't likely to slip into his bedroll because she wanted him too badly to refrain. As such, he'd lost his taste for the game. Seduction with Penelope didn't promise the same sweetness, the same heady sense of power.

And he couldn't go down the road to caring. Not again.

"True," he said simply.

This wasn't the time to get personal. With a measuring look, she subsided. A short time later, they reached a small craft with oars that had been pushed up on the shore. Shading his eyes, Tru glimpsed a small boat bobbing farther out on the waves.

"That's it," Zhara said. "We won't all fit, so we'll make two trips. Do any of you know how to row?"

Silence. *When the hell would we have learned?* He felt snarly. Soon Pen and Adrian wouldn't need him anymore. Not for protection. Not for anything. That knowledge dug into a ridiculously raw place—a place he'd thought scarred over for years. He'd believed himself so well protected that nothing could get inside his armor ever again.

"I'll need a volunteer for the first trip from your group."

"Me." Adrian glanced at Tru as if for permission.

He inclined his head in silent thanks. The kid's bravery made his job a lot easier. There was no way in hell he was leaving Penelope unprotected, and no way he would let her get in that boat without him. Adrian's offer simplified everything.

Soon the small craft had pushed far from shore, leaving Tru alone with Pen. She stood beside him, grubby but undaunted. She really thought these people could make a difference in her fight against O'Malley. He shook his head in disbelief. What must it be like to have that kind of faith? And hope? Painful, he guessed. Especially if things went wrong.

Such a damning combination of strength and doubt, of experience and naïveté.

"Do you think I'm being stupid? To trust them."

Tru looked out to sea. "Not if you're cautious. Keep sharp, listen for lies, and be ready for trouble."

She, too, gazed over the churning waves in uneasy silence. "I already saw signs of deception. Not in their faces, but in their auras." Her look said she expected him to make light of her mojo.

But he respected what she could do. He'd seen too much of the world not to. "Everyone lies. So that's probably natural to some degree. Somebody gleaming silver with purity, I'd suspect them of using some kind of masking spell."

"That makes sense."

"Glad I could help." And he meant it, astonishingly enough.

Deep blue eyes gazed up at him with entrancing candor. "Would you do me a favor?"

"Depends on what it is."

Pen's lips curved. "I want a kiss. For luck."

His heart gave a crazy lurch. Absurd to imagine that his touch could bring her any good fortune, but then, she must know that.

She just wanted the kiss. And he did, too.

"That I can do. For a moment I feared you'd found a dragon for me to slay."

"Not today. Well, not yet."

Carefully, he cupped her face in his hands and bent down. She lifted on tiptoes, lips parting for his. It was a slow, languid dream of a kiss, all brush and tease and sweetness, a heady precursor to the wildness that thumped like a drumbeat. Deeper, deeper, and with each sweep of tongues, she clung to him, so soft and warm that he could lay her down on the sand. Any gentleness would burn away until he took her with utter ferocity.

"Was that what you had in mind?" he asked against her mouth.

Her breath came in flattering gasps. "More."

Whether a request or an answer, he obliged as if it were both. By the time they finished, long moments later, her lips were rosy and bee-stung. He stroked the delicate curve of her jaw and she tilted her head, deliciously responsive. God, he wanted to make her come. She bore all the hallmarks of an unawakened woman.

He no longer wanted to bait her or use her for his entertainment. She had become more. Dear. Vital. *Precious*. And not in the casual way he usually used the endearment.

More like—

No. He snipped the thought.

Tru preferred pursuing pleasure for its own sake. He hadn't always been that way, but it was easier. Less painful. He'd suffered enough heartbreak for two lifetimes.

Mason would've been disappointed in the man he'd become.

A bitter smile twisted his mouth.

"Is something wrong?" She watched him, as if reading his expressions.

Tru offered a lazy smile—the I-don't-give-a-fuck smile that she hated. On the heels of their intimacy, the dismissal seemed to hit even harder. She stiffened her shoulders.

"Just the whole world," he said. "But never mind. We'll put it right, won't we?"

"Why are you acting like this? I thought—"

"That you fixed me? Sure enough, I'm a regular Quixote tilting at windmills now."

"I hate it when you get this way."

Me too.

A taut, angry silence fell between them. They didn't speak again until Jack returned with the boat. He signaled that they should wade out into the water and climb in. Tru waited for Penelope to make it into the craft, before gracefully leaping over the side. The lilt of the water offered an unsteady landing, but he managed to sink onto the bench without mishap. Jack took up the oars. Pen sat beside Tru but didn't appear happy about it. Even then, he was privately glad she'd chosen to sit by him rather than the sullen stranger.

That spoke volumes about his sanity. And maybe hers.

Whatever else could be said of Jack, the man knew how to row. In his hands they pulled cleanly through the waves and cut the distance to the larger boat. Which wasn't much. Just a small seafaring vessel. Perhaps it had been a fishing boat before the Change, long since retrofitted with patched sails. Rough work, but functional.

Adrian waited for them on deck as Tru followed Pen up the ladder. So did Shine and Zhara, who was clearly the captain. She gave the orders, telling Jack to pull anchor while the girl trimmed the sails. Tru's group did its best to stay out of the way. The wind puffed out the patched canvas and they drifted in the right direction. Wherever that might be.

"Sorry we haven't had a chance to talk much," the tall woman said.

Pen nodded regally. "I understand."

"You must have questions."

"Obviously. How did you know I was coming?"

Zhara smiled. "I read runes. Bones, too, if the situation demands. Augury isn't an exact art, but sometimes the information can be truly useful."

"How specific is it?" Pen warmed to the discussion, making Tru think she would be happy talking to the other woman for the duration of the journey.

He moved off and took a defensive position at the rail. It made no sense for strangers to wait until they boarded before attacking, but sometimes people behaved in incomprehensible ways. He felt no surprise when Adrian joined him. The kid would become a permanent shadow if Tru allowed it. He should do more to discourage the attachment.

But Adrian wore such an eager puppy expression. Tru couldn't bring himself to do it.

"Can you believe it?" Awe filled his voice, which cracked in that awkward adolescent way. He gestured at the wide-open ocean around them. Blue-green waves lifted and fell as the wind pushed the boat along.

"What, in particular?"

"All of this. I didn't even know people could *do* this."

He doesn't remember anything.

But Tru did. Once, people had flown. If Tru said so, Adrian would probably ask what spell had permitted that to happen. This boy remembered only the Changed world, but Tru was a child of both. Sometimes he felt the weight of that most awfully. Maybe it was suitable that he was twin-souled as well, man and lion, both unable to find where they fit. Years ago, he'd thought he'd found such a place, but it had been as temporary as a dream.

"The boat you mean?" he asked, realizing Adrian awaited a response.

"Yeah. I didn't even ride in a vehicle until I was fourteen."

"Was that when you were taken?"

The kid gave a jerky nod. Some wounds didn't bear exploration. If Adrian wanted to talk, he wasn't likely to be shy about it. Tension slid out of him, maybe when he realized Tru didn't intend to poke. He relaxed more as he asked questions about things he saw swimming in the water. Tru answered as best he could.

"Can you read?" he asked.

Adrian shook his head. "There was no call for it on the farm. Since then . . ." His voice trailed off.

Yeah, whatever he'd been doing hadn't required books. Tru's stomach churned. He'd love to kill whoever had tormented this young man. Not a clean death either. He'd go lion and play with the bastard for a while. The mental picture cheered him up.

"What's so funny?" Adrian asked.

"I'm picturing what it would be like to maul the guys who stole you."

A smile built in the kid's eyes and spread to his mouth. "You'd do it, wouldn't you?"

"Hell, yes."

"I never had that before. Somebody to fight for me. Even my dad . . ." Adrian shrugged. "He was pretty worn down, I guess. Tired."

"It can be a struggle."

Tru said the words, but he felt like puking over the side of the boat. Not from seasickness. Parents should look after their children. Protect them, no matter what. He had reasons for believing so strongly—only a few of which related to his own less-than-stellar childhood. But he wouldn't share with Adrian. Some failures were too private to speak aloud.

"You seem like you've known the Orchid for a long time." Maybe the kid had sensed it was time to back off the personal shit. He seemed to have a natural gift for knowing when to shut up and stay put. Invaluable survival skills.

"Long enough," he admitted. "Why do they call her that, anyway?"

That was something he'd never ask Pen. Not in a million years. It highlighted the difference between them too greatly, and he didn't want her to be a saint or a symbol of hope. He only wanted her in his arms, writhing and screaming his name. And the strength of that desire scared the hell out of him.

Adrian went somber, as if he was about to relate a religious parable. "The way I heard it, she was defending a kid from O'Malley raiders, just put herself in between him and danger. Before she could smite the bastard, he cut her. She killed him, but her blood spilled onto the ground, and wherever it touched the soil, an orchid grew, pale and red-veined. Sheer magic." The boy spoke the last word with profound reverence.

It was an amazing story—and Tru had seen enough of Penelope's gifts to believe it might hold some grain of truth. "Thanks for telling me."

As she never would.

"There are more stories, if you want to hear them. Miracles she's performed. People brought back from the brink of death."

"Not just now, I think." They'd only make him feel more inadequate.

"So what do you think the camp will be like?"

"I have no idea. But I hope it's civilized. I need a bath so bad I can't stand myself."

Adrian laughed. "Me too."

"Well, I wasn't going to say anything."

The kid punched him in the arm and then looked horrified. "I'm sorry, I didn't mean—"

"It's okay," Tru said softly.

"Seriously?"

"I promise I'll never hurt you. And I won't let anybody else, as long as I'm around."

"But you won't always be."

"I'll teach you to protect yourself. I haven't forgotten what I said before we jacked that truck."

Adrian offered a smile full of bright teeth. His dark eyes sparked with excitement. "Yeah, you did say you'd show me some stuff."

"And I will. We haven't had a chance with all the traveling, but there should be opportunity in camp."

"Thanks, Tru." The boy hesitated, staring out over the rail at the blazing sky. The late-afternoon sun was sinking into the horizon over a ladder of gold. "You know, if I *had* a brother, I'd want him to be like you."

Oh, kid. You wouldn't say that if you knew me.

THIRTEEN

An hour into the voyage, they lost sight of the coast.

Much later, they tethered the sailboat to a small dock on the far side of a sandy island. Pen stepped onto dry land and swayed. Plenty of distance from the prying eyes of O'Malley's thugs. Dozens of huts clustered in the island's interior reminded her of long-ago photos of Plains Indian settlements. Only, these were made of often-patched white canvas, shaped into low square blocks no bigger than two meters square. She hadn't seen smoke from fires when approaching the camp, but now the trails of silvery gray reached skyward.

She stepped closer to the settlement, and her senses exploded.

Magic.

So much magic.

Her knees gave way. Tru and Adrian each grabbed an arm, and she sank against Tru's easy strength. He didn't appear as solid as he was, all lean muscle and quick grace. The breath wouldn't stay in her lungs. Each sense pinged out until only sight remained.

She was lying on the ground. No, on the dock. Tru's concerned face obscured her view of the sky at dusk. Pale blue eyes against a much darker blue vista.

But then she was floating. Tru held her. His voice punched through the strange cotton that muffled sound. He was angry, shouting at Zhara, whose eyes had widened so that her irises were looped with white.

Magic.

Everywhere.

She felt the old impulse to teleport. Panic grabbed the base of her neck and twisted. The press of her ribs against Tru's implacable hold faded and softened. Some dark and deadly threat pressed up from her sternum. It bubbled inside her veins, seeping out of her skin. If she lost control in this place . . .

But Tru still held her. The memory of his kiss grounded her. Kept her solid and sane and *there*, snuggled in his arms. Their bodies had made promises she intended to honor. For him, yes. But for her, too.

Sensation returned to her skin. Words made sense again.

"Someplace indoors where she can lie down," Tru said. *"Now."*

She tried to reach for his face, to ease the tension that tightened the tendons of his neck and deepened his frown lines. But her limbs were leaden. She could only let her forehead fall against his chest. When was the last time she'd given herself so completely to another's care? Not once since going out on her own.

In the Changed world, placing trust in others was almost as frightening as a night full of monsters.

"Come on, Pen." *He's never called me that before.* Always, it was Penelope with a beautiful curl of his lip. "Stay with me. Eyes open, baby."

"I'm here," she whispered.

Eyes the color of an icy lake filled with a concern she'd never seen from Tru. But then he vanished and she saw only black.

She awoke in a squat hut filled with the soft glow of a single candle. Still wearing the same clothes. Still fighting that head-melting buzz of magic. But the dissonance had faded. She could make sense of individual auras, rather than drowning in a heavy wash of so many powers.

Tru sat on the floor, his back propped against her cot. After such a day, any other man would've used the moment of solitude to grab a quick nap. He kept his eye on the exit, a flap tied shut with rope. His rifle lay across his knees. Adrian was curled into a crescent shape in the far corner.

"Keeping watch," she said softly. The words scratched out of her throat. Every joint felt rusty.

He turned slowly, with no sign of surprise, as if he'd already known she was awake. Maybe he had. "I probably deserve that you sound surprised. But I'm not a complete bastard."

The backs of her eyelids felt lined with sandpaper. She blinked a few times, then tried to sit up. Tru met her by the side of the cot, preventing the movement.

"Tru, I'm fine."

"Don't fight me on this. You didn't see your face."

She made an exasperated sound, then relaxed beneath the pressure of his palms. "I just . . . I've never encountered so much magic. There are a *lot* of skinwalkers here. And people like me. It was overwhelming."

"No shit." He shoved his fingers through his hair, which made it stick up in odd places. Sand still clung to the skin along his cheek and forehead.

Pen took his terseness for anxiety. But she knew better than to call him on it or thank him for his care. If she'd learned anything about Tru—years ago, and now—it was that he didn't like to acknowledge the guts that bled beneath the surface. His unspoken concern would be enough. Safer that way.

Knowing he'd soon be gone did nothing to urge Pen to open up. Knowing he'd be disgusted by what he found inside her offered an equal deterrent.

"What's your lay of the place?" she asked, hoping for a businesslike demeanor.

Tru flashed her a quick, assessing look. Then he nodded, accepting her topic change. She wanted distance from the moment when her panic had dissolved simply because he held her.

"About two hundred people. Family units. Little kids and old people, even." He squinted, staring at some middle distance. "I've been everywhere, Pen. But I haven't seen this many people in one place since . . ."

"Since before."

"It's almost claustrophobic."

Pen traced his profile with her gaze. Long lashes angled downward and shaded whatever he hid in his eyes. To be among this many people all of a sudden had to be as overwhelming for him as the magic had been for her. Conventions and conversations, rules and responsibilities.

It was a wonder he was still there at all.

"What about their fortifications?"

"Solid," Tru said gruffly. "Only one harbor. There are gun batteries set up on towers, and the rest of the beaches are reinforced. I'd be surprised if there are many access points."

"You sound impressed."

He shrugged, then checked his rifle. She'd bet anything that he'd already done the same inspection a dozen times. Mason hadn't raised no fool.

"It's easy to be impressed by things I can't do."

Before Pen could follow up, footsteps sounded outside the shelter. "Penelope? It's Zhara. Arturi would like to speak with you, if you're feeling up to it."

"Then let him come see her," Tru called back.

Pen put a hand on his shoulder. "It'll be okay. Just stay with me, yes?"

His eyes dropped, looking at where her fingers curved against his flesh. "We have a deal."

She should've bristled at that blunt reminder, but she wanted it, too. Camp meant getting clean and fed, and maybe even privacy. She could hardly breathe for the possibilities. But the other change was his tone of voice. He no longer seemed to be taunting. More like . . . promising.

She shook the thoughts out of her head. Not only did she have business to attend, but she would be an idiot to believe this lion intended to stay caged. He'd run free soon enough. All she hoped was that it was sooner rather than later. She already relied on him more than she should. The voices that had called to her for years simply faded into the background when Tru was near.

Pushing off the cot, she crossed the small hut and opened the canvas flap. "I'm ready."

At her back, Pen heard Tru speaking quietly to Adrian. Then he followed her out into the gathering darkness. The ocean was loud, a constant crash of waves. But the sound of people was so much stronger. Chatter, hammering, the clink of utensils. Singing and a baby crying and the soft notes of a distant fiddle.

Unexpected tears pricked her eyes. She wanted to explain why, but no words came. This was so much bigger than she'd expected. So much more to defend. The weight of a duty she didn't yet carry kept her feet from moving. No wonder Tru avoided lasting ties.

But she also felt relief. The rumors had been true; they'd found a real, thriving settlement with a fighting chance. She was giddy with the possibilities, no matter the burdens of protecting such a treasure.

"This Arturo guy can wait." Tru stood beside her, his expression etched with concern. "You need to rest."

"No, I'm all right. Honest."

He maintained his dubious frown but took her hand. Held it. And they walked behind Zhara as she led them through camp.

Despite the urge to absorb every detail, Pen kept her eyes lowered and her concentration tight. Just the heat of Tru's palm. The even, assured cadence of his strides. To try processing everything at once would only put her back in that hut. And she wanted to meet the man who'd inspired this haven.

Zhara was outfitted more simply than she had been on the beach. No cloak, no small arms on her hip. She kept her hair neatly cropped, which accentuated the grace of her neck. Reaching another hut—one exactly like all the rest—she ducked inside.

Pen exchanged a swift glance with Tru before following.

And she stood face-to-face with a figment.

"It can't be," she whispered. "*You* can't be."

He sat behind a small table; maps and manifests scattered its surface and lined the soft walls. He stood, wearing a dumbfounded expression that matched her inner turmoil.

"Hello, Penny."

"Finn?"

A slight smile. He nodded. "Arturi, actually, but yes. You once knew me as Finn."

She rushed forward and embraced him. Just like that. No hesitation as she hugged a piece of her imagination made real. He smelled of chalk and wood smoke. Their laughter was matched in disbelief.

"What's going on?" Tru asked.

Pen faced him. "Do you remember back when I had an imaginary friend?"

"You were little. Kids do that."

"This . . ." She met the man's eyes again. "This is him. Grown up."

Tru turned the full power of his scrutiny toward their host. She tried to imagine what he saw but knew their perspectives would be entirely different. Arturi was thirty-ish. Tons of freckles added a ruddy cast to his fair skin. A lock of ginger hair hugged his forehead. His eyelashes were so pale as to be nearly invisible, making the blue of his eyes more prominent. An awkward smile was made all the more humble by crooked front teeth.

He was nothing special. Objectively, he looked like a human gnome, all soft and sweet-faced. But to Pen, seeing him in person was like learning dragons and mermaids really existed. Even in the Changed world, evidence of such magic still took her by surprise.

"This is Tru," Pen said, crossing back to his side. "He's the skin-walker who helped get me here."

"I remember you talking about a boy named Tru. Same person?"

She couldn't look at Tru. Couldn't do it, even though she knew it was cowardly as hell. The unexpected embarrassment was too much. "That's right."

"Why did she call you Finn?" Tru's expression remained wary.

"I was born in Finland."

Pen grinned at her nine-year-old self. "I just thought it was your name."

"That's right. But I never minded." A wistful smile touched his mouth. He seemed self-conscious about his teeth, because he didn't let them show.

"Wait, so he was real?" Tru huffed out a laugh. "That's almost a relief."

With a little flinch, Pen tried not to read too much into his off-hand words. She'd always thought herself mad. Had Tru believed the same?

"When the Change began in Europe, my parents managed to get us to Florida." Arturi's posture tightened subtly, the reflex of grief. But even through that grief, his voice remained almost hypnotic in its sure smoothness. "They didn't last long after that, so I stayed, even when the Change hit the east coast."

"Then you've been at this a lot longer than I have," she said.

He nodded. Try as she might, Pen could detect no magic within him. No ability to shift. No healing. Not even the strange aura given off by Zhara's ability to read runes. He was simply a man. An ordinary man, but one armed with a strange charisma that drew her attention. She had been in his head since childhood. She knew his fears and his hopes better than she knew her own. Maybe he knew the same about her. How could a man without magic speak to her across such a gulf of time and space?

When Zhara walked over to him, he wrapped an arm about her

waist. They made such an odd couple, with her dusky skin and slender, athletic physique—probably a good ten centimeters taller than he. But that quiet intimacy spoke volumes about their trust and affection.

Pen staunched the urge to retake Tru's hand. They'd let go sometime between the walk and stepping into the surreal. She missed the reassurance of touch.

Arturi's expression, however, meant an end to such impulses. She could hardly think of him by that name, so long had she seen his features in her mind and called him Finn. "I'm glad you found us," he said, words somber. "Zhara predicted your arrival, but now I must know. Why are you here, Penny?"

"To convince you to take down General O'Malley."

He nodded, as if that were the exact answer he'd awaited. "Then we have a great deal to do."

Pen inhaled through her nose. Despite her self-doubt and memories of old failures, she discovered a surprising measure of calm. Daydreams of an imaginary friend hadn't been the ravings of a lunatic little girl. Something unlocked inside her. *I'm not crazy.* For how many years had she traveled, surrounded by magic but still unconvinced of her own sanity? It had simply been a destiny no one knew how to interpret.

No fear here. Only what she'd been meant to do all along. These were the people she'd come to help.

Arturi changed his focus with the slightest shift of his gaze. "And you, Tru. I remember Penny thought very highly of you. Will you be joining us?"

FOURTEEN

Tru sidestepped the question, but what did they expect? That he'd sign up for some fairy-tale mission to dismantle O'Malley? He had as much reason as anyone to hate the general, but he also knew the difference between fights that could be won—and ones that were doomed from the outset.

Rather than press, Arturi assigned an escort to show them to their quarters. Adrian would share digs with a number of orphaned children. Tru went with him to make sure it was decent, but the kids were allotted plenty of space for individual pallets. They had free rein in the camp by day, so it wasn't as if they spent all their time trapped inside. Just a warm, safe place to sleep.

"You fine with this?" Tru asked.

"Sure. They told me there are washtubs set up over there." Adrian pointed to the far end of the settlement.

Tru made out a low wooden wall surrounding an outdoor bath, which was located close to a well. Water boiled on the fire. The town maintained a schedule. Because only males were allowed to use the facilities at the moment, he and Adrian walked over together to clean up. The arrangement was clever. He stood in a small tub and soaped up. Overhead hung a bucket with holes in the bottom. He pulled its connected rope to move the covering aside, which released water over his head. Others waited to use the bathing area, so he rinsed quickly and donned his travel-worn clothing. Then he waited for Adrian without being obvious about it.

On his way out, he asked, "Is there a laundry?"

"That way," a man answered.

Adrian didn't have any other clothes either, so Tru made his next question count. "Is there a place we can trade for supplies?"

"The quartermaster's in that tent," another man replied.

"Thanks."

Inside the tent, the air was dark and warm. Stuff cluttered every spare inch. He picked a path to the front, where a young woman sat in a camp chair, chewing a pipe. There was no smoke, so she must like the feel of the stem between her teeth. At closer glance, he recognized her as Shine, the quiet one who had escorted them from the coast.

"What can I do for you?" she asked.

"You have clothing?"

"Sure, as long as you don't mind homespun. What do you have for trade?"

He only had one thing anyone would want. With some regret, he dug the item out of his pack. It was an expensive survival knife with multiple attachments. Mason told him years ago that it had once cost almost a hundred dollars, but that wasn't how Tru knew its worth. The excellent quality blade had stood up well over the years, and it would offer invaluable help to anyone who practiced regular woodcraft.

Tru placed the knife in her hands. She turned it over, pulling out all the little tools to examine them. Eventually she said, "Two sets of clothing for each of you."

Because he suspected that she expected him to, he haggled. "Are you crazy? They don't make tools like that anymore. Any idiot can stitch up trousers and a tunic."

"But that doesn't take into account growing the flax, spinning it, and weaving it into cloth. The needlework is the least of the process."

"Six sets."

"That's ridiculous. We trade with the daredevils who knock off O'Malley's shipments. I could bargain for ten of these knives for less trouble."

"I doubt it. The markup is insane."

"Three sets," she said with a twisted upper lip.

"Five."

Adrian watched the proceedings with an apparent mixture of embarrassment and hilarity. But he kept his smile to a minimum. Bargaining was serious business.

"Four," Tru finally said.

"Sold." Shine took the knife and opened a trunk stuffed with layers of clothing. Every article had been crafted from raw homespun, which meant garments of pale, clean simplicity.

For the next few minutes, he and Adrian dug through the trunk, looking for four trousers and tunics that would fit. The design reminded Tru of a surgeon's scrubs, though it had been many long years since he'd seen a doctor wearing anything but a bloody apron more suited to a butcher than a man of medicine.

"Do you mind if we change in here?" he asked. "I'd like to get these clothes to the laundry. How much does that cost by the way?"

"I'll turn around," Shine said. "And there's no cost per se. Everyone pitches in. So as long as you're willing to take your turn in the laundry and the galley, we make sure the work gets done."

"What's a galley?" Adrian whispered.

"The kitchen, I think."

"Yep." Shine, it seemed, had very good ears. "You'll both take a turn cooking sometime in the next two weeks. You need to see Vern about getting on the work roster."

That sounded like hell. Tru would wash his own clothes and get his own food. But Adrian seemed pleased with the idea of fitting in and being needed. He beamed at the prospect of chores.

So Tru said, "Good idea."

Once dressed, the two parted ways. Adrian headed off to look for Vern, and Tru walked toward the tent he had been assigned. Or rather, the one *Pen* had been assigned. Arturi's people had assumed she would share with Tru. He didn't like the assumption, as it forced him into position as half of something. Mr. Penelope Sheehan. He had offered his heart and his life to a real woman once. He wouldn't repeat the mistake with a living goddess—a martyr in the making if ever he saw one.

Technically, he could leave now.

He'd kept his promise. That was the only thing that mattered to him. Not sex, anymore. Keeping his word meant everything. Mason had taught him that much, but Tru needed to get out while he still could.

Wearily, his steps turned toward Pen's tent. Inside the small space covered in pale cloth, he found little by way of amenities, just a cornhusk mattress and handwoven blankets for a bed. No other furnishings, not that they were needed. Most of the camp seemed to do their living outside with other people. The place couldn't have been established for too long. Defenses first. Then niceties. He'd proceed the same way.

Once inside, he saw Pen had bathed, too; she must have used a private tub or basin. One couldn't make the divine Orchid stand around dirty. Her skin shone with a sun-kissed glow, courtesy of their days on the road. Short, freshly washed hair gleamed with pale streaks. As ever, her deep blue eyes haunted him. Sometimes he saw them in his sleep, and he didn't *want* to.

Leave. Now.

He was about to make some excuse, but she forestalled him with a smile. "So we made it."

"Promised you we would."

"I shouldn't have doubted." She took a step toward him. "So . . . now or should we wait until dark?"

No question what she meant. Night was a few hours off. Instinct demanded he delay, as he feared touching her as he had few things in his life. Tru hadn't known such bone-deep dread since the early days of the Change when they'd all been trapped in the wildlife station, sure of nothing but the likelihood of an early, gruesome death. As he had then, he covered his fear with bravado and an easy smile.

"No time like the present."

She cocked a brow. "You're not exactly bursting with enthusiasm."

His grin felt sharp enough to cut his lips. "Sure I am. Men live for sex."

In turn, her expression became doubtful. He couldn't bring himself to offer assurances as she pulled off her clothes quietly. Of *course* she was beautiful: slim, delicate, but also strong with high breasts and long, lovely legs. He remembered the scar on her upper arm. She'd gotten it when she teleported out to save him. Surrounded in the snow by a pack of demon dogs, he'd been certain of his death. And she'd appeared out of nowhere, a nine-year-old girl ready to take on evil for his sake.

That only made it worse. They had history.

His body, when confronted with a gorgeous female, did what nature demanded. Cock hard, Tru skimmed out of his own clothes, knowing his head was too messed up for this. He should go. But this felt like closure. A business transaction, though it wasn't. It couldn't be, and that was part of the problem.

I can't do this.

But his body throbbed, making it all too plain that he could. *Not now. Not like this.* But later wouldn't be easier. To wait would only make touching more complicated. Better to complete the compact with the only sort of sex he'd had in four years. He was good at it, and nobody ever seemed to notice the difference. Only he knew how it *could* be.

Hiding a need for what he couldn't have, he stepped forward to kiss her. It wasn't a slow, tender kiss like they'd shared before, but more of his practiced work. He needed long moments to coax her mouth open. She was willing but not eager. He should have minded, but her distance helped. They both held reservations, which made him feel less alone.

Because he couldn't bear to make it awful for her, he kissed her throat and her breasts, caressed her sides, and stroked her thighs. By increments, her body softened. When Tru swung her into his arms and carried her to the pallet, she didn't resist.

There on the blankets, he stroked between her legs until wetness slicked his fingers. Her eyes remained cool and watchful, despite her body's natural response. He could draw a facsimile of readiness from her in this state of mind, but there would be no real connection. He took great comfort in that certainty.

This was an introduction to pleasure. Nothing more. He was no longer *capable* of more.

Once he was sure he'd prepared her adequately, he covered her. His cock slid inside smoothly. No flinch of pain across her features. No tensing of her thighs. Instead she framed his hips with her legs as he surged deep. Her welcoming body felt good, beautifully so. She was hot and wet and female. She was Pen. Old pain knotted up in his head to do battle with physical pleasure. He wanted more from her and he shouldn't, because that way lay madness. This was all he could have, aching and empty, despite how completely he filled her. Tru could permit only their bodies to touch because anything more intimate would wreck him.

He pumped in measured rhythm, focusing on his own responses— the only way to manage this encounter. No thought. No emotion. No memories. His head went Zen. She grew restful beneath him, moving just enough to offer the illusion of participation. An orgasm built gradually in his balls, an inevitable response to his movements, but Tru had disconnected. He pulled out and finished with few slippery jerks of his fist.

Pen lay still. "I thought you said you'd give me sighs and ecstasy."

"Not today."

Sheer release left him feeling better in the physical sense. Months had passed since he'd sought a suitable mate, and he'd only stayed with her for two weeks—a lonely woman whose husband had died. With no possibility of entanglement, she'd been content for him to stay for a while, in her bed, for the satisfaction of mutual needs.

Emotionally, he felt like an animal in a trap. Without another word, he rolled over and went to sleep.

FIFTEEN

Tru had left her once before.

Little more than a child at the time, she had already learned that people leave. Sometimes it was by circumstance, like when her mother died. Sometimes it was by choice. She'd never known her biological father, and Dr. Chris went off on his own, blaming himself for her mother's death.

But Tru.

Pen blinked up at the ceiling, although she couldn't see the canvas roof in the pre-dawn darkness. His departure had taught her that when people left by choice, the hurt cut deep in lasting ways. He *could* be with her. But he'd chosen not to stay.

The deep rasp of his even breathing filled the tent. She turned onto her side, propped on her elbow, and faced his back. *He's not gone yet.* But she had felt distance in his sterile kiss and perfunctory fuck. No, even that word implied more . . . passion. Tru was halfway gone already. Not even the lure of sex was strong enough to keep him on Arturi's island.

Why would he remain? He could roam as unencumbered as ever, seeking out the brief partnerships that seemed to define his adulthood. No sense sticking around for a half-crazy woman with delusions of saving the world. She wasn't that tempting.

She hadn't cried since that terrible day—the day she'd done so much worse than eat raw meat. Maybe that was a good thing. Her shell was tough enough to endure even the worst, all without needing to wipe away tears when there was work to be done. But she wanted to weep right then. For both of them. The orphans who couldn't even find a moment of solace with one another. That life could withhold any chance at happiness seemed beyond cruel.

Fearing she'd wake him but craving the feel of his skin, she edged closer. Her bare belly rested against his hip. Both of her breasts pressed the curve of his upper arm. When relaxed, his muscles revealed so little of his vitality. But she knew differently. She knew his strength, and that extended to the strength of his will. When he wanted to go, he would.

Soon.

Perhaps as soon as daybreak.

She didn't blame him for the way he'd behaved. Perhaps she should've demanded more from their brief encounter. But one of the offshoots of believing herself crazy for years was a deep sort of introspection. She was forever looking for signs of her own insanity. That meant resisting the urge toward self-delusion. From the start, she'd known that Tru would hold back, that the emotion she wanted was not within his power to give.

Pen used the tips of two fingers to brush a smattering of hair from his forehead. She petted down to his temple, to where the hollow beneath his cheekbones formed a deep shadow. Thick lashes fluttered just a little as his eyelids twitched in dream. What did Tru dream about?

All she had was that lonely nightmare. A rope ladder. Foliage all around. And Pen looking up toward a future that meant the end of something beautiful.

She banished that familiar, haunting scene and stared at Tru instead. He had the most beautiful lips. Leaning slowly nearer, she brushed her mouth against his. The thought of Sleeping Beauty and Snow White fluttered through her mind, but what use were fairy tales in a world so hideous? No happy endings. Not for them. And it wasn't as if a man like Tru needed rescue. Her magic, and even the solace she sometimes provided with her body, were intended for those whose minds could be lifted and whose hearts could be lightened.

She believed neither of Tru.

He stirred, his hand lifting to cup the back of her head. Such an automatic gesture. The sort of gesture a man would make toward a longtime partner, one he knew would always be there when he opened his eyes. Arturi had behaved that casually toward Zhara. Pen had seen so few loving couples in the years since the Change, with Jenna and Mason as her only other example. She wanted that trust and companionship with the greediest part of her soul.

But that wasn't to be. Not when she craved Tru's kisses.

Tightening his fingers, he pulled her closer. The brush of his tongue against her lower lip was an enticing promise. Take him deeper and risk more hurt when he left? Or wake him right then?

She didn't want him to rouse. Didn't want to see the recriminations in his eyes when he realized that dawn was only an hour off.

Didn't want him to stop.

Pen closed her eyes and sank into his kiss. Although she had not performed any ritual, she let her gentle, somnolent magic ease forth. Maybe it even affected her, because her heart's worries swept away like clouds sent east by the wind.

She'd never used her magic for selfish reasons. Others did. Never her. Not since the time she'd lost control. And then she had become the Orchid. Only healing. Doing good.

But Pen—the woman, not the saint—was selfish.

He would hate her when he realized. Maybe that was for the best, if she gave him a reason to go.

Easing into that lean, muscled embrace, she pressed deeper against his body. Blunt fingernails edged down to her scalp. He kneaded and clenched. Pen moaned into his mouth. Their tongues met as the kiss stoked a strengthening fire in her gut. Tru angled her head to plunge deeper. The rasp of his chin stubble made her shiver. She arched her head back. The invitation was well received as he sucked wet kisses down her throat. His teeth sank into that taut tendon. The gentlest bite.

She wanted more.

If this was her one chance with Tru, her last chance, she was going to learn every inch of his body. Storing up memories against the loneliness that was sure to come. Soon she would be the Orchid again. And the Orchid didn't yearn for a man.

Pen wrapped one hand around the back of his neck, pulling him in for another meeting of lips and tongues. He was more forceful now. Their teeth clicked once as he rolled half on top of her. She pushed deeper into her magic. If she went too far, she'd come up against his iron will. He'd know that she sprinkled sleepy dust over their last good-bye.

Daring to see the results, she pulled back and met his eyes. No panic there. No urgency to hit the door at a full sprint. No, what she saw tore a hole in her spirit and left it bleeding. Tru gazed at her with such overwhelming intensity, as if his drowsy self had no defenses. None. She'd stripped him back to some hidden core that left her shaking.

She regretted it. Right then. Regretted beguilement when she had no hope of keeping him. Because at that moment she'd made herself just as vulnerable.

But neither could she stop. His erection burned against her hip. Big hands with long, elegant fingers trailed down the center of her chest, then tightened on her breasts. He tugged at her nipple, twisting, teasing that hard peak. Replacing his fingers with his mouth, he suckled and licked. The gentle scrape of his teeth against her flesh shocked each nerve ending. A spill of liquid warmth wet the skin between her legs. She rubbed her thighs together in a restless dance.

"Need you, Tru. Don't stop."

The growl in his throat reminded her of the lion he kept caged in his skin. That primal sound set off firecrackers in her blood. Her arousal jumped from latent to demanding.

Pen pushed against his shoulders. He seemed perplexed at first, but then sank into the rustling cornhusk mattress. She stifled her guilt. Deal with that tomorrow.

The urge to rush rode her like a cruel master. But this was her only chance to be with him, just woman and man. Every other male either worshipped her or wanted her dead. Only Tru saw something else.

She trailed openmouthed kisses down his chest. The sweat had dried on his body, as if he wore the salt of the spraying surf. Licking, tasting that warm skin, she sank lower until the rigid heat of his cock pushed between her breasts. He thrust. Delicious images coalesced in her mind, tempting her to try what she'd never dared. She pushed her breasts together, until that sensitized flesh enveloped him. Tru groaned and thrust again, again.

But too curious to stay, she continued kissing until she reached his swollen head. She explored smooth, thin skin with her tongue and lips. Each wet caress dragged a moan or hiss from Tru—never fully-formed words. Half man, half animal. He bracketed her head with his hands. Pen glanced up, meeting his eyes. Naked hunger waited there.

She took his cock in her mouth. Sucking, relaxing her jaw, she took as much of him as she could. No man had ever dared demand such intimacy. Whereas she'd been able to disconnect on occasion when a man pushed between her thighs, she could find no such distance with Tru's shaft pressing the back of her throat. Didn't want to be distant. This whole encounter was meant to take more of him than she'd ever have with anyone else.

The hands that had held her in place tugged her up and off. Pen only smiled, then wiped her mouth with the back of her wrist. "You taste good."

Tru growled as she climbed astride his lean hips. The shaggy length of his hair fanned over the dark blanket. Just the barest grace of morning light bathed his skin in a rosy glow. People thought she was a goddess. But Tru . . . he was as divine as a man could appear, all sleek features and powerful limbs. Preternaturally beautiful. Clear blue eyes watched her with unblinking intensity, as if he might regard her the same way.

His hands molded along her waist, then smoothed up over her ribs before cupping her breasts. He idly flicked her nipples with his thumbs. Hard and ready, his prick nestled flat between her wet lips. He thrust gently, rubbing, teasing.

"I've never ridden anyone," she confessed. "I've never taken what I need. You make me want to."

She *was* taking. The fact he still languished behind a foggy curtain of sleep should've made her back off. He could wake up and leave— the inevitable. But her throat was tight. Her breath came in quiet, truncated gasps. This wasn't going to end until she knew exactly what she'd been missing.

Just a dream to him. Just a dream to them both. She felt hazy and groggy, high on her arousal and dimmed by the blanket of magic she'd laid over their conscious minds.

Pen lifted her hips, enough for Tru to position his thick, hard head at her opening. She sank down with a long groan, one he matched. At first she set a languid pace. She could feel each ridge of his cock as he pushed in, drew out, pushed in again. But the greediness she'd held back refused to wait any longer. Bracing her hands on his chest, she worked him harder, gaining speed and power.

Tru wrapped his forearms around her lower back. He bowed her body down over his until their chests pressed flush. His breath heated her neck.

The shaking tremor sprang from deep in her belly. Rich and full, her climax built until she became mindless for it, striving, taking Tru for all he'd give.

He clamped his hand over her mouth when she screamed.

Hard waves swirled her into a thick blackness, dragged under by a pleasure she'd never known. Dimly, she realized when Tru tensed, and she rolled away. His hot release spilled against her thigh. They breathed in tandem. The echoes of their gasps filled the hut.

Pen collapsed against his slack body. She nuzzled his neck as he drew her closer. A sigh of contentment—content on so many levels—eased out of her lungs.

And she knew exactly when her magic slipped.

Tru tensed. The hands idly stroking her back went still. He grabbed her upper arms and shoved her up.

"What the *fuck* did you do to me?"

SIXTEEN

She witched me.

Tru scrambled from the pallet and grabbed for his clothes. The faintest creep of light signaled dawn's slow approach. Outside, torches crackled some distance away. He smelled the animal fat, but the torches weren't enough to brighten the tight darkness in the hut. Better that way.

Pen's silence felt like an admission of guilt. And that stung like hell. He'd trusted her not to encroach. Not to disrespect his boundaries. Not to *take* what he chose not to give.

"Nothing," she said, but it was too late. She seemed to realize it, for she amended, "Not on purpose—"

"I don't care. Give Adrian my best, will you?"

Leaving the boy bothered him more than a little. The kid would feel abandoned . . . but better now than later. At least they had found safe refuge for him. Adrian would make new friends and fit in. Nothing to worry about. Saint Penelope would sort out any problems quick enough.

He packed fast because he was good at it. In the past ten years, since leaving Jenna and Mason's cabin, there had been only one place where he'd lingered for longer than a few weeks. That was the problem with this kind of sex. It came with unwanted emotional crap. He didn't need memories bobbing in his brain like deadwood swept up in a churning river.

"I don't have any regrets," she whispered.

Maybe he wasn't supposed to hear it, so he pretended he didn't. Tru shouldered his pack and pushed out of the tent into the darkness just before sunrise. A few people were already stirring, headed for the galley. He'd bet they ate a lot of seafood here, courtesy of the retrofitted fishing boats. With purpose to his step, he set off toward the dock, taking care not to draw undue attention.

An old guy slept at the bottom of a small boat. He stirred at Tru's approach. "You're later than Arturi said you'd be."

Tru shook his head, sure he'd heard wrong. "What?"

"I expected you last night," the man went on. "You oversleep? I'm Burke, by the way."

Scraggly bits of hair grew around the dome of his head, like a ragged tonsure. Though only a few teeth remained, he showed them off with a cheerful, uninhibited smile.

Between the hour and his mood, Tru really didn't have the patience. He curled his hand into a fist and decided not to play head games. "I just need a ride to the mainland."

The boatman sighed in exasperation. "I *know*. Just get in already, before the tide goes again. It's come and gone already. I was starting to think Arturi might be wrong about you, but you know he never is."

What the—?

Choking the inevitable question that the cagey bastard doubtless hoped to provoke, Tru hopped into the craft. Burke raised the sail and trimmed the lines, doing whatever he needed to ease the boat out to the dark water. Tru's inner lion rumbled with discomfort. Those instincts didn't like the open sea and asked when the hell he'd get back where they belonged.

We've come too far east. We were better off in the plains. Plenty of hunting and grasslands there, but the winters were deadly. Still, he'd worry about that when the time came. Plenty of time until the big chill.

While he adjusted the sails and lines to wind and current, the old man rambled on about the miraculous nature of what Arturi and his fine wife, Zhara, were doing on the island. How proud Burke was to do his part. For a brief moment Tru considered shoving his escort over the side, but since he didn't know how far they were from shore, he took that to be a bad idea. The lion agreed, so he gritted his teeth and sat quietly.

Hoping to aim the man's conversation in a new direction, he asked, "How can they be married? I haven't seen a priest in years."

"They said their vows in the new church, boy."

"The what?"

"Didn't you meet Preacher?"

Tru badly wanted to tip his head back and shut his eyes, but that would only unsettle the lion, unable to see anything, feeling only the slosh of the waves. Bad idea to provoke a big cat. So he stared at the old man. "I wasn't in camp long."

An evasion, sure. At that he was world-class.

"I guess. You can't miss him. Big son of a gun with wild red hair and beard halfway down his chest."

"Sounds like a charmer."

The old man laughed as if Tru hadn't spoken in an arid tone. "Not sure I'd describe him that way myself, but he's got a big heart. Arturi draws that sort, like your lady friend."

Tru's nerves tightened, but he ignored the reference to Pen. "So what's this about a new church?"

That should be a safe subject. Keep Burke from gushing such praise over Arturi. For a man like him to end up with a woman like Zhara, he had to be the fastest-talking motherfucker in the world. On those merits alone, he couldn't be trusted.

And you left Pen there, her and Adrian, at his mercy.

The guilt, too, he ignored.

"The Church of the Change?" Burke asked, as if new faiths had sprung up like ragweed.

"Uh-huh." Middle of the water, angry lion in his head—anything more civil was beyond him.

"It sprung up about five years ago, I guess. Services have some old words and some new ones. Mostly it's about helping each other and spreading hope around. It'd do you good to listen one morning."

"I'll bear that in mind."

"There's a mission on the coast here, if you're curious."

"Oh, yeah?" His tone said, *Who fucking cares?*

The old man reached for his hand and shook it. His finger palsied against Tru's palm. Then he pointed. "Sure. Eight kilometers from here as the crow flies."

Finally they drew close enough to shore that the ferryman stopped rowing. "You'll swim from here. I won't risk beaching her."

With muttered thanks, Tru hopped over the side, hoping the frigid water wasn't too deep. He could swim but didn't care to pit himself against the ocean. Fortunately, he found his footing and slogged to shore. His pack would need airing, provided he could find someplace to hang his things. At least the weather was warm enough.

He trudged out of the water onto the damp, sandy beach, a desolate stretch of ocean. Driftwood made monstrous shapes in the dawn darkness, but they didn't unnerve him. He'd been alone for almost half his life.

Briefly, he considered shifting, but it wasn't wise to do so this far from good game hunting. He needed to push inland before risking that, where he was more likely to find prey other than seabirds. Animals in flight really pissed off the lion—and there was nothing quite so pathetic as a lion roaring on a beach because his dinner squawked twenty meters overhead. So he flung his pack over one shoulder and set off.

Four days later, he'd changed twice. Slept a lot. Eaten plenty. Run a lot of hours with his pack in his teeth, which was faintly absurd. The

Change had culled the hell out of the country. Now the wide-open spaces were just that—a brave new frontier for anybody crazy enough to go exploring.

During his travels, he'd occasionally wondered what the rest of the world was like. How long before someone perfected a spell to talk to people in the Far East, to see about the damage there? Sometimes the Change was incredible because everything was brand-new. The only way to learn came through trial and error. Since Tru had always preferred reading poetry to educational texts in school, he didn't mind.

Living with the errors, however . . . That took a different sort of determination.

Nightfall found him in human skin, which was unlike him. Until he came upon the mission, he hadn't known why he was walking on two legs. He hadn't consciously made the decision, but he admitted to curiosity.

Let's call it that, anyway.

At one time the mission had been a church, the kind that serviced a whole county. It had half fallen down, shored up with primitive construction. A schizophrenic structure—part old world, part new. Salvaged parts were strewn across the yard. The place teemed with activity. He drew up short, watching young women bustle around. From the smell, he guessed they were making soap.

"Are you here for shelter or to help, son?" A motherly woman hobbled toward him with a welcoming smile.

Iron-gray hair wrapped around her head in an impressive coronet of braids, and her face showed more evidence of smiles than frowns. She wore the same homespun he did, perhaps courtesy of the island camp. He supposed that made her take him for one of Arturi's followers.

Tru had no explanation for his reply. It just came out—as crazy as four days in the wild that had offered no peace, only a discontented buzzing and memories of Penelope Sheehan.

"To help."

"That's excellent. You look like a strong lad."

It had been a long-ass time since anyone talked to him with instant trust and acceptance. He didn't show teeth or let the lion slip. Not even a little. Instead he followed the woman. From what Tru could tell, mostly kids and this lone woman ran the place. No weapons. No sentry. No guards. How could it possibly survive?

"What *is* this place?"

"The Children's Mission, of course."

Yeah, he'd gotten that much from the garrulous old man. What he didn't know was what they did . . . or why. She must have surmised his confusion, for she went on: "We're farmers mostly, allied with Arturi. Close enough for trade."

He supposed that was necessary. "So you send supplies back and forth?"

"And we keep a watch on O'Malley's people." She spat in the dirt as if the name left a bad taste in her mouth. "We have scouts, though they don't look like much. Our girls are good at going unseen."

"You've only women here?"

Dear God. If the general's men ever got wind of this place, they'd raid the hell out of it and burn it to the ground. The young ones would be worth big money. Tru felt sick.

She shook her head. "No, not all, though most of the boys are young yet. I suppose it'd be most accurate to say we're an orphanage, though that doesn't encompass the width and breadth of it."

Boys, too. Shit. Clearly, he was here for a reason. They needed protection. And the idea of so many vulnerable kids made him crazed—tapping into an old, lost part of his heart.

"What would you like me to do? I don't carry weapons, but I'll be able to fight off any trouble for you."

She astonished him by throwing her head back with a merry laugh. "Oh, my, you are a brave soul, aren't you? Skinwalker and bristling wild, but you haven't lost yourself to it yet."

Tru stared at her, puzzled.

"Don't worry about us, boy. I'm a fair hand with a charm. That's how I knew your nature. And this place is hidden."

"But I found it."

"Because Burke told you about us . . . and he set our mark on you." She indicated his palm. "I'm Mary Agnes, by the way."

Though he saw nothing on his skin, he remembered the old man's odd handshake. A huff of breath escaped him. He hated some things about the Changed world—like spells dumped on the unsuspecting. But that thought circled him right back to Pen. He was determined to wall her off like that crazy dude did in the Poe story. Maybe with more successful results.

"So you don't need me to stay, then." He didn't know why he felt so downcast.

She cast a friendly smile over her shoulder. "Need, no. Not per se. But willing hands are always welcome. Come or not, as you will."

SEVENTEEN

Pen joined the morning calisthenics as she had for the previous seven days. Routine was good. Routine meant she was getting stronger, not just in the way her body responded to daily exercise. Zhara drilled the troops with a combination of tai chi, strength training, and yoga. A niggling voice in Pen sounded very much like Tru's usual derision, so she worked all the harder. Anything to get him out of her head.

She could go for whole ten-minute stretches without thinking about him. Without reliving the betrayal in his voice when he had accused her of witchcraft. Without wondering why she hadn't begged him to stay.

Well, that last was easy enough to figure. She didn't make a habit of haggling with the clouds or pleading with a quiet copse of evergreens. Useless.

Adrian, however, was a different matter. He did his exercises like all the other teens, blending with the adults by way of their bodies, if not their maturing minds. But a surly reserve had taken the boy over.

She felt partly responsible.

As morning turned to full day, sweat streaked down her spine and between her breasts. She finished the last sun salutation and followed the others to find refreshments. Adrian slouched along behind her, his posture that of a kid told to take out the trash.

She forced cheer into her voice. "You want to help me today? I'm on fishing-net detail."

"No, thanks. I have lessons. Then two hours in the galley with Jules."

"Which one is he?"

"The condor. His wife's a crow."

"Xialle. That's right."

A wistful look softened his features, making him appear even younger than usual. "Can you imagine? Flying like that?"

But in a well-practiced maneuver, he shut down his wistfulness and trudged away.

Pen wanted to help him, but she didn't have Tru's rapport with the boy. At least Adrian was with other children, cared for and treated with respect. His lessons thrilled her the most. Actual books. Wherever Arturi's people had traveled, all coalescing on that little island, they seemed to value reading material as much as weapons. Every child learned to read and do their sums. Even some history, although that had already changed. Oral traditions took the place of established fact, but Pen could hardly tell the difference. She hadn't been to school since she was nine. Mason and Jenna had given her what formal education she could claim.

All she knew was that Genghis Khan had not been Russian, as Adrian's teacher claimed. Turkish, maybe?

She watched the boy slink off toward the classroom on the north side of the island. Head bowed, his freshly shaved scalp gleamed chocolate brown. He hadn't had a drink of water after his exercises, but nagging him would do no good. She knew from six days of experience.

Not for the first time, she wished Tru had stayed. Yes, for her. She missed him in ways that snuck up on her in the middle of the night.

The way light caught the blue of his eyes and turned them nearly transparent. The soft gravel of his voice, especially those moments when he teased her and his grin surprised them both.

But she also missed the way he had managed Adrian. Almost . . . effortlessly. As if he knew exactly how to reach past the boy's pride and his occasionally sullen shell. Although she liked to assume that was because of Tru's own nature, she knew that did him a disservice. Not everyone took the time. Tru had.

She gulped water, then pressed a palm against her breastbone, as if she could seal the hurt into a corner. Nothing about Tru had ever said he would stay. But that didn't keep her from wanting impossible things.

Idiot. How long had she waited for her mother to come back? In a world of magic, where she used her mind to talk to a young man she'd never met, where she could heal the wounded and sick, where she could teleport in times of trouble—*why* shouldn't her mother return? She'd held to that belief for years. Just waiting for Angela Sheehan. In a way, she wanted it just to prove Mason and Jenna wrong. They could shift. What right did they have to say her fantasy was any less plausible than their abilities?

The moment she'd grown up was the moment she accepted that even in the Changed world, death was permanent. And those girls . . . they would never come back to life.

"Pen?"

She huffed an exhale and turned to face Zhara. "Yes?"

"Arturi would like to talk to us both this afternoon. He has a task."

"A test, you mean. For me."

The woman's smile was slight. "One could say that, yes."

Pen bridged the question that had been bothering her for days. "You . . . you don't trust me, do you? Not like he does."

With a nod, Zhara led the way back through camp. They crossed between the lodging huts, passed the practice yard, where instructors already worked with students in martial arts and magic, and came to a small clearing down by the dock. The dark woman looked out across the ocean. Pen couldn't help but admire her sleek lines. She looked like a warrior goddess, all pride and secrets.

"Arturi has been my husband for three years. But he's known you intimately since childhood."

Pen blushed at the use of the word "intimate." In truth, she'd imagined Arturi—or Finn, as she'd known him then—as her first lover. They had traded secrets for years. She'd only later assumed that her imaginings were the product of an insane adolescent imagination. But knowing a real man had been on the other end of those first impulses lent a peculiar awkwardness to their new relationship.

She trusted Arturi. Being around him, however, was a different story.

"I have," she answered carefully. "But I can't help what came before. And I have no intention of allowing any of it to manifest in real life."

Zhara actually laughed. "Oh, I believe that. You look elsewhere for companionship now."

Pen bristled, wanting to protest Tru's hold on her. But Zhara had eyes, and her sight went deeper than mere senses. If Pen wanted the woman to trust her, she needed to admit the obvious. Or at least not lie about it. She held her tongue, squinting at where the water sparkled with bright orange streaks of sun.

"What I'm concerned with is that Arturi has never been wrong in his estimation of people."

Zhara squatted. From a bag slung over her shoulder she withdrew a set of carved runes. She cleared a flat space in the dirt, then tossed wooden tiles with a simple flick of her wrist. She pointed, circled her palm over the ground, mumbling something indistinct.

The hair on the backs of Pen's forearms stood on end. Zhara could probably articulate which parts of her ritual were essential and which were mnemonic devices. One day she might, if she found the right apprentice. More oral information, yet to be passed down.

"He has yet to misjudge a person's intentions," Zhara said, her voice slightly lower pitched. "Between his knack for reading people and my runes, we have yet to be betrayed. But we are no longer in agreement."

"What do you mean?"

She turned to look up at Pen. Her dark eyes held an equal measure of wariness and determination. "He insists that everyone here is aligned with our work. I say that someone on this island intends to betray him. Betray all of us."

The wind off the ocean was warm, but Pen shivered. She rubbed her hands along her upper arms. "And you think I could be that person."

"You don't say that as a question. No one ever doubted that you were clever." After quickly collecting her runes, Zhara stood. "But the Orchid is the stuff of new legend. Your reputation and your magic mean that no one can separate the woman from the myth. Least of all the man you befriended when he was a lost boy."

Licking her lower lip, imagining the salt she'd licked from Tru's sweat-slicked chest, Pen pushed her shoulders back. "This test, then. It's yours, isn't it? Arturi doesn't think I need it."

Zhara nodded, just the barest dip of her sharp chin. "And if you hurt him, I will have to kill you."

She made it so plain, so basic. Pen admired that honesty. If she were false, Pen would deserve that fate for betraying these people. Her intentions had always been pure, but now she needed them to be selfless, too.

When had that become a problem? Selflessness had always been an essential part of her unwanted reputation as a living goddess.

That was before Tru had revealed her as a woman who wanted more than adoration from afar.

The two did not need to be incompatible. She could be selfless and a woman who'd opened herself to the passion of a man. But only if that man was Tru.

Who wasn't coming back.

She acknowledged Zhara's threat with a direct gaze. "Understood. But there will never be a need. I am here only to help."

The air shimmered between them as they took stock of each other. Then Zhara's smile returned, the broad one that spoke to the generous nature beneath her military bearing. "He always said you were tough."

"You sound surprised that he told the truth."

"Not at all. Only surprised I like you as much as I do."

Pen offered a smile of her own, one much more rueful. "And you fight it, don't you? To try and keep him from succumbing to a blind spot."

"Like I said, no one else claimed you weren't clever. Come. He's expecting us."

But instead of walking back to headquarters, she continued on toward the dock. To Pen's surprise, Arturi sat on a rough-hewn bench. A fishing net stretched over his lap. He used a bone needle to restring the netting, patching holes. Taking his turn with the chores, just as everyone else did.

"Penny," he said, making room on the bench. "Glad you could join us."

Everyone called her Pen but him. She made a conscious effort not to refer to him as Finn, but he seemed reluctant to give up their old connection. Or maybe it was a nudge to ensure that *she* never forgot it.

She shrugged. "It was my turn."

"That it was." He nodded to the others assembled in a small circle. "You remember Jack and Shine. This is Preacher, Reynard, Miranda, and Koss."

Pen nodded to Preacher first, out of respect for his position as one of Arturi's most trusted advisors. The giant man had coppery hair and a beard that stretched down to mid-chest. She'd heard of Preacher, of course, and had even taken in his sermon two afternoons before. But that had been at a span of several hundred meters, with the whole of the island's population between them. Arturi was the brains of the organization, but it seemed Preacher was its spiritual center.

Reynard was a thin, wiry man with a bald head. The way he looked out through hooded eyes reminded her of Mason. A man who had seen too much, yet tried to carry on with life—if only because others expected it of him. A scar the shape of an upside-down horseshoe wrapped from his cheek around to the back of his skull. A brand of some kind? Pen tried not to stare.

"I know what you're thinking," he said with a grin and a thick accent. "'That man is surely Cajun.'"

Although Pen blushed, she joined in the others' laughter. "Would you mind telling me what you can do? All of you, actually, if it wouldn't be too rude."

"I'm a turkey vulture," Reynard said. "But I'm really an all right guy."

"Especially if you need someone with a wicked crossbow," Jack added.

Reynard touched the hilt of the weapon strapped across his back. "What, this old thing?"

Pen's grin widened. She liked him, even his inviting aura, which glowed with a rich earthen brown.

With a shamed blush, the woman named Miranda confessed to being a baboon. Pen couldn't understand the woman's reaction. Powers brought about by the Change were to be respected and feared, not thought a cause for chagrin. She wished she'd spent more time learning people rather than cultivating distance and awe. Tru would've been able to explain such a woman to her—a translator even among allies.

The young man named Koss, no older than twenty and thin as a willow branch, spoke with quiet enthusiasm about his animal self. "I'm a marmot. Sorta like a . . . well, like a big squirrel." He grinned with boyish sweetness that belied his place among Arturi's top people. "But little mammals get out of big trouble."

After the formalities, Pen relaxed. Just a little. She could do this. She could be one of these people without the need for the pretense of the Orchid. No one had mentioned that name, not here. Perhaps with Arturi leading the way, she could learn what it was like just to be Pen—helping him make this world a better place.

And maybe that would ease the deep ache in her heart. The ache Tru's leaving had caused.

"We gather here because there's work to be done," Arturi said, meeting each person's eyes in turn.

Pen hid a shiver as their gazes locked. It was like seeing an imaginary friend and an old flame made real, all in one man whose face remained unfamiliar. Absolutely disconcerting. Yet as always, something about Arturi made her pay attention. His calmness and his control over even the simplest situations screamed magic. But there was none. Just the strange charisma some human beings could wield.

"And," he continued, "because it's best to make plans in plain sight. Even those who trust us implicitly would begin to suspect our motives if we met behind closed doors, allowing access to only a select few." He gestured to their position on the docks. Workers moved here and there, attending to daily business. But any could stop and listen. The circle was that exposed. "We govern by their consent. What right do I have to bar them from listening, from adding their input? In this way, we build trust."

Zhara nodded, her head bent to the work in her lap. Quick fingers knitted at a hole in the fishing net until it was no more. But then she lifted her eyes, skewering Pen with a meaningful look.

I say that someone on this island intends to betray him. Betray all of us.

The woman's warning echoed in Pen's mind with a clear certainty. She'd do everything in her power to expose the traitor. No way had she traveled across the wrecked, blasted country, intent on defeating O'Malley and working toward a better way of life—only to lose to a turncoat.

"So," Arturi said. He waited until all attention had returned to him. The smile he offered Pen was gentle, almost apologetic. "Once again, the time has come for some of you to return to the mainland. Penny, if you want me to make war, you will help me do so by taking the lead."

EIGHTEEN

Tru had been at the Children's Mission for a week and a half. He knew all the children by name, and he kept waiting for his customary sense of entrapment to kick in. But this was different from most settlements. The residents didn't rely on him for anything. Sure, they seemed glad for his help, but it was patient acceptance rather than need. His flight instinct never activated.

He'd spent time in the tannery, making a few necessary items, and a couple of things that doubtless would never see the light of day. Yet there had been no controlling the impulse, and he tucked the finished product in his gear, shaking his head at his own foolishness. He wasn't a man given to romantic impulses.

Not anymore.

Life coalesced into a regular routine. Mary Agnes never raised her voice. Never whipped her charges. At first he'd wondered how one woman could manage the place, but in the Changed world, most kids had experienced trauma that stripped a portion of their innocence. It wasn't unusual to find a twelve-year-old organizing tasks for younger ones, which meant Mary Agnes maintained a capable cadre of assistants.

He'd hammered nails and sweated in the hot sun while trying to figure out why he wasn't already on his way west. The lion wanted to know the same thing. *What are we doing here? This isn't our place.*

After nearly four years, they were still looking.

Mentally, Tru separated his life into sections, like a novel. Part One: *Before the Change*. Part Two: *In Jenna and Mason's Care*. Part Three: *Looking for Home*. Part Four: *Home*.

And Part Five . . . was everything that came after Part Four. That was simple. It would be called *This Sucks*.

Only, the last few weeks hadn't. He knew why he'd bailed. Guilt, plain and simple. Because he didn't deserve to be happy, and he couldn't stick around where he might be. He couldn't let those empty spaces be filled. Pleasure led to peace, and peace meant he ran the risk of forgetting—and in a different way than he did when he went lion. As an animal, the past stayed with him but blurred and distant. Sharp, painful memories belonged only to his human half, of which the lion didn't always approve.

Usually, the big cat corrected.

He smiled a little and wondered if other skinwalkers had such talkative beasts inside their heads.

The smile turned into a quiet chuckle, which drew the eye of the girl working next to him. No surprise. He had been a surly bastard for ten days, and that afternoon he'd behaved no better during the mindless digging. The mission intended to enclose some farm animals once they finished the fence.

And if that's not the saddest thing I ever heard, the lion growled.

I know. You want to hunt. We'll go soon.

You said that a week ago.

With a faint sigh, he turned another shovel of earth. The girl beside him, Clary, was about thirteen, thin as a reed, but tough. Her eyes were watchful, and she never tolerated any nonsense from her younger charges. He'd seen raiders receive less obedience than this half-grown woman.

"Why do you keep looking at me?"

He smirked. "Because you're looking at me."

"You're sighing and making faces, like you're talking to folks in your head."

"Maybe I am."

"Does that mean you're crazy?"

Tru laughed. "Maybe. Probably. But I'm harmless."

"Mary Agnes says that's what all men claim," she said darkly.

"Some men are liars," he answered, more thoughtfully than her statement demanded. "But not all. It's up to you to winnow out the bad seeds."

"You must be all right. Nobody ever stuck around this long to help us without trying something with one of the girls before."

His blood chilled. "What happened?"

"We stabbed 'em." She touched the small knife strapped to her thigh.

Tru approved of her matter-of-fact tone. Mary Agnes didn't let any child out of her sight without self-defense training. He remembered being taught about stranger danger—to run and scream and find a trusted adult. In the Changed world, children were taught to stab anything that tried to do them harm. Not a bad policy.

"What if they have guns?"

Clary snorted. "They don't keep them if they do. And them on the island know better than to send hooligans our way."

Another couple of hours passed in silent, backbreaking work, but as they finished the last hole, a runner arrived. This kid was named Ben, gap-toothed, towheaded, and not more than six. He panted out his message in between gulping breaths:

"There's . . . a test . . . 'bout . . . to start!"

Clary perked up. "I'll be right there."

She grabbed her shovel and took off running. Rather than be left standing, he did the same. The lion growled in his head and showed a mouthful of teeth, but this time the big cat felt as curious as Tru did.

At the mission, Mary Agnes stood with a small team assembled.

He guessed these were the scouts she'd mentioned in passing—all girls, all around Clary's age. The woman couldn't mean to send them to spy on O'Malley's thugs? But he'd been around enough to know that you didn't make friends by passing judgment on people's business, particularly when that business remained unclear. So he stood quietly and listened.

"Arturi is sending a small team," Mary Agnes said. "They're targeting a slave shipment bound for the Big Smoke."

Toronto, he recalled. He didn't remember why it was called that before. With the fires and riots after the Change, it made perfect sense. The girls listened to the briefing with perfect attention, ready to play their role. Whatever that was.

"You'll watch and report back. Intervene only if it looks like our side is going to lose."

Intervene? He wondered what Mary Agnes thought her six girls could do against O'Malley's guards. Still, he didn't speak up. The woman had to know what she was doing or these kids wouldn't have survived.

"Understood," the tallest girl said. Bethany.

Mary Agnes went on: "I don't expect any problems, however. Arturi's newest recruit is reputed to be phenomenal. An inspiration to the western resistance for years."

Tru growled. Pen *would* be involved in this run the girls were meant to observe. That description couldn't apply to anyone else.

"I'd like to go with them," he heard himself say.

Finally, the lion snarled. *A hunt worthy of us and not more digging in the dirt like some mongrel.*

Mary Agnes shook her head. "I'm sorry. There's no way you can be as quiet as my girls. I won't risk them for your curiosity."

"I'll shift. In lion form, with sufficient cover, nobody will spot me unless I mean them to."

"You'll listen to Bethany?"

Though he was amused at the idea of taking orders from a teenage girl, he remembered that there had been adults who treated him like a leader when he wasn't much older. So Tru schooled his expression and nodded. The lead scout studied him as if taking his measure and deciding whether he could be trusted.

"I don't believe he'll endanger the mission," she finally pronounced.

"I won't."

Bethany turned to the other girls. "We leave shortly. Get your things."

"What would those be?" he asked Mary Agnes, once the kids dispersed.

"I forgot you don't know. Our girls use blowguns and poison darts. They once killed twice their number in O'Malley thugs, all without ever being seen." Her tone reflected pure motherly pride.

"Holy shit."

"Language. I don't know if you remember this much history, but in many wars, there was a children's crusade. This is the same."

"You taught them?"

"Of course I did."

"And you don't feel it's better to let them be innocent for as long as they can be?"

She shook her head, eyes fierce. "When they came to me, they were frightened, at the mercy of anybody stronger. Not anymore."

That much was true. Mary Agnes's children were confident and capable, ready to take on a team of O'Malley thugs with an eager glint in their eyes. They would become formidable men and women. So maybe it was best to let even this part of childhood change. Kids had borne more responsibility in other ages, and the human race kept plugging along.

We adapt and we hide and we abide.

"Thank you for letting me go with them. I have . . . a personal stake in this." He had no idea why he'd told her, except that her calm gray eyes invited confidence.

"I could see it in your eyes. You know the Orchid, do you?"

Biblically.

"As children, yes. Met up again recently."

Mary Agnes cocked her head. "Then why aren't you with her? Clearly fate's involved. It's a big world."

Ordinarily, a word like "fate" wound him up in knots, because if he was destined to meet up with Pen, then maybe everything that had happened in Part Four—*Home*—was also inevitable. That didn't set well with him. Not at all. For good or ill, he clung to free will because it meant he wasn't fucked no matter what he did. The choices he made in life made a difference.

"I respectfully disagree."

"You would," she said with a chuckle.

He puffed out a breath and walked away from the conversation before it could turn into an argument. Quickly, he shifted. He'd done it enough that there was no pain involved, though in the beginning it had hurt like being run over by a truck. Now it was smooth and practiced, magic easing the transition. He padded up to Bethany. His human aspect watched while the lion sat down on its haunches and sniffed the air.

Interesting smells. Sweat. Salt. Cooking meat. Sweet grass. Big, fat rabbit. He almost went after it, and received a nudge. Task. Hunting, at least. He waited patiently.

When the other humans assembled, the scouting crew had dressed in green. None of the girls twitched at seeing the lion. Brave females. He liked them all. He decided licking could wait. They all carried slender reeds. Sleepy, the lion lay down while Tru listened.

"A couple of things." Bethany held up a hand. "Like Aggie said, we're backup. We step in only if there's trouble." When the other girls acknowledged this, she went on, "Once they complete the run, we'll take charge of any kids on the truck and bring them back to the mission. The island's already crowded enough."

"Escort duty," a girl named Gretchen muttered. Her nose wrinkled.

The smallest girl of the bunch said shyly, "We were all noobs once. I came off one of those trucks."

Bethany nodded. "They'll be scared. They'll cry. It's our job to get them here so Aggie can fix them."

Simple was good. He understood his part. Watch the prey. He was unhappy he had to let others do the maiming, but he understood why it had to be so. This was to prove them worthy hunters. He was there to protect them, like cubs. Understandable, if very un-lion-like. But humans were odd, not always practical.

Bethany ordered, "Move out!"

NINETEEN

Pen closed her eyes as the spray washed over her face.

The boat wasn't fast, but the wind kicking up from the southeast threatened a hurricane's bluster. Dark, mottled clouds lined the evening horizon as if the sky were bruised. Another week had passed in preparations that had taken on a fearful tinge. A big storm had the potential to wipe out the island. The shelters could only protect so much of the resources they'd hoarded and scrimped.

But that wasn't her job. Arturi had outfitted her strike team with the best weapons in the settlement. She wore her cloak despite the heat, knowing its concealment would be invaluable when night fell. Or when the rains came. Beneath that protective layer of wool, she wore her complement of knives and a hip holster. The gun was refurbished, maybe a Beretta. Names meant less than functionality.

In the boat were troops. Her troops. Seven people. Seven names she'd learned by drilling their faces, voices, mannerisms, fighting styles, and family situations into her head. Reynard would scout as a turkey vulture with Jack as his heavily armed human backup. Miranda, always reluctant to shift to her baboon self, carried weapons as well. Koss, the marmot, never used armaments, and neither did two identical witch sisters. Last but not least was Zhara.

But no amount of preparation made a dent in Pen's nerves. She didn't enjoy leading under the best of circumstances, especially when the point of the operation was to test everyone's loyalty. Knowing whom to trust was as valuable as any sidearm.

And Pen dearly wanted to trust herself. She needed to know that in a moment of crisis, she could still protect her friends. Arturi had said as much. If she wanted him to make war, she had to be ready to do her part—as more than just a symbol.

He knew what she'd done. And he wanted to her to lead anyway.

Time to put that ghost in its grave for good.

"Queue up," she called over her shoulder.

Technically, as the most senior among their number, Zhara should be in charge, but this run, she served merely as a silent observer. If her runes had whispered any hint of events to come, she kept that knowledge close. Jack and Reynard sat side by side, faces turned toward the gathering storm. With his broad features and bulky frame, Jack was the most physically robust. He also carried the largest weapon—some automatic rifle that would've suited Mason years ago.

But the last Pen saw of Mason, he'd been carrying baby Mitchell in one arm and leaning the other against an upturned shovel. Jenna had been the one to wave good-bye. He'd been as big as ever. Only, much like the cabin he'd built into the side of a mountain, he blended with the Changed world. The weapons he and Jenna carried within them were far more powerful and resilient than guns.

Pen only wished she carried a portion of their strength. If they battled doubts, *ever*, they'd never let on.

But then, they had each other. They had perspective and trust, and someone always at their back. She wanted that more than she could stand. And those thoughts led her straight back to Tru.

After navigating the rowboats to shore, Pen and her crew made fast time. She checked each soldier trudging up the sandy beach. Her head count came out right, so it was time to get moving.

"We need to hit the highway by evening," she said, "or we'll never make the rendezvous. If that truck slips our net, those kids wind up in hell."

"Never happen, boss," Reynard said with an easy smile.

His aura glowed with sunny amber opulence. For Reynard, life meant taking every challenge and turning it into a dance. All laughter, at least as much as she'd seen—no matter the gruesome scar that cupped his face.

Pen nodded. "Good. Let's move out."

Before he shifted, Reynard called to the others, "You heard the lady. *Allons-y!*"

She fell into step beside Zhara. Despite the woman's obvious distrust—a distrust Pen didn't fault her for in the least—she was oddly companionable. They walked in silence. First up the beach. Then into the dense semitropical overgrowth that separated the ocean from the north-south highway. Zhara kept a long stride that never seemed to tire.

No one stopped walking. Strong legs on all Arturi's soldiers. Funny how Pen had come to think of them as belonging to her old friend. And she included herself in that number. Was it possible that some people were better at leading in crisis, while others were better at building quiet stores of hope? She liked to think that was possible. Then maybe the burden of command wouldn't seem so heavy.

"How did you meet him?" she asked Zhara. "If you don't mind my asking."

"You don't know? I assumed you knew everything."

Pen blushed. As if she'd peeked in on their wedding night. She wondered then how much of the connection Arturi had actually revealed. Its intimacy, but also its limitations.

"I haven't been in contact with him for years. That's why I thought he wasn't real."

Zhara lifted her chin. "He told me you come and go. That he's seen your fight for years."

"That can't be," Pen said, brushing a heavy clump of stringy moss away from her face. "He doesn't have any magic. I keep looking, but I can't see a single shimmer."

"I know. He's an odd one."

"And you just . . . accept that?"

A shrug lifted the taller woman's shoulders as she walked. "I have to. He's my husband and I love him. When no one else would even look at me, he made me his own. We keep each other safe."

Pen was more puzzled now than she had been when first asking about their relationship. Zhara seemed to take even more on faith than the rest of Arturi's people. It seemed almost . . . cruel. And to the woman he claimed as his helpmeet.

"I was General O'Malley's soothsayer," Zhara said softly. "His personal pet."

Despite the hot, humid dusk, Pen's heart iced over. She had never met the man in person, but she'd glimpsed his face in the minds of his countless victims. One memory she'd gleaned showed him standing on two bodies, his boots between their motionless shoulder blades. He'd looked about sixty years old, with white hair and a chunk missing out of his lower lip; and he radiated . . . absence. If the Changed world permitted something as antiquated as a soul, O'Malley had long ago sold his.

To think of spending any amount of time with the man . . .

Zhara glanced her way. Her dark eyes remained calm despite the way her voice deepened. "I can tell by your face. You know him."

"*Of* him. I've never seen him."

"Distrust will be the end of us. Hence exercises like this. When Arturi led a raid where I'd been held for years, he rescued me. But no one else would have me. They all feared that O'Malley had replaced my will with his. The magic I practice didn't end their suspicions. Voodoo. Witch. It was all the same to them."

"Arturi vouched for you."

"Yes. Always has."

And that's why you don't ask anything of him.

"And since then, we've been building," Zhara said. "No more battles unless we're forced to. I think . . . I think he's been waiting for this.
For you."

A corner of Pen's heart ached for the woman. What sort of man
did they all follow? Although she didn't think of herself as blind, willing to take orders from any old savior for the sake of releasing the
burdens she carried, she felt seduced by Finn. By the lilting voice in
her head she'd carried since childhood. Despite a plain exterior, he
carried a charisma that had her trudging through the bushes in the
dark. On the verge of a hurricane.

If she survived this, she was going to have a nice long chat with
Finn. And she wasn't going to do it while repairing fishing nets.

An odd shiver crawled up her spine.

She stopped.

Tree branches whipped in the wind; clouds obscured the moon
and stars. But Pen noticed magic all around, flickers of silver light. At
such moments, she wondered how everyone else saw the world. Surely
it didn't look like this. Like fireworks.

Reynard circled overhead, calling a warning. Unfortunately, she
didn't speak turkey vulture.

"Koss? What can you tell me?"

"They're coming. Diesel stinks."

"And in the trees?"

"We have company," Koss answered. "Backup, I think."

Ah, so that's what she felt. What she saw. She should've known
that Arturi would never put a plan in place without another to back
it up. Why risk lives because of one disloyal follower? Or one doubt-
ridden leader, for that matter. With a secondary team in place, he
could do it all.

He probably had another reason for sending Zhara along, too.
Pen could only guess.

But that wasn't her job. Much as she wanted to dissect Arturi's methods and learn from them, she couldn't while completing the assignment at hand.

Rain pattered on the leaves long before she felt the water on her upturned face. "All right, fan out. You know your positions. Jack and Miranda up front with me. The rest toward the back with Zhara. A dozen meters between everyone. Be ready to move as soon as the truck stops."

They crept over the road, half of them remaining on one side. Far, far in the distance, Pen saw an approaching light. She blinked, intending to banish the silvery glow if it was magic. She needed her earthy senses in full working order. But no, the light came from an approaching truck.

Two hundred meters to the north was a rest stop of sorts—just a flat place where the trees shaped a semicircle off the highway. Arturi had drawn the map that Pen emblazoned on her brain. The men behind the wheel would be tired. The guards would be hungry and restless, eager to take a piss. They would be in no mood to fight. That lack of vigilance would mean their defeat.

Still, she took nothing for granted. And she would've felt a whole lot better had one of her crew been a sharpshooting skinwalker who hid a lion within his lean muscles.

Tru was probably halfway to the plains by now, roaming as he longed to do. The gleaming edge of want that gnawed at her, day and night, explained why he felt so close. Just pure . . . *want*.

She shook free of that numbing refrain and positioned herself by the side of the pitted asphalt. There she started her ritual. Unable to see the driver's eyes, she took a stab in the dark. Face up to the turbulent sky. Down to her chest. And the words of thanks that fueled her power. The glare of the oncoming headlights penetrated her closed lids. She stretched out to find where a man's mind might be. Waiting. Waiting for the moment to strike.

A shot rang out.

Her concentration shattered, Pen rocked back on the soles of her feet and pushed to a low crouch. Mini bursts of light spouted from a machine gun where the others had crouched to wait. More gunfire followed.

"Halt!" she cried. "Cease fire!"

But the panic triggered the guards' return assault. The huge truck lumbered onward, driving at only a few kilometers per hour. And it wasn't stopping. Headlights shone twin beams of blinding light down the highway. They'd never be able to catch up if it continued northward.

Pen's mind ran ahead six chess moves. "Shoot the tires, engine block, whatever it takes to stop it!"

She sped through her ritual despite the fighting and gunfire. Even the pop of exploding rubber didn't distract her this time. Holding to her calm, she found the driver and replaced his thoughts with her own. It was a more aggressive move than she liked. Confusion was better. Less . . . disgusting. Because in giving the man her impulse to slam on the brakes, she gathered up the residuals of his base needs.

Their minds touched, the slither of a snake through her thoughts. He'd sampled the merchandise that morning, taking turns with another guard. Keeping each other's secret as they molested a pretty brunette.

Swallowing her bile, Pen released him and shoved her anger into his mind.

The truck ground to a halt, not ten meters distant. She shook free and shouted, "Go! Go!" Puddles splashed her shins as she ran.

Her team pounced. They traded fire with the guards positioned atop the trailer, six in all. Pen sped past the cab, knowing what she'd find there. A man with brains the consistency of mashed bananas.

She'd committed murder again. With her mind. *No, no, no—*

But dwelling on it would get her colleagues killed.

"Three minutes till the tail truck drives up," she barked. "Go now. Finish this!"

She met Zhara and Miranda at the rear of the truck. She wasn't supposed to be there, but the early gunfire had muddled their precision. With rain pelting down, they each grabbed corners of the filthy flaps. Miranda leveled her semiautomatic. On a silent count of three, they hauled back the tarp.

But Miranda didn't fire. Her plain features went slack. Pen realized why when she looked inside.

The truck was empty.

And in the distance, far sooner than she'd expected, came another pair of headlights.

TWENTY

"Something's wrong," Bethany whispered.

The lion agreed. There should be young on the ground, with the rest ready to fight. Instead they looked unsettled. Then one female rallied. She gave orders for the others to hide, leaving the first truck abandoned in the middle of the road.

Good plan. Like leaving a carcass for curious animals to examine. Exactly what these humans did.

Through the downpour, his ears pricked up at the sound of cursing as doors slammed. Men with guns crept around, but maybe they believed the threat was over—that the enemy had hit and run. Weapons hung from their hands as they performed a halfhearted search.

One of them said, "O'Malley will have our asses if we lose this truck. Smith, you take over the driving."

"At least it worked," Smith replied. "They went for the decoy instead of the—"

But before he could finish the sentence, he hit the ground on a flash of silver magic. His Tru half recognized that color as Pen's distinct shimmer. Only the magic was stronger, more violent. While the other guards stared into the sheets of rain, two shots rang out. Pen's team broke from cover to finish the job. The lion's muscles bunched, ready to protect her.

He could see, however, by her competent performance that she didn't need a bodyguard. The woman fought with both weapons and magic. Who could stand against her? The big cat rumbled in his throat, mane fluffed with pride.

The fight took no time at all. Bethany signaled for her team to emerge from the bushes, while Pen gave orders about siphoning gas. There was no use for such huge trucks on the island, and no way to get them there. The Children's Mission didn't need them either. Instead they would sit as a warning to O'Malley until they fell to pieces in the road.

"Change now," Bethany ordered, placing his clothes on his back.

As one, the girls turned to give him the illusion of privacy. The lion grumbled as it went, disappointed that it hadn't chased, clawed, or mauled anything.

Tru scrambled into his clothes as the girls pushed forward. Slaves clambered from the back of the second truck. Most were thin and weak, and over half of them were children. The tall woman from the island, Zhara, moved among the adults offering reassurance. She explained about the camp and offered invitations to join up.

"You can come with us now," she said. "Or you can make your own way. From this day on, you're free."

Most recognized that they had no hope of staying that way without help and a safe place to recover, so they went with her. Bethany took the same role with the kids. A few stayed with parents who had been in the truck, but the majority clustered around the six girls. Many were crying but quietly, as if they'd learned that noisy tears didn't earn comfort. Only punishment.

Pen had yet to notice him. She was talking to a bald man who used his hands as much as his mouth when he spoke. But as if she sensed Tru's presence, she turned. Rain sluiced down her face, her skin luminous. Not moonlight—not on such a night. She always looked that way, even at high noon. She shone with magic and the pure enthusiasm of a successful operation.

Before he knew he meant to move, Tru wove through the press of bodies. *So many prisoners.* His anger at General O'Malley swelled to intolerable proportions. Now that he'd seen the thin, grimy faces of the children wedged like sardines in the back of a truck, he *had* to fight. Even if he hadn't felt this incomprehensible pull toward Pen, he couldn't walk away. He had two compelling reasons to stay.

As he strode toward the witch, Penelope Sheehan, he felt no fear. At some point during the long weeks of brooding and digging post-holes, he'd said goodbye to the past. He could start again.

We're never going to the plains, the lion thought. But the complaint held no bite. The animal, too, found it revolting that cubs should be treated this way, instead of being taught to hunt and fed fresh meat.

Pen met him halfway. "I thought you'd be long gone by now."

"I had something to do."

"What's that?" Her deep blue eyes were wary.

Without asking permission, he kissed her. This wasn't the time for words. He'd find his poetry later.

"Cut the lights," the bald man said.

The road went dark and the engines died as Pen's crew followed her orders, stealing gas and stripping valuable parts.

Bethany stepped lightly to Tru's side, her eyes inquiring. "Are you going back to the mission with us?"

"Do you need me to?"

"We've only done this a hundred times, Tru. It's best we get these little ones home, though, before they really start wailing."

"They always do," Gretchen muttered. "Once they realize we won't beat them for it."

He arched a brow. "You girls have been . . . enlightening."

The scouts couldn't retreat as silently as they'd arrived, not with so many charges in tow. But it was amazing how quickly the rain swallowed them. Before long, only he and Pen remained amid a swirl of activity. He couldn't make out her expression, whether she was happy to see him or just surprised.

"Would you like me to come back?" he asked. "No deals. Just yes or no."

"Yes." Her answer came with flattering quickness. But maybe she only craved his company because he saw her as a real person. Because he challenged her and made her think, instead of bowing at her feet.

Well, if that was all she needed from him or all she wanted, he'd deal with it. With or without Pen, this was a worthy fight. And sure, it was laughable to cast himself in the role of hero, but if he could keep a few more kids from the backs of trucks like these, then it was worth stepping up.

"Orders?" The bald man came up to Pen once the work concluded.

"Reynard, yes," she said, giving him her attention. "Nice work. But who fired first?"

"Jack. His machine gun jammed and went off once he got it unstuck."

"But we recovered. Good." She let out a sigh that Tru heard as relief. "Now we'll return to the island with our new charges."

Zhara came to stand beside Tru. "What about him?"

"*He* can speak for himself," Tru said.

Dark eyes assessed him and found him wanting. "I'm sure."

Pen slicked wet hair off her forehead and tugged her cloak into place. The glow of her confidence was . . . intoxicating. "He'll be joining us."

"After he left you?" Zhara shook her head in disapproval.

"I was helping at the mission." That wasn't the reason Tru had gone, but Zhara didn't need to know that.

"Oh?"

Tru presented callused hands. "I've been digging for two weeks."

Hearing that softened Zhara's expression. "That was kind. I may have misjudged both of you."

Inwardly, he bristled. Had the woman been giving Pen a hard time? He opened his mouth to tear her a new asshole, but Pen put her hand on his arm. The pleasure of her touch ran through him until tense muscles eased. The lion wanted to rub his face all over her legs, but Tru decided it wouldn't be appropriate. He restrained the urge. Just.

"Let's move out," Pen said.

The others followed her off the road and quite a long distance to the beach. It was almost sunrise when Tru glimpsed two sailboats rocking out on the rain-chopped waves. *We're in for a hell of a storm.* He shaded his eyes, trying to judge whether the crafts would hold all of them.

"I think we can manage." Zhara was studying the boats, too. "But it will take a long time if we row everyone out. Can all of you swim?"

The prisoners were tired and starved, but they all nodded. They were willing to work for their own liberty; Tru couldn't object to that. He eyed the thunderclouds and sheets of rain that dimmed the dawn. Although the gales had subsided, a turbulent sea could be disastrous. Yet they couldn't stand on the beach all day, and the Children's Mission was hours in the other direction.

Pen did a head count. "Sound off by ones and twos. Then divide up. The rowboats each have enough room for the six smallest and weakest. Decide among yourselves." Once the group had split up, she pointed to the bald man. "Reynard will captain the first boat, with Miranda as his second. Make sure you have everyone when you climb aboard, and then signal me. We'll come after you."

Zhara tossed her an inquiring look.

"It seems best not to have all the bodies floundering in the water at once," Pen said. "If somebody runs into trouble, it will be harder to spot."

"Good thinking."

"Jack will captain the second boat with Zhara."

The first group swam out without mishap and prepared their craft for the journey. Tru didn't relish the ocean, but he'd do what he could to keep these people safe. One of the freed captives was a young woman with a kid around six or seven. Perhaps some pervert would have bought the pair for unspeakable purposes. He clenched his fists and tried not to think about all the kids they hadn't saved. Yet.

No way she could make the swim while carrying her son. And the rowboats had already departed.

"I'll take him," he said quietly. "He can ride on my back."

"Mama?"

"I'll be right there with you," she said, touching her son's cheek with heartbreaking tenderness.

Pen touched his arm. "Are you a strong enough swimmer to do this?"

"I wouldn't have volunteered if I wasn't."

Tru knelt so the boy could piggyback, then waded into the water. With a child in his care, he couldn't manage long, quick strokes. Instead he dog-paddled, riding the waves whenever possible. Neither fast nor elegant, he cut the distance to his assigned ship as best he could. The others quickly outpaced him. He just wanted to get the boy back to his mother in one piece, without saddling the kid with a crippling fear of the water.

By the time Tru arrived, the others had already climbed a rope ladder to the deck. Except Pen. She treaded water beside the boat. Her presence warmed him. Maybe she wasn't even waiting for Tru. Her care might be for the boy, or as simple as "no man left behind."

"You made it!" the boy's mother called.

Excited, the kid let go of Tru's neck and kneed into his back, pushing upright. Not a smart move.

A wave smashed Tru at just the wrong time, slamming him into the hull. His head went sick and spotty. He managed to shove the boy onto the rope ladder before being dragged under. The current spun him, and then he was under the fucking boat, so dizzy he couldn't remember which way led to light and air. Salt water pushed into his nose and throat, burning, choking.

Someone grabbed him by the arm. He had sense enough not to fight. Pen pulled him to the surface, where he spat and tried to clear his head. Her skin shone silver amid dark waves. When he rubbed a hand across his face, his fingers were slicked red with blood. Not quite a broken nose, but it hurt like hell.

"Let's get on board" was all she said.

But her eyes said a hundred other things—relief, determination, and even more he didn't dare assume—and he said it all back.

TWENTY-ONE

Sky blended with ocean. Pen scrabbled at the boat tossed on the waves. Rough streaks of distant lightning illuminated the panicked faces of its passengers, but only for brief seconds. The bright imprint lingered on her retinas even when the dark returned.

The ladder was slippery despite the rough rope. She tugged her weight out of the water, dragging hard against the pull of the sea. Her cloak hung around her neck like an anchor. Another jagged strike lit the sky in a flash of white. Looking up, she estimated another two meters of rope left to climb. Tru needed her to move. He was treading water just to her left, probably in need of medical attention.

A face hovered over the side of the boat. The shadows and sleeting rain obscured the man's features. But the glint of pale metal was unmistakable. She couldn't discern whether he held a knife or gun, only a quick warning of malice.

I'm going to die.

The living world slipped away with a quickflash bang. And then she was back in the water. She didn't hit with a splash—simply wound up there.

Teleported. I could be anywhere. How far . . . ?

Fabric tangled over her head. She whipped off her cloak and lost it to the current. Fighting for calm, she concentrated on the glimmers of magic. On one boat was Zhara's, a pale green. On the other she found Reynard's light brown cast, like very dry soil.

As long as she could see them, she could find the surface again.

But she was too distant now. Too far to swim for it. The shore was her only answer.

Where was Tru? She searched for that familiar ripened wheat aura—the same color as his lion's fur.

She kicked hard. Then harder still. Fatigue set into her muscles in the form of a seizing cramp. Her legs shuddered, losing coordination. Air turned toxic in her lungs. She burned from the inside out.

With all her strength, she sent out a mental shout. Hopefully she could reach Zhara and Reynard.

Go now, get to safety!

She broke the surface. A huge gulp of air righted her dizzy brain. She bellowed Tru's name before sinking back down. The urge to open her mouth and inhale was nearly overpowering. Salt water filled her mouth.

Conscious thought fizzled. *I teleported into the ocean. Not my smartest move.*

Hands grabbed beneath her arms. The unmistakable comfort of Tru's aura enveloped her in a golden glow that held the darkness at bay.

He bobbed into view.

"The boats are leaving!" The downpour almost consumed his words.

With no time to explain, Pen threw an exaggerated gesture toward shore. "Swim!"

Never had the urge to give up dogged her harder. Years had passed since she'd pushed her body to such a limit. Each pull of arm over arm seemed to do nothing. The shore loomed just out of reach between the waves.

But Tru didn't give up, which meant she sure as hell wouldn't.

The unfamiliar feeling that she worked beside an equal competitor egged her on. No one tested her as much as he did. No one pushed her as hard.

The calm she found felt like casting. She couldn't look up or down. No rituals now. She drew power from the strength of each precious breath. Her thighs cramped and her lungs felt pounded by a boxer's fists, all watery, bloody bruises.

Something brushed her foot. Another stroke . . . another touch, just against her toes.

The beach.

She dug deep for one last push. Walking first, then crawling, she hauled her weary body onto the sand. She curled over as her stomach balled like a fist. But she managed to keep from vomiting.

Tru collapsed next to her, his face turned toward the sky spitting fury. "What . . . the fuck . . . happened?"

Pen wanted to touch him, if only to reassure herself that they'd both survived. But cold and fatigue kept her still. She simply hugged the sand and waited for something to give—the storm or her will.

Eventually, as one, they stumbled to their feet. He reached for her hand. That simple gesture flayed her fear, revealing more steel beneath. Always more steel. She didn't break, not when others depended on her.

For the moment she chose to pretend Tru needed her.

The beach was deserted. Lightning cast eerie flashes down its long, unbroken stretch. Tall waves bit at the shore like hungry mouths.

"This way," she said, giving his hand a tug.

Just like when she'd been little. Always knowing where to go to find shelter.

She was hungry. So hungry. A whole evening's worth of spells had left her depleted. Colorful spots that weren't auras hovered in her line of sight.

"Are you sure? Pen, there's nothing here!" The wind stole his words, but his expression revealed doubt.

With what felt like a smirk—although she didn't have the energy for it—she nodded toward a rocky outcropping two hundred meters distant. Trees whipped on every side, but the ledge deflected the brunt of the storm. She knelt before the small opening.

"In we go," she said.

She shimmied through the narrow gap between two boulders. Once inside, she realized that the structure was likely man-made. No way these chunks of granite had always been part of the beach.

Tru stuck his head in, but Pen felt it more than saw. The black was absolute. A hard shiver overtook her as he crawled inside.

"Lost my cloak," she said, teeth chattering. She hunched into a ball. "I've had it for eight years."

For some reason, that made Tru laugh. He collapsed on his back, his shoulder pressing against her hip. "We almost died."

He curved onto his side and wrapped around her. After the first press of chilly cloth, she luxuriated in the deeper heat of his skin. The embrace felt right . . . easy. Arms and hands, legs and torsos—they curled into each other, both shivering from cold and exertion.

And fear.

Pen hadn't been so afraid for her own safety for a long time. And to have Tru beside her was equal parts terrible and wonderful. She wanted him safe. Safe and gone, if need be. But always safe.

"What happened?" he whispered against her temple.

She told the story with as much detail as she could recall since the impression faded with time and sleep.

A growl rumbled out of Tru's chest. "Someone was trying to kill you?"

"I couldn't see, not exactly. But I felt his intent. He wanted me dead." She shuddered, but not from the cold. "I don't know if he'd have done it then. I panicked and 'ported."

His hand on her upper arm went still. "I saw that. You were there—then not."

"And the boats?"

"They just took off, dammit."

"That was my decision. It's okay."

After describing the distress call she'd flung toward Zhara and Reynard, she tucked her forehead against his chest. She felt tiny compared to Tru. His heartbeat matched hers, still half frantic.

"Typical," he said against her temple. "Are you ever selfish?"

"I have you here alone, don't I?"

He ignored her attempt at flirtation. "Arturi put you up to this?"

The scorn in his voice rang stronger than she expected. She harbored her own doubts about her old friend's motives, but Tru's unspoken criticism made her feel defensive. As if she needed to protect Finn, or at least the memory of what he'd been to her.

"Arturi only wanted to prove to me that I could lead. I guess he was right."

As the lightning crashed and the winds raged, she shared the essentials of the last two weeks on the island. Tru reciprocated with the details of his time at an . . . orphanage? She couldn't concentrate.

"But the fact is someone tried to kill you," Tru said. "Arturi went fishing for a traitor. In the process, he loses you and keeps a killer on the island. And no one will know so long as we're stuck here."

God, he smelled good. Even now, drenched in salt water, he was the man she remembered. Two weeks didn't seem long in the scheme of a life. And she'd done her best to make that time productive. Moving on from him and what they'd shared. But the primal draw of his body was too much to ignore.

She burrowed into his arms. Her teeth scraped the skin along his upper chest. He groaned, tensed. For a second she thought he would push her away. Instead he found her buttocks and kneaded deep handfuls.

She was floating. Floating still. Like she was out on the waves.

"Pen?" The sharpness of her name dragged her out of that alluring darkness. "Pen, answer me."

"Here."

"When was the last time you ate?"

A sick fog crept over her thoughts. Nothing made sense.

"Morning," she said. "Before the boat ride to the mainland. I couldn't eat more. Stomach too jumbled."

"And you used your magic all night long." He gave her a little shake. "Pen?"

"Yes," she repeated, the word slurring to a stop. "All evening."

"Stay here." He took his body away. His warmth.

Pen clutched after him in the darkness. "Tru! Where are you going?"

"Hunting."

"The hell you are." She grabbed his hand in the dark, holding it between her breasts. "You answer me the same question. When was the last time *you* ate?"

His silence didn't mean the little cave was quiet. Waves and wind snarled just outside. "Also this morning."

"Best case, you manage to shift and go hunting. But you'll be weak. And you're still bleeding."

Long fingers found her face. He framed her cheeks between his palms. The warmth of his breath touched her just before his lips. He offered a soft kiss. "And what would you have me do, hmm? Let us starve?"

"Let me heal you first." She gripped his shoulders, deep into that lean muscle. He was impossibly solid, as if he could take a brick to the face and still grin. "You can hunt better. Be back here by morning."

He hesitated. "I hate to leave you."

"It's that or we both slip into exhaustion. No food. No way to replenish our bodies."

"You'll freeze to death." A panicky note she'd never heard from Tru edged into his voice.

Tru whipped off his clothes. Whatever he had, he piled on her in wet layers. "I'm going to go get food."

"No, wait!" She wouldn't let go of his hand. "One more kiss."

Touching his way back, Tru found her mouth. She tunneled her fingers into his hair and clutched tightly. He was warm and vital and colored with that gentle golden glow. As always. And she needed him safe. She kindled the magic, but he broke away, glaring.

"Goddammit, Pen!" Lightning lit him from behind. "That's not happening. And if you *ever* use magic on me again without my permission, we're done. You owe me a fucking apology for last time."

"Sorry," she murmured, feeling sleepy. "Nothing to lose now."

If Tru replied as he crawled back out into the storm, Pen didn't hear. She let the blackness have her.

TWENTY-TWO

Tru was furious.

His wounds weren't serious, and he'd hunted under worse conditions. Shifting helped, accelerating the recovery period. But more than that, he was furious with her all over again . . . for what she'd done before he left camp and what she'd just tried to do again. It hinted at a lack of respect for his free will, and that would be a problem. No matter the tugs of attraction, he couldn't be with someone who treated him that way.

Worry gnawed beneath his anger. They could deal with conflict once they were safe. She'd slip into a coma if he took too long, and that made his hands shake. He was the only thing standing between Pen and a slow death. People shouldn't depend on him; it didn't end well.

Not your fault, the lion said.

Maybe not. But something didn't have to be true to seem true.

Humans. The lion radiated disgust. *Let's hunt.*

Outside the cave, he slid smoothly into animal form. Raindrops spattered his fur. He shook, disgruntled, but remembered his mate was denned up, weak with hunger. That explained why he wasn't curled up beside her in the warm cave. He padded out over the sand, up toward the dunes covered in scrub. He sniffed, lifting his head into the wind.

Seawater, rotten vegetation, damp wood. Sand. In the distance, new scents beckoned. They made his mouth water, bright with temptation. He loped off, muscles limber. The lion let out a low rumble of pleasure that he was finally permitted to run, even if he didn't belong on this windswept beach. Like Tru, he'd learned to adapt.

Waterfowl. Rabbit. Squirrel. Not big enough game, and the first were too hard to catch. Deer would be good, but he was too close to the ocean. The lion couldn't range far. His female was starving.

He ran all the way to the distant trees, tracking a red scent, warm and delicious. The meat would be tangy on his tongue. His mouth watered.

The wild boar slept some ways off, tucked beneath the shelter of two intertwining trees. Ordinarily the lion would be wary of the huge creature with powerful tusks. But it lay quiet and unaware. Why would it expect to find a big cat hunting there? In the end, the fight was more like an execution. He crushed the boar's throat with powerful jaws, and ate. No niceties, no time. He towed the rest of the carcass back to Pen. That took a little longer than his kill, and his mouth ached by the time he dropped the boar outside the cave.

Weak and dizzy, Tru shifted, dressed in his damp clothes, and went about gathering firewood. It wasn't easy finding pieces dry enough to catch, but fortunately, the rocks had sheltered a few bits of wood at the base, perhaps blown in by a prior storm. The small pile wouldn't last through the night, but he only needed to cook enough meat to take the raw off. Efficient despite his worry, he used one of Pen's remaining knives to skin a portion of the boar and sliced the meat into strips.

More time trickled by as he struggled with the fire. Eventually he got the wood to catch and went to work. Because Tru had cut it thin for quick cooking, the meat was soon ready. Ducking down, he entered the cave and found Pen pale, far too still. His hands shook as he checked her pulse. Weak. Thready. But present. His head swam as he ate in desperate gulps. It wouldn't help her if he passed out.

Okay, he could do this. Refusing to succumb to panic, he propped her up in the curve of his arm. At that jostling, her eyes flickered half open—just a sliver of indigo. She opened her mouth to speak and he put food in it. They went on like that for countless minutes, until she stirred enough to reach for a slice of meat on her own.

"Feeling better?"

"Mmm." She was still eating.

Tru let her take over, but didn't move off. Not just because they needed to share body heat. He kept his arm around her, and his heart lurched when she snuggled against him. It had been years since a woman did that. Looked to him for more than sex. He waited for the usual panic about his past, but it never came. Though he was still angry, he owed her an explanation; he'd teased and promised paradise and then delivered mediocre sex, at best.

Maybe it was time to share the reason why. She deserved to know.

"There's a reason I act the way I do, Pen."

Her gaze flickered sideways as if to say she was listening, but her expression remained vague and dreamy. That made it easier. He'd never told anyone. How could he? He'd lost everything that day. There had been nobody left to tell.

"You already know I left Jenna and Mason when I was seventeen. I guess you were twelve? Nearly that?" At her nod, he went on, "I traveled for years. And I told you how I first learned to shift."

"It sounded terrifying."

"I thought I was going to die that day," he said quietly. "But then, the days run together, and it doesn't seem to matter. Birthdays, holidays, they're all gone. The only thing left is staying alive."

"I've been there." More meat. Her color improved, but she didn't look one hundred percent yet. Pen might not be snuggled up at his side if she thought about it, or if she was in possession of all her faculties. She might not ever again, after she heard what he had to say.

But for tonight, he could pretend it was her choice. That *he* was her choice.

"After years on my own, I started looking for a place to settle. And I found one."

"Oh?"

"It was a small skinwalker community in what would've been Pennsylvania. Not that pre-Change geography matters." Maybe he couldn't do this after all. Some things never stopped hurting, even after you forgave yourself. Talking felt like ripping open a wound that had almost scabbed over.

"I recall what the old maps looked like," she answered steadily. "North of here, yes?"

"Right. Well, like I said, small place, no more than ten families. I was around twenty, but I felt older. You know how it goes."

Of course she did. People grew up fast in the Changed world, or they didn't make it at all. No such thing as true innocence remained. Children were drilled on constant threats from the time they could understand spoken language: what to do about raiders, O'Malley thugs, and feral skinwalkers that had destroyed the demon dogs.

Pen had stopped eating. Hands folded in her lap, she watched him. Even in profile he sensed the weight of her regard. "Go on?"

Tru wanted to take his arm away, but she might see it as a rejection. So he sat still.

Remembering.

"There were all kinds of animals. Predator, herbivore, winged. Sometimes that diversity made for a challenge, but the leader was good at keeping order. He reminded me a little of Mason, and I guess maybe that's why I stuck around long enough for—" He swallowed. Cleared his throat. Otherwise his voice would've broken, making it impossible to go on with the quiet recitation.

"For Danni to catch my eye." He recalled those first weeks of courtship with a rush of adrenaline. So much. And so quickly. "We fell in love. Married in the skinwalker way. She was a cougar, closest I'd come to finding a proper mate. My lion didn't scare her like it did some others. You should've seen how the ferrets ran from us."

Pen didn't laugh. Her grave expression didn't tell him anything. Not that he could've borne sympathy. The only way to get through this was to ice it over, pretend the beauty and the agony had happened to someone else.

"I was there three years. We had a little girl, Laurel. Danni and I used to pretend to argue over what kind of big cat she'd grow up to be. Sometimes we wondered if she could shift into both cougar and lion. It's the first generation for this stuff, so nobody really knows."

He'd opened the door to so many memories. Too many. Laughter. Wrestling in a bed of clover. It hadn't been an easy life, but it had been . . . *good*. Laurel had his hair and her mother's eyes, brown velvet, like a doe. He missed them both with the fierce ache of permanent loss and unfulfilled potential. That was why he'd worked to keep their memory shut away, where it couldn't cut him as it did in his dreams. His lion form made it bearable, grieving with less ferocity. His animal self had a fatalistic bent about such things. No changing it. The world ran on the principle of tooth and claw. No use dwelling. The lion's cold practicality had saved his sanity.

"What happened, Tru?"

"There were purges," he said, not answering the question directly. "I'm not sure if you heard. News doesn't travel like it used to." Flicker of a haunted smile. "Zealots determined to cleanse our bestial taint. One day while I was out hunting, they found the settlement. 'Cleansed' it. When I got back, the houses were all smoldering, bodies everywhere but burned beyond recognition."

O'Malley had planted the seeds for the first purges, riling zealots up with talk of species purity. First he didn't think filthy skinwalkers ought to breed with humans. Then they ought to be rounded up and put in special camps where they could be watched. And finally, they should be exterminated. With his money and influence, O'Malley swayed a large number of folks to his thinking in the east. These days, it was safer to be a shifter out west, as Tru had learned the hard way.

"Danni and Laurel?"

"Gone."

No words were bleak enough to describe that moment when all the light burned away. Intellectually he knew that if everyone in town had proved no match for the invading force, he would only have perished with his family. But the thought offered no peace. No comfort. His lion and human soul were, for once, in perfect agreement. He had failed to protect his pride.

A few other hunters had also been away from town that day. He wasn't alone or unique in his bereavement, but the handful of men and women who walked away from that devastation couldn't turn to one another for comfort. The hills rang that night with howls and growls.

A few despondent skinwalkers had hunted down those responsible. Killed them in their beds. Some had strayed so far from their humanity as to slaughter families, too. Children. An eye for an eye, tooth for a tooth, Tru hadn't taken part. Danni wouldn't have wanted that. She had been a sweet girl, made of joy, and she'd have hated him if he painted her memory in blood. That alone had stopped him from joining the carnage. Instead, he ran into the wild. He grieved in silence and in his animal skin.

But the loss always remained, whether he ate or slept or fucked. For the past few years, nothing had mattered. Not a single impulse. Not whether he lived or died. Sometimes, he courted death, like when he'd targeted that O'Malley slave truck. Part of him had wondered, even then, whether a bullet in his brain would reunite him with Danni and Laurel.

"That's why I didn't want to touch you, after we reached the camp. From the beginning, I knew it would be different with you. Because we had history. You knew me back when I was a person . . . before I lost everything. And you made me remember, too."

"So that's why—"

"It wasn't good. And I *am* sorry. I didn't want to feel this. I was afraid." Stark words, but brave in their candor. "But . . . that didn't give you the right to do what you did to me, Pen."

"I just wanted to know . . . to see how other women felt for once. I thought you liked it." Her voice caught.

Tru realized she really didn't understand. "It's not about whether I enjoyed it. Sure, it felt great in the moment, but I wasn't ready then. You took what I didn't offer, and that's not all right."

"I'm sorry," she said. "I am. I didn't mean . . . I was just so disappointed—"

"I know. And that was my fault."

"Are you still mad?" she asked.

"Not now. I was, especially when you tried to whammy me a second time. I meant it when I said that can't happen again, or this won't work. You have to respect my decisions."

Her eyes shone with sincerity. "It won't. And I will, I promise."

"And *I* won't leave. No matter how scared I get." Tru couldn't believe he'd even consider doing this again, knowing how it could end.

I can't live through that again. I can't.

Danni and Laurel appeared in his mind's eye. It was a blessing he hadn't been able to identify their bodies because he only remembered them as they'd been in a field of gold, running toward him with laughter echoing to the sky. That moment, he carried tucked against his heart, and the memory had swollen to such size that he couldn't permit any other happiness to displace it. But there was room inside him again, even as his logical side urged him to run like hell, before it was too late.

"It wasn't your fault," she said softly.

As he'd known she would. Saint Penelope, who would solve the world's ills, martyr herself to death and never live. Never burn. Never suffer. In the hills, still smelling the smoke that marked his ruined life, he'd wept without reservation, without shame, for the first and last time. He'd cried until his throat was raw with it, before swearing he never would again.

Nothing remained of that life. For years he'd wandered. He became someone else, because the young man he'd been suffered too much damage to survive.

"Shut up," he told her.

His anger spiked . . . because of all things, he did *not* want absolution from her.

"Tru—"

"Don't you dare counsel me. A cause isn't love, Penelope. Love breaks you wide open."

TWENTY-THREE

Such sharp words should have cut her deeply. But she felt no anger. No loss. Just . . . emptiness.

Pen understood his pain. Only, she didn't feel it. Not the way he wanted her to.

Dawn had brightened the interior of their shelter, so that she could see the clear, transparent blue of his eyes. Nothing so uncontrolled as tears. Not from Tru. The break in his voice was telling enough.

The impulse to offer him succor almost gave her courage enough to make the effort. She could hold him. Comfort him. Help him endure the loss he'd carried for years.

But that was the point. He'd borne it himself. He had endured on his own, without the necessity of her intervention. Strong and resourceful, he was the ultimate survivor. The acerbic, cynical boy she once knew had grown into a man capable of love.

What did that say about her? Nearly ten years as Mason and Jenna's ward, and she had never cared that deeply about any human being.

Mama.

A sore spot in her chest ached around that single word. That thought disrespected her mother's life, as well as her deep, abiding affection for Jenna and Mason. But she'd never loved a man. Never with the passion and joy Tru had shown when describing his wife. His *wife*. That spot in her chest widened and blackened. Was she jealous of the woman he described, or of his happiness?

No, she was simply jealous that he'd felt anything, no matter the pain that followed.

He watched her too closely. No surprises there. People had always watched her, seeking a glimpse of proof she was as magical as the rumors insisted. Or as unhinged.

Both.

She turned away. "Don't look at me that way. Please."

"What? Like I'm pissed?"

"No, like I'm a freak."

"Whatever."

The storm had dwindled to nearly nothing, just a bluster without rain. Outside the shelter, gusts played with what remained of the fire. Tru would never respond to her pity, even if she felt it as deeply as a cut. But maybe she could make him understand. If Pen let him believe her a callous, distant martyr, he would never know her at all. And that hurt, too. Much more than she could admit.

"I killed a man last night," she whispered. The memory left her shaking. She huddled into herself, already missing the warmth Tru had offered with his embrace. So simple. Yet so easily taken for granted.

"You probably killed more than one." He spoke as if he couldn't quite grasp the turn of her thoughts. *Understandable.* "I was there, remember. And I don't think those knives of yours are for show."

"With my mind, Tru. I killed him with magic. I looked into the driver's memories and saw what he'd done to a little girl. And I didn't hesitate. Just turned his brain to pulp with a *thought*."

He shifted slightly, his gaze intensifying. His regard was a prickling heat across every inch of skin. "You can do that?"

"I can."

"I thought you were a healer with a few tricks up your sleeve."

"That too."

Pen dared look at where he sat cross-legged. He'd donned his shirt, but the neck hung open. She wanted to drag her tongue up from his pectoral to his jaw. Simply tasting. She could indulge for hours, learning what made him gasp and curse. To have that impact on a man—not one who needed her pity or her solace, but one who wanted to share the wonder of eager bodies coming together . . .

"Pen?"

He didn't sound angry. Just confused. She took a breath and fought the way her shoulders hunched.

"I can kill, too," she said simply. "That story I told you about being trapped, demon dogs everywhere?"

"Yeah?"

"That's not . . . exactly how it happened."

"You lied to me? Shit, and I thought you'd finally given me something honest."

She flinched. The meat provided energy, but strength would need to come from her will. "I wasn't prepared to tell you that I lost control. I lied when I said the dogs took out the guards. I didn't wait that long, because I didn't trust the guards to protect us. And even if they managed to ward off the attack, they'd only haul us up to O'Malley territory."

Tru tipped his head, as if he could see her secrets if he only looked hard enough. Maybe he could. After all, his pain and his anger were dragging out the truth. "What did you do?"

"Killed them. All of them."

"The dogs?"

"And the guards." Her breath caught. She swallowed it back. "And the five girls with me."

"The same way? With your magic?"

"I . . . lost control. This pain started in my chest and got bigger and bigger until I couldn't find my thoughts anymore. I just kept hearing those dogs. Those fucking *evil* dogs. They killed Mama in the snow and they were right outside, banging against the metal. Screams from the guards. And the girls wouldn't be quiet. They screamed, too. I couldn't see anymore. Just black, even though my eyes were wide open." She shoved at the tears on her cheeks. "I wanted them all to go away. That's what I thought. Just *go away.*"

The echo of that thought cut through years of defenses. She'd almost been able to convince herself of the lies she told Tru. Almost. But the desperation of trying to revive the girls in the van never let her go.

"I tried to heal them," she said. "I don't even remember their names. But they were dead. Just dead. And I'd done that. In my fear, I'd given in to an impulse that shouldn't ever be indulged. Not ever."

He listened in silence, and the raw scrape of her throat kept her grounded. "I've killed with knives—O'Malley's men—or in self-defense," she continued. "But until the raid last night, I hadn't killed with magic since that day. Inside I'm some blind, desperate *evil* thing. How could I ever open up to anyone, knowing what lurks in me, ready to blow?"

Tru sat very still. His anger remained obvious, in the tense tendons along his neck and his fisted hands. She wanted to look away, but seeing the exact moment he shut her out was important. She needed that proof he would stay gone for good this time, not teasing her heart with the hopeful possibility of another return. But his expression remained almost . . . blank.

Then he seemed to make a decision. He scooted across the scant distance between them. And took her back into his arms. "Hold on to me," he whispered.

Pen melted. She gripped his torso, her head tucked low. She didn't cry, not anymore, but the shaking wouldn't ease. Heel to crown, she shook with relief. His deep, hushed words soothed her frayed nerves. She felt protected, even from herself.

He stroked her hair in a lulling rhythm. "You never let up, do you?"

"If I let up for a second, I kill. Indiscriminately. How am I supposed to live with that?"

The shudder that rippled across his strong shoulders took her by surprise. "And you think that makes you, what—special? Or freakish? Pen, I live with that all the time."

She stilled. Her hands pressed against the skin of his back, up under his shirt, but she needed to see his eyes. "Your lion self?"

"Imagine how hard it was to hold him back after those bastards murdered my family."

"It tore you up."

He nodded tightly. "It did."

"And yet you're here with me? Why? I don't understand."

"Don't . . . ?" Tru rubbed her upper arms with agitated strokes. "How can you not get it? Pen, my mom hardly gave a shit if I lived or died. I might not have told them enough, but Mason and Jenna set me right. Without them, I never would've been man enough to fall for Danni. To father a child, for chrissake. But you act like you never even met them, let alone learned what love looks like."

Pen tipped her head up and found his jaw. She licked him there, just as she'd imagined. "Can I tell you something, Tru?"

He stared down at her, eyes wary. "What?"

"I didn't want you to come back."

"I almost didn't. I started to leave a dozen times."

The salt of sea water and sweat tempted her to take another taste. She nuzzled closer. Her nose pressed against the tight beat of his pulse. She kissed him with her mouth open. Licking. Then sucking. A scrape of teeth. Beneath the shirt, his skin gave way to the press of her nails.

Tru groaned her name.

"But you came back," she said. "I saw you and my heart cried out. So now I have something else to live with. It just *is*."

The fingers digging into the flesh of her hips went still. "What is?"

"Wanting you." She sucked at the place where his neck met his shoulder. That taut tendon bunched beneath her nips and bites. "I want you, Tru. And I don't like being out of control. It's dangerous. But you make me want to get lost in something so much bigger."

"Passion isn't the same as violence."

A shift of her legs meant she straddled him. His erection pressed against her belly, hot and hard. "Feels like it. Feels like we could rip each other apart and it wouldn't be enough. Tell me that's not how it is for you."

"Pen—"

"Tell me, and I'll stop."

With a tilt of his wrists, he bent her back and found her throat. The growth of his stubble scratched her skin in a delicious rasp. He sensitized every nerve, drawing her outside of her own mind. He repeated every lick and nibble and bite, as if he'd memorized the way she tried to claim him.

He threaded fingers into her hair and tugged. "And if I tell you that's *exactly* how it feels?"

"Then I'd ask you to make love to me."

"Here? Are you sure?"

"About what, making love?" She pressed her breasts against him, arching slightly. He had to be able to feel the damp heat between her legs. "I said I want you."

The light outside had taken on a soft, golden pink hue. Seabirds cried against the wind. Storm gone. Day begun. Pen locked eyes with Tru and felt the world shift beneath her. She didn't just want his body, although that new impulse was stronger than she would've liked. She wanted him to pry her open and shove some feeling under her skin. Lust. Hurt. Anger. That it didn't matter should've bothered her more, but the greed didn't allow her to be picky.

"What do you have in mind? One night? A dozen?" he asked against her mouth.

"I . . . don't know. This is new for me. And I'm scared, too."

In making the admission, as he had, something deep in her blood eased. Relaxed. Softened in such a way that only anticipation remained. Because Tru was strong. He was a survivor. And if anyone could see her through to the other side of this madness, he could.

But this man would never be hers. She understood that on an even deeper level than before. His heart belonged to another, while hers simply ached to be heard. With a silent oath, she vowed never to impose like that. He'd had the love of his life. He'd lost her. Never would Pen ask him to risk that again. And for her own sake, the one-on-one responsibility for another person's happiness and safety was too great to bear.

They could share this, though. Share a moment of freedom in a world that had stolen so many choices. She ached for that transcendence, no matter how brief.

"Show me how it can be," she whispered. "Tru, help me lose control."

TWENTY-FOUR

She's trying to distract me with sex.

And it was working. Her warm weight, her desperate arms around him—Tru wasn't immune to that from any woman, but with Pen, it carried extraordinary allure. Instinctively he knew she didn't ask men for this. Ever.

Which meant he was special.

He exhaled a soft breath against her mouth to still her nervous words. She gazed at him. Wide-eyed. Fierce. Full of doubts. So *completely* unlike Danni's straightforward joy. For the first time, he could hold another woman without that sharp splinter of regret because she wasn't the right one. Lost was lost, as the lion said, and the heart moved on. He didn't feel guilty about it anymore because Danni would understand. She would have hated how he spent his most recent years, drifting instead of living.

"Stop talking," he whispered, dropping a kiss onto Pen's nose. "That's the first step. And then unhook your brain. It's easy. I barely use mine anymore."

Tru stole another kiss to prevent her from protesting. The silly darling meant to defend him; he just knew it. He deepened their contact with soft strokes of his tongue, lips playing with hers. She would decide how fast to go, how deep, when to press and taste, when to retreat. He let her guide it all, knowing she could command her own seduction better than he. Women led with their minds.

She kissed him with voracious hunger, quivering from head to toe. Without seeming aware of the motion, she bucked against his hard cock. The friction drove him crazy, but this wasn't about him. At least not entirely.

So he did what he'd wanted the first time he really touched her, when he'd massaged her shoulders. Gently, he turned her on his lap. The round curves of her ass nestled against his erection. The heat of her made him groan as he wrapped his arms around her shoulders. With a tilt of her head, she offered access to her neck. Short hair made her throat irresistible, all gorgeous swanlike grace, arched and vulnerable. He swooped to kiss the spot just beneath her ear and trailed his teeth down her nape. Her shudder told him she liked it, so he bit and licked down the smooth skin until she writhed against him, pushing her ass down in his lap.

Not seduction. Pleasure. He just wanted to make her feel good, and she had to know it. No distance either. He was right there with her, aching. He yearned to be inside her, but she needed to think of nothing but her body and her pleasure when the time came.

Still nuzzling at that delicious neck, he cupped her breasts. Through the well-worn fabric of her shirt, he pricked the hard points of her nipples. He teased with slow, deliberate strokes, counterpoint to the teeth on her throat, and then applied more pressure with his palms. Pen arched on a little breathless cry. He stroked up and down her torso in a gentle glide, avoiding her breasts this time, just teasing ribs and hips.

"Oh, please," she whispered.

A touch to her knee. "Here?"

She shook her head and leaned farther into his arms, head on his shoulder. Her chest rose and fell as her knees bent, splayed wide. That deliberate, open-legged pose was the same as a spoken request, bold and luscious. His own hand trembled when he caressed a path over her hip to the tie on her trousers. The strings fell away, loosening the fabric. Just the sound of his breath, hers, and the waves lapping on the shore. The quiet turned him on more, adding another layer of intensity. Tru delved with delicate flourishes. First just forays, a bare caress of heat over her lower belly. She raised her hips. A whimper, deep in her throat.

He was afraid because he wanted her too much. His cock twitched when he touched her hot, slick labia. She jerked—not trying to get away, but to press closer. He brushed her clit, fingers working smoothly inside her. Mental images, straight from her deepest fantasies, bombarded his mind and left him dizzy with desire. Tru complied with those unconscious instructions. Slide, press. He eased one finger inside and hooked it. When Pen gasped and relaxed her thighs, he slipped another finger inside her.

"Yes, *yes*," she moaned.

More pictures. This time he didn't question them. Instead, he lifted her to her knees above him, facing him, and leaned in. Pen tasted of salt and woman, rain sweet, and she screamed when he lashed his tongue against her clit. She clutched his head, her knees wobbling, and he held her in place while he feasted. Slow lick. Gentle glide. Tracing her lips with his tongue. He spread her with his fingertips and claimed her with slow, deep thrusts of his tongue.

Her fingers tangled in his hair, moved his head where she wanted it. Tru let her take what she needed. Bucking, she didn't speak anymore, at least not in words. And when she came, she tasted like heaven.

But he wasn't done with her yet.

While Pen shivered from her orgasm, he positioned her on his lap and freed his cock at last. She felt relaxed and peaceful in his arms, while he was anything but. He didn't touch her with his fingers; she'd be too sensitive. Instead he fitted his cock between her thighs, nudging her sex. The wet heat maddened him.

Need to be inside her. Soon.

Pen offered a dreamy, puzzled look as if wondering what they could accomplish at this angle. Her innocence delighted him. God knew, he hadn't made love to a woman in years; he'd only fucked. And Pen had never made love in her life.

He was about to change all that.

"Ready to go again?" he whispered in her ear.

She shivered, as he knew she would. Sensitive neck. Sensitive ears. She was made for his touch, places he loved to linger. Some men were all about tits, thighs, and ass, which he liked fine, but a beautiful throat drove him wild. It was as if she wore her hair short just to tempt him with glimpses of her nape when she bent to some simple task. That soft, pale flesh was made for his mouth, his teeth.

"Dunno. Convince me."

Tru nipped her earlobe, tugging. Then he lifted her enough to wedge the head of his cock at her core, so she could feel the heat and the pulse. Anticipation gathered between them.

"I'll die if I don't have you." A lick along her neck. Then a push, so that the damp kiss of her body on his levered him even higher.

"That's . . . pretty persuasive." She sounded breathless. Elated.

For this moment, they were just man and woman. Elemental. No other concerns touched them. He risked touching her clit once again. Just a whisper of a caress, but she reacted to it with a moan and a series of tremors.

"Do you want me inside you, love?"

First time he'd used that endearment in years, yet he felt no pain. The wound was scarred but healed. For better or worse, he was a different man—harder in some ways, stronger in others. He wouldn't let Pen down. He'd give her everything he had. No more running.

"Yes."

That was all he needed to hear. Thrusting all the way in, he propped himself back on his arms. She caught on fast. If she leaned forward and he angled away, they found the perfect position. Together. That spot would make her scream like a crazy thing.

"You feel so good." Inadequate words. She was wet silk and starlight, arching over him, away from him.

They wouldn't finish like this, but he wanted her to feel the intense pleasure first. A few strokes and she was gasping. Pen set the pace, her movements jerky and mindless. She grew wetter, the slick sounds of their bodies so dirty and perfect. Her ass worked against his pelvis, muscles tensing and relaxing in concert with the pressure on his aching prick. An orgasm tingled at the base of his spine, building, building.

Hang on. Not yet.

She was almost there. Almost. And so was he.

"Touch yourself," he growled in her ear. "Your breasts, your clit. C'mon, Pen. Feel this. Feel me."

With a little sob, she did as he commanded. Hands on her own breasts, plucking at her nipples, and then lower, fingers furious between her thighs. Her movements quickened as he thrust, and he wrapped his arms around her waist, wanting her so close he could die of it.

It has to be now. Has to be.

Tru spun her just before she came a second time. In the movement, he almost slid out of her, only the tip of his cock lodged inside. Pen clawed his back for interrupting, her face a study in thwarted passion. He pulled her back down ever so slowly.

He bit her lower lip. "That's it. Hurt me a little. I like it. I can take it."

She dug her nails into his back, deeper, deeper, as she worked her pussy on his rigid shaft. Bigger. If anything, the pain made him harder. He swelled inside her because he'd made her this desperate.

"So hot. Wet. Tight. Mmm, Pen. *Pen.*"

Tru lost all ties to logic. Her eyes widened, luminous and blue as midnight. He could live in them, swim in them. Breasts against his chest. He wanted to taste her nipples, suck on them for hours to see if he could get her off. *Yes.* And that cute little divot of a navel. *So pretty. So sexy.* His head whirled with her. Lips parted, pink and rosy. He kissed her to taste her gasps. They belonged to him, just as she did.

Beautiful woman. Mine.

He kissed her as she came, as *he* did, lips and teeth and tongues wild as she tensed in his arms, grinding, grinding, until her motions slowed with weary satiation. His balls tightened. The orgasm crashed over him like an avalanche, endless streams of pleasure that rocked him head to toe, and he fell into the primitive satisfaction of filling her.

Not until afterward did he realize that he hadn't pulled out. Tru didn't mind—though maybe she would. She hadn't promised permanence. Since he'd failed one family, she might not consider him partner material—and with good reason. With determination and effort, he quieted his doubts.

"So," he whispered into her hair. "Was it good for you?"

TWENTY-FIVE

Pen couldn't have answered with words if the future of the human race had been at stake. She mumbled something formless and pressed her forehead against Tru's shoulder. Her bones had turned molten. The skin she'd worn her entire life felt too large, too heavy to carry. The sound of her heartbeat and ragged breathing blended with his soft murmurs.

Whatever she'd been, whoever she'd been—gone now. But the new woman might be strong enough to take her place.

She must have slept. Exhaustion and satisfaction conspired to steal hours. Warm hours spent with Tru, surrounded in the false peace of their little sanctuary. Eyes blinking open, she found only the darkness of gathering dusk. The warmth of her companion was gone.

The sharpest moment of panic receded when she saw Tru sitting just outside the entrance. His hunched shoulders, elbows draped over his knees, took up most of the view. Only slivers of fading light gleamed along the edges of his hair and the lines of his taut jaw. He looked to the east. That simple change of direction lifted a hopeful bubble in her gut. There was nothing to the east but the water and the island. Had Tru been peering westward with that same thoughtful intensity, she would've prepared herself for the worst.

Sitting up, she realized the source of her warmth. She was wrapped not in his arms, as she'd dreamed, but in . . . her cloak. It was filthy and had ripped along the hem, but it had not been lost to the ocean's pull.

Although Pen barely stirred, that slight noise must've been enough to catch Tru's amazing senses. He turned to watch as she crawled numbly out into the open, the cloak around her shoulders.

"Where did you find it?"

His slight smile flipped her heart. "About a kilometer from here. I went for a walk."

"Oh?"

She didn't want to press. Not in a way that would demand assurances. But knowing his intentions might make them easier to bear. Walking on his own, pacing, waiting for the right moment to go . . . she feared that outcome, even though he'd said he wouldn't leave.

"Pen?"

"Hmm?"

"Come sit. Please."

He scooted to the side on a giant hunk of driftwood, making room for her in front of the slight fire. More meat sizzled, the tangy scent dragging a fierce growl from her stomach. She settled beside him. Her inner thighs and stomach muscles ached in ways she'd never known. A little painful. But mostly in a way that made her smile privately.

With their shoulders and hips pressed side by side, they stared into the fire. Pen wondered when, if ever, she'd be able to breathe again. Nothing was so simple when her insides were consumed by this new need, by this unexpected infatuation. She tugged the cloak around herself, then thought better of it. She wrapped one end around Tru's far shoulder. They tucked in together, surrounded by the smells of the sea.

"I spent those two weeks at the Children's Mission, working mostly. I haven't in a long time. Not for anything but survival anyway." His mouth tightened into a firm line. "And even then, I don't know how much I actually wanted to see the next morning."

A lump had formed in Pen's throat. She forced it down. "And now?"

"When I saw those kids in that truck last night, I knew I had to help. That can't continue." He faced her, their lips so close. "But I'd be lying if I said you aren't the rest of my reason for sticking around."

"Why? You fulfilled your promise. I didn't ask anything else."

"Did what we shared this morning feel like an obligation to you?"

"No."

"Good. Because it wasn't."

She pushed snarled hair off her forehead. What she wouldn't give for a bath, or clean water for a quick wash. Their intimacy made her uncomfortably aware of how she must appear to him, when such concerns hadn't bothered her for years. In fact, their world didn't reward looks. It was best to blend in. But for Tru, she wanted to be sexy.

"Then . . . why?"

"Damn, Penelope, it's like we don't even speak the same language."

He stood up, letting in the ocean breeze. Pen stared into the fire and tried to pretend his words hadn't hurt. Always one step off, the woman everyone respected—even feared or revered. But no one ever saw her as an ordinary person; that was the drawback to the legend.

For the best. She wasn't ordinary.

"I can't change who I am," she whispered. "Believe me, I've tried."

"I'm not asking you to change." He paced the stretch of sand on the other side of the fire. A fine spray of grit caught the wind with each step. He was barefoot. Somehow, his naked feet struck her even more forcefully than his bare chest. "How can you be so optimistic about the whole damn world but not about yourself?"

"My magic, you mean."

"Your *neck*, Pen."

She drew her head back as if he'd just shouted. His words struck her that forcefully. "My . . . ?"

"I *adore* your neck. And your eyes. Do you know how long it's been since I thought the word 'indigo'? Maybe when I read it in a poem, years ago. But that's the color you use to stare at me."

Heat shivered up her spine, along the tops of her breasts and across her cheeks. Never. Not ever had she imagined such a treasure. So shocked, she said the first thing that came into her head. Pure instinct.

"Yours are like a clear piece of glass with the sky behind it."

He grinned lazily. "Is that what you think? Well, feel free to continue."

But Pen ducked her face away, embarrassed by the sudden impulse to tell him everything. How the long lines of his sculpted torso made her want to start their lovemaking all over again. How his deep, smooth voice narrated sexy fantasies in her daydreams. How the weight of his leg thrown over hers as they lay nestled together made her feel safe and protected.

Tru served up the meat on a flat stone he'd washed clean. "I see it, you know."

She stopped midmotion, a piece of pork halfway to her mouth. "What?"

"What you think. What you really want me to see." He tapped one temple. "You show me, loud and clear."

"Is that how you knew this morning? How to . . . ?"

He returned to the driftwood, kneeling this time. "How to touch you? Yes." A crooked grin shaped his lush mouth. "I'm good, but not *that* good."

"Last night, out in the water, I found Zhara with my thoughts and told her to go. I wonder if she heard." Pen shrugged. "Maybe I've been sending out signals all along, but never strong enough to know for sure."

"Too many people bowing to you, not enough arguing."

She jerked her knee out from under his palm but couldn't help a laugh. "They don't bow!"

"Queen Penelope."

It was an easy move to drop to both knees, where he pantomimed a subject bowing before royalty. But rather than continue the joke, he tugged her down on the sand with him. She laughed again. The darkness closed over them while Tru settled his body along hers. The fire snapped a gentle song.

"I'm being candid now," he said, placing a kiss on her forehead. "I'm here because I enjoy you. Now you say it back and we can stop." He found her ear, his voice a low purr. "Because I don't want to talk anymore."

Pen shivered. The heat she'd felt that morning rekindled in an instant, his words burrowing straight to her primal core. Greed. Lust. Safety. All of it tied up in Tru and how he made her burn.

"I'm with you because I enjoy being with you."

They made love on the beach as the stars came out. Pen saw them overhead, blazing through a clear evening sky, as Tru entered her again. Then more stars when she closed her eyes. Nothing but feeling. It was easier this time. Easier to turn off her mind and simply bask in his attention. Such a gift, one no man had ever thought to give her.

Damp summer air cooled their skin as they lay together, using her cloak as their bedding. Feeling soft and free of gravity, Pen idly stroked his abs. He radiated so much of his lion strength and grace that she almost expected a fine down beneath her hand, like an echo of his pelt. But his skin was smooth, warm, beautiful.

"You'll make me blush with thoughts like that," he murmured.

"I don't mean to," she said defensively. She hadn't realized she was broadcasting pictures again.

"Keep it up, and I'll insist you say it out loud."

Pen ducked her face against his side, hiding a broad smile. "May I ask you something? About Danni?"

Although his respiration increased and his stomach tensed, he gathered her close. "You can ask, Pen."

She heard the quieter message, that he might not answer. *More than fair.*

"You said you married in the skinwalker way. What did you mean by that?"

"We made a commitment, made promises like we were standing before a holy man. I gave her a necklace I'd found on my travels. She gave me a jade figurine her mother brought back from some trip to China decades earlier." He swallowed. "I couldn't find either in the aftermath of the attack. Looted, I think."

"I'm sorry." She pushed up to her palms and looked down at his stricken face. "I know you think I don't understand love, and that . . . well, I wouldn't argue too much. But I do know grief. And empathy."

"Too well, I think. You feel for the whole damn world."

His gentle teasing didn't hurt so much now. Maybe their time together was easing her back from the rigid defensiveness that kept her so closed and tight. If only that were true.

She found a lopsided smile. "The world doesn't make me feel like you do."

They both stilled. Pen's heart thudded, realizing how vulnerable her words left her. This was Tru. But who was he, exactly? She had become obsessed with a man on the verge of just as many changes.

He shared her grin, which melted another layer of ice. Such a thaw promised pain, but she felt as if she could move and flex and run for the first time in years.

"What shall we to do tomorrow, Queen Penelope? More pleasure? Or back to work?"

"Work, I think." She flicked her gaze eastward, where the moon sparkled white light over the calmed waves. "Someone tried to kill me last night. If I can get closer, I'll know who. Zhara said there was a traitor on the island. I can't help but think the two are one and the same."

"You won't be safe." His voice gained a sharp, intimidating edge. But rather than shrink from it, Pen absorbed that fortifying sound.

"Yes, I will," she said softly. "Because I have a plan."

"Oh? Now that sounds dangerous."

Pen tugged him off the sand and back into the shelter. The quiet was soft and enveloping, with the waves a distant rush. She pulled Tru down to lie upon her cloak, kissing, touching with more assurance. The path from intention to action was becoming easier to navigate.

"What about your plan?" he asked against her throat.

I adore *your neck.* She shivered at the memory, then tipped her chin back to offer more. "Tomorrow, I think. There's nothing to be done till then."

"I'm not going to like it, am I?"

"Nope."

"And why's that?"

"Because it will mean trusting Arturi. Completely."

Tru stiffened. "I don't think I can."

"I know," she said, touching his face. "All I need you to do is watch my back. And keep that lion of yours at the ready."

His nasty, gorgeous grin was barely visible in the dim light, but it covered Pen in exquisite goose bumps. "That I can do."

TWENTY-SIX

Just before daybreak, scouts from the mission found them. Tru wouldn't have heard their approach without feline senses. Mary Agnes had been right. The girls were good. Clearly, they'd been searching for Pen and him. There could be no other reason for their presence. He stepped into sight, frowning when they trained their blowguns on him.

"Don't make us kill you," Bethany said.

"Why would you want to?" He made sure to keep his hands in sight.

"One of the boats never made it back to the island. All aboard are missing, including Zhara."

"Shit."

"Arturi thinks we did it?" Pen strode from the rocky outcropping with a pleat between her brows.

"We were instructed to find survivors if there was a shipwreck. You're the only two we've encountered."

"That doesn't mean we're guilty," Tru snapped. "That storm was terrible. They could've sailed south to find safe harbor."

Bethany shook her head. "Zhara would have predicted such possibilities on her runes."

"Only if she thought to cast for it," Pen said, taking a step toward them.

The girls trained their weapons on her. If one of them spooked, the poison would be quick and lethal. Without thinking, Tru stepped in front of her to shield her with his body.

She flashed him a surprised look. He wanted to smile, despite the mess they were in. Perhaps spending her life protecting other people—and atoning for the lives she'd taken—left her unable to imagine anyone risking his safety on her behalf. But Tru didn't need the protection of the Orchid. Eventually she'd figure out that he needed *her*.

"What are your orders?" he asked Bethany.

"To bring you back to the rendezvous point, where Arturi's guards will take you both in for questioning."

Tru glanced at Pen, brows raised. *Do we go with them?* She cocked her head, thinking. Then she nodded. He hadn't been able to do that with anyone since Danni. With a gentle pang, he remembered how they'd discussed the little one with a tilt of the head. *Laurel wants another sweet. Can she have one?* Brow creased in thought, then a negative head shake. *She's had enough.*

With his start in life—a druggie mom who let him raise himself on TV, junk food, and video games—he shouldn't have survived the Change. That he had sometimes mystified even him. The fact that he'd landed, at fifteen, in a better home than he'd ever known was also inexplicable and astonishing. He'd found a place more than once, and he believed in magic. It was impossible, the way it sparkled all around him. Particularly in Pen. So if lightning could strike a man like him, it could strike again. It had, in fact, despite his reluctance.

Because Pen nodded at the girls, he stood down. From Mason he'd learned that a man could listen to a woman without being weak.

"Very well," he replied. "Escort us. We won't resist."

It should have been absurd when the scouts surrounded them, three in front, three in back, but their movements revealed brisk purpose. This wasn't the first time they had served as Arturi's mainland enforcers. They marched down the beach; he gauged the distance at a couple of kilometers.

Mary Agnes had some means of communication with the island— she'd proven that once before—so he wasn't shocked to find a small boat waiting. The men on board wore green armbands. He'd seen them around the camp, hard-faced military types with more scars than he'd had hot dinners. Of course, if Pen wanted to scramble their brains like eggs, they couldn't do a damn thing to stop her. He wondered if Arturi knew the truth about her powers.

"Report?" the leader asked Bethany.

"We found no trace of anyone else. No signs of wreckage either."

"Is there much trouble with piracy around here?" Pen asked.

It was a good question, but the guard still growled. "Shut up. Speak only when spoken to." He gestured to his men. "Apprehend the prisoners."

Two men leaped from the boat and splashed toward them. Within seconds they twisted Tru's arms behind his back, binding his wrists. They treated Pen likewise, just as roughly, and the lion snarled. Tru didn't realize he was making the sound low in his throat until the leader cuffed him on the side of the head. Not a real blow or he'd be dizzy. More like a bad parent would give to his noisy kid.

"Is that all?" Bethany asked.

The girl no longer looked so sure of her mission. Nor did Gretchen. For all their poise, they were young and Tru had worked beside them. Surely they didn't believe he'd kidnapped Zhara, stolen a boat, and hidden the evidence so completely that nobody could find a trace.

Pen seemed wary now, too. *This isn't how Arturi would do things,* her blue eyes said.

But he wasn't so sure. He didn't have her faith in the little man. If someone stole his woman, Tru would definitely bind and beat some motherfuckers. More surprise from Pen. Had she caught that mental image?

Now wasn't the time to explore why they could share pictures in each other's heads. They had trouble to deal with—and he didn't want to involve the girls.

Once they rowed out of range of the blowguns, they could mutiny. Was she there, seeing the plan he laid out? He couldn't feel her. Couldn't see any of her mental images. But she inclined her head. Warmth swelled within him both at her faith and her willingness to fight.

If Pen believed these weren't Arturi's men, he'd kill them.

Without protest, they climbed in the boat. The craft was small enough that they should be able to crew it by themselves, provided she could find the fucking island. Provided they weren't executed as soon as they landed without guards. A lot of ifs, but he would follow her, Penelope Sheehan, not the Orchid.

Waves and oars swept them from shore. Tru sat quiet while the men rowed. There were four of them, front and back, all armed. The weapons wouldn't help. A couple minutes later, Pen caught his eye. It was time.

She struck. Her mojo distracted the others because one guard screamed, his hands clawing the sides of his head. The men leaned in. Stopped rowing. "What's wrong? What the hell . . . ?"

Precious seconds elapsed while the guards argued about what to do. That delay gave Tru the chance to execute a partial shift. Most skinwalkers didn't possess such fine motor control, but he'd been shifting for a long time, and he'd learned some tricks. His forearms changed. He slashed the ropes with his claws. Partial shifting required less energy, and it was good sense not to go full-lion in a small boat.

The claws, however, kicked ass. He tore out two throats before the bastard realized he was free. Pen killed the screaming man cleanly; she'd prolonged his agony only to keep the others occupied. The last guard flung himself over the side. Tru slashed his hamstring before he hit the water. Blood drew predators, and the idiot's flailing would attract them even faster.

"If he makes it to shore," Pen said calmly, watching his progress, "he'll die of infection."

"Probably."

With a deep breath, Tru let the claws melt away, brought back human skin and fingers. He flexed to relieve the ache, and his stomach growled, but it was no worse than a hard workout. He'd be fine until they found food. When he glanced up, he found Pen watching him.

"Weird?" he asked.

"I haven't seen anyone partially shifted since . . ."

"The Change?"

"Yeah."

Memories flashed of bestial men with half-canine, half-humanoid features. Likely, she remembered that terrible trip through the woods as well as he did. Better, maybe, because she hadn't been running on pure adrenaline. Tru recalled monsters, sure. But when he thought about that day, he only remembered making Mason proud for the first time. Despite his bad attitude, it had meant so much when the big man gave him a rifle and acted like he believed Tru could save somebody.

"I can control it," he said.

"I know you can."

"I don't know how many people enjoy shifting as much as me. I experimented a lot, early on. Wanted to see what I could do, how far I could push it. Did I freak you out?"

"No, I wasn't scared." She paused. "And . . . you weren't either."

He arched a brow. "Why would I be?"

"I told you about how I lost control. I could hurt you." Her expression was grave.

Tru laughed, waving a hand in dismissal. "Don't be dumb. I trust you."

Some of her ideas were ridiculous. If she'd spent half the time he had, playing with her powers instead of worrying about them, she wouldn't worry about going supernova. But this probably wasn't the right moment to offer his opinion on the subject. Pen took things so seriously . . .

Finally she said, "I don't know if you should."

Ignoring that, he took up the oars. "Now which way, cap'n?"

After a moment of contemplation, she pointed. "It's a fair trip without sails. We can take turns."

"A fair trip" turned out to be an understatement. With four men rowing, it might not have seemed so long, but with only Tru and Pen to pull the boat through the waves, the journey felt endless. His arms burned like brands by the time Pen glimpsed the rise of land behind him.

"How'd you find it?" he asked then. "Do you have a perfect memory for cartography or what?"

She shook her head, seeming a little abashed. "It's Arturi. I can feel him, like a warm spot in the back of my brain. He's been there ever since I was a little kid."

"Right. Your friend, Finn."

He still didn't trust the guy, even if she'd known him forever. The little man would be more unpredictable with the loss of his wife. When men loved, they didn't stay rational. He ought to know. Tru resolved to be wary, but he'd follow her lead.

Untold moments later, he hopped onto the dock to moor the boat. The larger craft Reynard had captained bobbed in the harbor, safe and sound. At least that many had returned safely.

No guards waited for them. Nothing seemed out of the ordinary. If Arturi knew his wife had been kidnapped, why wasn't the island covered with patrols?

Foreboding swelled as Tru trudged the stone-lined path toward camp. "Arturi's *here,* right?"

Pen nodded. "He's just up ahead."

Nobody seemed alarmed. No amped-up security measures. Instead, kids took lessons and people did their calisthenics. Workers went about their business, with women at their looms and men gutting the morning catch. A few settlers gazed in awe at the woman beside him. Two people dropped in obeisance as she passed. Had Pen been wearing a skirt or robes, they would've kissed the hem.

"That is *not* right," he whispered, stifling a smile.

"You're telling me."

"I wasn't just talking about that, actually. The whole atmosphere feels off. They should be upset. And preparing for battle."

Worry glazed her deep blue eyes. "I agree."

"Can you tell anything about the little guy's mood?"

"I don't receive from him anymore. We're not in each other's minds the way we were as kids."

He felt pleased as hell to hear it. Tru would never share his woman; he'd claw out somebody's intestines first. Pen cut him an odd look. *Shit, did she see that?* Her narrow look indicated she had. The pattern so far, then, suggested that strong emotions broadcast mental pictures back and forth. *Good to know.*

Are you sure about this? The lion wondered. *We could have* six *females to serve us. Less work.*

Tru stifled a laugh. *That's what* you *think.*

Moments later, they found Arturi in his tent, and he seemed remarkably untroubled. "You were gone longer than I expected. Reynard said the conditions were terrible. But I'm glad to congratulate you on your success!" He glanced behind them, as if he expected more people. "Where are Zhara and the others?"

Fuck me. He doesn't know.

The message from the island to Mary Agnes had come from the traitors, not Arturi. Which meant Pen had the honor of bearing bad news, and Tru knew, historically, what happened to the messenger.

TWENTY-SEVEN

Pen sat down. Heavily. The strength in her legs puffed away like a gust of steam. "You don't . . . ?"

She wanted to ask Arturi a different question. Obviously he didn't know about Zhara, and she had no need for him to confirm in words what shone from his open features. But she dearly wanted to know whether he loved his wife; it was absurd but important.

What's it like, old friend? Is it terrifying? Glorious? Maybe both? She saw both sides of the coin at once. Because if Arturi truly loved his wife, that bond had better be worth the pain Pen was about to inflict.

Tru sat beside her. He seemed weary but alert, his mind like a bright beacon shining inside hers. Just images. Images of detention cells and Arturi's men hauling them out of the tent, never to be seen again. Those freeze-frame fears were more than enough for her to sense his wariness.

"Finn, I have bad news."

She used her nickname on purpose. *Hear me. Trust me.* And with plain, calm words, she described all that had taken place since she left the island. Empty truck. Swim to safety. Assassination attempt. Arrest. She didn't even leave out making love, although she omitted a great many details.

The complete truth.

Anything less would not help Zhara, and it might even lead to those detention cells Tru had imagined.

But each word drained more color from Arturi's face. His freckles became more prominent, like a blotchy sunburn. He raked shaking fingers through his reddish, overlong hair. "She wanted the test. She *insisted*. When I would've trusted you right away."

"I didn't ask for your faith," Pen said quietly. "And her intuition was right."

"Yes, and I should have listened." His heavily accented words were a low mumble. To come so far after the Change and be reduced to such a moment of weakness. It left Pen shivering inside. Nothing could ever be taken for granted. "I should have believed her warnings. Now . . . Christ, Penny. My *wife*."

Tears shimmered in his eyes, giving Pen all the answer she needed. He loved Zhara. Very much. She was no woman he'd chosen out of sympathy or obligation. And he was in agony.

Is love worth it?

She stuffed her selfish question back down into her heart.

Before Pen could offer him counsel, Tru cleared his throat. It sounded more like a truncated growl. "I'm going to ask this because it's important. Will you hear me out?"

The air between them crackled with an energy Pen could nearly see. Other than her foster father, Mason, she had never been closer to another man. To see them square off with such animosity in their postures and on their faces made her want to shrink back—or yell at them for tugging her loyalty.

Arturi nodded. His eyes still glowed with a sheen of grief, but they narrowed in suspicion.

"Could Zhara have been in league with O'Malley's people?" Tru asked.

"*No*."

"Let me finish." Tru's voice remained steady. "Pen said she was a soothsayer for O'Malley, yes?"

Another curt nod from Arturi.

"*And* she insisted on a mainland raid to test Pen's loyalty. Had Pen been killed, the person responsible could've told you any number of lies. Made her out to be the traitor. All those plans you've been making? Crushed, because the Orchid—your symbol of goodness and hope—was dead. Wouldn't that suit O'Malley?"

With slow movements, Arturi stood. He crossed to lean on the edge of his desk. Pen kept her thoughts wide open, looking for any sign of his intention or ideas, but nothing came. Either they had outgrown their connection, or he had learned to keep secrets from her.

"All true," he said quietly. "And yet I would cut my own throat before I believe it."

Tru held his gaze. "Tell me why."

"Tell me why I shouldn't assume, right now, that you sabotaged the missing ship."

"Because you know me, apparently. You sent Burke to the dock, waiting to sail me to shore."

Pen flinched. She cast a quick glance between the two, seeing the truth. No matter how resigned she'd been to Tru's leaving, she didn't like the idea of anyone else knowing her vulnerability. Not even Finn.

"And yet, against type, you returned. What am I to make of that?"

"Then you know why I came back," Tru said tightly. "So don't give me that bullshit. I'm here for Pen, and I nearly drowned swimming a six-year-old out to his mother's arms. Tell me I sold that kid out. Or that I'm planning to put a knife in Pen's back. I *dare* you."

Silence lengthened between them, turning the air in the tent hot and difficult to breathe. Pen found the moment to ask her question after all, although her motives were far less personal now. "Finn, do you love her?"

"Yes." His voice broke on that one word—blurted without hesitation.

"Why did she doubt it?"

"She told you that?"

"Not with so many words," Pen said quietly. "But she seemed almost jealous of our . . . history. Seemed to think you were hiding things from her. I want to believe you. Me, of all people, Finn. But I can't if you lie."

Tru's pride swelled like a bright sun in her mind. She held it back. No time for that sort of emotion to cloud her judgment.

Arturi's shoulders hunched. He looked down at his hands, which were stained with ink and chapped from the chores he completed alongside everyone else. "I thought I was mad," he said. "Completely mad. Even with all the changes we've seen, nothing ever explained how I knew you. So I told her as little as possible. To be frank, I thought she might leave me if she knew the full extent of our connection."

A sense of companionship unlike any she'd known took up too much room in Pen's lungs, making it hard to breathe. That Finn could've shared her ideas of madness. Her fears. Strange, but she'd never even considered the possibility. Why would she? Until a few weeks ago, she'd believed him a figment of her imagination.

But she needed to focus on Zhara. With a frown she asked, "What do you mean, leave? She loves you dearly. That much shines from her."

"Maybe now," Arturi said. "But she was . . . wounded by O'Malley. Deeply. She had a twin sister. But O'Malley wanted to punish Zhara for an inaccurate prediction. The runes failed him, and he needed a scapegoat. He forced her to choose between the slaughter of ten slave children and the death of her own sister."

"Jesus," Tru whispered. "That sick fuck."

"When I helped liberate that camp and saved her life, she was grateful. Even more so when I defended her from those who believed her a spy for O'Malley." The lines around his eyes tightened. "I took her affection as an extension of that gratitude."

Pen arched her neck to stare at the canvas ceiling. The pain of what she was beginning to patch together gathered behind her eyes as a sudden headache. It blocked out even the hazy images from Tru's mind. Arturi and Zhara loved each other. But doubt had kept them from trusting that love. Now they might never have the chance to make it right.

Not fair. Not by half.

She took Tru's hand. He squeezed back.

But Arturi spoke first. "How is it possible that I knew you at all?"

"Funny, isn't it? We still ask for answers, even now."

"I have no magic. Not a speck. All these years, fighting to see the next day. Nothing. Except for you."

Tru had gone quiet and still. But Pen did her best to focus on her friend. "I think it was me. All these years, it was my ability. Sending out images. Reading them in return. Like . . . a conduit? Even if the other person had no magic to speak of."

"But why me?"

"Why not you? Look at what you've accomplished here! Surely that counts for something. Surely . . ."

She blinked. Her eyesight jumped to black, as if a light had been shut off in her brain. All she saw was color. Auras. Tru's radiated beside her with the warm golden glow she had come to associate with safety. Beyond the tent's confines, other magic swirled and blended with human chatter.

"I have to go outside," she whispered.

"I don't know if I can let you do that, Penny." Arturi's words held an apology.

But even as she understood his caution, she could not obey. She stood, knocking her knee against the table.

Tru gripped her hand. "Pen, talk to me."

"I need to go." She swallowed. "But I can't see. Help me."

"Can't see? What's going on?"

She didn't wait for either man, only groped toward the exit flap. Arturi offered one more warning. "Stop now. Please. I don't want to bring in the guards."

"The guards who look identical to the ones who nearly killed us both?" Tru snarled.

"I only have your word for that."

Arturi made a move to prevent her leaving, but Tru met him with a low growl in his throat. Literally caught between them, Pen lost her patience. She tickled inside her own mind and found a tiny dose of magic to match her impatience. Both men let go of her arms.

"Goddammit, Pen," Tru muttered.

"Quiet now. Both of you. And listen."

She straightened her shoulders. Most people who'd heard the rumors believed her to be divine. Pen knew better. But at that moment the whys and hows of her magic no longer mattered.

"Arturi Mäkinen, you are my friend." Pen barely recognized her own voice. She should be panicking, not being able to see a damn thing. Yet no panic came. Only a certainty that made her feel as divine as her reputation. "But if you think a detention cell will keep me confined, you're very much mistaken. And if you hurt this man in any way, we will stand on opposite sides forever. I don't want that to happen."

"Pen?" Tru's voice was a light, no matter the darkness. "Tell me."

"I can't see," she whispered. "Just auras. I need you. Guide me outside."

"If you can't see, you need to sit your ass down. Rest. Get a witch doctor in here. Or hell, heal thyself."

"Tru, he's outside."

"Who?"

"The man who tried to kill me on the boat. His aura. It's bright and murky at the same time. You need to come with me, to see who it is."

Arturi pushed past her, muttering something about guards, although she couldn't tell if he intended them to seize her or the traitor. She grabbed his forearm. "Stealth, Finn. Quiet feet. Quiet words. He'll be desperate if he's found out."

"Who saw you arrive?" he asked.

"Everyone we walked past. If he has friends, he'll know of our presence. He'll know that we've spoken."

Tru put a hand on her waist. She remembered having seen Arturi do the same to Zhara, and she sighed quietly. "I think you have it wrong," he whispered.

"What?"

"Your plan. You don't want me to be one of them, right? Only acquiescing because of your reputation? Because I won't."

The celestial feeling was slipping away. Only Pen remained—a woman blinded by powers she couldn't control. A clawing panic worked up her throat. "Tell me," she managed.

"Better that whoever it is thinks we've been arrested."

Arturi's disbelief was obvious when he asked, "You would agree to be detained?"

"Believe me, I'd rather not." An image popped into Pen's mind, of Tru's lion self raging against the idea of confinement. "But if we walk out there now, all on the same side, then we'll have no cards to play."

"But if the Orchid and her lover are detained, he can continue his plan," Arturi finished.

She shivered at his assessment of her relationship with Tru. In so many ways, in her mind and heart, they were just Pen and Tru. That's all she wanted to be at that moment, but they had so much to do. "You're right. You both are."

"Wouldn't have expected you to say that with a smile on your face," Tru said.

"I can admit when I'm wrong. I rather like it, in fact. Helps me trust the people I'm with."

"Well, here we are," Arturi said. "A matter of trust."

Tru's growling lion sounded crystal clear in her mind. "Seems like."

"Then lead us away in chains." Pen found Tru's hand. He wouldn't let anything happen to her. Although the dark was still just as terrifying, she needed to hold on to this odd, otherworldly sight. Just for a little longer. "But make sure to take us past the temple where Preacher delivers his sermons. That's where the traitor is. Right now. He needs to see us being led away as captives. And we need to see who he is."

TWENTY-EIGHT

The cage had actual bars.

Tru hadn't expected that. In a camp like this one, he'd expected something a lot less horrifying. The cages weren't big enough for a man to stand, so he sat on top of rusted metal that bit into his thighs. A faint scent of musk lingered. Perhaps they'd used the pens for animals.

Pen turned her face blindly, tracking the bastard with the aura that matched the man who'd intended to kill her. Maybe the same one who'd made Zhara disappear, too. That was where things got murky. Without proof, they couldn't guarantee her intuition was correct. Whether Tru believed her or not wasn't the point.

"You there?" she whispered.

She had to know the answer if he showed up on her radar, but he answered anyway. "Crowd's getting big."

Pretty much everyone on the island had come to see the show. They gathered just beyond the cages. Muttering. Judging. Arturi took charge of the proceedings as the settlers asked about how the traitors would be dealt with. He'd shocked the hell out of everyone by announcing Zhara's disappearance, and things had been chaos ever since. The man's charisma calmed them, but then someone pushed to the front of the crowd.

"Arturi."

Tru recognized the voice and strove for a better look.

Jack. Fuck. That guy was captain of the second boat. The same man who had come with Zhara to meet them, and whose gun had fired early during Pen's rescue operation. How had he gotten there? And without the rescued prisoners? When Tru glanced at her, Pen was staring right at Jack.

"That's him," Pen whispered, her eyes still vague. "I'm sure of it."

"What do you mean? He's human."

"No, he has powers. I don't know what kind—maybe teleportation? Something elemental? But his aura keeps getting brighter. I think—"

"Pen, it's not an exact science. Just give it to me."

She licked her bottom lip, which she'd worried to chapped redness. "I think some other entity has been disguising his magic, shielding his memories. But it's leaving him now."

"Infiltrate the island, then let him take the fall? Sounds like O'Malley."

Pen nodded. "Now maybe I can get a sense of what happened to the other boat."

As the crowd muttered its discontent, Arturi turned and lifted his brows. "What is it, Jack?"

"I know you err on the side of peace and forgiveness, but surely even you cannot forgive what these two have done." Jack turned to the crowd with a showy gesture. "They came to you under false pretenses, betrayed your trust, murdered your loyal men, and gave your wife to her greatest enemy."

A low rumble ran through the crowd. Tru's heart clenched. He recognized the signs of rising bloodlust. Since the purge where he'd lost Danni and Laurel, he'd learned when to linger and when to run like hell. This *wasn't* the time to be trapped in a cage. If Arturi handled this wrong, he'd get them both killed.

Arturi turned, his face cold as a glacier. "Oh? And how do you know?"

That quieted the throng for a few seconds as they mulled the question. A sick wave of restless tension snaked through the crowd. Tru noted the men with hands on their weapons, eyes ready for trouble. But he couldn't tell where their allegiance lay.

Jack lifted his brows. "Excuse me?"

"No formal reports exist at this time," Arturi said. "Yet you've made a specific set of allegations. Where did you obtain your information?"

"It's simple deduction." Jack shrugged. "Their ship didn't return, nor did any of the people on it. Zhara is missing, and those two are caged. Why would you do that if they weren't to blame?"

More noise from the mob, whispered speculation, hushed words that sounded like a nest of snakes.

"Is it true?" a latecomer asked. "Has Zhara been taken?"

Arturi never broke eye contact with Jack. "The first two statements are true, undoubtedly. But how did *you* manage to return? Why do you have no knowledge of the others? Or Zhara?"

"*I* have proven my loyalty. The strangers are to blame! We must execute them before that witch brings General O'Malley himself down on our heads."

A cheer rose up from the crowd. Soon enough, they'd gather sufficient enthusiasm for a stoning, a drowning, or a hanging. Jack seemed to have collected a fair number on his side, whether by bribes or persuasion. Arturi proved his position, however, by raising a hand for silence, and the response came immediately. Only the sound of breathing and the rustle of their clothes could be detected over the constant drone of nearby waves.

Arturi didn't back down. "You never answered the question, Jack. How did you come here alone?"

Tru looked toward Pen, who appeared deep in concentration. "Anything? Any proof to get us out of this?"

"The boats separated in the storm, but that's all he's letting me see."

"We're nearly out of time. I don't like this."

"Me either," came another voice.

Tru spun on his knees to find Adrian fiddling with the lock. It wasn't a sophisticated mechanism, just impossible to reach from the inside. Within seconds, the boy freed him and opened the mechanism for Pen. She stumbled out into Tru's arms. Unfortunately, that choice gave Jack an excuse to move against Arturi.

"The prisoners are escaping! Death to any who stand against us!"

A gun went off. A woman screamed. The first man fell. Copper stench filled the air, and children wailed.

Arturi shouted, "No! No fighting!"

But it was too late.

The scene melted into chaos as the mob divided into a small civil war. Few of the combatants carried guns, but plenty used fists and blades and blunt objects. Kids ran underfoot, tugging at pant legs and sobbing. Tru fought the urge to shift because that would only add to the mayhem, but the lion wanted to establish his place at the top of the hierarchy.

Instead keeping low, he asked Pen and Adrian, "You two okay?"

Before they could reply, a man lurched toward him. Tru took him with a fierce roundhouse to the jaw followed by a kick to the knee. The pop said his aim was dead on, and the man moaned as he fell. Tru took up a defensive position, fighting anybody who got too close. His stance warned that he'd beat the living fuck out of anyone who messed with Pen or Adrian.

It was no bluff.

Pen didn't use her magic. Tru guessed that was because she feared a crucial lack of precision, that she'd wind up brain-damaging the wrong people. She needed more faith in her capabilities, but this wasn't the time for a self-esteem lecture. Adrian took a couple of steps as if he wanted to fight, but Tru shook his head.

"They'll come to their senses sooner or later. You don't want to create bad blood for no reason, just because you got swept up."

With a faint sigh, the kid nodded. Good sense. Plus, he was small. He needed a hefty growth spurt and a good couple of kilos before attempting any ass-kicking. Though Tru had been thin around the same age when Mason took him in, he'd been much taller.

Despite the bedlam, Arturi's forces fought with more organization and more confidence. Most of that, Tru had to admit, came directly from the small man who shouted orders with precision and calm. He might not be a fighter himself, but he was a hell of a commander. For the first time, Tru saw what Pen admired in Arturi. This man could lead. He made people want to fight for him, to win for him. No matter what. He was the kind of guy who could make a real difference in the Changed world.

But only if we put down General O'Malley first.

It might be a suicide mission, but Tru believed in the goal. There was no guarantee this crew could turn the world into a better place, but it damn sure wouldn't happen if they didn't try. And trying was the first step.

After Arturi's people restored order, the camp was a mess. Fifteen bodies, with Jack among that number. Twice that many had been wounded.

Arturi shuffled like a walking dead man among the injured, his eyes haunted with sick regret and what Tru could only imagine to be fear for his missing wife. It was impossible to know how many of those who fought for Jack were on his payroll and how many had just gotten caught up in his rhetoric. Or if O'Malley was behind the whole uprising.

Which put Arturi in a hell of a predicament.

Did he trust the survivors, or execute them? If he banished them, they could get a warning to O'Malley that his agent had died. Traitors might even know enough to alert him about plans to raid the fortress. For now, the prisoners who had certainly fought for Jack stood tied in a line. Twelve men, two women, and a young boy.

Tru didn't envy Arturi his decision. *What a fucking mess.*

"Do we have a truth teller anywhere in our midst?" someone asked.

Although Tru had heard of that particular magic, he'd never met anyone who admitted to the talent. A walking lie detector only made people nervous.

But Arturi knew his people—his particular talent, which must've made this uprising especially difficult to endure. His forehead slick with sweat, he looked over sea of faces. "Will you come forth, my friend?"

Shine pushed to the front of the crowd. "Yes, I will," she said softly.

"She's a truth teller?" asked Reynard. Tru was glad to see the scarred Cajun among the faithful, though he wasn't surprised, given how well the man had performed under Pen's direction.

Even with a puffy lip and a black eye, Shine smiled as if she had enjoyed a good dustup. "Enough to let me figure out whether somebody's bluffing me in matters of trade."

Preacher joined them then. "And I'll vouch for the girl's word."

"As will I," said Arturi. Turning, he addressed the crowd. "Do all of you agree to stand by Shine's ruling? Though Jack was right, in that I am a man of peace, I will *learn* how to make war. My enemies will have reason to fear me before the sun sets."

Quiet assent came in reply, a murmured "yes" from each of his people. A few leaned on one another, shaking and in tears. They had considered this place a sanctuary. *But death crosses the sea, the sand, and mountains just the same. There is nowhere it cannot reach.*

One by one, Arturi assessed each suspect. "Are you loyal to me?"

A pause, an answer, and then a nod or a head shake from Shine. She nodded ten times—eight men, one woman, and the boy all passed her judgment. Two men and a woman remained.

"They lied," Shine said decisively. "I don't know if they're loyal to Jack, but they're *not* loyal to you."

Pen clutched Tru's hand, but she didn't speak up. This wasn't the time for the Orchid to intervene. She hadn't founded this camp or led these people. Arturi needed to show strength here or he'd lose his supporters. *A house divided against itself cannot stand.* Oddly, he remembered Abraham Lincoln had said that in some speech he'd studied in school. *Wonder what Honest Abe would make of the Changed world?* Then he realized Arturi might be the Abe Lincoln of their time, which gave him a weird, proud chill to witness the small man make what might turn out to be a historic decision.

The female suspect clung to her partner's hand, tears in her eyes. For their part, the two men seemed stoic and resigned. They didn't speak a word in their own defense. They didn't plead for their lives.

"Are you newly come to the camp?" Arturi asked each in turn.

At first the question puzzled Tru. Surely Arturi knew everyone already, but the theater inherent in the commander's bearing provided the answer. If they were fresh refugees, they might not feel a connection to the leader yet. Arturi wanted no possible room for public doubt when the time came to render judgment.

"No," came the reply, thrice over.

"That's true," Shine said.

"Are you loyal to Jack?" The question had to be asked.

There could be no doubt in the crowd's mind. Arturi did all he could to keep from being perceived as a tyrant. Again, they said no. But even Tru could see the sick fear boiling away beneath their eyes. He didn't know why they bothered. If he knew somebody could tell the difference between truth and falsehood, he'd come clean and die spitting defiance. But not everyone shared his brand of crazy.

Shine shook her head. "They're lying."

Arturi pronounced their fate to a crowd as silent as the grave. "Then hang them all."

TWENTY-NINE

The blindness faded during the trial. Almost as if each of Shine's stark replies held magic of a healing kind, Pen could see a little more and a little more. The first thing she glimpsed with clear, stark precision was the grief on Arturi's face. Jovial and kind, he had been reduced to the role of a judge where the stakes were life or death.

She turned to Tru, blinking a few times to bring his features into focus. When had she ever seen him appear so solemn? But he was a survivor. He would soak this into his soul, blunting the edges until the memories became easier to carry. That was his strength, even more so than the lion he carried beneath his skin.

Arturi, however . . .

"Do you trust me?"

Tru frowned. "Why wouldn't I?"

She touched his cheek. The place around her heart tightened as he leaned into that caress. "I need to go to Arturi. Now. Alone."

"Enough with the Orchid crap."

"Not like that." She glanced to where Arturi oversaw the preparations for the hangings. Preacher, Shine—no one even looked at the leader who was being consumed by his responsibilities. "He needs a friend. Someone who won't judge him."

Tru adjusted where he sat, forearms draped over his knees. The sun was setting, which cast his features in a deep blood orange. Even his irises took on that glow, making him seem even more like a big cat. He released the tension in his jaw on a heavy exhale. "Do what you need to."

She was tired. Exhausted, even. But not like she suffered after using her magic to excess. Her mind had been worn down by the emotion of the previous few weeks. All new. All hard to interpret. But she had nothing on Arturi's pain.

With a kiss to Tru's bare forearm, she stood and made her way across the small central clearing. Smoke hung heavily in the air as the dead were cremated. Smoldering piles of canvas marked where four residential huts had nestled beneath a scrub tree. But most of the island's scars would not show. They would be housed inside disillusioned hearts. Particularly Arturi's.

If he lost hope . . .

The whole community might topple.

In years past, people had opportunities to try and waste and fail. They'd only start again. But who knew how many more chances humanity had left? Pen had traveled the length and breadth of North America, much like Tru, their lives crisscrossing. She'd seen isolated clusters of human beings huddled against the world. A few rare instances had even permitted skinwalkers and practitioners of magic to live among them.

Never once had she seen a place this civilized, this integrated. A place so full of potential.

Her knees shook as she walked to Arturi. A part of her did not want this task. To kill in self-defense, or to kill O'Malley's people as she aided those who'd been taken . . . that seemed easier. Standing by to watch three seemingly ordinary people hang would take another level of strength. For Arturi, and to honor what he'd worked to build, she would do it.

She took his hand.

Arturi seemed to pull himself out of a daze. He looked at her, then down at their joined hands. "Penny."

"We've made it through dark times together. Before."

"We did. Now I feel crazy for a different reason."

Cold shivered under her breastbone. "Oh?"

"This," he said, waving his other hand at the whole scene.

What he indicated encompassed good and bad. The people who held guns on his behalf and the traitors who awaited their fate. Huts decorated with paint on the canvas stood alongside those stained by black smoke. At the mess hall, a duty roster waited. The provisions tent provided a rudimentary commerce system that gave everyone an incentive to work. And babies. Children. Everywhere.

Pen felt a foreboding she couldn't understand. "What about it?"

"What's the use?"

She flinched.

He shook his head sadly. "I mean it, Penny. What use is struggling to build, when destruction is so much easier. I wonder if it's our nature."

Tru had often accused her of being unable to open up. She knew he was right. That impulse to hide her feelings was not easy to overcome. Safer to hide it deep down.

Which is why her anger and frustration came as such a surprise.

"Don't you dare," she whispered, words clipped. "Don't you *dare* give up on this."

"I can't argue now. Please. Stop."

"No, I won't." She jabbed a finger toward the scene before them. "Look at what you've done here."

"I've lost control here."

The dejection in his voice sent a shiver up her back. This was beyond a simple case of regret or loathing in anticipation of the hangings. It was even more than losing Zhara. The combination of events was crushing him. But what would these people be without their leader?

"You've lost no such thing," she said. "Otherwise today's anarchy would've continued. You would've been facing the complete destruction of the island, not a few charred huts. Settlement gone. Little experiment over." She nodded toward the quiet crowd that awaited his direction. "They need you, or there's nothing left here."

He turned stricken eyes away from his followers, leveling his gaze at Pen. Tears shimmered, unshed. "And tell me how I'm supposed to lead them when she's gone?"

"Zhara?"

"Yes," he said tiredly.

Pen blinked. A deep grief tugged at her, but not just for Arturi. She grieved for Tru and the family he'd lost. When a man's reason for living was gone, what purpose did he have? Tru had buried everything, just kept walking. On an instinctual level, she knew that Arturi was not that strong. He could lead hundreds, one day maybe thousands. But he needed a personal connection to make it real.

She had that in common with him. The world had become, to her, a series of distant encounters and deeds done. Tru had shown her another reason for fighting. Maybe Zhara had provided her husband with the same earthly grounding. Everything else became . . . theory. All purpose with no heart.

"We're ready, sir," said one of his men.

The condemned stood on stools beneath the island's largest tree. The willow dripped thousands of limp limbs, its leaves shimmering with countless tiny movements. By contrast, the three prisoners didn't move. They waited with their hands behind their backs and their necks bound by nooses.

Arturi's expression took on a hard gleam. He strode forward and regarded each of the traitors in turn. Pen could only watch, unsure of his state of mind. She glanced back to where Tru sat with Adrian. They looked so mismatched—the tall, wiry man and the round-faced boy who worshiped him. A twinge of affection for both nearly drove her to abandon Arturi. She wanted to go and hold them both close.

But for the future, for a *good* future, she stayed put.

"Do you have any last words?" Arturi asked one of the men. The husband and wife had refused to say anything to Arturi.

The second man sneered. "This settlement will burn, fearless leader. All of it."

"Why do you hate it so?"

"This is no longer a world meant for sharing. It's for taking."

Arturi's head bowed. His shoulders lifted on a heavy exhale. "Taking," he said quietly, perhaps so quietly that only Pen and the condemned heard. "I suppose so. And now I take lives."

He signaled to a nearby guard and turned his back to the willow. Pen met him there, stopped him with a hand to his shoulder. "You need to see this," she said.

"Why? I cannot stand it."

"You're the leader, Finn. If you can't watch the outcome of your own judgments . . ."

Tight lines scored either side of his mouth. He nodded. And when the bodies dropped, he watched the entire time. Until there was only stillness and quiet.

When it was over, she took his hand again. "But this isn't the end. Tell me you realize that."

"I know nothing now." Blasted eyes begged for what she couldn't provide. Answers. Comfort. The promise of a future. "What do I do?"

"Plan with me. Help me. Jack passed as human because someone wanted him here, hidden—maybe to stir discontent. He survived and returned, which means the boat didn't crash in the storm. It *must* have been an O'Malley setup." Energy zipped up from her toes as the scope of their task became clear. "You know he won't have her killed. She's like a toy he lost and wanted back. That means there's a chance we can save her. And we can take him down. Once and for all."

He shook his head. "This is our home. How do we mount an army with these people?"

"You knew I could lead, although I didn't want to. And you know, deep down, that your people can fight. Don't they have the same incentives? Loved ones taken? Lives threatened? A future to win?" She took his upper arms in her hands and gave a little shake. "Tell me how this is supposed to end, if not with us fighting."

"Giving up."

"That's right. And you might as well have done that when the Change began and saved yourself the trouble. But then you wouldn't have found Zhara." She gentled her voice, feeling more than she should. Knowing she was talking about Tru, not just Arturi's wife. "Tell me she isn't worth fighting for."

He paled in that peculiar way of his, where his freckles became even more pronounced. "I can't do it alone. I would, but I'd die trying. I'm . . . Penny, I'm not a warrior. And I don't want to fail her."

"Don't worry about that." She smiled slightly. "We know warriors."

Glancing toward Tru, he nodded. "You keep one on a leash."

"Not even close," she said with a laugh. "And don't let him hear you say that. I'll be dodging his wounded pride for days."

"Thank you, Penny."

"You're the only person who still calls me Penny."

"I'll stop if you want."

"Don't you dare," she said, echoing her admonishment from before. But this time she felt as if she'd truly connected with Arturi as a man. A person. Not the memory of a friend who had once inhabited her brain. She gathered him into an emotional hug—two lost children grown up. So many of those who'd survived the Change felt that way to Pen. Lost souls. Holding on to whatever good that was left.

"Good." He stepped out of her embrace and straightened his shoulders. "Then we have work to do. May I borrow one of your knives?"

She watched with fierce pride as he took a blade and returned to the willow. He cut the ropes himself, as guards lowered the dead to the ground. "Dispose of them," Arturi said. "Shine, take their possessions for the commissary. Their goods and their lives are forfeit."

When Tru came up beside Pen, she leaned into his body. The

strength she'd mustered to help buoy Arturi was quickly fading. They were signed up for a suicide run. One that would make or break the future of post-Change civilization. A shudder worked across her shoulders.

"You did a good thing," he said.

"Do you think so? Really?"

"You're all he has. Until we get his wife back."

Despite her happiness that Tru was on board, she couldn't help the fear that dogged her. "And if I'm wrong? If Zhara is already dead?"

"Then he'll have a stronger reason to fight."

"Maybe I *can* tell. Find her, like I did on the boat. Or the way I found Arturi all those years ago."

"Knowing one way or the other might affect our strategy, but it's not essential."

"But he'll be crushed if she's dead." She saw it clearly then, almost a portent of things to come. Arturi, a shell of himself, barely speaking. The leader of this tiny haven gone.

"That won't change needing to take this to O'Malley. You know that."

His eyes had grown somber. Heavy-lidded, almost flippant in their regard—same as always. But a deep, dangerous fire burned within their depths. The lion wanted to end this. Not out of revenge. Not out of the need to claim territory. But to rid the world of a cancer that would eat at the balance of all remaining life.

She looked to where the small man already directed Reynard and Miranda in the gathering of provisions and weaponry. Preacher stood over the recently departed, head bowed.

"I do know. And deep down, I bet Arturi does, too. But I can better prepare him for the worst."

Tru's expression had hardened for reasons she couldn't discern. "Do what you think you must."

"Just . . . don't let go of me. Please?"

"I'm not going anywhere. I already said I won't run."

With her fingers twined with Tru's, Pen shut her eyes. No rituals this time. No incantations. Just a true knowledge of what she sought. Zhara. Needle in a haystack. So many auras across the whole of the continent. But geography gave her a sense of where to look. Only a day away. Somewhere close, perhaps along the coastal highway. Farther and farther, she pushed out away from her own mind. Floating on clouds. Soaring with birds. She wondered if this was what Tru felt when he became an animal, giving himself over to another element that lived inside him.

She squeezed his hands. He squeezed back. And she kept going, flying, searching. Dimly, she became aware that her knees had given out. Tru held her on the ground, her head against his shoulder. That reassurance only gave her more strength. Pushing. Looking for the woman they all needed to be safe.

A glimmer of pale green. Like a new leaf.

"Zhara," she whispered.

The green glowed a little brighter.

Then, a bright flash of red. Hard red, as if a hue could taste like blood. Iron. Bitterness. The face of General O'Malley coalesced in her mind, along with an aura the same color as a heart sliced out of a gaping chest. Not the same person. But whoever worked with O'Malley possessed magic that rivaled hers.

And that evil magic pushed back. *Hard.*

THIRTY

Tru caught Pen as she fell.

Her stricken expression spoke of unseen terrors. He drew her into his lap, quietly angry that she'd taken the responsibility upon herself. If Arturi couldn't cope with a crisis, he wasn't much of a leader. If Tru held any hope that Danni had been taken rather than gutted, he would've chased that faint promise to the ends of the earth. He had little sympathy for a man who seemed willing to give up at the first sign of resistance—little sympathy and less faith.

Pen roused, a hand to her temples. "O'Malley has protection."

"Magic, you mean? More than his usual thugs?"

"Exactly. Maybe even what kept Jack shielded all this time. But at least I found Zhara. She's alive."

"Right now? I don't care. You need to eat something and get some sleep." To Tru's surprise, she didn't argue, which spoke volumes about her energy level.

She even let him carry her to her assigned tent. In the morning, they could plan and mobilize. The big drawback to mounting such an operation was the necessity of leaving the camp undefended. Not every citizen would—or should—participate, but those who went had to worry about their loved ones.

As he laid Pen down on the pallet, he said, "We should take the vulnerable personnel to the mission. Mary Agnes's charms should be strong enough to hide them, leaving everyone else free to fight."

"That's a good idea," she said groggily. "I'll tell Arturi."

"Tomorrow."

No need for a watch. The worst had already happened—treachery from within—and even General O'Malley would need time to break Zhara. The old man's brutality might be legendary, but Arturi's wife had thwarted him once before. Tru doubted she would give up the camp's location, even under the worst torture.

Though he lay down beside Pen, he didn't sleep much. He sensed an imminent sweep into epic events and didn't like the current of the river. He didn't believe Arturi was strong enough to lead on his own. The man needed a lieutenant, someone to provide the steel in his spine. If Zhara wasn't found, that steel would come from Pen. Tru didn't kid himself that she cared for Arturi beyond their experience as children. But she would sacrifice personal happiness on the altar of duty. She had that trait in spades.

Maybe she'd inherited the tendency from her mother, who died trying to save her only child. That experience, compounded by her guilt over the girls she'd accidentally killed, meant Pen didn't know how to step back and just *be*. Everything needed to be larger than life. With every fiber of his being, he resented that she had been the one to crack his defenses. A normal woman would've been ten times more preferable—a simpler woman who didn't see the world in terms of all that could be saved, but rather something that must be survived.

But there was no point in wishing. He'd learned that long ago.

At dawn, he rolled away from her, avoiding her restless hands, and went looking for Adrian. He owed the kid an apology.

The boy was already up and working through a series of exercises by himself. Tru recognized the desire to be self-sufficient. He watched for long moments without interrupting and let Adrian decide when they would speak. Tru understood firsthand that such power mattered to a young man who had known relatively little of it.

Eventually, the kid wrapped up his workout. "Did you need something?"

"First, to thank you for helping Pen and me."

"I didn't do it for you," he said, tone angry.

"I know. But thanks. Second, I need to tell you I'm sorry."

"What for?" From his hunched shoulders, he knew the answer.

"Leaving."

"You never promised you'd stay."

Tru folded his arms and gazed off toward the water. "I should have said good-bye in person, though. I was mad at Pen when I took off, and that had nothing to do with you and me. It was wrong."

"I'm used to it. My old man did the same thing."

"Took off?"

Adrian shook his head. "No. Treated me like I don't matter."

Ouch. The sad part was, the kid's tone held no self-pity, just a matter-of-fact assessment. "You know that's not true, right?"

"When a thing's accepted by most people, they take it for true. That's good enough."

"Not for me," Tru said. "I'll make it up to you."

With a slight smile, the boy looked almost rueful. "Careful. That sounded like a promise."

"It is one. Do you forgive me?"

"For not saying good-bye?"

"That, and making you feel like you're not important to me."

The slump in Adrian's shoulders spoke louder than any shout. "Why would I be? I'm just some kid you hauled out of a slave truck."

"Walk with me," Tru said.

They turned from the training area and headed toward the dock as the sun came up. He needed to tell Adrian his story to make him understand. So as they walked, Tru explained how he'd survived the

Change. Told him about Mason, how the guy had taken him in although he had no reason to be kind.

"He said it was because he needed another man who could stand guard, but . . . I wasn't much of a man back then."

"Like me," Adrian muttered.

"See, that's the thing. Now I think Mason saw in me the man I could be. With a little help. And that's kind of how I feel about you."

"I don't even know what you're getting at." Although he faced the ocean, Adrian slid his eyes to follow Tru. Wary. So afraid to hope.

Laurel had been much easier, a dear daughter with a sunny spirit. No dark corners. But then, for every short year of her life, she had never once doubted she was loved, that she was wanted. The pain of her memory still burned, but it was a good pain now. Even if losing his family had nearly killed him, Tru was a better man for loving them. Love hadn't made him small or weak. It had opened his heart to things he never believed possible. He wanted to give Adrian some of that maturity, and so he spoke words he'd thought he never would again.

Making promises. Taking responsibility.

The lion needed a pride.

"You're family now," Tru said. "Just like I was to Jenna and Mason. That means I won't walk out on you again. In fact, I bet in three or four years' time, it'll be the opposite. You'll be the one to go. But I will hunt your ass down if you do what I did to my foster parents."

"What's that?" Adrian was almost smiling.

"Leave and never come back. I bet they're worried as hell about me." One day, he'd get back to Mason and Jenna. He liked to imagine them in the cabin, doing well, healthy, happy. As safe as the Changed world allowed.

Adrian nodded. "That was kind of mean."

"I wasn't thinking about them. I just wanted to see the world. Find my place in it. And it's not like I can just call home."

"You'd have to live right next door."

Wow. That was how the world had altered in a generation. Chills washed over him. In Tru's time, the word "call" meant phones. In Adrian's, it meant yelling for somebody, or maybe a magical thing like they did from the island to contact the mission. No technology anymore. He and Pen were among the last bridges, joining what had been lost to what would come after.

Seabirds whirled overhead, catching Adrian's attention. He followed their haphazard flight as the breeze carried the scents of salt and dead fish. "I forgive you," he said at last. "Mostly because I don't know that anybody ever said sorry to me before."

Tru grinned "You shouldn't get used to it."

"I won't." He shook his head. "You don't want me to call you—"

"No. It's fine." He wasn't sure he could handle being Dad or any of its permutations. *Not yet anyway.*

They arrived back to camp as a group milled around the training yard. At first Tru thought trouble might have resurfaced. His hands curled into fists against the urge to claw. What she'd seen of O'Malley's magical defense had intimidated Pen, who had nerves of steel. The same news would start a screaming riot among the rest. So he bit down on his urge toward violence and restrained the restless lion.

Closer inspection revealed neither a protest nor a demonstration. This audience was attentive, waiting for Arturi to speak. Probably platitudes about giving and sharing and building a better tomorrow. With Adrian at his side, Tru took a position in the back of the crowd and crossed his arms. Several hundred people had gathered, while he scanned the crowd for a particular short-haired woman with a silver glow.

"Yesterday was a sad day," the short man said quietly.

At once, the whispering came to a halt. Tru had never seen that kind of reaction without a thin veil of magic, but this was different. Arturi possessed an unnameable quality that made people want to hear his words.

"It was a day when we learned that those with whom we have planned and dreamed might not be trustworthy. Treachery cuts especially deep because it makes us doubt ourselves. Why did I not see this?"

The strategy was bold, asking aloud the questions these people must be posing to themselves. Wondering if they could really believe in Arturi.

"It's because I'm just a man," he went on. "I believe the best of people until they prove otherwise. I have to. Otherwise we're all just mindless animals, shooting or mauling each other for a drink of water. Enough blood has been spilled to poison the land a thousand times over. If our crops do not grow, it's because we haven't worked hard enough, not because of some witch woman with a lazy eye." His audience laughed a little at this.

"I believe there will come a time when unity will make a difference, when we will fly from the ashes like a phoenix and stand against our oppressors. I believe that because I must, and because Zhara taught me that there is no adversity so great we cannot overcome it."

He paced a little, his gestures refined, restrained. And yet he *had* them. Tru couldn't have identified the moment, exactly, but staring around at the rapt faces, he knew they would fight and die for this man.

In truth, so would he.

The magic of simple human hope.

"I believe because I must. Because it's all I have. What little we've built here, they would take from us. They would grind us down for no better reason than profit. They took everything from me, I thought. I fell into despair." Another candid admission, but the words did not ring with a politician's calculated artifice. Arturi did not seem to speak with any thought toward how his words would be received. In another, a more ambitious soul, such influence would be off-putting. "But who among us has never known loss?"

Heads were shaking, faces soft with memories of those taken, those lost. Tears glittered in the eyes of many. Arturi's voice was the magic, Tru decided. Soft and full and hypnotic. Even the accent served him well, an exotic lilt to lure the ear.

"But the Orchid came to me and she reminded me that I have *not* lost all that matters." A buzz of excitement, then. To most, the Orchid was a symbol. "That I still have all of you and your faith, however little I deserve it. If you will follow me—I say 'if' because I will compel no one to fight in my name—then I say it's time we took the battle to General O'Malley. He took my life, my *wife*, and I want her back. I want everyone as safe as she will be in my arms once again. So, what say you, friends? Do we go to war?"

"War," came the thunderous response.

Someone thumped his fist against his palm, and the noise ran through the crowd like wildfire, an ominous cadence. Like primitive war drums. A call to the end. Watching this fervor, Tru wondered if General O'Malley felt cold fingers of dread dragging down his spine for reasons he couldn't explain.

THIRTY-ONE

Pen stretched alongside Tru for the third morning in a row. As she had on each of those mornings, she awoke feeling tired but energized. The camp was lean now. Hard work had stripped everything back to the bare essentials of material and personnel. The shipments of non-combatants to the mainland had taken place on the first day of preparations. The only people left on the island were Arturi's soldiers.

That those soldiers included boys and girls as young as twelve didn't surprise her at all. Even younger children from the mission would join their ranks. The Change had not been kind to the young. But at least they had been given the tools, training, and guidance—the ability to fight back. The real victims were those O'Malley held prisoner, whether child or adult.

She lay naked against Tru's side. They had made love silently the night before. Words weren't as necessary when they shared images that slid from suggestion to reality. He literally read her thoughts when she fed him pictures of what she wanted and needed. He was opening her, slowly, to a new way of communicating. Her body seemed particularly adept.

She couldn't get enough of him. Touch, taste, sound—she lapped up every moment. *This is Tru. This is the woman I am when I'm with him.*

The dawn broke with garish summer colors. She traced the sleek line of tawny hair that bisected his chest, down to his navel. His morning erection rose up to meet her, as a slight smile tipped his mouth.

"The hour is nigh," he said. "Grant a soldier's last request?"

"If this were the morning before we strike, I'd give you anything you wanted."

"Oh? That sounds promising."

"As it is, we have two weeks of travel ahead of us."

He looped a hand around her waist and snuggled her hips firmly against his. "It's not going to be a summer camping trip. O'Malley will have people all through the east. Plenty of danger to deserve a morning BJ."

"No way."

His tickling was instantaneous and merciless. Pen threw her head back, laughing, begging him to stop. Tru levered atop her body and parted her thighs with his knee. The laughing trailed into a long moan as he slid into her slick channel. One long, firm push. His languorous rhythm didn't last long. Such a sleek, beautiful body—all lean lines and responsive muscles.

Pen marveled at the difference between Tru and her previous lovers. Nothing altruistic about this moment. She knew he would take the pleasure he needed, just as she would take hers. That sharing became easier, more natural. Greedier. As if every slam of his quickening hips were an affirmation of their bond.

She was alive. With Tru, she was *so* alive.

Only when he lay sprawled across her, both breathless and satisfied, did Pen's thoughts return to the day ahead. As she had been practicing, she pushed her mind away from the island, searching, attempting to discern the lay of O'Malley's people. She had been surprised to learn how few of his rank possessed magic. Either that, or the malicious force she'd encountered—that blood-red aura—possessed the power to cloak their opponents.

No army had ever gone into battle more blindly.

But giving up was not an option. She would fight with Arturi until the threat was no more. Or until she saw her mother again.

That unhappy thought urged her to burrow deeper into Tru's arms, snuggling closer to his warm safety. Elegant, callused fingers stroked her bare arms, her breasts, her hips, in a lulling rhythm—more hypnotic and comforting than sexual. Pen's breathing evened and slowed.

A rope ladder.

Looking up toward a distant treetop.

She *must* climb. But to do so would be the end of her world. The end of her life.

I gave you my all, love. I did, I did.

Pen screamed and sat upright. Gasping now, clutching the blanket to her chest, she scrambled out of bed and into her clothes. Free of her lasting nightmare since making love to Tru, she had thought the nightmare gone. But her throat closed around another shriek as grief chilled her skin. Now its horror magnified, strong and bone-deep, when she understood exactly what she stood to lose.

Tru edged onto his elbow, looking impossibly disheveled and sexy. "Bad dream?"

"Yeah," she said, throat parched. *But more than a dream.*

She understood that now. Years of believing herself crazy because of Finn had been proven wrong. Her dream had been with her nearly as long: the need to climb, and knowing that to do so would tear her to pieces. The strength of that prophecy sat firmly in her mind like a history yet to be written.

She would be lost to Tru. Her guts twisted as if trapped by a vise.

He knew what it was to lose and fight and endure. All she could hope was that he'd keep the reins loose. His caring held the potential to make her selfish. That was the last thing Arturi and Zhara and the whole community needed.

Tru would suffer again. He would lose another woman who loved him.

Pen squeezed her eyes shut. *Love.* She loved him in ways she'd never thought possible. Now their future together would last only a matter of days, not years.

Maybe it wasn't true. Maybe she was only imagining the worst possible scenario. She didn't mind dying, because part of her had died a very long time ago. The memory of her mother's blood on the snow wore a numb spot on her heart, one that might never return to sensation. To shed her fatalism had been a lifelong battle.

But she dreaded causing Tru another round of hurt. The openness he'd fostered in her was not without reciprocation. She remembered the scarred, callous man he'd been when reluctantly helping to liberate that slave truck. Had she done something hideous in loving him? In leaving him vulnerable to another loss?

The island came to life around them. With fewer people, the settlement appeared bigger and less inviting. Less like a home. More like an abandoned military encampment. Shine had stripped the galley and the commissary clean, with the domestic supplies heading out to the mission with the non-combatants. Koss and Reynard oversaw loading military provisions onto the last boats. Soon every soldier would take to the swamps and highways and woods, in search of the monstrous human tyrant that must be culled.

In silence, sitting in the flap of the hut, Pen ate dried meat and drank herbal tea while watching the bustle of activity. No matter her gifts, the knack for organizing such an endeavor was beyond her. Tru emerged looking sleepy, unbelievably delicious, and a little mistrustful—watching her with questions he had yet to ask.

He shook his head and blanked his expression. After tugging a homespun shirt over his head, he raked his hands through his hair by way of a morning beauty ritual. Wild. Powerful. A little reckless.

"Good morning."

A knife of dread slipped between her ribs. She was going to hurt him. And that tinge of wariness in his voice said he knew as much.

Now she understood—so clearly—why he'd left the island by himself. A clean break. But her mother, a nurse's aide, had told her the truth about ripping off bandages. Quicker didn't hurt less. The fallacy had been perpetuated by battlefield doctors and nurses unable to endure the agony of removing wrappings one slow, merciless inch at a time. The process, repeated across dozens of soldiers a day, gnawed at their nerves until the medics needed relief. Faster meant less pain for them, not for the patients.

To break it off with Tru now would only be doing herself a similar favor. He deserved every minute they had yet to be afforded. Maybe in time, as he had done with Danni, he would be able to look back on these days with gladness.

He touched her cheek. "What is it?"

Pen blinked, surprised to find herself shedding silent tears. Her heart hurt. It *ached*. Whatever resignation her mind and even her soul had accepted about events to come, the part of her that longed for a future with Tru was already grieving.

"Tell me."

She shook her head. "You'll think me silly."

"I doubt that."

"Just my thoughts getting away from me." Quickly dashing away her tears, she turned away from his probing, icy blue eyes. He would stop her if he knew. It was wrong to deny him that option, but she hadn't had a choice in the matter since she was nine years old. "I'm just nervous about getting under way."

Those eyes she loved, so clear, so pale, dug deeper. A frown cut between his brows and twisted his mouth. "I thought we were past this, Pen."

"We're not," she said tightly. "You'll just have to trust me."

She turned to join the others, but Tru caught her arm. He dragged her closer—a standing version of the embrace they'd only just shared. His scent wrapped around her like a lover's tease and a security blanket all at once. "I *can't* trust you. The only thing I can trust about you is that you're looking for a way out."

"A way out?"

His frown melted into a sneer. He shoved her away, just enough to end their contact. "Away from us. You'd run as fast as I did, given half a chance."

"That's not true!"

He shook his head and lifted his shoulders in a weary shrug. "You know what? Forget I said anything. It's a waste of breath with you sometimes."

Her skin stung as if she'd been slapped. Pen only stood there as he stalked away, hands shoved into his trouser pockets, the line of his shoulders rigid. He was insane if he thought this was what she wanted. The idea of a quiet, safe life as his woman made her glow from the inside out. But what manner of person would she be if she ducked out of the whole world and let it rot while she indulged in her man?

A happier person. Maybe even a saner one.

She grabbed her duffel and left the tent. Arturi had assigned particular individuals to dismantle the shelters. Everyone had a duty. Hers, apparently, was to question the very course of her existence.

Four hours later, she boarded the last boat off the island. Arturi stood on the docks, looking back at what they left behind. Maybe one day they would return, rebuild, renew. But for the moment this meant the end of all he'd accomplished.

Unlike Pen, who was melancholy, Arturi seemed eager. He boarded the sailboat with a grin. Something of the friend she'd long known shone from him, and she wanted very much to understand how he had regained his center. Hers had been obliterated.

"Smile, Penny," he said, standing by her side. "It's a good day to begin a journey."

"Oh?"

"Zhara has sayings and such for almost every occasion. One was 'A sunny afternoon holds no malice.'" He shrugged. "Maybe they came from her people in Haiti. Maybe she just made them up to keep her own balance when times got tough. But she said them often enough that I started to believe them. All of them."

Pen noticed his phrasing. *Zhara has sayings.* Present, not past tense. Whatever dark place he'd plummeted into was well behind him. To her old friend, this journey was not only well under way, but the battle was won and the war concluded.

"You shouldn't be here with me, though," he said. "Where's Tru?"

She looked out over the waves as they sailed west. The bright glint of sunlight off the water stung her eyes and reminded her of the tears she'd shed. "He isn't in the mood to speak to me at the moment."

To her surprise, Arturi caught her by the upper arms and looked directly into her eyes. His height meant they stood face-to-face. A glimmer of distress passed over his features. "Do not waste these moments. Don't. You owe it to those who have lost."

"Is that why Zhara held so many doubts about your feelings for her?" She couldn't help the sharpness of her words. He was cutting way too close to the quick.

"If I'm unable to tell my wife, entirely and completely, how I feel about her, I will regret it like no other failure in my life. That is a mistake too painful to be made by more than one person in this world."

He nodded to the aft railing, where Tru stood next to Adrian. They laughed about something, with Adrian pointing to the shore. Pen's breath caught. Not for the first time, she found herself standing next to Arturi when she desperately wanted to be with those two.

Maybe Arturi was right. She might not be able to tell Tru the entire truth about her vision, but she could spend what time remained with him. And she could tell him the truth about her feelings. Now. Before they made landfall and the hunt began. Before she faced her death.

He might never care for her as he had loved his wife, but surely he harbored some affection. The pain Arturi lived with—and might need to live with forever, if they weren't successful—seemed like the worst possible sort of remorse.

She nodded to her friend and wove back across the ship's deck, passing the soldiers who would make war on O'Malley. The waves rocked her footsteps but not her focus. She reached the railing and stood to Tru's left, with Adrian on his other side.

He spared her a glance, then returned his gaze to the ocean. "How's the commander?"

"Hopeful, actually. It's good to see."

"Is that why you're so chipper?"

His hint of mockery didn't sit well, but she probably deserved his scorn. She hadn't been up front with him about so many things. Maybe this . . . maybe this would be different.

"No, I think that's for another reason," she said softly. "Tru, can I talk to you for a moment? In private?"

THIRTY-TWO

Tru kept his expression quiet, not showing his anger. He merely nodded and moved farther down the rail. If Pen thought he would make it easy for her to pass off some speech about how they needed to focus on the mission, she didn't know him at all. He'd *always* been a fighter.

"I just want you to know that I . . . well, that I love you." In speaking those words, her mouth twisted as if she'd bitten into a crab apple.

"Sure you do," he said. "I can tell by the way you treat me."

Her expression fell.

What was he supposed to say? Love didn't look like this, at least not what he'd known of it. Even if she was scared, she could turn to him if she trusted him. She'd been in fucking *tears*. Instead of revealing what was on her mind, she'd clammed up. Said "trust me" like he was a primitive tribesman who needed her to interpret signs before he set off on an ocean voyage.

His relationship with Danni hadn't been perfect—they had both been young and dumb—but Tru knew how it should work. Give-and-take. Plenty of talking that, sure, could lead to fighting. But conflict opened the way to greater understanding. When there was only silence and distance, nothing permanent could grow. And that made him sad for so many reasons.

"You don't believe me," she said.

"Love is huge, wonderful, and terrifying, and it kills you to lose it, but even with the pain, you wouldn't do anything different."

And if she felt that for him, she wouldn't be so sad-faced right now, like she'd just confessed to a terminal illness. Love meant joy, every bit as much as it held the potential for loss.

"You mean Danni."

I mean you. Because you're going to break my heart just like she did, only it won't be through circumstances beyond your control.

How did I fall for such a closed-off female?

Told you we'd be better off with six, the lion said lazily.

Quiet, you.

Tru didn't speak or form the pictures in his head that would let her understand. He maintained the distance between them, just like the space between their hands on the rail. She had small scars on her fingers, gained through hard work, just like everyone else. The Orchid liked to pretend she wasn't above the messiness of everyday life, but maybe deep down, she preferred her untouchable persona. Flowers didn't bleed, or hurt, or cry. She'd rather keep going down this path, toward mindless self-sacrifice. People could talk about her goodness after she died.

At the first indication of trouble, she'd raced right back to that behavior. Saving the world. He felt like a fucking *ass* for thinking he was special enough, important enough, to be the man to her woman. But it wasn't enough. *He* wasn't enough.

"I let you in," he said. "Despite my better judgment, I did. I *knew* it was a bad idea—"

"Because you were hurt before."

God, she didn't understand anything. While she might be the most magically gifted human on the planet, she had the emotional understanding of a child. That didn't set well with him either, as if he'd taken advantage of her naïveté. Sure, he could make her come, but he couldn't reach her on any other level.

"No, Pen. It was a bad idea because you don't understand how relationships work. You don't care about building a partnership. That's not love. And if you don't get the difference, I'm through trying to explain it to you. Remedial class is over."

Tru moved away, unwilling to listen to more of her justifications. It didn't take long to make landfall, where the others were waiting. The rest of the day was long, spent bidding farewells and laying plans. He stuck by Adrian, who would accompany the militia to General O'Malley's stronghold. They would divide the force there, one for diversion and one to lead a small group into the belly of the beast. Tru intended to be among the latter. No one could deny his combat experience and aptitude for killing.

Once Bethany and the scouts from the mission joined them on the beach, they moved out. Arturi gave no more speeches. Tru had a little more faith in him now. No telling what the man could accomplish if he managed to rescue his wife and defeat the greatest opponent to rebuilding any kind of civilization. O'Malley had been quoted often as saying that chaos was good for the bottom line.

To Tru's mind, the old general was a dinosaur. The Changed world didn't function on capitalist principles anymore. Most people were too busy just trying to meet basic needs to care about stockpiling wealth. Only a rare few, like the general, had used the Change to springboard to a position of power. There were other private empires, but none so vast or strangling.

If we can put him down, it will give people some breathing room.

Big if.

After the noon meal, Tru shifted and scouted ahead, looking for a good place to camp. He had company this time, a couple of skinwalkers from Arturi's camp—a male marmot and a female crow. They made an odd team, but the bird flew ahead, calling warnings until they ran into their first problem just before dark.

It was a pain in the ass that they had to shift back in order to discuss what she'd seen. Tru averted his eyes as they dressed. "There's an encampment up ahead," the woman said. "We could go around, but we'll lose time, and they've got traps set up around the perimeter."

Tru shook his head. "We can't risk it after dark. Our numbers are too great for such a delicate maneuver."

"We should go back and report," the man said. Tru had forgotten his name. Koss, maybe? Generally, he didn't recall unless it was a kid or someone he especially liked. Kids needed to be remembered because people often acted as if they didn't count.

The skinwalkers returned in human form. No sense in burning extra energy to shift for the run back to the others, who moved at a steady speed a few kilometers behind. That meant running, but all of them were lean and strong, a side benefit of their abilities.

By the time they rejoined the small army, however, Tru was tired. He let the woman fill Arturi in on what they'd found. He felt Pen watching him, but he wasn't in the mood. Instead he listened as Arturi decided how to handle his first combat dilemma.

"Xialle, do you get the impression they're waiting for us?" he asked at last.

Xialle must be the crow.

"They're waiting for something," she answered. "They've dug in, established defenses all along the road."

"Mines, probably," someone said.

Everyone knew—and feared—that the general had access to an old cache of claymores from one of the great wars. The mines worked on a simple, deadly principle, and no one had the expertise to disarm them. Such knowledge belonged to the world that had been lost. But the old bastard would maim using whatever technology he could get his hands on, until he ran out of stockpiled ordnance or someone cut his throat. Tru would enjoy being that someone.

"I might be able to find them before our troops go in," Pen said.

Of course. Her magic could do damn near anything except make her happy. Tru folded his arms, mouth set.

"How?" Arturi asked.

"Technology feels different from living things. So if they've laid mines, there will be . . . dead spots in the ground." She appeared to struggle to provide even that much explanation, but the short man nodded.

"How close do you need to be?"

"I'm not sure. I've never done anything like this before."

She had scanned for Zhara from a crazy distance, but the effort had cost her. And O'Malley's pet spellcaster had nearly melted her brain. Tru wanted to object, but this was her favorite thing to do—save the day and amaze the masses. *Yeah, that's right, Pen. Add to your legend. Make it so nobody can speak of you without reverence.* He kept his mouth shut, but he simmered through his silence.

"Do you want to try?" Arturi touched her arm lightly.

Tru ground his teeth, even though the man's touch wasn't sexual. He just . . . didn't like it. In twenty-seven years, damn few things—or people—had belonged to him. In his heart, it felt like Pen did. Which made no sense. She didn't know how to give herself to one person. She was better at sowing her magic far and wide, a gift for the madding crowd. And that sure was easier than letting somebody really crawl inside her. It would feel like having her guts ripped out if something went wrong, because life was a fucking crapshoot that way. No one had a choice where to get off the ride. Sometimes it spun and dumped you on your ass. Sometimes you staggered out dizzy and smiling.

And she didn't understand *any* of that.

"I think I have to," Pen replied.

"I need my journal and graphite." Arturi gestured and the items came quickly in response to his urgent tone. "I'll map the area as she uncovers them. We'll have to figure out a way to detonate them before it'll be safe to move in."

"One thing at a time." But Pen was smiling.

And why not? She was about to make herself *useful* again, as if she lacked intrinsic value without her powers. That idea hit him like a hammer against the skull. *That's what she thinks.* If she couldn't do her thing and make the world a better place, what would she be? It *must* have to do with her mom.

Pen came out of the station, looking to protect me. But she couldn't control her mojo. And it cost her mom's life. That same loss of control had killed innocent girls. Now she feels she has to use those powers, maybe until it kills her, to be worth those sacrifices.

Stupid woman. Didn't she know a good mother would risk her life for her child, regardless of intelligence, appearance, or ability? Bad mothers . . . well. Tru knew all about them, too. As it turned out, maybe his mother's indifference had been for the best after all. Because he'd never once wondered how she'd feel about his lion self.

"Then go on," Arturi said. "We'll work out the logistics for our first battle afterward, though I think it best to strike under cover of darkness. I hope they won't be expecting us to mobilize as fast as we did."

Preacher put up a hand. "I have some ideas in that regard once the Orchid's done."

Understanding her actions didn't sweeten the pain of watching Pen kill herself slowly—and for the greater good. Beatific deeds couldn't be everything. Not in a whole and happy life.

As shadows lengthened around him, Tru bolted down another meal to fortify himself for the coming night. Then he shifted once more, and in lion skin, he slipped off to do a little preparation of his own.

THIRTY-THREE

Pen drank the water Shine provided, then ate tough jerky with meticulous bites. Her headache only intensified. She was a healer. She should be able to get her own agonized brain through the next few hours. But the sizzling pain would not abate.

The sun had set, replaced by a fragile moon. Just a sliver of light against a wholly black backdrop. She and the four-person recon team had crept forward along three kilometers of overgrown forest. Every few hundred meters, she sat and concentrated on the vibrations of the earth. She couldn't describe them as anything else. The planet had a pulse, from underground rivers to the creeping crawl of worms. The mines took up area that felt like dead space in her head.

Gritting her teeth, she opened her eyes to find Arturi sitting beside her. He'd been with her every step. While she appreciated his encouragement, she wished another man held her hand.

She needed Tru's love. She needed his faith that the world deserved a better future. And those two things seemed incompatible. The pull to be selfish shimmered off of him like his golden aura.

"Three hundred meters due north, behind a fallen L-shaped tree." After a gulp of water, she forced back the blaze of pain. "One hundred meters northwest, between two elms, one of which is scarred by a lightning streak."

Arturi read his compass and made notations in a leather-bound journal. It looked ancient, with yellowed pages fattened by humidity and frequent use. "Advance. Five hundred meters. Hold position there."

He helped Pen stand, with her arm around his shoulders. Her knees shook. Her backbone felt made of moss. Dizziness slipped her vision toward a charcoal gray that had nothing to do with night shadows.

"Penny?" Arturi gave her a gentle shake. "Come on now, old friend. Stay with me."

"I'm here. Go."

She would not lose to O'Malley. Fear of using her magic had stayed her hand for too long, made her terrified of losing control. Of using all that she had. That wasn't an issue now. Arturi deserved every ounce of strength she could muster.

Although she couldn't remember much of the journey, she found herself at another rallying point. Fire burned behind her temples. She ate again, drank again, but nothing stemmed the tremors shaking her limbs. Concentrating produced nothing, as if her magic were nothing but an extinguished ember. Just . . . black.

For a brief moment she panicked. What was she without the forces warping her mind and determining her fate? She was not a warrior, not really. She wielded knives for self-defense, as a last measure. And she was not the leader Arturi could be. Too many people feared her to listen and relate. Awe got in the way of camaraderie.

But that panic gave way to a vision unlike any she'd ever dared permit. A life of her own. Quiet. Settled. Simple responsibilities and simple joys. Making love to Tru, sharing laughter as well as passion. Children one day, with Adrian there, too. He would grow into a fine man with Tru as his example. They would nestle in a cabin somewhere safe, like Mason and Jenna had forged for themselves, but near enough to open plains so that Tru could indulge in the hunt.

The image was so clear and so perfect that she nearly wept. Her hands shook as she pressed them to her eyes—whether to make it go away or to hold it close, she didn't know.

In the dark, eyes pinched shut, her momentary lapse toward fantasy gave way to the return of the powers that defined her. There was a land mine. She pictured a void in the soil. But rather than be relieved, she bowed over her thighs and sobbed. "I can't," she gasped. Again and again.

She just couldn't do it anymore.

Exhausted.

So unspeakably tired.

And the life she'd imagined with Tru wouldn't rematerialize. She only saw the nightmare of her death. Pen . . . the only one left to save Zhara. That ladder. That choice.

I gave you my all, love. I did, I did.

"Find him." Arturi's voice echoed somewhere nearby as a sharp, whispered hiss. "I don't care where he is. Find Tru."

She felt disembodied, skin cold and numb. Her head was a bloated mass of thoughts that wouldn't make sense, no matter how she forced the pieces together.

Arms closed around her. "Can't," she whispered again. "No more."

"It's okay. I'm here."

"*Tru.*" The tremors intensified, this time out of relief. "My head. It hurts. Splitting apart."

"I got you." He gathered her up, lifting her from the leaf-strewn ground. But then the words he spat were anything but gentle—more like a human version of his lion's roar. "Not again, Arturi. Do you understand me? You find another way."

"She didn't tell me," came Arturi's steely reply.

"She never does. Don't you get it? And she never will."

Pen cringed at their harsh words. The pain burrowed under her skull and tapped from the inside out. *Heal thyself.* But she couldn't find the concentration to ease her own hurts.

Instead she did the next best thing. She tucked into Tru's arms as he carried her back from the front lines. Temporary tents, forged from the remnants of the island's canvas huts, occupied a clearing. No one lit fires, but a sense of homey companionship layered over the glade. Even Pen felt it, something larger than her pain. Yet always distant. A reward she couldn't accept.

But nothing mattered so much as Tru's mouth against her skin. He kissed her, murmured words he probably meant as comfort. Only, she heard the tension and pain in his deep rumble. She tightened her hold, forearms crossed behind his neck.

"I saw us," she whispered against his neck. "We were married. Adrian was with us."

"When? Just now?"

"Yes. When I thought my powers were gone. I could see a simpler life." Grief along with hunger twisted her stomach. "But that's vanished now. Can't find it. Tru, please, help me."

He edged into a tent and laid her down on a rough blanket, holding her close to his body. She shook beneath the calming hands he ran along her skin. "Tell me more."

The break in his voice reminded her of when he'd been younger, on the cusp of manhood. She had thought him a god, all dark hair and skin as pale as his blue eyes. Fierce. Fearless. Just the opposite of how she'd felt, trapped in her own mind after the first horrors of the Change.

"I'm going to fail you, aren't I?"

"By wearing yourself down to nothing," he said. "By throwing yourself on O'Malley's sword. Any number of ways. But yes. You will." His hands tightened, as if willing away the future he predicted.

Pen wanted it gone, too.

"I don't want to." She struggled to sit, but he held her still and forced a strip of dried meat into her unsteady hands. "I saw us *happy*. Do you know how that felt?"

"Peaceful."

"Peaceful," she said, the word like a shudder. "And safe and real. And . . . friendly."

He chuckled softly. "Friendly?"

"Welcoming. When people are glad to see you. I don't remember the last time I felt that way." She forced herself to nibble the jerky. A memory filtered through the pain as it receded. "Like how it was that first winter, before Mama died. I was a little lost, but I knew I was cared for and loved. You could've been a real brat about me not talking. But you never lost your patience with me. How could I let you die?"

The soothing palms went still. "Let me die?"

"With Jenna. On the snow." More memories burst open. She'd been safe in a bunker with her mother. But demon dogs had cornered Tru where he stood guard over Jenna's unconscious body. "I saw it all happen. Knew I had to do something. I just . . . teleported. For the first time, I think now, it was to go *toward* danger. But I wanted you safe. I didn't know . . ."

"You didn't know your mother would be killed."

The sob she expected to pummel out of her chest didn't come. She'd cried for her mother, too many times to count, all within the safety of dark nights. No one to know. But that grief was a dull ache compared to such a fresh hell.

She blinked up at Tru in the nearly dark tent. The layer of gold in his aura illuminated his face, but she knew that wasn't what her eyes saw. Her magic, maybe. And her heart.

"She made a choice," he said softly. "Just as you did. Hell, just like I did. I'd run out in the snow to help Jenna make her way home. Can you get that, Pen? Choices. You have to make them, no matter your gifts."

Tempting. So tempting.

Touching Tru's face, she traced the swoop of his cheekbone and the line of his jaw. "And what if I chose you. What would that mean?"

"Telling me the truth. *Always.* Not shutting me out, even if it's easier. Taking care of yourself, so that we have a chance at a future."

Something else. Something deeper. She felt it in him like a shiver, or like a jab of electricity. Her brain hurt. But she relaxed in his arms, her mouth tucked against warm skin. He tasted of salt and of Tru, the only man who'd ever treated her like a woman to be loved. Not a goddess to be worshipped or feared or even used.

An image pinged in her mind. Must have come from Tru, because she'd never seen anything like it. A closet. Shoes didn't match on a rack, but they formed a pattern. Brown, black, brown, white. Neckties hung down like colorful stalagmites. And in the corner was a very young version of the man she loved. Bony knees were pulled up to his chest, arms wrapped fast around them. Dark hair dipped over his eyes. Outside, a man shouted at his mother, just one of her casual overnights. They never looked in the closet as their fight raged.

Young Tru, not even important enough to beat. He ducked tighter into the corner.

Pen gasped. Shook her head. Light-headed, thirsty, she held on by the slimmest thread. "Jesus, Tru. Now who isn't being honest?"

"I won't argue. You're tired, and you've rubbed a goddamn hole in my patience."

"No, you said that if I were to choose you, I'd need to tell the truth. But it goes both ways. You don't want me to simply take care of myself." With the meat gone and her strength returning she crawled to her knees. They faced one another, tummy to tummy. With both hands shaking, she framed his face. "I saw you. I saw what you just gave me. That fear and loneliness."

"Pen, stop."

"You want me to choose you. Let the world go to hell, so long as we have each other. That's it, isn't it?" She kissed his cheeks, even when he tried to push her away. "Tell me what it's like when I help Arturi. When I go to him. I need you to say it. Otherwise you're a martyr just like me, not admitting what you want."

A dark tremor shook out from his aura, like a tidal wave pushing to shore. He angled a palm behind her head and pulled her close. Their mouths met in a fierce rush. He kissed her with more passion than he'd ever shown. All tongues and teeth and deep, greedy breaths.

He eased her back to the blanket, his long body tight above hers. But she didn't feel seduced, only claimed. Hands everywhere. Legs pinning hers. Lips along her collarbone and down to the neckline of her shirt.

He reached that barrier and bowed his head, forehead against her sternum. A long, low growl pushed out of his chest. His shoulders shook, but with anger or leashed passion she couldn't tell.

"Yes," he rasped against her skin. "I need you to choose me. I can't just be the guy who scrapes you off the ground at the end of the day." He lifted his head, features tight with pain and yearning.

For a split second she again found that image she loved. Her and Tru. Happy.

The risk was huge. To refute the idea she wouldn't survive this war. To believe, instead, in something . . . beautiful.

"I choose you." She touched his hair with trembling fingers, then trailed one down to his mouth. That lower lip was still swollen and wet from kissing her. "If you'll have me."

THIRTY-FOUR

The pleasure of Pen's words astonished him, even as Tru wrestled with doubt. She meant them *now*, but he wondered how long it would last. Until the next time Arturi needed her to do some impossible thing? Maybe. But if he didn't take a risk, he didn't deserve her. Nothing came with a guarantee.

"If?" he repeated with a half smile. "When I came back, I came back to *you*."

"It hurt when you didn't believe that I love you."

He got that. But . . . "It's not just the words, love. It's about the way you treat your mate. Words, on their own, have no meaning."

"I *do* treat you differently from everyone else. The others all know."

"Okay, Pen. Since you don't see what I'm getting at, I'll show you." He pulled her between his legs and wrapped his arms around her, face against the curve of her neck. God, he could sit like this forever. "Touch matters. Not just words. About what you said on the boat . . ."

"Yes?" She sounded so scared.

"I fell in love with you the first time I touched your breasts."

"Back *then*?" Astonishment colored her tone.

"Then," he said. "Afterward, you called me an asshole, and you told me I should be better than that. Remember what you said?"

"You asked why I thought that, and I said 'because you're Tru.'"

He smiled at the memory. "That was the first time anyone ever said my name that way, like it was a good thing to be me. I was yours, then, but I didn't think you'd ever be mine. I love you, Pen. I tried to leave because I didn't see it ending well—not with the way you try to carry the world—but I want you so bad I can't sleep at night. I stay up just to look at you." Tru punctuated each word with a kiss down the side of her neck.

A shiver swept through her, delighting him. "Wow."

"You see the difference, my heart? I'm not sad, telling you this. It's not a bad thing. I'm happy you're finally willing to hear it."

"But you've been happier."

It took him a moment to connect the dots. "Are you comparing yourself to Danni? Don't. My life with her was good, but I love *you* just as much."

"You do?" She shifted in his arms, visibly astonished.

"Woman, your mind never ceases to amaze me." The words weren't a compliment, and by the way she stiffened, she knew it.

"The way you talked about your wife—" Her voice caught on the last word and he heard her longing.

Hadn't he wanted that sense of belonging? It seemed she did, too. Tru eased her from him, though not for the reasons she seemed to fear. In the dark, his eyesight was sharp enough to note her pretty face clouding over.

"You want the promises," he said.

"Only if you mean them."

"I don't make vows I don't intend to keep. Will you bind yourself to me tonight? Will you be my wife?"

Those were not the words he'd spoken to Danni. That night, they had both been wild, playful, laughing. *Let's stay together forever,* followed by breathless kisses and the sparkling heat of a summer night. This was a somber moment, a weightier one, but no less sweet, like the darkest berries heavy with juice at the bottom of the briar patch—worth the pain of picking them.

A nervous breath escaped her. "You'll have to tell me what to say."

"The words just need to come from your heart. But I'll go first if that makes you feel better."

"Please," she whispered.

The lines of an old poem whose author he could no longer remember came to him, perfect for the moment. "Come away, come, sweet love/The golden morning breaks/All the earth, all the air/Of love and pleasure speaks/Teach thine arms then to embrace/And sweet rosy lips to kiss/And mix our souls in mutual bliss."

Her eyes went wide and dreamy in the dark.

"Penelope Sheehan, I love you more than the sunrise over the ocean, more than freedom. I would die, willingly, to keep you from a moment's pain. I promise you the full strength of my back and spirit in our shared journey, all the days of our lives. I will never forsake or betray you. I am yours to my last breath." Tru took her hands in his and brushed each palm in gentle reverence, and then he took her mouth in an utterly carnal kiss. Dual promises of both respect and desire.

She took a breath once they sat back. Although shimmering with nerves, her voice didn't waver. "You woke me up, Tru, like I wasn't finished until I found you again. Only with you am I whole, a woman capable of giving and receiving love. You made me believe I could be more, and I will spend my life working to make you as happy as you make me."

"I take you as my wife," he said softly. "From this day forward."

"I take you as my husband, from this day forward." Her echoed words gave him a pleasurable little chill.

That definitely needed to be sealed with a kiss. There were no witnesses, but in this world, their promise—their kiss—was enough. To again have someone who belonged to him . . . dizzying.

Mine. Oh, Pen.

"I have something for you. For us." Tru fumbled in his bag.

"A present?" Her tone was joyful, matched by a broad smile.

The Orchid probably didn't receive many gifts. People might assume that nothing they possessed was good enough. That had to suck.

"I suppose . . . more of a wedding gift." He found the matching leather bracelets he'd crafted during the long nights at the mission.

The work was primitive, not high quality, and certainly not on par with old-world wedding rings. But her expression lit up when he reached for her wrist to fasten the small ornament.

"You made this for me?"

He nodded. "I didn't know if this day would come. But . . . I hoped, even when it didn't make sense."

"Hope doesn't." She gazed down at her arm as if he'd wreathed her in shining jewels. Then she took the other bracelet from him and bound it around his arm, symbolic of the promises they'd made. The circle, likewise, representing a love without end.

The future was uncertain.

But tonight? He would make love to his wife. Tru flashed a series of images at her, opening himself completely, and she responded with a siren's smile.

"If the lady has no objections?"

"She has none. In fact, I'd go so far as to say she's eager."

"No headache? I've heard sex is a good cure. Natural endorphins."

"It's still there," she admitted. "But you make it better. You make everything better. You always did."

He couldn't claim he'd experienced some instant connection with her as a child—that he had been waiting for her to grow up—but he'd always known she was special. He'd wanted to protect her, even then. Those feelings had grown into something so powerful that they were his heart and soul. *She* was.

Pen shivered and reached for him. The pictures in her mind reflected the devotion sweeping through him, pulsing over them both like a river. He smiled, because she gave back that emotion in a rushing flood. His cock went hard as a spike in response, though it had been sitting at half-mast during their impromptu ceremony. She simply had that effect on him.

"God," he growled into her throat. "I'm gonna enjoy this."

"Me too."

They'd never done this before—made love with their defenses completely down, hearts and minds in tune. In fact, he couldn't say he'd ever done that with anyone. As of that night, the act was brand new. *My wife.* It was different from Danni, to whom he'd given a boy's heart and a boy's enthusiasm. Pen claimed him as a man, who had been beaten, broken. But he'd come out stronger on the other side, strong enough to be the man she needed. His hands trembled as he stripped her clothes, punctuating each article with kisses along the skin he revealed.

Tru meant to go slow. Be soft and gentle. Take hours kissing and licking until Pen was lost in a dreamy daze, but he couldn't. Not with her dirty pictures in his head, already aroused by the wildness he fed her.

She wasn't passive, waiting to be pleasured. Not this time. Instead she tugged at his clothes with eager hands. She nuzzled and bit and licked, just as he did.

When Tru bent his head to her breast, she clutched his hair and kissed the top of his head, writhing like a wild thing in his arms. Tempting nipples urged him to suck and nip. He gave her a faint edge of teeth. She cried out. *More,* demanded the heat in his head. He couldn't possibly do all the things she wanted—not *right* now—yet those ideas maddened him. He wanted to do everything. He wanted to *own her* completely with his body.

"Take me," she moaned. "Tru, love me. *Fuck* me."

He lost all control. They rolled onto carelessly strewn blankets, arching and tugging, mouths clinging, legs tangled. She bowed under him, eager to take him, and he palmed her thighs wide, teasing with slow strokes against her hot, slick lips. Pen bucked and clawed at his back. The pain sparked him to greater desire, as it always did, because it meant she was lost in him, just as he was lost in her. The heat of her lust sizzled in his head, flashing graphic images he couldn't resist.

With a soft roar, he rolled her to her stomach. He'd wanted her like this for so long. Pinned under him. Helpless, impaled on his cock. Now he would have her that way. Rather than acting unsure, she lifted her ass and gave him a look of pure sultry temptation over one shoulder. He couldn't stand any more.

In a long, hard thrust, he took her from behind, hands on her hips. She accepted his length as if she had been made for this. Her back arched in the most graceful inward bow, sweet bottom pushing back in time to his strokes. He laid his body against hers and nuzzled his face against her neck. Covering her. Claiming her.

"Ah. Ah." Small moans escaped her, but they only mingled with his harsh breaths. Not protests.

She loved this. He felt it in her body and her mind, each time she moved. That pleasure drove his own desire to insane heights, until he thought he might die of it. *More. More. Yeah.* He fed her his lust, and she shook with it, her pussy drenched around him. Tight and pulsing, she rocked, growled in her throat—his own lioness.

"Come for me, wife." The words were enough, coupled with a deep stroke.

Pen gasped her climax, and he bit the back of her neck, holding with his teeth as his orgasm consumed all thought. Dual sensations mingled until he couldn't tell where his body ended and hers began. He shook from head to toe and his vision grayed. He held still to keep from passing out entirely. Not the right note for their wedding night, even if it happened due to the best sex he'd ever had.

"Damn," she said eventually.

That pretty much summed up his thoughts. When he could trust himself, he rolled off and pulled her into his arms. They cuddled, sticky with sex and sweat, as night noises sounded all around them. *Even the bugs sound like music tonight. This must be love.*

Holding Pen, he imagined that a feeling like this could last all his days, never slipping away like moonlit water through his hands.

THIRTY-FIVE

Pen awoke a married woman.

She lay in Tru's arms, surrounded by a warmth and peace she couldn't deny. Her sacrifices would mean nothing if she denied herself such a basic need. They had made love through the night, once when she felt surrounded by nothing but Tru and the quiet darkness. He adored her more deeply than she ever imagined, learning and exploring. Then, just before dawn, he had come to her again, his mind and heart open in terrifyingly beautiful ways.

And always the same promise, though it went unspoken. That she could have this for the rest of her life.

All she had to do was trust.

She inhaled and stretched, relishing the flex of his hand at her hip. The purr in his throat was positively feline. Though stripped raw and aching in so many new places, she could have loved him all over again.

But that gorgeous, sultry ambition was cut short by a distant explosion.

"Shit," Tru rasped, sitting upright. His hair was a snarled thatch, and reddish-brown whiskers shadowed his sharp jaw. "What the hell was that?"

Pen could've stretched her mind out toward the sound. The new way she controlled her magic would make it an easy task. But she was still light-headed and not entirely sure of herself. A little time. Time to make certain she didn't slip back into the realm of giving too much—so much that she risked more than her health.

"Let's find out," she said.

Tru pushed the blanket off his thighs. Sweet life, he was beautiful. The dark hair that dusted his skin made her want to leave every care behind. Just stay there. The two of them, safe and loving.

But his smile was even more enticing. "Now that's more like it."

Balance. She could balance her two lives. Tru wasn't going to run from this fight. He was too damn *good*, no matter how his callous shell occasionally got the better of him. That she had brought such goodness back to the world filled her with a power she'd never known. Not magic. Just the knowledge that her life had affected one person so greatly.

They dressed in silence, with quick purpose. Pen strapped her knives around her waist, then tugged on her cloak. Tru outfitted himself simply in the cargoes he'd stolen the day he stopped that O'Malley's truck. The closer-fitting, more rugged material would serve him better than loose homespun. He looked lean and fierce, especially in his expression. Determined. Fearless.

And if she endangered herself needlessly, she would upset that determination. The worst she could do was split his concentration between the demands of an emergency and anxiety about her. That realization rang clear like the chime of a bell.

She grabbed his arm as he made for the tent flap. "I won't make you worry."

A frown revealed his confusion. But softness soon took its place. He glanced down to where their hands joined, with each wrist banded by the bracelets they'd exchanged. "I'd appreciate that."

He dipped close for a swift, sweet kiss. Pen soaked up every beautiful sensation, as well as how her heart eased its nervous twitch. *She beat more steadily now.*

Out in the clearing, their ragtag soldiers had gathered around Shine, Reynard, and Miranda. "O'Malley's goons in the distant encampment have been sniping our people as they demarcated the mines," Shine said. "The explosion occurred when one of the workers was tagged and fell onto a mine. Luckily he was the only casualty."

Arturi and Preacher emerged from the forest cover, with boyish Koss working with Bethany's reconnaissance team. Pen smiled tightly as they approached, marveling at the change in her old friend's posture and attitude. Arturi didn't just walk; he *strode*. A mirror of Tru's determination reflected in his expression, despite his jovial features and kind eyes. If anything, that contrast made his resolve all the more impressive. O'Malley had turned a peaceful man into a wartime leader.

She wondered if the general had any idea what his greed and violence had unleashed.

As was his style, Arturi greeted a number of people individually. That included Pen. "Good, you're well. I was worried." He flicked his eyes toward Tru, with a look that was almost penitent. "We'll find another way," he said softly. "I promised you."

Tru tucked Pen against his side, his arm at her back. "I'll hold you to that."

But then Arturi was a leader again, declaring his intentions to the several dozen people assembled to hear him speak. "Preacher and I have discussed tactics, based on reports from our scouts," he said, indicating Koss and the mission girls. "Any minute now, more explosions will go off. These have been calculated to create confusion along the enemy's perimeter." He paused, seeming to understand just how intently his people craved his words—his assurances. "Today we strike, and we claim our first victory. Our hope is that information we'll gather in the camp will help reveal O'Malley's exact location, as well as provide intelligence about how to infiltrate his headquarters. Preacher has your assignments. Go now."

Minutes later, Pen and Tru tramped through the woods at a fast clip. They were on the verge of battle. When would it come, her death? When would she be forced to say good-bye to Tru? She gnawed jerky as she walked, despite her unsettled stomach. Energy was more important, so she choked down the rough breakfast.

"What of scouts' reports that their people are ill?" asked Miranda, who trailed Preacher.

"We must never let our hope for the best-case scenario cloud our anticipation of the worst." Preacher held a low-hanging branch aside and ushered their small team through. He locked eyes briefly with Tru, his beard shaped around a smile. "But the reports are that their water supply has been tainted."

Tru only matched his grin and walked on. Pen caught up with him, tugging on his arm. "What is it?"

"I took a walk yesterday when you were working."

"A walk."

"Yup."

"Had you shifted?"

"Yes, I had."

Pen caught his humor, although she couldn't understand its origins. "And?"

"I may have used their freshwater reserves as a latrine. And then encouraged the other skinwalkers to do the same."

She giggled like a little girl being told a dirty joke. "That's remarkably crude."

"I like to think of it as clever and resourceful."

"That, too."

They came to the launch point for the operation. Pen looked around, sizing up their small band. Miranda had taken the baboon form she seemed so reluctant to assume, all for the betterment of the operation. In marmot form, Koss was such a small creature—almost unnoticeable, which was his great asset. Overhead, Jules and Xialle circled in their bird forms, condor and crow. A simultaneous dive from both would signal the start of the operation. With the skies covered, Reynard had decided to stay human. He and Preacher carried intimidating weaponry, while Bethany and the mission girls had taken to the trees with their poison blow darts.

Fifteen people total. Arturi knelt at the forefront, a lone human male. No special gift from the Change. But without him, their cohesion and discipline would splinter.

"Everyone has a task," he said. "Keep to your individual missions and the rest will fall into place."

Pen could've sworn he intended his words just for her. She needed the reminder. Her job was to trail the more physical team members, such as Tru, but to keep within range of the defenses. Confuse the guards as quickly as possible. Resist the urge to kill them outright, knowing such magic only depleted her too quickly. "It's a marathon, not a sprint," Arturi had said. And then she would possess enough reserves to heal the fallen.

A woman beside Pen was staring at her with wide eyes. "I can't believe I'm going into battle with the Orchid," she whispered.

Pen flinched on the inside. But what was such a soul to do? The myths about the Orchid would be hard to dispel. There was safety in being something *other*, but there was also loneliness.

"Did you know that some orchids live their entire lives feeding on fungi? They're beautiful and exotic, definitely, but still parasites. It bothered me when I learned they weren't as pure as they appear." Pen extended her hand despite her flabbergasted expression. "My name's Pen. What's yours?"

The woman almost backed away, as if a touch would be too much to bear. But Pen held her gaze, steadily, hoping to make this first step with someone who must be as scared as she.

Slowly, as if reaching out across a great distance, the woman took her hand. "I'm Maya. A healer."

"Then we have that in common. We're in this together, Maya. Don't forget that."

Maya nodded in apparent understanding, but cradled her hand against her chest like a mother with a babe.

At Pen's side, Tru belly-crawled into position. He whispered, "They'll come around. Keep at it, love." He brushed a kiss on her cheek. "See you on the other side."

The caw of a crow.

Everyone looked up to see Jules and Xialle dive straight down in deliberate unison.

"Hold," hissed Arturi.

A bright, deafening explosion heralded the start of the violence. Three more mines rocketed plumes of fire and soil into the sky. Tru shifted, the last of the skinwalkers to do so.

"Three more mines," Arturi said, arm lifted to hold back his troops.

Another explosion. Another.

Pen's ears rang, and her nose clotted with the acidic stench of explosives. An image triggered in her mind—an image from Tru, no matter that he had assumed his lion form. She saw a flash of his grief as he'd approached the burned-out wreckage of his town, where his family had been murdered. Focusing hard, she gave him a picture of her own: the matched leatherwork on their wrists. The roaring pain in her head eased. His focus became as clear and sharp as hers, no matter that his heightened senses must be reeling from the explosions.

She snatched up his bracelet where it had fallen after his shift. After safely looping it around her knife belt, Pen and the remaining humans gathered the skinwalkers' clothes and shoved them into backpacks. Maybe someday, hundreds of years from now, skinwalkers would no longer feel the compulsion toward modesty.

But that day wasn't now. It would never be unless Arturi's small army succeeded.

The last explosion rocked the ground beneath Pen's knees. Arturi lowered his arm. Tru led the skinwalkers' charge, his compact, powerful legs tearing through the forest. Clumps of dirt flung up from beneath his great paws.

Arturi, Pen, and the other humans ran in pursuit, with Reynard and Preacher at the forefront. The stink of smoke and singed earth filled Pen's nose as she ran. Huge mine craters looked like the planet trying to swallow a meal. She could only hope her efforts the night before had identified the mines' locations.

If not . . .

No. She closed down that surge of guilt and responsibility. She'd been able to do no more. They would find another way. And even Pen was not so naive as to assume the assault would result in zero casualties.

Fire licked at a wooden barricade where a mine had thrown showering sparks. Men in plain drab uniforms scurried with water buckets and weapons, as if uncertain what problem to tackle first—the fire, or the oncoming assault.

Arturi's faithful fanned out across the clearing, scattering in what looked like a random assault. True to their instructions, each individual performed only his or her task. Tru provided cover for sneakier, smaller skinwalkers such as Koss. His massive paws slashed and hacked through the unwary. But he was not bulletproof.

Pen slid to a stop within ten meters of the barricade. She ducked behind a fat tree trunk, where leaves from a dozen autumns clung to her boots like wet paper. Concentrating, she focused on a guard in the lookout tower who leveled his machine gun. He was a killer. A thief. A man of such malformed conscience that the list of deeds she discovered in his mind flipped her stomach. Pen swallowed a surge of bile—and squashed the impulse to see justice done with a twitch of her will.

Magic, yes. But in control.

Instead of murder, she dazed him. The trick seemed almost elementary after the magic she'd wielded recently. The man simply . . .

lowered his weapon. He stared up at the sky, as if tracking a forma-
tion of geese.

Miranda, so powerful in her baboon form, bounded up the watch-
tower and savaged the guard. Tru slammed against the gate with his
bulky, muscled shoulder. He threw back his head and roared . . . such a
roar, like the sky split open to reveal an angry god. That would definitely
terrorize his opponents, because even Pen's arm hair stood on end.

What an amazing creature.

Mine.

The gate's loosely fastened chains gave way to the force of his
battering-ram body. He mauled another guard as smaller skinwalkers—
marmot, ocelot—slipped inside. All ready to take the encampment
apart.

It was working. Arturi's plan was working.

Pen shook her head at her own hubris. She might have forged her
reputation as the Orchid, but she knew the limits of her potential.
Magic was magic, but a human body had limits. And if there was
anything Arturi and his people represented, it was the superiority of
civilized cooperation over single-minded barbarism.

She was just another cog in a well-oiled machine. What a wonderful thing.

With a tight grin, she sighted another guard and turned his daz-
zled eyes to the sky.

THIRTY-SIX

The lion let Tru lead, or at least co-lead. Even his animal self understood the importance of this first battle. The timing needed to be precise. Such a fight required incredible trust. One unsteady hand on the trigger and he was dead. Yet he had no fear. Some risks were worth taking.

Cordite and gunpowder scented the air, acrid in his sensitive nose. The first shots rang out, and he launched himself at a bearded sentry in battle fatigues. The general still outfitted his men as if this were some guerrilla war. Tru's full weight took the man down, and he didn't waste time on finesse. With powerful jaws, he clamped the enemy's throat and crunched. He spat blood and shook his head, crouched low to avoid gunfire.

Some men wandered about in confusion, dazed by something his mate was doing. Animals swarmed over the grounds, some skinwalkers, others sent by those gifted with magnetism. Some of the enemy were sick from tainted food and water. Yet the blast of the mines had provoked others to action, and they fumbled for their guns. Too slow. It would cost them.

Movement. Noise. Tru sprang away into the shadows as a spray of bullets spattered the ground where he'd been standing. *That's right.*

Shoot at me. Mouth open in a feline laugh, he circled the perimeter. The smaller mammals went after ammunition and ankles, scurrying the moment a thug wheeled to aim. Larger ones fought with raw savagery. Screeches, growls, and howls split the night.

O'Malley's men shot wildly, but most of them carried big guns, which didn't perform well in up-close-and-personal combat. Only a few possessed pistols or knives, but they lacked skinwalker speed. *We have magic in our veins. Just try and stop us.*

After the first wave concluded, Tru made another run. Tall man, hat. Smelled of old meat and strong liquor. The lion rumbled in disgust.

He tracked his prey for long moments as the male tried to rally his people. "What are you doing, morons? Fight! There can't be too many. They're not soldiers. They're not *trained*. O'Malley will have our asses!"

The others responded to his commands. Their aim improved, and Miranda took a bullet to the chest. She went down in a spray of blood, dwindling back to a human female as she died. Tru's anger sparked bright as fire. The tall man kept shouting, but Tru had stopped listening to the words.

That's the dominant, the big cat thought. *Time to take him down.*

He stalked closer, using crates as cover. Arturi's second wave of soldiers, all equipped with rifles, fired from various positions around the camp. Copper scented the air as more guards fell. Campfires blinded the defenders, making it difficult for them to see targets in the dark. None of Arturi's allies ventured so near the mêlée, leaving the close fighting to the skinwalkers.

Smart.

The enemy wasn't.

A man lurched into his path. Tru hamstringed him with a swipe of one paw. The gun dropped from his hand, and the lion pounced. Digging with both front and back claws made for a gruesome death.

The screaming startled some of the men so badly that they broke and ran. More shots rang out, dropping the deserters as they tried to find safety in a landscape teeming with Arturi's second wave.

Nowhere to run. And no time to play. With resignation, the lion efficiently finished the kill, though it would have been more fun to prolong the writhing and screaming. Tru didn't share that inclination— the big cat had a cruel streak.

One leap later, he slammed the enemy's would-be commander to the ground. The man flailed beneath him, trying to lay hands on a gun that had bounced away. Coolly, the lion bit down on the his spinal column, and that irritating movement stopped. The man's rapid, terrified breathing said he wasn't dead. His incoherent whispers said he wanted to be.

This one, Tru didn't kill.

Paralyzed, the commander could still prove of some use in an interrogation. As the battle concluded, Tru grabbed him without regard for his injuries and dragged him back toward the command post. Arturi's troops were full of wild excitement, having tasted the idea that their unconventional tactics could best a larger force—through a combination of magic, mundane weapons, and misdirection. Already someone was playing the drums, thumping out a triumphant rhythm. Later Tru would make sure Adrian was safe, check on the scouts from the mission, and find Pen to celebrate, just as soon as he finished up this grim business.

Back in human form, he dumped O'Malley's hound on the ground outside Arturi's tent. There was no way to knock, so he clapped his hands together twice as he'd noticed the others doing. Funny how little courtesies survived, even in the Changed world.

Arturi poked his head between the flaps, looking downright exhausted. And now that he was no longer "on," Tru saw how worried he remained. If the man had slept more than two hours in a row since Zhara disappeared, he'd be surprised.

"What's this?" Arturi asked, glancing down at the prone, whimpering form.

"He looked like he was in charge, so I thought he might know something useful. Like exactly where we can find the general."

They had always known a rough location, based on information Pen gathered long ago, but the mountains were vast. Without more specific coordinates, they might need months to track the bastard. Time Zhara would not have.

Evidently Arturi thought the same because he muttered, "Get him inside."

Tru dumped the prisoner on his wounded back. He wouldn't feel pain because of the paralysis, but any man would find the absolute vulnerability of the position horrifying.

"I know you can talk," he said. "And you will."

"Fuck you," the guy spat.

"This is how it's gonna go. If you cooperate, if you tell me what I need to know, then I'll kill you quickly. No pain. No suffering."

The other glared. "You're going to kill me regardless."

"See, that's where you're wrong. If you refuse, I'll get a healer in here. She'll close the wound. But you'll live on as a cripple. Nobody here will wait on you. Don't worry, though. I'll make sure you get enough food and water not to die. But cleaning you up?" Tru shook his head. "Sorry. You'll have to sit in your own filth. And meanwhile, Arturi and I will make it clear to the others that they can do whatever they want with you."

O'Malley's man drew in a breath, eyes wide with horror, but he tried for bravado. "So? It's not like they can hurt me."

"Of course they can," Tru said silkily. "There are places where you still feel pain. Your face. Eyes. Tongue. Throat. Parts of your shoulders. Maybe your upper arms. And I'm not sure if you're aware of this, but people who've been enslaved often develop endless creativity when it comes to torture."

"I won't let them kill you," Arturi added quietly. "But keep you? Oh, yes. Most of my people would *love* to get their hands on you."

Whether by threat of cruelty or because of what he'd already suffered, the man broke. "I can give you coordinates. I will. Just don't make me live like this."

The bastard was a true coward. Giving up? No way. Tru would fight on as long as he still drew breath. But not this piece of shit.

Tru produced a blade, but Arturi only said, "I'll send for Shine."

The small man stuck his head out of the tent and called for a runner. When the trader appeared, she was out of breath and pink-cheeked from the celebratory dancing. Tru heard the party in full swing now. Everyone was so proud—and they'd earned the chance to cut loose.

"What's up?" She was a cool one, calmly ignoring the man on the ground. Business as usual.

"Just a little truth telling," Arturi said.

"Go on, then."

Arturi knelt beside the prisoner. "Where is General O'Malley's base? Be as specific as possible."

In a quavering voice, the man gave latitude and longitude.

Shine nodded. "He's telling the truth."

"No one has used coordinates in years," Arturi said. "but an older citizen should know how to chart it."

Tru nodded. "What about Burke? If anybody could do it, I bet it's a seasoned sailor. Is he still with us?"

"He didn't stay at the mission if that's what you're asking," Arturi glanced at Shine. "Do you know if Burke survived the fight?"

"He did, sir. Yes. Stayed with the riflemen."

"Get him in here," Tru said. Arturi made the order less peremptory with a gracious smile.

Shine ran to do his bidding.

The request had served another purpose. While the trader was gone, Tru kept his promise. He spiked a knife into the man's heart and stopped it dead. By the time Shine returned with Burke, he and Arturi had dragged the corpse behind the tent for later disposal.

Cold, yes, but necessary.

Tru left then, knowing the others could map and navigate better than he. Best to let everyone play to their strengths. Finally, he felt free to look for Pen. On the way, he grabbed a string of smoked meat. His belly rumbled after the long fight in lion skin, and he required protein to get back on even keel.

He expected to find Pen hanging back, playing the Orchid, while she watched the party with longing eyes. Instead, to his delight, he found her drinking among the victorious. They weren't calling her Orchid either.

Pen sprang to her feet, more than half drunk. The smell of fermented fruit wafted around her as she took a step toward him and stumbled. She beamed as if her clumsiness was hilarious—and it was, rather. Tru put an arm around her. Music washed over him, pounding drums and vibrant strings. Simple instruments and simple melodies had survived the Change. So had they.

His heart, which had been hers for the longest time, swelled at seeing her as a flushed and exuberant woman. Not separate. She didn't seem aware of any burdens, though that could be the alcohol churning in her veins. Maybe his hopes had merit after all. Maybe this woman could be his wife without feeling she'd given up something valuable in trade. God knew he never wanted her to *settle* for him. Not when he loved her so much.

"Glad to see you," he said softly into the curve of her neck.

"It went well." Her voice was a little slurred, her smile sunny. "Tru, this is Xialle's partner, Jules. And there's Maya and Koss, and you know Reynard." She grinned. "They're my friends." Such a proud little stress on the word, like she'd never had any before.

Maybe she hadn't. The idea of her being so lonely broke his heart.

She wouldn't be anymore. He'd see to it. As he'd told her before, he kept his promises.

"A pleasure," he told the group in general. "I'm Tru. Pen's husband."

Hours later, after the party wound down and he carried his laughing wife back to their tent, he realized few moments had ever been prouder than that one—when he introduced himself as Pen's man for the first time.

THIRTY-SEVEN

Two weeks had passed, as near as Pen could tell. All she knew for certain was the full moon had come and gone, as had her menses, which began the day after their victory celebration. It was her second cycle since becoming intimate with Tru.

In the beginning, she'd been frightened when he released his seed within her womb. The idea of bearing a child held a terrifying power, like staring into the sun until her eyes saw only black. But since declaring themselves to one another, Pen hoped that one day they would bear children. A new future. A new life, created by two people who loved each other.

She stood by as Burke used Arturi's compass and the light of a fading evening to check their position. The waiting was growing tedious, just walking and searching. Inside, where her mind worked without impediment, she prepared herself for the possibility that a baby wasn't meant to be. The only couples she'd known to conceive were both skinwalkers—or both human. The Changed world meant there would always be children who needed security and guidance, yet she couldn't help longing for a son with Tru's soulful eyes and poet's soul. A quiet, strong harbinger for a better future.

Adrian clung to him like a vine, absorbing Tru's experience and attention as a plant would light and rain. She looked up from the star charts and found them across a clearing, engaged in a lesson in martial arts. The air was thinner and cooler up in the Appalachian foothills, but Tru had stripped his shirt. Twilight shadows accentuated the flex and play of his lean muscles as he demonstrated a low, aggressive fighting stance. Watching him move that way, out where everyone could see, seemed even more intimate than within the confines of their private tent. She could stare all she liked.

My husband.

Adrian did his best to mimic the move. She smiled when Tru feinted left and managed to take the boy down. But it was a close call. Adrian was getting *much* better.

The best part of their relationship was the easy camaraderie. Even if she had been able to protect Adrian long enough to get him to Arturi's camp, Pen never would have formed such a special bond.

Tru extended his hand, pulling the boy to his feet. A flick of Adrian's upper body sent Tru hurtling to the ground. Flat on his back, face to the waning moon, he only grinned.

Pen's heart twisted with such emotion. She turned away from where Burke and Arturi bent over a tree stump, then pressed a fist over her heart. She loved Tru so dearly that it bordered on pain, but a pain that reminded her that she still drew breath.

"He's a good man, Penny," Arturi said at her shoulder. "But then, you've known that for some time."

She smiled. "Intuition, maybe. Certainly not magic. Just . . . believing what he was capable of being. Only, I didn't know what he was capable of being to *me*."

Arturi's eyes looked very dark in the evening shadows. But even without a great deal of light, Pen sensed the strong tug of his sadness. "Another day off, I think."

"Yes," she said, knowing his thoughts were with Zhara. "One more day."

"When the scouts return by morning, we'll know enough to plan our assault. With any luck we'll be able to proceed as we did against the last two encampments. Magic and skinwalkers and bullets." He clenched his jaw. "We will win this thing."

She grasped his hand and gave it a squeeze. "Yes, we will."

A screech drew their attention. The familiar shape of Reynard's turkey vulture form swooped across the night sky—nearly black on black. An image of blood slashed over her line of sight, like a wash of red paint.

"Something's wrong," she whispered. Out of the corner of her eye she saw Tru and Adrian jogging to meet them. She held out a hand. "Wait! Watch for where Reynard lands!"

She couldn't follow the flight of the bird, not when the night and that smear of red muddled her vision. Tru nodded once. He sighted Reynard, even as the ungainly vulture angled toward the treetops. Shadows seemed to erase his form.

Another screech, this from a different bird. A crow. "That's Xialle." Arturi's voice held a note of unease. "Neither was due back until morning. Six hours, at least."

Xialle's caw cut a shiver across Pen's skin. If she'd thought Reynard difficult to follow, she had absolutely no chance of tracking a crow at midnight.

"Find Jules, her mate!" Arturi called to the camp. "And follow her. We'll bring healers once they're found."

"You assume they're injured." Pen's throat felt thick around the beat of her heart.

"You don't?"

"Something's not right," she said again. "But I don't think they're injured. Neither of them flew any different than usual."

An image flashed in her mind. From Tru. Just a picture. Reynard in human form, sprawled on a carpet of brown pine needles.

She took off at a run, dead on toward where Tru had stalked into the woods. Arturi huffed a rhythm at her back. He kept pace despite his shorter legs and stockier build. Always at the front, just like her. Maybe that's why she had been drawn to his mind, to his soul. Even as a child she'd needed that leadership, feeling grounded in the companionship of one who felt as she did.

"Tru! Where are you?"

He called her name, and she pounded through the undergrowth to a small clearing. Pine trees at this altitude. The nip of cooler night air in her nostrils—sharper, colder than down by the sea.

She and Arturi pushed through the scrub and clinging branches, emerging into the clearing. Others followed them. Reynard lay, just as she'd pictured. Tru knelt over him with a thumb to the man's throat, but she could've saved him the trouble. The faint glow of Reynard's earthen-brown aura told her that he yet lived.

"Pen, come see what you can do."

She liked that Tru had come to a quiet understanding. He still respected her as much as ever and encouraged the use of her powers. But she always felt the good, dependable boundaries of his love. Risking too much would chip away at that love, at the trust they'd been steadily building.

She knelt beside their fallen comrade. Hands shaking, she touched his head and his inner wrist. The skin at both locations was cold, clammy, almost rubbery. Life pulsed beneath her fingertips, but in a way that knotted fear at the base of her skull.

This isn't Reynard.

On a hard shudder, she opened her eyes in the hope of disproving her mind's cringing conclusion. The body lying before her certainly *looked* like her friend.

"Pen, talk to me."

She looked up to find Tru's anxious expression. "Can you . . . ?"

Letting her voice trail off, she didn't know what to say. How to explain. An old fear resurfaced for the first time since meeting Arturi in the flesh—that she was crazy.

Tru circled around their fallen comrade and knelt just behind her, one arm around her shoulder. "You need to tell me. For all our sakes."

"I don't think this is Reynard."

She said it with her eyes closed so she wouldn't need to see the quizzical looks that passed between Arturi and her husband. Their silence told her enough.

Tru's hand swept up to her nape, gently massaging there. "Can you save him?"

"That's just the thing," she whispered, fearing words would bring condemnation. "I don't think I should. He doesn't . . . feel right."

Backing away from Pen, away from the body, Tru said, "Bethany, bring an article of clothing from Reynard's possessions. Quick. His life is at stake."

While the young scout ran back to their makeshift camp, Tru shifted. The ease of his transformation no longer surprised her, but she never failed to be impressed by the animal he became. And in her heart, she breathed a little easier.

He wasn't condemning her. He was helping her.

The lion ranged forward, gaining a measure of respect from those who'd congregated in the tiny clearing. They simply backed away, silently, in quiet deference. He was treated with just as much awe as the Orchid, but Tru never let himself be trapped by their respect. It was just a part of him. She envied that ease.

The scout returned, panting softly.

Pen took hold of a grubby olive-green T-shirt. "You're sure this is from Reynard's things?"

"His tent mate said as much," Bethany said. "I'm sure of it."

Nodding, Pen extended the garment toward her lion mate. Tru's wide, dark nose roamed over the cloth. His nostrils quivered on each inhale. He crossed back to Reynard's motionless body, poking at his armpits and groin, at his hair follicles and the soles of his feet.

A low rumble sounded in the lion's throat. His mane bushed up, a sure sign of aggression. He flicked his tail repeatedly, scented the wind, and growled so that the bass harmonics echoed across the clearing. Pen shivered. That warning was loud and clear.

Arturi shook his head. "I don't understand. *That's* Reynard."

"It may have been," Pen said. "But he's . . . changed. There's a different tint to his aura."

She knew fear was holding her back. It wouldn't take much to reach out to him, to feel his mind as she'd done with any of O'Malley's enemies. What if Reynard's consciousness still existed in there somewhere, kept captive by a spell? For the sake of information and to help their fallen friend, she needed to try.

With Tru still in lion form, she reached out for Arturi's hand. "Don't let go of me. Close your eyes and think of wildflowers you picked for me that time."

His mouth opened in shock. "Penny, that was a long time ago."

"I know," she said. "But you still remember them."

He nodded, his expression haunted. The image came to her then — a bouquet of blue and white flowers he'd picked when she was no more than thirteen. She'd half believed the gesture one of her own making, just the lonely longings of a girl on the cusp of adolescence. But Finn had been real, and the man she knew as Arturi presented her with the image of those flowers, from a past they should not have been able to share.

Using that thought like a lifeguard's buoy, she swam in after Reynard.

The clutter in his brain was sticky, noxious with the stink of all things *wrong*. Someone had been in there. Recently. That wash of blood red was visible now, lurking underneath Reynard's pale brown aura. Using her thoughts, her magic, she ripped away the deceit. Kept digging. Wading deeper. Fear soaked her mind like a chemical burn.

A scream.

A *man's* scream, deep-throated and tortured.

She ran to it, heaving those disgusting smells and blinking past a haze of scarlet. There, deep in his brain, waited Reynard. He was a shriveled, cowering thing, like a baby left on a rainy doorstep. She approached cautiously, looked around, recalling blue and white flowers. That memory steadied her breathing.

"Reynard? What happened?"

"Witch."

"I'm not a witch." She knelt next to his fractured persona—all that remained of him, other than the body sprawled outside, far away on the forest floor. "I'm here to help."

"*Witch* did it."

"You have to tell me who. Please. Otherwise more will suffer. Tell me, Reynard."

He shivered, twitched, cried out again. "Zhara!"

Pen recoiled. She stumbled away and fell, crawling backward on her hands and feet. The truth of it hit her hard between the eyes. Whatever had happened to Reynard, he truly believed Zhara was responsible. But she couldn't leave him.

"Let me heal you," she said. "Please. We can bring you back. You can tell me what happened."

"A trap. Heal me and she walks among you."

"Reynard, you have to be mistaken. She was kidnapped, remember?"

"Don't believe it!" He sobbed, curling deeper into himself until what remained of Reynard was almost invisible. "Please! Not like this! End it, Orchid. Please."

The comrade she'd known would never have called her by that name. That impression of seeing a babe in the rain hit her again. He was going to be trapped that way. Forever. In this place of poison and rot. The funny, sarcastic spirit she'd known was gone.

Crying tears that might be only in her mind, Pen looked away when she ended his life.

Wildflowers. Blue and white. *Get me out of here.*

She catapulted out of that space on a hard gasp. Tru rushed to her side, practically knocking Arturi aside as she doubled over and retched. Shivering that wouldn't stop claimed control of her limbs.

"Jesus, Pen," he whispered against the top of her head. "What happened?"

"He was in there, but buried. That force working for O'Malley had warped him." Her teeth chattered, and her stomach growled for food despite the knots of dread. "Tru, he was crying. Begged me to end it. He was so scared, just . . . *wrecked*. I had to."

Tru kissed her head. "Any word on Xialle?"

"Her mate found her," Arturi said.

Pen could hardly look at the man. What if Reynard was right? What if that malevolent force working for O'Malley really was Zhara?

What if Jack hadn't been the only traitor on that island?

"I have to see her," Pen said, struggling to her feet.

"Oh, no you don't." Tru caught her by the shoulders and forced their gazes to lock. "You aren't going into another injured mind, not like that."

"You smelled it, didn't you? That he wasn't the same man anymore."

He nodded, mouth compressed.

Giving her husband a desperate hug, she held on tightly. And she tucked her lips right next to his ear. With words no louder than an exhale, meant for his sensitive ears alone, she whispered why it was so important that she ask Xialle one last question.

THIRTY-EIGHT

It's started, then.

Deep down, Tru had known it was inevitable. The days leading up to the raid had been just a temporary dream. Pen would do what she felt she must for Arturi's cause, no matter the cost. Maybe he should admire that dedication. Instead he only knew a cold knot in the pit of his stomach.

She's my wife, *and she's going to kill herself.*

But he didn't protest. Instead, for the first time in days, he closed up. His head went quiet. No mental pictures shared between them. Pen glanced at him sharply, but she didn't ask why. She must know. She'd said she chose him, and he'd only asked her to take care of herself. Today she would forsake that promise for Arturi—to find out whether his wife was, in fact, a traitor. Tru followed the rest of the small group through the forest. Cradled by her husband, Xialle looked no better than Reynard.

Jules glanced up, his face a study in misery as he held his woman. "Can you help her, Pen?"

Pen. Not Orchid. She had made that much progress, at least, toward becoming her own person and stepping out of the shadow of her good deeds.

Yet at the request, she came forward as she always must. Tru closed his eyes, but he didn't leave as he had when she remote-sensed the minefield. Even if she didn't love him enough to put him first, he'd stand by her. Funny. He never thought he'd end up married to a fucking heroine, but it seemed that need ran deeper in her than anything else. He should have known, really. Some things set early in life. This was her imprint.

He'd never love this about her. He could accept it, though. Had to, in fact, because it wasn't going away. Tru hadn't imagined he'd spend his life righting wrongs, but fine. If Pen had a permanent compulsion to save the world, then they'd fucking save it. Since he couldn't deal with life without her, he'd be the muscle at her back and the arms that held her in the night. No man relished the idea of being a background player on the stage of his wife's life, but he'd take what he could get.

Bearing witness to Jules's utter despair provided a harsh alternative. He could lose Pen forever. Give up on her. On them.

Not gonna happen.

Maybe that made him pathetic—holding out hope for what might never be right. Tru hunched his shoulders and strangled a sigh as she dove into Xialle's head.

No, the lion said. *It means you love your mate.*

And how do you feel about her? Weird to ask, but it was pure skin-walker. Both halves of him needed to be in accord.

I'd like it if she could shift. I miss hunting with Danni.

He'd never had this conversation before. *So do I. But otherwise?*

She's ours, the lion replied, as if that answered the question.

And really, it did.

The moment she came out of the other woman's head, weak and shaken, he caught her, as he'd been doing for weeks. As he ever would. Whether he agreed with her decisions or not, he'd support them. Mason had taught him that much about being a man. Taught him how a woman ought to be treated. The guy probably hadn't intended to impart those lessons through his interactions with Jenna, but that was

how Tru had learned men and women could share more than screaming matches that ended with slamming doors and abandonment.

Tru cradled his wife in his arms; she gazed up at him, her face
pale, eyes full of hell. Xialle was dead. She, too, must have begged for
release from whatever the witch had done. Mercy killing was a hard
fucking task, especially for someone like Pen. Twice in one day? He
wanted to rip O'Malley to shreds.

Soon, the big cat promised with cold delight. *Soon.*

Jules wept, rocking Xialle in his arms. Long moments passed before he could speak. "Who did this to her?"

"Yes, what happened?" Arturi asked.

Pen wet her lips with her tongue. "Reynard said it was Zhara. I
had to find Xialle to confirm."

The small man was already shaking his head. "She wouldn't. Never."

"They believed it," Pen said softly. "And they feared her."

Tru bit back a frown. "Maybe she wouldn't have before, but O'Malley
might have broken her. If she's turned on us, this whole mission might
be pointless."

"Even if that were true—and it isn't—our mission is *not* pointless."
Arturi wore a hard look, as if argument might be dangerous. The ex-
pression sat better on his affable features than Tru would've guessed.
"Slaves remain imprisoned inside the compound. We must destroy
O'Malley."

Still, Tru didn't know if he wanted to rescue a traitor. "We might
rethink our plan and focus our efforts on taking out the general, then
freeing the captives."

Arturi folded his arms. "You're holding your wife *right now*. If
someone took her from you, if they presented evidence, no matter
how compelling, that she wasn't the woman you loved, would you
believe them?"

No fucking way. The answer came from a primitive part of him,
echoed in the lion's growl. And like that, he saw the man's point.

"Not without seeing it with my own eyes," Tru said. "If I found her and she tried to kill me, I might believe. *Might*. But I don't know I'd give up hope that she could be fixed, that she could come back to me. I'd want to think she loved me enough to *fight* her way back." His hold tightened on Pen.

"You comprehend my position perfectly. Our plan proceeds unchanged."

"Give Pen a few minutes to recover."

Arturi nodded. "We need to see to the bodies anyway."

The leader of the resistance summoned soldiers and directed them to Reynard. Jules needed longer to be convinced that Xialle was beyond saving. There, on the mountainside, they held a quiet service. Preacher spoke a few words where the fallen were buried side by side. It was a solemn moment, one to bring home how much everyone had sacrificed.

Yet nobody appeared to harbor doubts. If they turned craven, then these brave souls died for nothing. The collective resolve firmed, heartening Tru. This might have started out as a motley group of traumatized survivors, but they had united in common purpose.

"Are you all right?" he asked Pen softly, knowing she wasn't.

If he were a little braver, he'd open up to her and offer warmth to compensate for the anguish she'd endured. But he couldn't, knowing he'd only deluge Pen with his own fear. She didn't need the negative messages, and he didn't have a strong filter on what he shared. Maybe once they grew more practiced, he could pick and choose. Today, not so much. So the door stayed closed.

"Every time I kill that way, I feel like I lose a little more of myself."

"So *stop*. A knife works just as well, I promise."

"But there's still pain. They didn't deserve more. I can do it so they feel nothing. It simply . . . ends."

Just because you can, doesn't mean you should.

But Tru chose not to argue. She'd made the choice, so she would live with the consequences. He didn't want to change her, even if her decisions drove him crazy. She must feel the same way about him; any relationship called for compromise.

After the joint funeral, as dawn lightened the eastern sky, Arturi gave the order to move out. They faced a day's hike, according to their aerial scout. Now only Jules, the condor, remained to provide reports on fortifications. He didn't look up to the task, but when the boss man asked, "Do you want a break?" Jules shook his head.

"It will be worse if I'm not busy. And O'Malley owes me." *In blood,* the man's bleak face said.

Tru imagined how he'd feel in the same circumstances. He'd lost one family. Losing Pen might kill him. But no. He wouldn't end it, even then. That wasn't in his nature, but spending the rest of his life without her, wandering, would be the nearest thing to hell without standing in flames. He'd caught glimpses in her eyes as they traveled—she didn't expect to survive this final fight.

Which made what he'd done stupid beyond all understanding. Loving her? It wasn't like he could help that. But *marrying* her? Shit. But deep down, he'd hoped that maybe the promise of a future with him would be a lure strong enough to keep her from making the ultimate sacrifice—trying to save a world that didn't love her back.

Pen, he thought. *Ange would want you to live . . . and be happy. That's all.*

But he didn't speak those words aloud either.

He fell in with the rest of Arturi's army. They still appeared a ragtag bunch as they trudged up the mountain, but looks could be deceiving. Although the scouts were among the most dangerous of their number, the young girls offered no hint behind their quiet, innocent faces. They would slip in first, kill the sentries. Pen and the other mystics would handle magical defenses, then she intended to go after the mad witch.

For her sake and Arturi's, he hoped it wasn't Zhara.

As for himself, Tru would lead the few remaining skinwalkers to the general. If they had a sample of his scent, their task would be simpler. But the man was slippery as a snake. Nobody had seen him outside his mountain stronghold in years.

By the time they arrived at the base of the path Jules had discovered, sunlight slanted through the tangle of tree limbs with a distinctly orange cast. After a short hike to the first checkpoint, the mission scouts tackled their first assignment. As evening fell, Arturi gave last-minute instructions without displaying even a hint of uncertainty. Tru admired his conviction, even as the sinking in his stomach worsened. He didn't feel as if he were about to defeat a great enemy.

He felt like he was about to lose everything he loved. Again.

"We hold here until we hear from Bethany," Arturi said. "Once she gives the all clear, we go in. Is everyone ready?"

Just as he'd done with the previous encounters, Preacher provided specific assignments, giving people tasks according to their strengths. His precision made Tru think he had military experience, before he found religion.

Whatever happens, this is it. Either way.

He went to find Adrian then. The boy wasn't happy about being left out of the final attack, but since he was young and not especially well trained, he would prove a liability.

Consequently his mouth was sullen, but his eyes were scared. "I want to fight."

"We need you to watch our backs," Tru said.

"Bullshit."

"Be safe." He gave the kid a half hug. "I'll see you soon."

Pen put a hand on his arm as the girls disappeared into the brush that framed the path. He couldn't hear even a rustle from their steps. Amazing, really. Mary Agnes had achieved miracles with her charges.

Tru glanced down at his wife, memorizing the beauty of her upturned face, those indigo eyes, and the rosy curve of her mouth. Tears stung, thickening in his throat, but it wasn't the time to be a sensitive pussy. It was time to give her the strength to do what she must. No matter what. Even if it meant leaving him behind.

God, no. Don't make me do this. Don't.

He found the resolve to kiss her, knowing it might be the last time. "I love you, more than anything."

She clung to him, her lips sweet as nectar. Maybe this was his big destiny: loving people and letting them go. If so, then it fucking sucked.

"Me too," she whispered, arms tight around his neck.

He drew back then, because he wasn't done. No more touching—he couldn't bear it—just the power of his words, setting her free. Jules wheeled overhead, a shadow of wings among the trees. "Believe, like I do . . . You won't hurt anybody you don't mean to. You're the motherfucking Orchid. Now go kick some ass for me, Pen."

THIRTY-NINE

Pen watched her husband walk away, ending their farewell. Although, in truth, they'd been saying good-bye over and over during the last arduous hike to the fortress. Without access to Tru's pictures of the world—his memories, his fantasies—a hollow had opened in her mind. This was different from when he'd left the island. They hadn't been living inside of each other then, sharing every inspiration.

She could call it off. They could run away, back down the mountain, to be free of these burdens. But one look at the way Arturi's troops fanned out across the glade put an end to that momentary lapse in concentration.

Everyone had a job to do.

Pen's was to destroy a witch.

She'd spent the last half day in a semi-trance. Walking. Preparing. Always eating. But all the time reliving the moments inside those fractured, ruined minds. Reynard and Xialle. The dead who'd blamed Zhara.

The feel was all off. She didn't know what had happened to them, but nothing about their possession had even hinted at Zhara. No sense of her spirit. No glimpse of her mind. Just that blood-red aura, all sticky and bitter in her thoughts. When she searched from the island, looking for Arturi's wife, she had seen Zhara's leaf-green aura. Distinct. Unmistakable. And then the shock of blood and pain.

There existed two entities. She was nearly sure of it.

But even now, there was still so much she didn't know about magic and the Changed world. If such a creature existed, she hadn't yet encountered it. Leave it to O'Malley to harness and exploit the greatest potential for evil.

The battle began with the crack of an automatic weapon. A Klaxon added to the sudden chaos. Pen's heart slammed into high gear; she could rocket to the moon on her adrenaline. Best of all, she carried Tru's blessing.

Now go kick some ass for me, Pen.

Only as she crawled over a low embankment, gunfire everywhere, did she realize how much that must have cost him.

Her knees clotted with mud as she chased the shock troops closer to the battlements. A huge fortress loomed before them. Rows of stripped tree trunks made it look like a fort from pioneer days, which seemed oddly fitting. If O'Malley was the invading force with technology and supplies, she was part of the pesky native population that wanted them gone. She considered herself lucky she'd learned so little about history before the Change. Precedent might very well say that the natives always lost, but she didn't want to know.

Detonation charges exploded at the base of the main gate. Near-suicide runs made by the forward-most skinwalkers. As soon as their human duty was dispatched, they scurried away in their animal skins. Pen couldn't see past the sudden haze of smoke and flashes of fire. But her job wasn't to make sure the others were safe.

The chaos intensified as O'Malley's people responded with massive artillery. How long had they been stockpiling such weaponry? For just such an assault? Pen smiled at that, liking the idea her ragged band was worth so much hassle. And it still wouldn't be enough to keep O'Malley safe.

The last she glimpsed of Tru was the flick of his tail as he bounded through the wreckage of the fortress door. She exhaled and shut her eyes. It wasn't her job to keep him safe either, although that fact cut a sharp twinge of pain across her heart.

She followed as part of the second wave. Humans and those with other powers. The guards were easy to find, easy to muddle and confuse. They rankled with a proud scorn that rubbed her mind the wrong way. She slipped deeper into a trance of her own making. Her eyes were open, but she didn't see the same way. Something deeper, far down inside her, was taking control.

Shaking with a brief flash of terror, she grounded herself in the truth. She was stronger now. More practiced. More mature. The motherfucking Orchid.

She ran until her lungs burned on each inhale of cordite and charred wood. With a thud, she slammed up against the external wall of stripped tree trunks. The position would give her body cover as she sank deeper into her mind. Eyes closed—sight was almost a distraction now—she found the five closest guards. Depraved, ugly thoughts of killing throbbed in her mind like rotting sores.

She twisted her magic. And killed all five.

The energy in her cells sank. Although her stomach was a liquid mess after being in those foul minds, she grabbed a hunk of cooked meat out of her satchel and shoved it into her mouth. Choking down food was the least disgusting thing she'd need to do that night.

Without those five guards, the covering fire at the external wall was almost nil. Arturi's remaining people surged forward. She caught sight of him in the crowd, face tense, eyes determined. Her Finn, all grown up.

They locked gazes, exchanged nods. She turned away and ran into the fortress.

Almost as soon as Pen raced across the threshold, cloak furling out behind her, a hard wall of sensation smacked against her brain.

She staggered. The back of her head connected with the leg of a look-out tower. She sank into the loam, seeing stars and blood red. The entire fortress was protected by that hideous aura.

Her intrusion was not welcome.

Too goddamn bad.

Pen used her hands to drag her reluctant body to its feet. Splinters dug into her palms—unpleasant, but a reminder of anything outside of the chaos of her thoughts.

Something else was trying to get in. Get into her brain.

So that's what had happened to the others. This . . . *thing* shoved inside and took control. With that much power, no telling what thoughts it could implant. Maybe even that the culprit was Zhara. Pen held out that hope.

Shrugging out from that invading touch took all her strength. She shoved back. *Hard.* And headed toward the source of the energy.

Everywhere, volleys of gunfire and even more detonations. Pen only saw them as shades, like the after-images of a dream. She was too focused on the churning evil battering at her head. Running again, she hugged the edges of the compound. Last thing she needed was a bullet to end her mission.

She wanted to go down fighting.

Tru had been near to tears, she thought. *He let me go.*

As if he knew that she didn't expect to live to see the morning.

Pen forced that heartache aside, focusing instead on the scarlet glow around a dilapidated woodshed. Such an innocuous little thing. The two-by-two-meter shed didn't look big enough to house any-thing, let alone such a tremendous power source. She crept nearer, but the effort was like shoving magnets together the wrong way. The force didn't want her any closer.

But Pen was determined. If this was where the battle ended for her, she would at least see her enemy.

Her short hair stood on end as she walked, forearm over her face as if guarding against a stiff wind. She blinked and coughed as the energy forced its way into her mouth, tasting of putrid meat. A roar of anguished frustration sounded like a train barreling full speed into her ears.

Hands shaking with the effort, she reached for the shed door. It was unlocked. The wood flung open as soon as she touched the handle.

A moment of odd calm swirled away the mayhem. She stood motionless, looking down at a shriveled, warped little creature. Perhaps an ordinary woman once, the thing now seemed like a troll out of a twisted fairy tale. Sparse gray hair grew all over her head and down over her face. Her spindly arms were spread wide, manacled to the shed's walls. Her feet, too, were chained.

Warped and snarling, the thing smiled.

And attacked.

Pen flew back three meters and landed on her ass. She scampered off to the right of the shed, away from the physical dangers of the battle. From a tucked-in position behind a rusted wreck of a car, she huddled close to the metal and fired back at her opponent.

The dream space she entered was unlike any she'd ever experienced. Like walking through someone's mind, only she didn't know whether that mind belonged to her or to the creature. Maybe they created the battlefield together. Swirls of deep red and silvery white coalesced all around. No ground. No sky. Nothing but the feel of dripping, decaying thoughts seeping into hers. The gnarled woman's cackle scratched like steel wool over Pen's nerves. She took a deep breath to block out the ever-present stink, closed her senses to the sounds and the vile bitterness that burned acid-strong in her stomach.

Die!

The one word echoed so clearly that she thought it must have been screamed. But like the cackle, it was all in her mind, in that bizarre dream space.

Who are you?

Die!

Pen worked harder, digging past the spongy mass of the creature's defenses. Images coalesced. A woman during the initial days of the Change, when it had first reached the east coast. Nearly two decades ago. Taken hostage by the man Pen knew to be O'Malley, only younger and stronger of body.

Torture. Such suffering as she'd never imagined. She watched as the woman was beaten and electrocuted, then left to heal on her own, alone, crying, until she begged for another beating just to be granted some semblance of human company.

Years.

Decades of abuse.

Pen threw up the meat she'd choked down, but the grisly images wouldn't abate. Over and over, the woman had been stripped of her will. All that remained was this filthy, cowering beast of a human being.

Why didn't you fight back? You had magic!

The devilish mind stuttered. Cried out. Pen saw nothing but fear—fear the thing had harbored of her abilities. Fear of all magic in the wake of the Change, even her own. Even when faced with an enemy that had stolen her freedom and erased her identity, she hadn't fought back. By then it was too late. Torture erased the woman's autonomy, her own desires replaced by nothing beyond pleasing O'Malley.

His misshapen pet.

Pleasing him meant providing cover. No wonder people had never known the fortress's location, and why the shipments of slaves seemed to vanish into vapor. Complete magical camouflage.

Did you kill Reynard and Xialle?

Trespassers. Threat.

And Jack?

Ruse!

Pen had never been inside a mind so narrowly focused. Every

higher thought had been dissolved across year after year of agony. Nothing remained but reflexes and gut instinct. How could a person empathize once divested of all trace of humanity?

Let me help.

But the woman screeched like a dying animal and flung another tidal wave of magic, burning Pen's skin, flaying her defenses until she felt skeletal and exposed. Rather than fight that pain—it took too much energy—she let it sink into her marrow and ravage her muscles. No stopping it now. She would win this with her magic or she would die on the spot.

Although her confidence had increased to the point where she no longer needed it, she sank into her old ritual. She pressed her hands flat together, even while her palms seemed lined with razors. Turned her eyes to a sky she couldn't see for the eddies of blood. Tucked her chin to her chest, when her ribs threatened to collapse under the battering weight of pure malice.

"Mama, I need you."

She flung open her mind on a bellow of pain. The blood color sank into her eye sockets until she saw nothing else, just that nauseating haze. But the force of her blast carved out a tiny space of silvery light. Dizzy now, she kept pushing, pushing back.

The raging force of her potential, unleashed on a single creature.

The red faded by degrees to a sickening puce. Light and dark switched places, like the image of the sun that stays behind closed eyes. Shivering, crying, Pen reached down inside the woman's consciousness and broke her in two.

The cackling wrath ceased as Pen hit the ground. She panted. Dirt clung to her sweat-soaked face and palms. The beat of her heart was unnatural—clipped and loping. Far too fast. She smacked parched lips. The ends of her toes and fingers were numb, as if all the blood in her body had been conserved in more vital places.

She blinked until the real world took the place of that viscous dream space. Around her, the battle still raged. Muscles quavered like a newborn foal's as she pushed up from the dirt to a sitting position, huddled against that rusted-out car.

Arturi's people still needed her. She should go. Get up. Help.

But Pen lowered her head and sobbed.

FORTY

The lion crept behind enemy lines. For this last mission, Tru had yielded control because he was distracted, worried about his wife. That lack of focus could lead to dangerous mistakes. Better to rely on the feline hunter and concentrate on success. The cat knew how to kill; he took great pleasure in it.

Of the skinwalkers who had begun the fight with him, only the marmot survived. Koss scampered ahead, scouting terrain. Sniffing, the big cat padded along while magic sparked in the air. His fur bristled as if touched by a static charge. Something big was happening, somewhere. Gunfire popped and men howled. But none of it was his business.

He was stalking bigger game.

He avoided the war machines, reeking of old pollution and grimy with years of accumulated dirt. The light would be gone soon, harder for the enemy to tell friend from foe. If O'Malley didn't hate skinwalkers so much, he might have recruited more animals to fight, but his thugs remained confined to human skin. The lion shook his head with pity and disgust.

The main building rose before him. Old. Huge. Those small, wily females had said the largest force waited for the rebels in the courtyard, leaving the interior lightly defended. He circled, testing and trying to find the best way in. The old man would hide in there, bellowing orders to the people he expected to die on his behalf. Not how a proper male behaved. But all the power in the world couldn't stand against simple resolve, and the lion had both determination and cunning.

He decided where to enter, through a fragile square window with no guards in sight. Launching through the glass, his fur protected him from the shards that sprayed everywhere. The assault wasn't as quiet as he preferred, but this wasn't his native hunting ground. The lion crouched in wait because guards would respond to the noise he'd made, unless they had all been sent outside. The old man would not be so foolish.

A door slammed open to reveal two men who stank of sweat and smoke. The lion took a great leap and knocked them down together. Their weapons clattered away. One of them pissed; that potent stench filled the air. That enraged the beast, so he the killed the urine-stained one first with a swift rake of his claws. He crushed the other in his jaws until the death rattle gurgled from his throat. The lion spat. Putrid-tasting flesh. Unworthy. He squatted over their useless guns and sauntered away, tail lashing with satisfaction.

The hallway stretched before him. He found no clues except the stink the guards had left. They might have been sent to check on the noise, which offered the best chance of finding their leader quickly and quietly. Afterward, he'd stand over the carcass and roar. The lion didn't lose.

Koss scurried ahead, keeping out of sight. Though the lion lost track of his small partner, he was comforted to know that the marmot would warn him before any enemies approached. The smoky-sweat trail led deeper, through other rooms. His human self noted that this was a nice place, lots of salvaged luxury items from the pre-Change world. Fine paintings with gilt frames. Everything gleamed. But the animal wasn't impressed. The floor was hard and slippery, no traction for his claws, and it stunk. People who lived there had stunk up the place with terror smells.

The muted noises of distant conflict made him prick up his sensitive ears. Then another closer sound registered. Human voices, not far. An argument? But he didn't pay attention to the words. Just the anger in their tone. Hard to say how many, but that wouldn't matter. He'd kill them all.

It might be helpful to stop and listen. We might learn where O'Malley is.

The lion obeyed his human half and waited as Koss scampered back with a chatter of warning.

"I'm telling you, this place is cursed," said one guard. "We need to get the hell out."

"The general will hunt us down like dogs if we do. If we die, it better be at the hands of the enemy."

A new voice added, "You wouldn't *believe* the shit I've seen today."

"Just keep a sharp eye peeled. There's no way these hedge witches and skinwalkers take us out. We're the closest thing left to a fucking military outfit left in this godless hellhole."

"Speak for yourself," his cohort replied. "I'm going before it's too late."

A gunshot rang out. "Anybody else feel like deserting?"

The lion crept around the corner. Three guards stood over a body, stationed where the hall intersected with corridors leading off in several directions. Two of them wore shocked expressions, as if they couldn't believe what the other had done. Their shock left the door wide open for a stealthy strike.

With a few slices of Tru's paws, the surviving guards died. Blood smeared the tiles where their bodies fell. He leaped over their corpses, surging toward the final confrontation with the human responsible for enslaving so many innocent souls. Excitement pushed through his veins, spiking to new levels. The big cat savored his triumph even as he kept moving. His tail lashed like a victory pennant.

He let the marmot take the lead once more. *Scout on, little friend.*

The scent trail grew stronger. More fear. More men. Up ahead, there would be greater resistance. He must be approaching the room where the old man lurked like a spider spinning his web. The coward was too weak to fight his own battles like a proper warrior, instead sending his thugs. But there was no escaping the lion.

With a tiny paw, Koss waved him on. Nothing scary here, it seemed. The lion passed into the next room, which was full of strange items, most of which he didn't recognize. They smelled odd, but there was no prey to be found. He padded silently closer to O'Malley.

As he crossed the threshold, red light flared all around him. A carved head screamed. Both halves of him—human and feline—recoiled, dancing away from the sound. It was both awful and unnatural, as if someone's voice had been bound into the statue itself, trapping it for all eternity, to serve as the old man's alarm. The red light made it impossible for the lion to pass the barrier and rush farther into the house. This smelled dangerous.

Koss had been too small to activate the magical trap; he danced on his back legs—an apologetic stance. But that didn't solve the problem. The lion stalked around as the shrieking continued. Three guards assembled on the other side of the red light, watching. Waiting. Aiming their rifles. Their bullets would tear him up.

The lion focused his wrath on the screeching head. He reared up and swiped with his front paws. The statue smashed to the ground and shattered into fragments. At the moment of impact, the sound stopped and the light died. He crouched beside the emptied shelf, out of the gunmen's sight. They would have to get within claw's reach if they wanted to fight.

A stupid one stepped into the doorway, close enough for him to leap. He took the human down in a powerful lunge, clamping his throat, crushing fragile flesh. But the other two still fired their weapons. One bullet struck Koss dead center. The marmot died, his small body blasted apart, as the lion fought back the pain of losing a good comrade.

Bullets sprayed the area, biting into the floor all around him. One hit him in the flank, and he roared his fury and his pain so that it echoed through the house, warning his enemies he was coming. His next attack carried him onto the chest of the guard who didn't turn to flee. He killed that one in a single ferocious slash. The other he ran down like a terrified gazelle.

The man wept and pleaded for his miserable life. "Please, just let me go. I'll get the hell out of here. Nobody has to know."

The lion stared down into the whiskered face, yellow teeth, and bloodshot eyes. Terror wafted from the man's skin in unbearable waves; he was hardly able to breathe with the weight on his chest. Amusement curled through the lion, chased by vague satisfaction. He existed to see his enemies brought low.

In reply, he growled low in his throat, ignoring the throb of his injured thigh. Blood trickled from the wound, which meant he couldn't waste more time. Already he had waded through too much human garbage, slowing him down. If wounded again, he might not fare so well when he finally found the old man.

Underneath the big cat's weight, the guard shut his eyes, doubtless knowing he would find no mercy. He had willingly served evil and could not be permitted to live. The lion ended him.

Tru pushed to the forefront of the mind he shared with the lion. He had established enough distance from his earlier fears to concentrate on the endgame now. *Thanks,* he told the big cat. *I've got it from here.* Better if he was in charge to calculate his odds of survival—and with his leg leaking all over the place, it didn't look good.

What the hell. Let's rock-and-roll.

He padded forward. From two rooms away, he heard O'Malley

shouting, "Where the fuck is your A-game? You're the worst trained sons of bitches I ever had the misfortune to employ. None of you's worth the bullet it'd take to put you out of your misery."

"Then we'll just leave, sir," came a reply. "Because I don't think we're winning this fight. They have too much magic. Too many sharp-shooters. Men are just dying, quietly, and we can't even see what from, not a mark on 'em—"

"Pussies!"

Showtime. Tru nudged through the next room, body low to the ground. His lion half wished for tall grass to conceal his movements, but he settled for skulking behind furniture. Tru wondered if he should shift, go back for some guard's weapons, and try to snipe them from around the corners. Pick them off, since he didn't know their numbers. Hard to tell from movement, no way to tell from smell. These bastards all reeked the same.

But no.

His wound would only be worse in a human body, plus he'd suffer lingering weakness from the shift. Better to go out roaring as king of the jungle.

Pen. I love you.

Before Tru charged in, he opened the way to her and channeled that picture like a river. Even if it was messy and awful, he wanted to share his last moments with her. His, hers, whatever. He'd take whatever she sent back. No more secrets. No more fear. Just them, souls together, even if they spent their last moments apart. Their connection should be strong enough to surmount the distance. He hoped.

You're everything, he thought, knowing she might not pick up those words. But she'd see his devotion in the picture of the life he'd wanted for them both. Maybe, if he focused hard enough, she'd even hear the words, this one time.

I gave you my all, love. I did, I did.

He bounded into the room, where O'Malley stood screaming at two guards. The old man didn't have a weapon. No hesitation, no doubts. Tru knocked them down before anyone raised a gun, and he slaughtered them fast. His claws savaged soft skin and tougher bone, leaving O'Malley helpless. He expected the cowardly monster to bargain, maybe, as if a lion would accept terms of surrender.

But before he closed for the final kill came the unmistakable sound of rifles being cocked. Tru froze. Glanced up. He hadn't scouted the room before committing—that had been the marmot's job. Up above, he found a whole gallery of snipers with their weapons trained on him.

The old man was smiling.

"Not as smart as you thought, eh, skin-filth? Did you really think I'd send all my troops away? Your people will fight to the death outside, but they won't be able to touch me in here. It's an instant kill zone." The general raised his arm, ready to order Tru's execution.

The lion closed his eyes. Only a miracle could save him now.

FORTY-ONE

Eventually Pen found her strength.

She held her head with both hands as if her brains would leak out her ears like whipped cream. Nothing worked right. The whole universe might be crammed inside her skull. What would happen if she opened herself to so much magic but couldn't refasten the door?

Staggering away from the ruined car and the little woodshed, she managed to keep low and tight to the edges of the compound. An eerie stillness had fallen over her senses. She saw violence but couldn't hear the sounds or smell the stink on the wind. Full night meant shadows running among bursts of gunfire and flames that ate at the barricades.

But no more blood red. The witch was destroyed.

She propped her arm against a piece of wood that looked to be an old pillory. Maybe O'Malley put his men in the stocks. Leaning there, she felt something cold creep up her spine. It wasn't the witch, but some other awareness, her mind wide open to so much energy in the world. If the Change could be spoken to, she was doing so just then.

Arturi.

She pictured him as an old man. Always on the short side, he was a little stooped and walked with a cane. Zhara was there, her beautiful dark face still smooth, but her hair tinged with sharp streaks of silver. Arturi addressed a huge collection of onlookers. Tens of thousands—numbers she hadn't seen since before the Change, when people had filled enormous sports stadiums. Hard to believe.

But there was Arturi. He raised his hands. And he spoke of hope and resurgence, using that same intoxicating calm he had so perfected. A leader for the ages.

Pen blinked, trying to find her way out of the powerful vision. Perhaps the magical world was compensating her for the death she still expected. She could see Arturi's success in her mind, even if she never saw it in person. Because if she believed in one prescient vision—so good and clear and beautiful—then she had to believe her nightmare would come true, too.

And that meant finding Zhara. Pen would reunite the lovers and make sure that future happened.

Tru.

Tears seeped out of the corners of her eyes even as she pressed on, deeper into the compound. The screams of the dying echoed in her ears now, her senses slowly returning to the physical world. But she dreaded movement forward. That wobbling progress, which grew stronger by the step, dragged her toward the moment when she would give up Tru forever.

Smell was back, and taste—the sickly bite of blood, where she'd chomped the inside of her cheek. Then came touch. The pressure of her boots striking soil with each step. The feel of wind and the heat of fire against her skin.

Ahead awaited a long series of tall metal cages, all draped in tarp. They looked like semi trailers—the same kind that had once been her voluntary prison. The chicken-wire frames and metal support beams were the echoes of a long-ago nightmare. She'd thought herself so clever then. Before Tru. Before she'd learned all he had to teach.

Arturi limped around a distant corner, bleeding from his foot and thigh. Preacher, who was covered in the gore of battle, supported their leader's body. Pen signaled them with a wave of her hand. Shouldering their rifles, the pair hobbled over as quickly as they could. Arturi's face was covered in sweat. In the orange firelight of burning wood, his freckles were dark splotches against pale, slicked skin.

"The witch?" he asked, panting.

"Dead. Zhara?"

"No sign. These cages next. We can afford to release the prisoners now that the fighting has died down. The girls are ready to escort them back out into the forest to the rendezvous."

"I should tend your leg," she said.

"No time. Let's do this."

Pen swallowed her protest and nodded. Together they ripped the canvas off the ragged chicken wire. Inside, prisoners of all ages, shapes, and colors—mostly naked, some wounded, all near starving—cowered back with their arms around one another. Breathing calmly, Pen sent her magic out to them. Just a touch of softness to ease their fear.

Still no Zhara. Not among a hundred prisoners.

"Where is my wife?" Arturi called. "Her name is Zhara. O'Malley's pet. Someone, please. Tell me!"

Pen caught a general impression of sadness in reply to the question. Sweet earth, what if the woman really was dead? Pushing her senses, she tried to find a glimpse of Zhara's leaf-green aura, but too much magic swirled around the compound—a whirlwind that blunted her ability to pinpoint one individual woman.

Bethany slipped forward with her troops, of which only three remained. Their young, grim faces attested to the rigors of the conflict and the losses they'd suffered. With her usual aplomb, Bethany took charge of removing the prisoners from their detention cells. Preacher covered their exit.

One captive grabbed Pen's hand as she loped out, her gait tired and uneven. "The dark lady. She is in chains. North tower, awaiting the old man's bidding." She grimaced. "At least, she was."

Pen thanked the woman and slugged Arturi on the arm as she ran. "This way!"

The scenery felt eerily familiar. She saw a gun turret and a lookout tower, both shrouded in a concealing treetop. A rope ladder led up and up, to where a dead guard draped lifeless over the side.

My nightmare.

I'm not ready.

In her vision, however, Pen hadn't been able to see anyone else. Just the ladder . . . and the compulsion to climb. Suffering awaited her if she did.

But she wasn't alone. She turned to find Arturi coming up behind her.

"There," she said, glancing skyward. "She's O'Malley's prize, kept away from the fighting."

Hope lit his face. He reached for the ladder, but Pen stopped him. "You can't. Your leg. I'll go."

I gave you my all, love. I did, I did.

She froze.

That was Tru's voice.

The whole time, Pen had assumed those final, heart-stricken words would be hers. Instead, Tru spoke them. He was the one in danger. And he was saying good-bye. Cold streaked her skin and sank talons down to the marrow of her bones.

You promised, her heart screamed. *You promised we'd be together forever.*

Only at that moment did she realize the hideous injustice she'd perpetrated. Not only had she misinterpreted her vision, she'd asked Tru to commit to a woman who had no intention of living. To make promises when she had no goal of honoring them. Not really. She would forsake all others for as long as she breathed, but what was the use of her sacrifice if she courted death so diligently?

"I have to go," she whispered.

Not waiting for Arturi's reply, she sprinted across the compound. Love gave her strength, yes, but so did dread. The sheer terror that she would be too late. Although her lungs ached, scorched by flames and smoke, they had nothing on her tortured heart.

I'm coming, Tru.

The main building was huge and labyrinthine. But the Orchid didn't abide walls. And she didn't tolerate threats to the man she loved.

Bursting through the front door, she did what she'd never thought to do again. Only one other time had she let go with such wild abandon. Her magic had been propelled by fear and desperation. She'd not been able to distinguish friend from foe.

That was long ago.

She sensed the gold aura of her mate—so much stronger in her mind than anyone else—and shielded him.

Then she detonated a bomb of pure magic.

The concussive force of her spell knocked Tru back against a wall, knocking his head against a marble fireplace. He went still. All around, fire sprang up as if the room had been doused with gasoline.

As for the snipers in the gallery, they *melted*. Not just their minds. But their bodies, too. Agonized cries bounced off the high ceilings until they were no more.

Pen kept running, seeing that scene unfold. Banging through a set of double doors, she vaulted over corpses that bore Tru's claw marks. Her side ached. Her mind rattled like a rock in a bottle. But all she wanted was to see him whole and well. The fire would reach him soon.

Into the general's inner sanctum, she coughed and searched through the dense smoke and flames. Twisted puddles of human remains dripped off the upper balcony and coated the sleek marble floors. Some bodies were turned inside out. Some looked how humans would appear if their bodies were the tallow that fed a candle's flame. Liquefied.

She found O'Malley first. Just a wreck of a man.

Funny, that her magic had let him live.

He coughed into the crook of his elbow as the smoke became a crushing weight in Pen's lungs. Kneeling on the foul devil's chest, she whipped out her knives. Killing him with her mind would be too generous. Instead she gutted him from stomach to sternum. He flailed, choking his last breaths.

Pen turned and used her mind to pinpoint where Tru had been blasted. His aura was so faint, nearly invisible amid the bright orange glow of the fire. She raced to his side, finding him almost defenseless in human form.

"Tru!"

She ducked under his armpit, trying to lift him. But he was big and heavy. Instead she stood and grabbed his wrists. Inch by inch, she dragged him out of that burning bedlam. Her shoulders ached, ready to pop out of their sockets. But she didn't stop. Couldn't stop.

Not now, Tru. Please, my love. Not like this.

She barely got him past the threshold of the upper balcony before O'Malley's sanctum collapsed. Vibrations shivered through the ancient building. Mortar and hunks of plaster rained down from the ceiling.

Drawing on her last stores of energy, she dug deep into Tru's unconscious mind and shook hard. *On your feet!*

He jumped to wakefulness. Sitting up, he grabbed his head and growled in pain. "Fuck, my head!"

"Sorry," she said, grabbing him around the waist. Tugging. Urging. "We gotta run. *Now.*"

"Pen, what the hell?" He blinked amid the ash and flame.

"Shut up and move."

With one last shake of his head, he pushed to his feet. Only then did she realize the bullet wound that had ripped open the meat of his thigh. Later. She could heal him later.

The building began its slow, decaying collapse. Tru leaned heavily on her for support, until he regained his bearings. Then it was just a matter of compensating for his injury. They ducked falling debris.

Always forward. Pushing on. Pen couldn't breathe past a hard cough lodged in her throat.

With one last mental search of the burning wreckage, she found what remained of O'Malley's consciousness and ended his life.

Just to be goddamn sure.

She and Tru burst into relatively fresh evening air. Behind them, the citadel burst apart in a fierce wave of heat. The glow of her magic formed a bright triangle of light that stretched skyward, as ash sprinkled down like light snow. Pen and Tru just *ran*.

Only when they emerged past the outer barricades of the fortress did they slow. His adrenaline must have flagged because he began to limp heavily. They gasped, leaning against a tree, arms trembling as they held each other.

"I hope Arturi got Zhara out," she whispered.

Tru stopped petting her back. He pulled away, his tense expression illuminated by the distant flames. "What do you mean? You don't know?"

"I heard your call. You needed me." She swallowed, where the pain of so much smoke had been replaced by thick tears. "I couldn't leave you to die, my love. Arturi had his mate to save. I had mine."

Shuddering, Tru pulled her into a fierce embrace. He didn't speak for the longest time, just held her as she held him. Desperately. As if they'd just survived the absolute worst the Changed world could throw at them.

Maybe they had.

"You chose me," he said, his voice deep and rough.

She stroked the damp hair back from his face, smoothing, over and over, just to prove that he was alive. "I made a promise. One I intend to keep for as long as I'm able. That means taking care of us. I'm sorry it took so long for me to see how important your love is to me. Nothing can take its place. Nothing else is worth fighting for. *Your* love, Tru."

He gathered her close. There in his mind, he shared the image she'd been unable to hold steady. Their future together. A home. Safety. Children. Peace. And all the love they could fit into one beautiful lifetime.

Pen wept until her chest ached with it. Even Tru's eyes weren't dry.

"I should heal your leg," she said. "So we can make it to the rendezvous."

"You're a wreck. I can make it."

She was about to argue with him but stopped short. He was Tru. He knew his limits, and most times he knew hers better that she did. She nodded, then helped him into the clothes she'd carried on her back. He was shivering but strong enough to make it to camp. There, they could eat, heal, rejuvenate. And celebrate.

Just before they set out, she took his wrist and re-fastened his bracelet. "Can't forget this."

He closed his fingers over hers and squeezed. For once, her magnificent poet was speechless.

They propped each other up, shuffling away from the past as it burned. Ahead, at the rendezvous, she glimpsed a familiar leaf-green aura. Zhara. There was grief in their camp, with so many dead, but there was also elation and the adrenaline of having won an impossible fight. With O'Malley eliminated and the heart cut out of his empire, Arturi's little band could rebuild. A real future—maybe even the glorious one she'd envisioned.

"Almost there, my love," she said. "Our friends are waiting for us."

Smiling, he lowered his head to hers for a kiss.

EPILOGUE

It was a splendid day to get married. Again.

This time Tru wore a brand new suit, hand-tailored for the occasion of the finest linen the weavers could produce. He stood before Preacher waiting for Pen to become his bride all over again. After everything they'd endured, he shouldn't be nervous.

And he wasn't. Much.

But he didn't relax fully until she came into view wearing a watercolor-blue dress, walking toward him across the field of flowers. The sun burnished her hair, picking out the gold streaks. She moved toward him in time to the music while their friends watched with affectionate approval. That she'd chosen him once seemed incredible. For her to do so again was miraculous. He was the luckiest man alive.

Pen reached his side, and Preacher raised his hand to stop the pipers. "Dear friends," he intoned. "We gather to join this man to this woman in the sight of the earthly and the eternal. The only law of life is love. Without it, life is nothing, and without love, death has no redemption. If we learn nothing more, let it be this."

The crowd murmured its assent, for this was the teaching of the Church of the Change. Tru had heard far worse foundations for faith.

He smiled into Pen's eyes, listening as Preacher continued. "Penelope and Truman, do you both come before this company of your own free will and with free hearts to pledge to each other?"

"I do," Tru said. His heart sang at hearing her soft reply in perfect time with his.

"Then repeat after me: I, Truman, in the name of the great spirit that resides in us all, by the life that courses within my blood and the love of my heart, take you, Penelope, to be my chosen one. I promise to love you wholly for all the days of my life, and even into the great beyond, where we may meet, remember, and love again. Your path is now mine. May our shadows never part."

On a deep, shaky breath, he spoke the words as a soft light gathered around Pen. The onlookers gasped a little, but not in dismay. The light show didn't surprise him, only drew a tender smile. He loved everything about her, even this incredible magic.

When her turn came, Pen spoke her vows in a firm voice. Preacher beckoned Adrian forward. The boy came bearing an old chalice that had been salvaged from some ruined cathedral. It was tarnished silver, ornate, full of a sweet-smelling wine.

The cleric took it and drew Tru toward Pen with a hand on his shoulder. "Drink ye both from the cup of love."

Symbolic, certainly. They bent their heads together and tipped the goblet up, rich red trickling into nearly touching mouths. The task proved messy but unexpectedly delicious, just like life in the Changed world. The audience laughed a little when they bumped noses, and Tru heard the soft "ahhh" when they kissed.

"Hey! We haven't gotten there yet," Preacher said, laughing.

Tru stood back with a wicked grin, loving that he could make her glow like that. And when Pen was happy, she actually lit up the world around her. Fucking magical, his wife. Or . . . she would be his wife soon, officially, in the Church of the Change as well as the private skinwalker way. She'd never get away from him now.

"I now pronounce you husband and wife. May your love endure eternally. *Now,* Tru, kiss your bride."

With great eagerness, he did. Flower petals rained down soft, white, and delicately scented. Pen twined her arms around his neck, leaning into him—the female embodiment of bliss, of all his dreams. *She chose me,* he thought in pure wonder. *All over again.*

After the ceremony came a banquet, dancing, and more congratulations than Tru could answer. Pen never left his side. He'd given up hope it could ever be like this between them. She had seemed so convinced that they wouldn't make it down from O'Malley's mountain, and yet they both had.

Later, Arturi—with Zhara in tow—came to offer his congratulations. "So how long will you two lovebirds be out of commission?"

Tru glanced at Pen, brow lifted in inquiry. She was the one with the world-saving vocation. "My heart?"

She offered a secret smile. "Indefinitely, I think."

Arturi's mouth gaped open. "But there are still so many people to rally, Penny. We took out O'Malley, but the damage from his tyranny has yet to be healed. It may take years to see real progress in the recovery."

"I wish you well with that, my old friend. But as it turns out, I don't need to save the world. I only needed to help *you.* Now that I have, I've found a new calling."

"What do you mean?" the small man asked.

Zhara tilted her head. "Pen has interesting news for her husband. We should grant them some privacy." She led Arturi toward the refreshments: honey cakes and fruit, fresh cheese and flat bread.

"You're really walking away?" Tru asked.

"I had a revelation when I staggered away from the witch. My brain was a mess. Completely defenseless, I think. And I saw the future. Not just some idea of how things could be, but a vision as real as any history yet to come." She glanced toward Arturi, where he stood facing his wife, his arms crossed behind her back. "All these years, the voices, the doubt. I was meant to help Finn. He has Zhara now. That will keep him strong as he puts the world to rights."

"What do you mean?"

"That vision? It was of Arturi at the head of a new Changed government. Real civilization. Decades from now, all gray hair and wrinkles. But with that same fire in his eyes, and Zhara at his side. His strength." She took his hands. "That's not my future. It's theirs. I have to . . . I have to put our family first."

"Are you telling me . . . ?"

"I think so," she said with a shy smile. "It's early days. We'll know for certain in a few weeks. If I'm right and you're willing, I'd like to head west for our honeymoon. I don't want to travel when I get big, and it would be a comfort to have the baby near Jenna and Mason. I might need their help." She paused, studying his face.

Pure joy rushed through him. Where he'd had nothing, now he had everything. Tru pushed out a shaky breath and swept Pen into his arms for a kiss that would leave no doubt as to his reaction. "I didn't think I could ever feel like this again," he whispered into her hair.

"I'd given up hope. I thought there was something wrong with me for the longest time, that I was crazy. I never imagined I could embrace such joy."

"We'll take the trip slow. In stages. It should be easier now that we don't have to worry about O'Malley's slave gangs. We can even drive one of his vehicles, though the roads will be shit."

"Where are you going?" Adrian had come up behind them, a closed look on his face.

He thinks we're making plans that don't include him. That he'll be left behind again.

"Talking about heading west to see our folks and settle down," Tru answered easily. He didn't need to look at Pen for confirmation. This was right, and her accord filled him with warmth. "You willing to head out day after tomorrow?"

The kid's face lit up. "Yeah. That would be great."

Tru winked. "Don't come looking for us until then, though. We're going to be busy." Pen nudged him, but Adrian was laughing, ducking his head and making a face.

Tru had all kinds of ideas. Nuzzling his face against Pen's neck—her so-delicious, sexy-as-hell neck—he whispered a few words only she would hear. A little shiver tickled through his wife, the woman who had married him twice. That would never stop amazing him.

"Try to behave," she murmured back.

He quirked a grin. "Why? You love me when I'm bad."

"I love you all the time."

"So you do." He lifted her into his arms and carried her off to the roaring approval of the gathered guests.

No need for farewells. They were all friends, and they'd see one another again. Visits would be made. Tales would spread, mouth to ear, as they did in the Changed world. Whispers carried on the wind. Winged skinwalkers would ferry messages between settlements. The wheel spun on.

Arturi might, in fact, alter the course of history. The Dark Age could brighten in days to come. Civilization might rise in a different and better direction. But Tru wasn't looking that far down the road because he held his beloved in his arms. And anywhere, anytime, that Pen smiled at him, his whole world shone bright as daybreak.